Become our fan on Facebook **facebook.com/idwpublishing**
Follow us on Twitter **@idwpublishing**
Check us out on YouTube **youtube.com/idwpublishing**
Instagram **instagram.com/idwpublishing**
deviantART **idwpublishing.deviantart.com**
Pinterest **pinterest.com/idwpublishing/idw-staff-faves**

978-1-63140-366-8   18 17 16 15   1 2 3 4

COVER BY
SAM SHEARON

EDITED BY
JUSTIN EISINGER

EDITORIAL ASSISTANCE BY
LESLIE MANES AND
ZAC BOONE

COLLECTION DESIGN BY
RICHARD SHEINAUS/
GOTHAM

Ted Adams, CEO & Publisher
Greg Goldstein, President & COO
Robbie Robbins, EVP/Sr. Graphic Artist
Chris Ryall, Chief Creative Officer/Editor-in-Chief
Matthew Ruzicka, CPA, Chief Financial Officer
Alan Payne, VP of Sales
Dirk Wood, VP of Marketing
Lorelei Bunjes, VP of Digital Services

IDW founded by Ted Adams, Alex Garner, Kris Oprisko, and Robbie Robbins

The X-Files created by Cris Carter.

THE X FILES

WHIRLWIND page 1
by Charles Grant

RUINS page 135
by Kevin J. Anderson

WHIRLWIND

By Charles Grant

ONE

The sun was white and hot, and the wind blew ceaselessly.
Annie Hatch stood alone on her ranch house porch, one hand absently
rubbing her stomach as she tried to decide what to do. The late-morning sun
made her squint, the temperature already riding near ninety.

But the wind that coasted across the high desert made her wish, for the first
time in a long time, that she were back in California.

It hissed softly through the brush, and whispered softly in her ear. Of course,
she thought; you could also just be a doddering old fool.

A quick smile, a quicker sigh, and she inhaled slowly, deeply, taking in the heat,
and the piñon, and, so faintly she might have been imagining it, a sweet touch of
juniper.

Wind or not, voices or not, this was, all in all, far better than Hollywood.

That was where she and Burt had made their money, so many years ago it might
have been a dream; here was where they had finally made their lives, no dream at all.

A breath of melancholy fluttered her eyelids closed for a moment. It wasn't easy
being a widow, even after fifteen years. There were still too many times when she
thought she heard him clumping back from the stable behind the house, or whistling
as he fiddled with the generator, or blowing gently on the back of her neck.

The wind did that to her, too.

"Enough," she muttered, and strode impatiently to the end of the porch, leaned
over the waist-high, rough-hewn rail, and looked down the side of the adobe

house to the stable. She whistled twice, high, sharp, and loud, and giggled silently when she heard Nando curse, not very subtly letting her know he hadn't finished saddling Diamond yet, was she trying to get him trampled?

A second later he appeared in the open doorway, hands on his wide hips, glaring at her from under his time-beaten Stetson.

She waved gaily; he gestured sharply in disgust and vanished again.

"That's cruel," a soft voice said behind her.

She laughed as she turned. "He loves it, Sil, and you know it."

Silvia Quintodo looked at her skeptically for as long as she could. Then she grinned broadly, shaking her head as if at a child too angelic to be punished. She was a round woman, face and figure, with straight black hair forever caught in a single braid that hung down her back. Her skin was almost copper, her large eyes the color of a starlit night. Today, as always, she wore a loose, plain white dress that reached to mid-shin, and russet deerskin boots.

"You're staring," she scolded lightly.

Annie blinked. "I am? I'm sorry. My mind was wandering." She stared at the weathered floorboards. "I guess I'm just feeling my age today, dear."

Silvia rolled her eyes—*oh, please, not again*—and returned inside to prepare an early lunch.

Annie thanked her silently for not feeding the self-pity.

In truth, she knew she wasn't so bad for an old lady of sixty-one. Her face was narrow, accentuating green eyes and dark, not quite thick, lips; the lines there were more from the sun than her age. Her hair was white, but softly so, cropped short and brushed straight back over her ears. Practical, but still lovely. And her slender figure was such that, even after all these years, she was still able to turn more than a few heads whenever she drove into the city or up to Santa Fe.

It was good for her ego.

Oh brother, she thought; it's worse than I thought.

What it was, was one of those days that crept up on her now and then—when she missed Burt so much it burned. There was never any particular reason for it, no specific thing that jogged her memory. It just happened. Like today. And the only cure was to take Diamond and a canteen and ride into the desert.

Maybe, if she were brave enough, all the way to the Mesa.

Sure, she thought; and tomorrow I'll wake up and find Burt beside me in bed.

A snort behind her made her jump.

She whirled just as Diamond thrust his head over the rail, his nose catching her stomach and shoving her back a step.

"Hey!" she said with a scolding laugh. "Knock it off, you big jerk."

He was already in bridle and saddle, a short black horse with a rough diamond blaze between his eyes. Nando stood beside him, grinning, one hand on the animal's rump, his stained brown hat pushed back on his head.

"Serves you right," he told her smugly. He could have been Silvia's twin, not her husband, save for the ragged streaks of gray in his hair, and the fact that his broad blunt nose had been broken too many times for him to be rightly called handsome. Those who didn't know him figured him for an ex-boxer or an ex-Marine, not the foreman of a ranch that wasn't much of a ranch anymore.

Annie made a show of ignoring him and his rebuke. She adjusted her straw Western hat, fixed the strap under her chin, and swung her legs easily over the rail. Without pause or hesitation, she grabbed the horn and swung lightly into the saddle. Only then did she look down at him. "Not bad for an old lady, huh?"

"The day you get old, Seora," he answered solemnly, "is the day I stop shoveling horse shit for a living and start selling bad turquoise to the tourists up Santa Fe."

Diamond shook his mane impatiently.

A warm gust made them turn their heads, but not before she saw the expression on his face.

When he looked back, he was somber. "It talks."

"I wouldn't know."

He shook his head slowly, not quite sadly. "You know. You always know."

She grabbed the reins angrily. "I know nothing of the sort, Nando." She was prepared to cluck Diamond away when Nando tapped her leg. "Now what?"

He reached behind him and pulled out a canteen. Grinning again: "No rain, no water." He tucked it into the silver-studded saddlebag.

She thanked him with a brusque nod and guided Diamond across the side lawn to a break in the double split-rail fence she had painted white the year before. Once through, she followed it around to the front, checking the grass inside to see where it was dying.

Everywhere, she realized; everywhere.

Despite the extraordinarily expensive, undoubtedly wasteful belowground system her late husband had installed himself and had connected to one of the score of deep wells on the ranch, the grass seldom survived intact all the way through the summer. Still, she thought as the ranch drifted away behind her, wasteful or not, it was better than nothing.

At least it had color.

At least it had life.

"All right," she snapped to the shadow that rode beside her. "All right, that's enough, Annie, that's enough." Her right hand held the reins lightly; her left hand rested on her thigh, and it trembled.

She ignored it, concentrating instead on the rolling land ahead, automatically checking for wind or flash-flood damage to the narrow wood bridges Burt and Nando had built across the several arroyos meandering across the four thousand acres, glancing to her right every so often at the high heat-brown hill that blocked the sun each morning. Like the exposed knobby root of an ancient, distant tree, it flanked the recently paved road that led east to the interstate and west to the Mesa.

To the reservation.

She couldn't see it from here.

The hill crossed the road a half-mile ahead, still high, still marked with thorned shrubs and tufts of grass sharp enough to slice through a palm, still studded with large brown rocks and partially buried boulders.

Like a wall to keep the rest of the world out.

Or to keep the Konochine in.

For some, however, it wasn't high enough or strong enough.

They left to see what the world outside looked like, to discover what the world had to offer besides life on a reservation.

For her, it was Burt, and a brief but lucrative career in Hollywood; for others, unfortunately, it was prejudice and pain, and ultimately, a grave too far from home.

Diamond shied suddenly, forcing her to pay attention, to glance quickly at the ground for signs of rattlesnakes. They'd be out now—the sun was high and warm enough—coiled deceptively still on whatever rocks they could find.

She saw none, and frowned her puzzlement when the horse began to prance, telling her he wasn't thrilled about approaching the ranch side of the hill.

That's when she saw the buzzards.

Five of them circled low near the two-lane road, and she mouthed a sharp curse as she nudged the horse in that direction. There weren't many cattle left; she had sold most of them off not long after Burt had died, and seldom replaced the ones she lost. Every so often, though, one of those remaining found a way through the barbed wire that marked their pastures. Sometimes they tumbled into an arroyo; sometimes a rattler got them; sometimes they just couldn't find the water or the food and simply gave up, laid down, and died.

Closer, and she saw a van parked on the sandy shoulder, on the far side of the fence that ran along the blacktop. Vague waves of ghostly heat shimmered up from the road, blurring the vehicle's outline.

"What do you think?" she asked Diamond. "Tourists?"

The desert beyond the Sandia Mountains was beautiful in a stark and desolate way, with flashes of color all the more beautiful because they were so rare. It was also a trap. It wasn't unusual for an unthinking tourist to pull over because he wanted to walk a little, stretch his legs, check things out. It also wasn't unusual for the heat, and deceptive distance, to combine to lose him.

One minute, you could see everything; the next, you were alone.

Sometimes he didn't make it back.

Another twenty yards, and Diamond pulled up short.

"Hey," she said. "Come on, don't be stupid."

He shook his head violently, reaching around to nip at her boot, a sign he wasn't moving another inch.

She glared helplessly at the top of his head, watching his ears twitch in agitation. Forcing him would serve no purpose. He was as stubborn as she, and most definitely stronger.

"Can you say 'glue'?" she muttered sourly as she swung out of the saddle and ordered him to stay put. "Idiot."

Dusting her hands on her jeans, she trudged toward the van, scanning the area for whoever it was who had been stupid enough to leave it.

She hadn't gone a dozen yards when she heard the flies.

Her stomach tightened in anticipation, but she didn't stop. A check of the fence revealed no breaks in the wire, no toppled posts. The van itself was a dusty dark green, streaked with long-dried mud.

"Hello?" she called, just in case.

The flies sounded like bees.

The wind nudged her from behind.

She stepped around a sprawling juniper, and her left hand instantly clamped tightly to her stomach.

"Oh God," she whispered. "Dear Jesus."

It wasn't a lost cow.

There were two of them, and they lay face-down, arms and legs spread, unnaturally twisted. Flies crawled in undulating waves over them, thick and black, drifting into the air and drifting down again. Not five feet away, a buzzard watched, its wings flexing slowly.

It snapped its beak once.

Annie spun away and bent over, hands on her knees, eyes shut and stomach lurching, her throat working hard to keep the bile from rising.

She knew the bodies were human.

But only by their shape.

Even with the flies, even with the sun, it was clear they had been skinned.

TWO

T he sun was white and hot, and there was no wind.

Traffic in the nation's capital moved sullenly and loudly, while pedestrians, if they moved at all, glowered absently at the ground, praying that the next building they entered had its air conditioning working. In this prolonged July heat wave, that wasn't always the case.

Tempers were short to nonexistent, crimes of passion were up, and blame for the extreme discomfort was seldom aimed at the weather.

The office in the basement of the J. Edgar Hoover Building was, according to some, a working monument to the struggle of order over chaos.

It was long, not quite narrow, and divided in half by the remains of a floor-to-ceiling glass partition from which the door had long since been removed. Posters and notices were tacked and taped to the walls, and virtually every flat surface was covered by books, folders, or low stacks of paper. The lighting was dim, but it wasn't gloomy, and as usual, the air conditioning wasn't quite working.

In the back room, two men and a woman stared at a series of red-tabbed folders lying on a waist-high shelf. Each was open to the stark black-and-white photograph of a naked corpse, each corpse lying in the center of what appeared to be a tiled bathroom floor.

"I'm telling you, it's driving us nuts," the first man complained mildly. He was tall, solid, and a close-cropped redhead. His brown suit fit too snugly for real comfort. His tie had been pulled away from his collar and the collar button undone, the only concessions he made to the barely moving air. He wiped a hand over a tanned cheek, wiped the palm on his leg. "I mean, I know it's a signature, but I'll be damned if I can read it."

"Oh, put your glasses on, Stan," the woman muttered. She was near his height, her rounded face smooth, almost bland, with thin lips, and narrow eyes under dark brows. Unlike his clothes, her cream linen suit could have been tailored. "That's no signature, it's just slashes, for crying out loud. You're the one who's driving us nuts."

Stan Bournell closed his eyes briefly, as if in prayer. He said nothing.

"It's the bathroom that's important," she continued, her voice bored. It was clear to the second man that she had been on this route a hundred times. She pulled a tissue from a pocket and dabbed at her upper lip. "It's easier to clean, it's too small for the victim to hide in or run around in, and—"

"Beth, Beth," Bournell said wearily, "I know that, okay? I've got eyes. I can see."

The second man stood between them, hands easy on his hips. His jacket was draped over a chair in the other room with his tie, and the sleeves of his white shirt were rolled back twice. His face was unlined, and his age could have been anywhere from his late twenties to his mid-thirties, depending on how generous the estimate was.

Right now, he felt more like fifty.

The bickering had begun the moment the two agents had stormed into the office; the sniping had begun once the folders had been laid out.

He took a step away from them, closer to the work shelf. They were both right.

He had read the files several days ago, at his Section Head's request, but he didn't tell the agents that; their tempers were frayed enough already.

He sniffed, and rubbed a thoughtful finger alongside his nose.

All five victims—or at least, the five the FBI was thus far aware of—had first been attacked in other rooms of their respective homes. Houses, not apartments; suburbs, not cities. All signs indicated little or no struggle after the initial assault, indicating knowledge of the attacker, or near-total surprise. They had been chloroformed just enough for immobility, then dragged elsewhere. All were women, all in their early twenties, and all had been murdered in their bathrooms.

Strangled with either an unfinished belt or rawhide strap, their bodies stripped to the waist, and a razor taken to their chests.

One slice each.

None had been raped.

Beth Neuhouse groaned and plucked at her blouse. "God, doesn't the air conditioning work in here? How can you work like this? It's like a sauna."

Fox Mulder shrugged unconcern, then pushed a hand back through his hair.

He checked each black-and-white in turn, his gaze flicking over them increasingly rapidly, as though he were reading.

"Well?" Bournell asked. "You got a magic trick for us? You got a rabbit we can chase?"

Mulder held up a hand to hush him, then slid the pictures from their folders and laid them out in a line. A moment later he switched the second and fourth.

"Mulder," Neuhouse said, "we haven't got all day. Either you've got something or you don't. Don't play games, okay?"

Mulder straightened, and almost smiled. "Beth, get me a sheet of paper, please?" His left hand gestured vaguely toward the other room.

It was his tone that moved her more than the request. Those who had worked with him before had heard it at least once. One of the older agents had said it was like the first bay of a hound that had finally found the scent; you didn't argue with it, you just followed.

And you made sure your gun was loaded.

Bournell frowned. "What? I don't see it."

Mulder pushed the photographs closer together and pointed. "It's there. I think." Sudden doubt made him hesitate. "I'm—"

"Here." Neuhouse thrust a blank sheet into his hand. She stared at the bodies then, and her voice quieted. "I've been looking at those women for over a month, Mulder. I'm seeing them in my sleep."

He knew exactly what she meant.

In many ways, the black-and-whites were as bad as looking at the bodies themselves. Although the color was gone, violent death wasn't. The only thing missing was the smell, and it wouldn't take much effort to bring that up, too.

"So what do we have?" Bournell asked.

"I'm not positive. It's kind of crazy."

Neuhouse laughed quietly. "Well, this is the place for it, right?"

Mulder smiled. No offense had been meant, and he hadn't taken any. He knew his reputation in the Bureau, and it no longer bothered him. He was a flake, a maverick, a little around the bend on the other side of the river. He worked as much from logic and reason as anyone else, but there were times when he didn't have to take every single step along the way.

There were times when abrupt intuitive leaps put him ahead of the game.

Sometimes that was far enough to have it called magic.

Or, more often than not, spooky.

He put up with it because that reputation came in handy once in a while.

"Come on, Houdini," Bournell complained. "I'm frying in here."

Beth aimed a semiplayful slap at his arm. "Will you shut up and let the man think?"

"What think? All he has to do is—"

"Here," Mulder said, slapping the paper onto the shelf, indecision gone. He grabbed a pen from his shirt pocket. "Look at this."

The others leaned over his shoulders as he pointed to the first picture, but she wasn't the first victim. "The cut runs from just over her right breast to just under the left. In the next, it's the reverse."

"So?" Bournell said.

Mulder pointed again. "It could be the killer leans over and just cuts her." He straightened suddenly, and the others jumped back when his left hand demonstrated an angry, senseless slashing. "It could be, but I don't think so. Not this time." He pointed at the third woman. "This is clearly most of a letter, right?"

"R, maybe, if you combine it with the next one over," Neuhouse answered, glancing at her partner, daring him to contradict. "I know that much."

"Damn sloppy, then," Bournell said.

"For God's sake, Stan, he's slashing her! What the hell do you expect?"

Mulder copied the slash marks onto the paper, turned, and held it up.

They stared at it, puzzled, then stared at him—Bournell in confusion, Neuhouse with a disbelief that had her lips poised for a laugh.

"He's writing his name," Mulder told them. "He's letting you know who he is." He exhaled loudly. "One piece at a time."

\\\\\\\\\\\\\\\\\\\

The luncheonette was two blocks from FBI headquarters, a narrow corner shop with a long Formica counter and a half-dozen window booths, most of the decor done in pale blues and white. The windows had been tinted to cut the sun's glare, but it still threatened Mulder with a drumming headache whenever he glanced out at the traffic.

Once done with the sparring duo, he had grabbed his tie and jacket and fled, stomach growling unmercifully, his head threatening to expand far beyond its limits. Even now he could hear them arguing, with each other and with him, telling him, and each other, that he was out of his freaking mind. Killers did not write their names on victims' bodies; at least, they sure didn't do it in classical Greek.

And when they finally, reluctantly, accepted it, they demanded to know who the killer was and why he did it.

Mulder didn't have any answers, and he told them that more than once.

When it had finally sunk in, they had stormed out as loudly as they'd stormed in, and he had stared at the door for nearly a full minute before deciding he'd better get out now, before the echoes of their bickering gave him a splitting headache.

The trouble was, stomach or not, the nattering and the heat had combined to kill his appetite. The burger and fries looked greasy enough to be delicious, but he couldn't bring himself to pick anything up, even for a taste. Dumb, perhaps, but still, he couldn't do it.

A siren screamed; a police car raced down the center of the crowded street.

In the booth ahead of him, two couples chattered about baseball while at the same time they damned the heat wave that had been sitting on Washington for nearly two weeks.

On his right, on the last counter stool, an old man in a worn cardigan and golf cap listened to a portable radio, a talk show whose callers wanted to know what the local government was going to do about the looming water shortage and constant brownouts. A handful were old enough to still want to blame the Russians.

Mulder sighed and rubbed his eyes.

In calmer times, it was nice to know his expertise was appreciated; in times like these, exacerbated by the prolonged heat, he wished the world would leave him the hell alone.

He picked up a french fry and stared at it glumly.

The radio announced a film festival on one of the cable channels. Old films from the forties and fifties. Not at all guaranteed to be good, just fun.

He grunted, and popped the fry into his mouth. All right, he thought; I can hole up at home with Bogart for a while.

He smiled to himself.

The more he thought about it, the more he liked the idea. In fact, he thought as he picked up the burger, it sounded like exactly what he needed.

He was finished before he realized he had eaten a single bite. A good sign.

He grinned more broadly when a woman slipped into the booth and stared in disgust at his plate.

"You know," his partner said, "your arteries must be a scientific wonder."

He reached for the last fry, and Dana Scully slapped the back of his hand.

"Take a break and listen. We're wanted."

She was near his age and shorter, her face slightly rounded, light auburn hair settling softly on her shoulders. More than once, the object of one of their manhunts had thought her too feminine to be an obstacle. Not a single one of them had held that thought for very long.

Mulder wiped his mouth with a napkin, the grin easing to a tentative smile. "Wanted?"

"Skinner," she told him. "First thing in the morning. No excuses."

The smile held, but there was something new in his eyes. Anticipation, and a faint glimmer of excitement.

Assistant Director Skinner asking for them now, while they were both in the midst of cases still pending, generally meant only one thing.

Somewhere out there was an X-File, waiting.

"Maybe," she said, as if reading his mind. She snatched the last fry and bit it in half. An eyebrow lifted. "Or maybe you're just in trouble again."

THREE

Twilight promised the desert, and the city at the base of the Sandia Mountains, a pleasantly cool evening. The heat had already begun to dissipate, and a wandering breeze raised wobbly dust devils along the interstate that stretched from Albuquerque to Santa Fe. Snakes sought their dens. A roadrunner streaked through a small corral, delighting a group of children who didn't want to leave their riding lessons. A hawk danced with the thermals.

On the low bank of the Rio Grande, beneath a stretch of heavy-crowned cottonwoods, Paulie Deven snapped pebbles and stones at the shallow water, cursing each time he hit the dried mud instead.

He hated New Mexico.

The Rio Grande was supposed to be this wide awesome river, deep, with rapids and cliffs, all that good stuff.

But not here. Here, he could almost spit across it, and most of the time it hardly held any water. You could forget about the cliffs, and rapids were out of the question.

He threw another stone.

Behind him, he could hear muffled music coming from the trailer his parents had rented from the developer until their new house was finished. That was supposed to have been three months ago, when they had arrived from Chicago. But some kind of permits were wrong, and then there was some kind of strike, and… and… He snarled and threw another rock, so hard he felt a twinge in his shoulder.

He thought he was going to live in the West. Maybe not the Old West, but it was supposed to be the West.

What his folks had done was simply trade one damn city for another. Except that he had belonged back in Chicago; back there the kids didn't get on his case because of the way he looked and sounded.

A light fall of pebbles startled him, but he didn't look around. It was probably his pain-in-the-ass sister, sliding down the slope to tell him Mom and Dad wanted him back in the trailer now, before some wild animal dragged him into the desert and ate him for breakfast.

Right.

Like there was anything out there big enough to eat something built like a football player.

"Paulie?"

He glanced over his left shoulder. "You blind, or what?"

Patty sneered and plopped down beside him. She was a year younger than his seventeen, her glasses thick, her brain thicker, her hair in two clumsy braids that thumped against her chest. He wasn't exactly stupid, but he sure felt that way whenever she was around.

She pulled her legs up and hugged her knees. "Not much of a river, is it?"

"Good eyes."

"They're fighting again."

Big surprise.

Ever since they had moved into the trailer, they had been fighting—about the house, about the move, about his Dad being close to losing his job, about practically anything they could. A damn war had practically started when he'd taken some of his savings and bought himself an Indian pendant on a beaded string. His father called him a goddamn faggot hippie, his mother defended him, and Paulie had finally slammed outside before his temper forced him to start swinging.

Patty rested her chin on her knees and stared at the sluggish water. Then she turned her head.

"Paulie, are you going to run away?"

He couldn't believe it. "What?"

She shrugged, looked back at the river. "The way you've been acting, I thought... I don't know... I thought maybe you were going to try to get back to Chicago."

"I wish." He threw another rock; it hit the mud on the far side. "You ever think about it?"

"All the time."

That amazed him. Patty was the brain, the one with the level head, the one who never let anything get to her, ever. He hated to admit it, but he had lost count of the number of times she had saved his ass just by talking their folks into forgetting they were mad. Running away, running back home, was his kind of no-brain plan, not hers.

The sun died.

Night slipped from the cottonwoods.

A few stray lights from the trailer, from the handful of others on the other lots and the homes on the far side, were caught in fragments in the river, just enough to let him know it was still there.

Suddenly he didn't like the idea of being alone. "You're not going to do it, are you?"

She giggled. "You nuts? Leave this paradise?" She giggled again. "Sorry, Paulie, but I've got two years till graduation. I'm not going to screw it up, no matter what." She turned her head again; all he saw was her eyes. "But then, I swear to God, I'm going to blow this town so goddamn fast, you won't even remember what I look like."

He grinned. "That won't be hard."

"And the horse you rode in on, brother."

"I hate horses, too. Their manure smells like shit."

A second passed in silence before they exploded into laughter, covering their mouths, half-closing their eyes, rocking on their buttocks until Patty got the hiccups, and Paulie took great pleasure in thumping her back until she punched his arm away.

"I'm serious," she insisted, her face flushed. "I'm not kidding.

"Yeah, well." He watched the black water, rubbed a finger under his nose. "So am I."

Angry voices rose briefly above the music.

A door slammed somewhere else, and a pickup's engine gunned to launch the squealing of tires.

Off to their left, beyond the last tree, something began to hiss. Paulie heard it first and frowned as he looked upriver, trying to see through the dark. "Pat?"

"Huh?"

"Do snakes come out at night?"

"What are you talking about? What snakes?"

He reached over and grabbed her arm to hush her up.

Hissing, slow and steady, almost too soft to hear.

"No," she whispered, a slight tremor in her voice. "At least, I don't think so. It's too cool, you know? They like it hot, or something."

Maybe she was right, but it sure sounded like snakes to him. A whole bunch of them, over there where none of the lights reached, about a hundred feet away.

Patty touched his hand, to get him to release her and to tell him she heard it, too. Whatever it was.

They couldn't see a thing.

Overhead, the breeze coasted through the leaves, and he looked up sharply, holding his breath until he realized what it was.

That was another thing he hated about this stupid place: it made too many sounds he couldn't identify, especially after sunset.

Every one of them gave him the creeps.

The hissing moved.

Except now it sounded like rapid, hoarse whispering, and Paulie shifted up to one knee, straining to make out something, anything, that would give him a clue as to who was out there and what they were doing.

Patty crawled up behind him, a hand resting on his back. "Let's get out of here, Paulie, huh?"

He shook his head obstinately. It was bad enough he was here because his folks had had some shit-for-brains idea about starting over, when they already had a perfectly good business back up North. He definitely wasn't going to let the buttheads here frighten him off.

City boy.

They called him "city boy" at school, their lips curled, their voices sneering, unimpressed by his size or the glares that he gave them.

Yeah, sure. Like this wasn't a city, right? Like they didn't have traffic jams, right? Like people didn't shoot and stab and stomp each other here like they did in Chicago, right?

The dark moved.

The hissing moved.

"Paulie?"

He swayed to his feet, trying not to make too much noise. His hands wiped across his jeans and curled into fists. Now they had made him angry.

"Paulie, come on."

"Go back up," he ordered without turning around.

Something had definitely moved out there, probably a bunch of wiseass kids trying to creep toward him. He took a sideways step up the uneven bank; his foot nudged a short length of dead branch. Without taking his eyes off the dark, he reached down and picked it up.

"Paulie."

"Go up!" he snapped, louder than he'd intended. "Damnit, Patty."

Staring so hard made him dizzy. It was like trying to pin down the edges of a black fog.

His free hand rubbed his eyes quickly and hard, but nothing changed.

There just wasn't enough light.

This, he thought, is really dumb. Get your ass outta here before something happens.

An arm snaked over his shoulder, and he bit so hard on a yelp that he choked.

Patty's hand opened to show him the dim gleam of a gold cigarette lighter. He took it and half-turned, his expression demanding to know when she'd started smoking. He realized the ridiculous timing when she flashed him a *not now, stupid* grin and jerked her chin to turn him back around.

His own smile had no humor.

He shifted the branch club until it felt properly balanced. Then he took a bold step forward and squared his shoulders. "Listen, assholes, you want to get lost, you want to get hurt, your choice."

No one answered.

Only the hissing.

He held the lighter up and sparked it, squinting against the reach of the flame's faint yellow glow until his vision adjusted. There were shadows now that slid away and slid toward him as he raised the light over his head and moved his arm from side to side. The trees moved; the leaves turned gray; the bank took on contours that didn't exist.

"Hey!"

Another step.

"Hey!"

Another.

The breeze touched the back of his neck and twisted the flame to make the shadows writhe.

They kept coming, still whispering, and he gripped the club more tightly, angling it away from his leg, ready to swing at the first face that broke through the dark into the light. It wouldn't be the first time he smacked a homer with just one arm.

A low branch brushed leaves across his right cheek and shoulder before he could duck away.

He thought he heard Patty snap his name, but he wasn't sure. All sound had been reduced to his sneakers sliding over the ground, to the breeze tucked into the branches, and to the whispering.

He frowned.

No; it wasn't whispering.

It was, as he'd first thought, hissing. But strange. It wasn't like snakes at all, but like something… no, a lot of things brushing roughly over a rough surface.

Voices whispering.

He faltered, and licked his lips.

Okay, so maybe it wasn't people out there, and Patty said it probably wasn't snakes, and it sure wasn't the river.

So what the hell was it?

The breeze moved the leaves, and he looked up quickly, looked back and smiled.

That's what it was—someone dragging a branch along the ground. Leaves; the hissing was the leaves.

Growing louder.

Suddenly the lighter grew too hot to hold. He cursed soundlessly and let the flame die, whipping his hand back and forth to cool his fingers off, and the metal, so he could use it again in a hurry.

Timing now was everything.

He would wait until the asshole was close enough, then he'd turn on the light and swing at the same time. The jerk would never know what hit him.

He listened, a corner of his mouth twitching, his body adjusting slightly so that he was almost in a baseball stance.

Batter up, he thought; you goddamn freaks.

Louder.

No footsteps yet, but that didn't matter.

He checked back, but couldn't see his sister; he looked ahead, and made out a faint shadow that, because of virtually absent light, seemed taller than it ought to be.

Louder.

Very loud.

City boy, he thought angrily, and flicked on the lighter.

He didn't swing.

His sister screamed.

He couldn't swing.

His sister shrieked.

So did Paulie.

FOUR

Assistant Director Walter Skinner sat behind his desk, hands folded loosely in his lap, and stared absently at the ceiling for several seconds before lowering his gaze. He was not smiling. On the desk, in the center of the blotter, was an open folder. He looked at it disdainfully, shook his head once, and took off his wire-rimmed glasses. Thumb and forefinger massaged the bridge of his nose.

Mulder said nothing, and in the chair beside him, Scully's expression was perfectly noncommittal.

So far, the meeting hadn't gone well.

The entire transcript of a six-month wiretap on a Mafia don in Pittsburgh had been misplaced, and Mulder, arriving first, had walked straight into the teeth of the storm Skinner directed at his secretary and several red-faced agents. Mulder had been the target of the man's temper before, and he slipped hastily into the inner office with little more than a *here I am* nod.

Then he had committed the protocol error of taking a seat without being asked.

When Skinner walked in, his face flushed with exasperation, Mulder wasn't quick enough to get to his feet, and the Assistant Director's curt greeting wouldn't have melted in a blast furnace.

It had been all downhill from there, even after Scully arrived, with Skinner raging quietly against those whose carelessness had imperiled an important investigation.

Mulder bore it all without comment.

At least the man wasn't raging against him for a change, which had not always been the case in the past.

Then, as now, the bone of contention between them was usually the X-Files.

The FBI's law enforcement mandate covered a multitude of federal crimes, from kidnapping to extortion, political assassination to bank robbery; it also permitted them to investigate local cases when local authorities asked them for assistance and the affair was such that it might be construed to be of potential federal interest, generally involving national security.

Not always, however.

Occasionally there were some cases that defied legal, sometimes rational, definition.

Cases that seemed to include instances of the paranormal, the inexplicable and bizarre, or the allegation that UFO activity was somehow involved.

X-Files.

They were Mulder's abiding, often single-minded, concern, and the core of his conviction that, X-File or not, the truth was not always as evident as it appeared to be. Nor was it always liberating or welcome.

But it was out there, and he was determined to find it.

And expose it.

The cost was immaterial; he had his reasons.

Skinner thumped a heavy hand on the folder. "Mulder…" He paused, the lighting reflecting off his glasses, banishing his eyes unnervingly until his head shifted. "Mulder, how in the name of heaven do you expect me to believe that this murderer is actually writing his name on his victims' chests?"

It was the tone more than the words that told him the Director was actually concerned about something else.

"I thought it was obvious, sir, once the patterns had been established."

Skinner stared at him for several seconds before he said, flatly, "Right."

A glance to Scully told Mulder he wasn't wrong about the Director's focus; it also told him he had somehow stepped on someone else's toes. Again. As usual.

He was, as he had told her more than once, a lousy Bureau dancer.

There in fact were few things that frustrated him more than internal Bureau politics. He supposed he should have known, given the personalities currently involved, that it would have been more politic to let either Neuhouse or Bournell come up with the solution on their own. He should have only been the guide. Suggesting instead of declaring.

And, given the personalities involved, he should have also guessed that one of them, probably Bournell, would have complained that Mulder was trying to steal the case, and thus the credit, from under them.

"Sir?" It was Scully.

Skinner shifted his eyes; the rest of him didn't move.

"As I understand it, there's a serious time constraint here. By his already estab-lished schedule, the killer is due to strike again within the next two weeks. Possibly sooner. Anything Agent Mulder is able to give them at this stage, any guidance he can offer, despite the pressure of his own caseload, can only be helpful, not an interference."

Mulder nodded carefully; his other reaction would have been to laugh.

"Besides," Scully added blandly as the Director replaced his glasses, "I doubt Mulder thinks this one is strange enough to tempt him."

Skinner looked at him, unblinking. "I can believe that, Agent Scully."

Mulder couldn't decipher the man's expression. He couldn't forget that it had been Skinner who had once shut down the X-Files on orders from higher up, from those who didn't like the way Mulder learned too much of what, from their point of view, didn't concern him; nor could he forget that it was Skinner who had ordered opened the X-Files again, and Mulder suspected the Director hadn't had much support.

It was confusing.

Skinner was neither all-out enemy nor all-out ally. Despite the profile of his position, he was a shadow, and Mulder was never quite sure what the shadow was, or what cast it.

"Excuse me, sir," he said carefully. "Am I being reprimanded for lending requested assistance?"

"No, Agent Mulder," the Director said wearily. "No, you're not." He rubbed the bridge again, this time without removing the glasses. "The record shows I called you in. It doesn't have to say what we talked about. But next time, do me a favor—save me some trouble and phone calls, and let someone else figure it out for a change. As Agent Scully suggested, be the guide."

He didn't smile.

Neither did the others.

Finally, he slapped the folder closed and indicated with a nod that they could leave. But as they reached the doorway, he added, "Greek, Mulder?"

"Classical Greek, sir."

The man nodded. "Of course."

Mulder resisted the temptation to salute and followed Scully into the hall, where she suggested coffee in the cafeteria, iced tea for him.

"You know," he said as they made their way down the hall, "I appreciate the support, Scully, but I don't need defending. Not really."

She looked up at him and sighed. "Oh yes you do, Mulder."

He looked back blankly.

"Trust me," she said, patting his arm. "On this one you'll have to trust me."

His temper didn't flare until later that afternoon.

He had been halfheartedly sorting through a half-dozen new cases dropped on his desk for evaluation. His Oxford-trained expertise in criminal behavior, and his natural talent for discovering patterns and traces where none seemed to exist, were natural magnets for investigations that had suddenly or inevitably run into a roadblock.

He didn't mind it; he enjoyed it.

What made him angry now was the admittedly unfounded suspicion that Bournell and Neuhouse had deliberately set him up for a reprimand. They were not incompetent. They were definitely not stupid. Given enough time, they would have undoubtedly seen what he had seen; and the Bureau was crawling with experts—either here in the city or out at Quantico—who could have reached the same conclusions.

He leaned back in his chair, stretched out his legs, and stared at the closed door. A droplet of sweat rolled untouched down his cheek.

He couldn't help wondering if They were after him again—the unseen powers he had labeled the Shadow Government; the people who knew more than they let on about the truth he himself knew existed in the X-Files.

It wasn't paranoia.

On more than one occasion, they had tried to discredit him, and thus have him fired.

On more than one occasion, they had tried to kill him.

And Scully.

Only the fact that he had somehow attracted friends in that same gray land of shifting shadows kept him alive and functioning, and he knew it.

Now it was possible They were at it again. Nibbling at him this time. Distracting him. Possibly hoping to force him into a careless mistake on one of the cases he needed to study. He had learned the hard way that there was only so much Skinner and the unknowns could do to protect him.

"I should have told them it was Russian," he whispered to the floor.

And laughed.

Suddenly the door slammed open, nearly spilling him out of the chair. Bournell stood on the threshold, pointing at him. "Mulder, who knows old Greek?" the agent demanded hoarsely.

Mulder shrugged. "I don't know. Old Greeks?"

Bournell blinked slowly, took a step into the office just as a hush of cold air spilled out of the vents. He made as if to close the door behind them, and changed his mind. Instead, he slipped one hand into a pocket.

"Priests, Mulder. Seminarians. Teachers in a seminary. Preachers, Mulder. Ministers." His free hand took a slow swipe of his tie. "People, Mulder, who study the Bible."

Mulder waited patiently, unmoving. He suspected it wouldn't exactly do to mention that the list might also include professors of ancient languages, archaeology, and who knew what else. Not to mention immigrants who had been schooled in Greece. Or nonacademic scholars of at least a dozen different disciplines, both scientific and otherwise. The man was excited about something, and he didn't want to throw him off.

"I got to thinking," the agent continued, a finger tapping the face of the closest filing cabinet. "You were right about the Greek part, and I've kicked myself a dozen times for not noticing it before. But I have to tell you I think you're wrong about the name."

Mulder sat up slowly, drawing in his legs, tilting his head, eyes slightly narrowed. "How?"

"I was in a fraternity in college."

"A sorority would have been more fun."

Bournell glared at him in faint disgust until he lifted a hand in apology.

"Okay. So you were in a fraternity. What does that have to do with—"

"Alpha Chi Rho, it was." He held out his right hand; on it was an impressive signet ring, a faceted dark ruby centered in gold. He took a step closer so Mulder could see it more clearly. "On the rim, Mulder. Check out the rim."

He did, saw the three raised letters, and held his breath.

The hand dropped away. "Chi Rho. The symbol for Christ, Mulder." There was glee in his voice, in the way his hand danced at his side. "That's what he carved: Chi Rho." A sharp nod, a slap of the hand against his thigh. "Those women aren't hookers, that would be too easy. But I'll bet the farm and farmhouse there's something about them, a connection, that a religious fanatic might find to be… I don't know, sinful."

Mulder sat back, admiration clear. "I'll be damned."

Boumell smiled, rubbed his palms together, and glanced toward the vent. "Man, it's like an icebox in here. Your thermostat busted or what?" He headed for the door, grabbed the knob, and paused before leaving.

Mulder watched his shoulders tense, and relax.

"Hey, thanks, Mulder. No kidding. To be honest, I don't know if I really ever would have seen that Greek stuff. I've had this ring forever and hardly ever looked at it. But I just had it cleaned, and when I was putting it on this morning… well, it got me thinking, you know? And the next thing I knew I was looking at it like I'd never seen it before."

He hesitated, about to say something else, then nodded his thanks and closed the door behind him.

Mulder didn't move for a long time.

FIVE

Sheriff Chuck Sparrow took off his hat, wiped a forearm over what was left of his hair, and slapped the hat back into place, yanking the brim down hard. "What do you think?" the woman beside him asked, her voice tight with the effort not to lose her dinner.

Sparrow shook his head. The best he could figure, either somebody was in sore desperate need to practice his tanning skills, or there was another one of those damn cults holed up in the hills again. Either way, it didn't take a brain surgeon to see that he was in for a hell of a lot more work than his inclination wanted.

They stood side by side near the mouth of a small cave, on the west side of a solitary low hill two miles west of the Hatch ranch. Sprawled in front of it was what was left of a steer, ants and flies now vying for the right to rid the dead animal of whatever they could take.

"What do you think?"

"Donna," he said, "I wish to hell I knew."

She was a tall woman, her figure hidden in boots, baggy jeans, and a man's shirt about a size too large. Her short brown hair was brushed back over her ears, and on her right hand she wore the biggest silver ring Sparrow had ever seen. Her Cherokee was parked on the shoulder, fifty yards away; his patrol car was behind it.

She jutted her chin toward the cave. "You look in there?"

"Yes," he answered with exaggerated patience. "Yes, I looked in there."

"And?"

"And fourteen different kinds of shit is all what I found, all right? Bones. Little bones," he added hastily. "The usual crap."

"I read that they use them, you know. Kind of temporary, so to speak."

He scanned the hillside, squinted at the vehicles. "Now don't take this wrong, all right? But there hasn't been a damn mountain lion around here for nearly as long as I've been working this job. And in case you hadn't noticed, they don't generally skin their meals before they eat them."

"I don't need your sarcasm, Chuck."

No, he thought; what you need is a good swat upside the head, keep you from bothering the hell outta me.

The trouble was, this was the fourth animal he'd come across in just over a week slaughtered like this, and not a single sign, not a single print, not a single goddamn hint of what had killed them. Or rather, what had stripped off their hides. For no reason he could put a finger on, he didn't think they had been killed first. He reckoned the creatures had either died of the shock or had bled to death.

Just like he was about to die of the smell if he didn't get out of here.

He brushed a hand over his mouth as he turned and walked back to the car. Donna followed him slowly, humming to herself and snapping her fingers.

The thing of it was, Sparrow thought as he slid down the shallow ditch and took two grunting strides up the other side, if this was confined to just animals, there wouldn't be such a stink of another kind in the office.

That there were also three people dead, obviously of the same thing—whatever the hell that was—had put the fire on. So to speak. And every time someone called in with another claim, it was Sparrow who personally checked it out. It wasn't that he didn't trust any of his deputies. Thirty-five years roaming the side roads of the desert, talking to the Indians in Santo Domingo, San Felipe and the other pueblos, getting to know the hills and mountains until he could walk them practically blindfolded, did that to a man—made him the so-called area expert, even when he didn't want to be, hadn't asked to be, and would have given his right arm just to be plain stupid.

He reached in the driver's-side window and grabbed the mike, called in and told the dispatcher what he'd found and where. While Donna watched him distrustfully, he ordered a van to pick up the carcass, and a vet standing by to handle the examination. When he was finished, he dropped the mike onto the seat and leaned back against the door, arms folded across a chest nearly as broad as the stomach below it.

"You think you might go talk to Annie?" She stood in the middle of the two-lane road, sketching senseless patterns in the dust that turned the blacktop gray.

"What for?" He waved vaguely to his right. "Her place is too far away."

"Might be one of hers."

"Probably," he admitted. Then he gestured toward the hill, meaning what lay a mile or so beyond, what some of the locals called the Konochine Wall. "Might be one of theirs, too, you ever think of that?"

She didn't look, and he smiled. Donna Falkner didn't much care for the Kono-chine. For years they had refused her offers to broker whatever craftwork they wanted to sell; once they had even chased her off the reservation. Literally chased her, yelling and waving whatever came to hand, as if they wanted to drag her up Sangre Viento Mesa and drop her off, just as they had done to the Spanish priests and soldiers during the Pueblo Revolt over three hundred years before.

The difference was, the Spaniards never returned to the Konochine. No one knew why.

Now there was a middleman, Nick Lanaya, who worked with her, so she never had to set foot on the reservation at all.

"Satanists," Donna suggested then, still toeing the blacktop, hands in her hip pockets.

Sparrow snorted. He had been through the entire list of the usuals, from Satanists all the way to half-assed dopeheads who thought they could bring on a better world by chopping the heads off calves and goats. None of them, as far as he knew, killed like this, or killed both animals and people quite so ruthlessly and left the bodies behind.

But then, he wasn't an expert there, and he sighed as he finally admitted that maybe it was time to bring those experts in. Pride and getting nowhere fast were getting him crucified in the papers.

\\\\\\\\\\\\\\\\\\\

Two men sat on a hillside, their loose-fitting clothes as brown and tan as the ground around them. The first was old, his straight hair dull white and touching his bony shoulders. The planes of his face were sharp, the dark skin crevassed around the mouth and deep-set eyes. There was a necklace of rattlesnake spine around his neck.

The second man was much younger, but not young. His hair was still black, pulled back into a ponytail held by a braided circlet of gold and turquoise. His knees were drawn up, and his hands dangled between them, long fingers constantly moving like reeds in a slow wind.

When they spoke, which wasn't often, it was in a combination of bastard Spanish and Konochine. "Father," the younger man said, attitude and voice deferential and weary, "you have to stop it."

The old man shook his head.

"But you know what he's doing. He's damning us all."

No answer.

The younger man reached for a tuft of grass, stopping himself just before he grabbed it. The blades were sharp; had he pulled, they would have drawn blood. He grabbed a stone instead and flung it hard down the slope.

Below was the road that led out of the gap, past Annie Hatch's ranch to the interstate. Behind was Sangre Viento Mesa.

"People are dying, Dugan," he said at last, abandoning honorifics for first names. "He takes them as far away as Albuquerque now." He didn't turn his head; he knew the old man wasn't watching. "It's gotten too big to hide. They're going to come sooner or later, the authorities. We won't be able to keep them out."

The old man touched his necklace. "They can come, Nick. They can look. They won't find anything."

"And if they do?" the younger man persisted.

The old man almost smiled. "They won't believe it."

Donna watched the sheriff's car speed away, dust swirling into rooster tails from its rear tires. She knew his ego had taken a fierce beating because he hadn't yet been able to locate the cult behind the atrocities, but she didn't think he or the city police were looking in the right place. Haunting the downtown Albuquerque bars and sending undercover men to the university wasn't going to accomplish anything but pay out more overtime.

She squinted at the sky, saw nothing but a wisp of a cloud that looked lost amid all that washed-out blue.

The *Journal* and the *Tribune* were screaming for someone's blood, and if Sparrow didn't watch out, it was going to be his.

Not, she thought sourly as she headed back to her car, that it was any concern of hers. He was a big boy. He could take care of himself. Just because he never paid her any mind whenever she tried to give him a hand, just because he thought she was a little off-center, just because he never gave her the time of day unless she asked him right out…

"Shit," she said, and kicked at the Cherokee's front tire. "Idiot."

She swung herself in, hissing sharply when her fingers grabbed the hot steering wheel and snapped away. A pair of colorless work gloves lay on the passenger seat, and she slipped them on, glancing in the rearview mirror, then looking toward the hill and the cloud of flies that marked the steer's carcass. Her stomach lurched; a slow deep breath settled it.

This wasn't like her at all.

She had seen worse out in the desert, and much worse in town, after a knife fight or a shooting. She had no idea why this spooked her so much.

A quick turn of the key fired the engine, and another glance in the rearview nearly made her scream.

A pickup more rust and dust than red streaked directly toward her rear bumper, sunlight exploding from the windshield, the grill like a mouth of gleaming shark's teeth.

She braced herself for the impact, but the truck swerved at the last second, slowed abruptly, and passed her so sedately she wondered if it had really been speeding at all, if it hadn't been her imagination.

A look to her right, and the other driver stared back.

Oh God, she thought.

A gray hat pulled low, black sunglasses, long black hair in a ponytail that reached to the center of the man's back.

Leon Ciola.

She didn't realize she was holding her breath until the pickup disappeared ahead of the dust its tires raised; then she sagged against the seat, tilted her head back, and closed her eyes. Air conditioning spilled across her lap; she shivered but didn' t turn it down or deflect it elsewhere. She kept her eyes closed until she couldn't stand it. When they opened, she was alone; even the dust had gone.

Go, she ordered as she swallowed dryly; go home, girl.

It took her ten minutes before she could take the wheel again without shaking, another ten minutes before she realized she wasn't moving and tromped on the accelerator, ignoring the machine gun that rattled beneath the carriage, fighting the fishtail until the vehicle straightened, and the sun made her blind to everything but the road.

Home first, and a drink. Then she would call Sparrow and tell him Ciola was back.

She had a feeling the sheriff would be royally pissed.

The younger man stood, mock-groaning as he rubbed the small of his back and stretched his legs to relieve the stiffness. He tried again:

"Dugan, we can't let this happen. It will ruin everything we've worked for."

The old man didn't rise, didn't look back. His gaze seemed to focus on the dust clouds in the distance. "We can't stop it, Nick."

"Maybe not, but we can stop him."

"We don't know for sure."

But damnit, we do, the younger man thought angrily; we know damn well it's him, and we're doing nothing about it. Nothing at all.

Asked softly: "What if you're wrong?"

Nick shook his head, though he knew the old man couldn't see it. "If I am wrong, what have we lost? The Anglos come in, they look around, they go away, we're left alone. What have we lost, Dugan?"

Answered softly: "What is ours."

Again the younger man shook his head. This was an argument as old as he, and older: let more of the world in, it can be done without loss, we have television and radio, for crying out loud; or, keep the world out because it has nothing to do with what makes us what we are.

It was the reason the young were leaving, many of them not coming back.

In a single motion so rapid and smooth it seemed like no motion at all, the old man was on his feet, dusting off his pants, checking the time by the sun. Without speaking he walked to the top of the hill, Nick following to one side and a step behind. When they reached the crest, Dugan pointed to the pale ghost of the moon.

"One more night and it will be done."

Nick said nothing, and the silence spelled his doubt.

"One more night." The old man took his arm; the way down into the valley was slippery and steep. "It takes faith these days, you know." The hint of a smile. "A lot more than it used to, I'm afraid. But it is there."

It wasn't the faith Nick worried about. He had it, too, and even during his time in the outside world, he had kept it.

It wasn't the faith.

It was the killing.

It was what the killing would bring.

SIX

M ulder strolled into his office whistling. It was the kind of day that began with a gorgeous, unreal sunrise, Hollywood at its best, and carried that promise so well, he was half-afraid he was dreaming. The heat wave had broken three days before, bringing springlike temperatures to the capital, light showers at night to wash the streets, and a steady breeze that had thus far kept pollution from hazing the blue sky.

Leaves weren't dusty, the flowers were bright… it was so utterly perfect, it was damn close to sickening.

But he'd take it. He wasn't that much of a fool.

It took a second for him to notice Scully in his chair.

"Morning," he said brightly.

Since the meeting with Skinner, he had resolved two more knots in two more cases that had been bugging him for weeks. For a change, the agents involved were openly and immediately grateful; egos weren't bruised, and two more of the bad guys were on their way to capture.

He also wasn't surprised that Beth Neuhouse, unlike Bournell, hadn't come around to apologize for her behavior. In fact, he hadn't seen her for a week, another sign that life was good and maybe he'd been mistaken about the reprimand setup.

All he needed now was a generous supply of sunflower seeds, and things would be perfect.

"So what's up?" he asked, dropping his briefcase beside an overloaded desk.

Scully reached down beside her, and tossed him a plastic bag.

He caught it against his chest one-handed and held it up. It was a half-pound of sunflower seeds. He smiled. A sign; it had to be a sign. The smile turned to suspicion. "You hate it when I eat these things. It gets messy. You hate messy." He hefted the bag. "What's the catch?"

She shrugged innocently and reached down again, into her own briefcase. She wore a green suit and loose matching blouse fastened at the collar.

"What's the catch, Scully?" he repeated, tossing the bag onto his desk.

She held up a folder, waggled it, and placed it in her lap almost primly.

He stared at the folder, at her, and at the sunflower seeds. They were definitely a sign, and he had no intention of reading it.

Scully smiled faintly at his expression. "Don't worry. You'll probably like this one."

He waited. She settled back in the chair. "So, what do you know about cattle mutilations?"

"Oh, please, Scully, not that again, please." He crossed to a wheeled office chair and dropped into it, swiveling around to face her as he crossed his legs at the knee. He wasn't going to answer what was obviously a rhetorical question, until he realized he had to. She was preparing him, preparing his mind for something "ordinary" didn't describe.

"All right." He clasped his hands loosely, elbows on the chair's arms. "Depending on who you talk to, you either have half-baked cults that demand bizarre sacrifices—cows being the animal of choice—secret government experiments in immunology based on actual and potential chemical warfare, chemical warfare tests alone, or…" He looked at the ceiling. "Or experiments with alleged alien-based technology." He shook his head slowly. "To name a few."

Without responding, she flipped open the folder. "The cattle are either bled, they have sections of hide and/or muscle and/or organs removed—"

"—or they're just sliced all to hell and left in the middle of a field for some poor farmer to fall over. So what? You know this isn't the sort of thing I—" He stopped, and they looked at each other.

He had almost said, "need to know."

He broke contact first, staring at the tip of his shoe. "Where?"

"New Mexico."

He barked a laugh. "Cattle mutilations? Right. Near Roswell, I suppose. Come on, Scully, give me a break. I'm not about to get into that—" She held up a pair of photographs without comment.

After a moment he took them; after another moment, he placed both feet on the floor and leaned over, elbows now resting on his thighs. It took a while for him to understand what he was looking at, and when he did, he inhaled quickly.

At first they seemed to be little more than solid masses of stained white and gray lying on what appeared to be bare earth. Sandy, grainy, maybe desert ground. A blink to change the perspective, and their forms resolved into the carcasses of animals that had been skinned, stripped in some areas right to the bone. There was virtually nothing left of their heads but exposed skull.

"The one on the left," she told him, "hadn't been found for a couple of days."

Its eyes were gone, and a closer examination showed him swarming ants, and a few flies the photographer hadn't been able to shoo away. Its hind legs had been twisted from their sockets; its mouth was open, the tongue still there, but it was much smaller, thinner than it ought to be, and evidently raw. Although there were shadows, and although he tried, he couldn't spot any pools or traces of blood.

He glanced up, frowning. "Blood?"

Scully nodded. "I know, I've looked, too. If it's exsanguination, it's almost too well done. Otherwise… " A one-shoulder shrug. "cauterization is about the only other thing I can think of. Based on the pictures, that is. To know exactly, we'll have to talk to those who were at the scene."

At her direction, he checked the photograph on the right.

"Now that one," she explained, "was found, they think, only a few hours after it happened. The eyes are gone there as well, but I can't tell if they've been surgically removed or…"

She didn't finish; she didn't have to.

"The blood thing again," he said, looking from one exhibit to the other.

"Right. And again, I don't have an answer for you. Not based on what we have now.

Look close at the hindquarters, though. Twisted, just like the other one. I doubt if they're still in their sockets. There was a lot of force exerted there, Mulder. A lot."

"Meaning?"

"Too soon, Mulder, you know that. Most of the hide is gone, although—" She leaned over and pointed."—it looks as if there are still some strips around the belly. Maybe between the legs, too. With all that muscle tissue gone or shredded, it's hard to tell."

He looked up. "This isn't just skinning. What do you figure? Flayed?"

She nodded cautiously, unwilling as always to commit until she had seen the evidence firsthand. "I think so. I won't know until I've had a good look for myself."

Then she handed him another pair.

Puzzled, he took them, looked down, and rocked back in the chair, swallowing heavily. "Jesus."

People; they were people.

He closed his eyes briefly and set the pictures aside. He had seen any number of horrors over the past several years, from dismemberment to outright butchery, but there had been nothing as vicious as this. He didn't need to look at them more than once to know this was something different. To put it mildly.

Flayed.

These people had been flayed, and he didn't need to ask if they had been alive when it happened.

"Skinner, right?" The Assistant Director would have flagged this for him as soon as it had arrived.

Scully nodded as she pushed absently at her hair, trying to tuck it behind one ear. "The local authorities, the county sheriff's office, called…" She checked a page of the file. "They called Red Garson in the Albuquerque office. Apparently it didn't take him very long to think of you."

Mulder knew Garson slightly, a weathered, rangy westerner who had breezed through the Bureau academy at Quantico, less with considerable skill—although he had it in abundance—than with an almost frantic enthusiasm born of a man determined to get out of the East as fast as he could. Which he had done as soon as he could. He was no slouch when it came to on-site investigations, so this must have thrown him completely. It wasn't like him to ask for anyone's help.

"Mulder, whoever did this is truly sick."

Sick, deranged, or so devoid of emotion that he might as well not be human.

He grabbed a picture at random—it was a couple, and he was thankful that what was left of their faces was turned away from the camera.

"Tied? Drugged?"

Scully cleared her throat. "It's hard to tell, but initial indications are…" She paused, and he heard the nervousness, and the anger, in her voice. "Indications are they weren't. And Garson doesn't think they were killed somewhere else and dumped at the site."

He rubbed a hand over his mouth, bit down on his lower lip thoughtfully.

"Autopsies by the medical examiner, a woman named Helen Rios, are inconclusive on whether they were actually conscious or not at the time of death. The lack of substantial quantities of epinephrine seems to indicate it happened too fast for the chemical to form, which it usually does in abundance in cases of extreme violence."

"A victim's adrenaline rush," he said quietly.

Scully looked up from the report. "Right. Something else, too."

He didn't know what question to ask.

"They appear to have been dressed at the time of the assault."

He shifted uneasily. "Wait."

"Shards of clothing were found around each of the scenes. Not even that—no more than bits. Strips of leather from boots or shoes. Metal buttons."

"Scully, hold it."

Her hand trembling slightly, she dropped the folder back into her briefcase. "The pathologist says they either died of shock or bled to death." She inhaled slowly. "Garson, in a sidebar, seems to think they were frightened to death, that they were dead before they hit the ground."

Mulder waved her silent. "Scully, these people—forget about the animals for a minute—these people were attacked by someone, or a group of someones, flayed until their clothes were shredded and their skin was taken off." He gestured vaguely. Shook his head. "You're saying—"

"*They're* saying," she corrected.

"Okay. Okay, they're saying it happened so fast, epinephrine hadn't had time to…" He smiled without humor and looked blindly around the room. "Scully, you know as well as I do that's damn near impossible."

"Probably," she admitted. "I haven't had a lot of time to think about it."

He stood abruptly. "You don't have to think about it, Scully. There's nothing to think about. It's practically flat-out impossible."

"Which is why we have to be at Dulles first thing in the morning. Stopover at Dallas, we'll be in New Mexico by one their time." She raised a finger to forestall a response. "And remember: practically is the right word here, Mulder. That does not mean definitely."

He stared at her briefcase, spread his arms at all the work yet undone he could see in the office, and said, "What?" at the twitch of a smile on her lips.

She didn't have to answer.

He usually reacted this way when a clear X-File landed in his lap. A switching of gears, of mindset, excitement of one kind changing to excitement of another. Impossible, to him, meant someone else had decided there were no explanations for whatever had happened.

But there were always explanations.

Always.

His superiors, and Scully, didn't always like them, but they were there.

Sometimes all it took was a little imagination to find them. A less hidebound way of looking at the world. A willingness to understand that the truth sometimes wore a mask.

"There's something else," she added as he reached for the sunflower seeds and his briefcase.

"What?"

She stood and brushed at her skirt. "There was a witness to one of the killings."

He felt his mouth open. "You're kidding. He saw who did it?"

"She," Scully corrected. "And she claims it wasn't a person."

He waited.

"She said it was a shadow."

Brother, he thought.

"Either that, or a ghost."

SEVEN

A low fire burned in a shallow pit.

Smoke rose in dark trails, winding fire-reflected patterns around the large underground room before escaping through the ragged round hole in the ceiling.

Shadows on the roughly hewn rock walls cast by shadows seated on planks around the pit.

Six men, cross-legged and naked, their bodies lean and rawhide-taut, stringlike hair caught in the sweat that glittered in the firelight, their hands on their knees. Their eyes on the flames that swayed to a breeze not one of them could feel.

Over the fire, resting on a metal grate, a small, flame-blackened pot in which a colorless liquid bubbled without raising steam.

A seventh man sat on a chair carved from dull red stone, back in the shadows where the rite said he belonged. He wore no clothing save a cloth headband embedded with polished stones and gems, none of them alike, none bigger than the tip of a finger. In his right hand he held the spine of a snake; from his left hand dangled the tail of a black horse, knotted at the end and wound through with blue, red, and yellow ribbons. His black eyes were unfocused.

Eventually one of the six stirred, chest rising and falling in a long, silent sigh. He took a clay ladle from the hand of the man on his left, dipped it into the pot, and stood as best he could on scrawny legs that barely held him. A word spoken to the fire. A word spoken to the smoke-touched night sky visible through the hole. Then he carried the ladle to the man in the chair, muttered a few words, and poured the boiling liquid over the seventh man's head.

The man didn't move.

The water burned through his hair, over his shoulders, down his back and chest. He still didn't move.

The horsetail twitched, but the hand that held it didn't move.

The old man returned to the circle, sat, and after shifting once, didn't move.

The only sound was the fire.

\\\\\\\\\\\\\\\\\

A lone man waiting in the middle of nowhere.

He stood in the center of a scattering of bones—coyote, mountain lion, horse, bull, ram, snake.

And from where he stood, he could see smoke rising above Sangre Viento Mesa, rising in separate trails until, a hundred feet above, it gathered itself into a single dark column that seemed to make its way to the moon.

In the center of the smoke-made basket the moonlight glowed emerald.

The man smiled, but there was no humor.

He spread his arms as if to entice the smoke toward him.

It didn't move.

He was patient.

It had moved before; it would move again.

And after tonight, when the old fools had finished, he would make it move on his own.

All he had to do was believe.

Donna rolled over in her sleep, moaning so loudly it woke her up. She blinked rapidly to dispel the nightmare, and when she was sure it was done, she swung her legs over the side of the bed and sat up, pushing hair away from her eyes, mouth open to catch the cool air that puckered her skin and made her shiver.

The house was quiet.

The neighborhood, such as it was, was quiet.

Moonlight slipped between the cracks the curtains left over the room's two windows, slants of it that trapped sparkling particles of dust.

She yawned and stood, yawned again as she scratched at her side and under her breasts. The nightmare was gone, scattered, but she knew she had had one, knew it was probably the same one she had had over the past two weeks:

She walked in the desert, wearing only a long tee-shirt, bare feet feeling the night cold of the desert floor. A steady wind blew into her face. A full moon so large it seemed about to collide with the Earth, and too many stars to count.

Despite the wind's direction, she could hear something moving close behind her, but whenever she looked back, the night was empty except for her shadow.

It hissed at her.

It scraped toward her.

When she couldn't take it any longer, she woke up, knowing that if she didn't, she was going to die.

She didn't believe in omens, but she couldn't help but wonder.

Now she padded sleepily into the kitchen, opened the refrigerator, and wondered if it was too late, or too early, to have a beer. Not that it mattered. If she had one now, she'd be in the bathroom before dawn, cursing herself and wondering how she'd make it through the day with so little sleep.

She let the door swing shut with a righteous nod, yawned, and moved to the back door.

Her yard was small, ending, like all the other yards scattered along the side road, in a stone-block wall painted the color of the earth. Poplars along the back blocked her view of the other houses even though they were too far away to see even in daylight, unless she was right at the wall.

Suddenly she felt much too alone.

There was no one out there.

She was cut off, and helpless.

The panic rose, and she was helpless to stop it. Running from the room did her no good because she could see nothing from the living room window either—the rosebushes she had spent so much time training to be a hedge fragmented her view of the road, erasing sight of the field across the way.

Trapped; she was trapped.

A small cry followed her to the door. She flung it open and ran onto the stoop, stopping before she flung herself off the steps. Cold concrete made her gasp; cold wind plastered the tee-shirt to her chest and stomach.

I am, she decided, moving back into town first thing in the morning.

It was the same vow she made after every nightmare, and it made her smile.

Oh boy, tough broad, she thought sarcastically; think you're so tough, and a lousy dream makes you a puddle.

She stepped back over the threshold, laughing aloud, but not loud enough that she didn't hear the hissing.

The smoke rose and coiled and swallowed the emerald light.

Mike Ostrand was a little drunk.

Hell, he was a lot drunk, and could barely see the dashboard, much less the interstate. The gray slash of his headlamps blurred and sharpened, making the road swing from side to side as if the car couldn't stay in its proper lane.

This late, though, he didn't much give a damn.

The road from Santa Fe was, aside from occasional rises not quite hills, fairly straight all the way to Bernalillo, and into Albuquerque beyond. Just aim the damn thing and hold onto the wheel. He'd done it hundreds of times.

He hiccuped, belched, and grimaced at the sour taste that rose in his throat, shaking his head sharply as if to fling the taste away.

The radio muttered a little Willie Nelson.

He wiped his eyes with one hand and checked the rearview mirror. Nothing back there but black.

ack.

seventy.

re really lucky, he'd be home by two and asleep by

e it as far as the bedroom. Two-five if he couldn't get

a giggle, and rolled down the window when he felt a

not, he knew enough to understand that cold air blasting

infinitely preferable to dozing off and ending up nose-

ead through the windshield.

od.

ible was steady.

declared to the road. "Steady as a rock and twice as hard."

another belch.

It ha_____ ,ood night. No, it had been a great night. Those pinheads in Santa Fe, thinking they knew ahead of the rest of the world what the next artsy trend would be, had decided he was it. Living collages, they called it; the desert genius, they called him.

"My God!" he yelled, half in joy, half in derision.

After a dozen years trying to sell paintings even he couldn't abide, he'd sliced a small cactus in half, glued it to a canvas, added a few tiny bird bones and a couple of beads, called it something or other, and as a lark, brought it north.

They loved it.

They fucking loved it.

He had meant it as a thumbed nose at their pretensions, and they had fallen over themselves trying to buy it.

The wind twisted through the car, tangling his long blond hair, tugging at it, threatening a headache.

Five years later, twenty-five carefully assembled when he was roaring drunk canvases later, his bank account was fat, his home was new, his car was turned in every year, and the women were lined up six to the dozen, just waiting for his living desert fingers to work their magic on them.

It almost made him sick.

It didn't make him stupid.

Trends were little more than fads, and he knew full well that the next season might be his last. Which was why he needed to hole up for a while, work through an even dozen more projects, and get himself out before he ended up like the others—flat broke and saying, "I used to be someone, you know, really, I was," while they cadged another beer from a stranger in a strange bar.

The speedometer topped eighty.

The headache began.

Acid bubbled in his stomach.

The back of his hand scrubbed across his face, and when his vision cleared, he saw something to the right, just beyond the edge of the light.

He frowned as he stared at it, then yelped as the car followed his stare and angled for the shoulder. The correction was too sharp, and he swung off toward the wide empty median, swung back again, hit the accelerator instead of the brakes, and yelled soundlessly when the right-side tires bit into the earth off the blacktop.

The car shuddered.

He froze—turn into the skid? turn out of the skid?—and watched in horror as the low shrubs and deep ditch charged him and veered away at the last minute, putting him back on the road.

Sweat masked his face.

His bladder demanded immediate relief.

His left hand shook so much he thrust it between his knees and squeezed until it calmed.

"My God," he whispered. "Jesus, man, Jesus."

Twenty-five, he swore to himself; he didn't care if it took until dawn, he wouldn't go faster than twenty-five all the way home.

He wasn't sober, but he sure as hell wasn't as drunk as he had been.

The speedometer reached fifty.

He saw the needle, saw it climb again slowly, and decided it would be all right. Sixty, no more; he'd be home quicker, and that was okay because he was a menace to himself out here.

A hard swallow, a deep breath, his right hand flicking the radio off because what he didn't need now was interference with his concentration. Just watch the road, pay no attention to anything that—

He saw it again.

Just a suggestion of movement running with him on the other side of the ditch. Which was impossible. He was doing sixty-five, for God's sake, there wasn't anything except another car that could go that fast.

He squinted a stare, broke it off when the car began to drift, and licked his lips. There wasn't anything over there.

Good God, there couldn't be anything over there. It was the headlights, that's all, running along a row of juniper maybe, or some piñon, rock, something like that. His eyes caught the strobelike reflection, and the scotch turned it into something that paced him.

That's all it was.

He wished the moon were a little brighter.

Forget the new canvases, he decided a half-mile later; the hell with it, he was done. He had enough money, the house was paid for, what the hell more could he want?

The car jumped sideways when something slammed into the passenger door.

He yelled, and watched his hands blur around the wheel, watched the road blur black to gray and black again, screamed when the car was struck a second time, and looked over to see what drunken idiot was trying to run him off the road.

There was nothing there.

When he looked back, it was too late.

The highway was gone. All he could do was cross his arms in front of his face, close his eyes, and scream.

There was no fire, no explosion.

Mike Ostrand hung upside down in his seatbelt, listening to the engine tick, listening to the wind blow through the open window.

Listening to the hiss he thought was the tires spinning to a halt.

A few seconds later, he blacked out when something reached through the window and touched his arm.

EIGHT

La Mosca Inn sat between the Rio Grande and a high adobe wall that fronted the road. Eight units extended left and right from a central two-story building that housed the office, a large flagstone waiting room cooled by a small sparking fountain, and a restaurant large enough to seat one hundred without elbows and voices clashing. Spanish tile on the roof, shade provided by cottonwood and mountain ash, and a single huge Russian olive in the center of the courtyard.

Scully sat on a wood bench that ringed the massive tree, facing the arched entrance whose elaborate iron gates were closed each night at, the proprietor told her, precisely midnight. She let her eyes close, and touched a finger to her forehead, to trap a droplet of sweat that had broken from her hairline.

"Feeling better?" a voice rasped beside her.

"Not really."

The day had gone wrong from minute one: she'd overslept and had to race to the airport, only to learn that the flight had been delayed. For an hour. Then two. Once airborne, she had planned to set up her laptop computer, so she and Mulder could go over what details of the case they had.

It didn't happen.

Roller-coaster turbulence rode them all the way to Dallas, making reading the computer screen a nauseating experience; she spent most of the time trying, and failing, to doze. Then a series of thunderstorms ringing the Texas city forced them to swerve wide into a holding pattern until the squall line had passed. Another hour lost, and so was their connecting flight.

"Cursed," Mulder had said at one point. "This whole thing is cursed."

By the time they landed in Albuquerque, she was ready to believe in curses; by the time Red Garson had sped them in his Jeep out of the city, north to Bernalillo, she was ready to spend the rest of her life walking.

The man beside her shifted to get her attention.

She opened her eyes and smiled at him wanly.

Red was as Mulder had told her, a tall, lean, middle-aged man whose lined face and hands spoke of time spent in the mountains and the desert. She had no idea where he'd gotten his nickname, because his blond hair was pale, his blue eyes dark; part of his left ear was missing, bitten off, he told her, in a fight with a man who had a strong aversion to spending the rest of his life in federal prison.

Hardly a stereotypical FBI agent.

When he smiled, only his lips moved; he never showed his teeth.

He jerked his thumb over his shoulder. "You think he's fallen asleep?"

"I doubt it."

A pickup chugged past the Inn, backfired twice, and left a curl of black smoke behind.

"Dana?"

She nodded to show him she was listening.

"Why does he call you Scully all the time? I mean, you do have a first name."

"Because he can," she answered simply, without sarcasm, and didn't bother to explain. Just as it would be hard to explain why Mulder was, without question, the best friend she had. It was more than just being partners, being able to rely on each other when one of them was in danger, or when one of them needed a boost when a case seemed to be going bad; and it was more than simply their contrasting styles, which, perversely to some, complemented each other perfectly.

What it was, she sometimes thought, was an indefinable instinct, a silent signal that let her know that whatever else changed, whatever else happened, Mulder would always be there when he had to be. One way or another.

At that moment she heard a footfall and grinned. "Here he comes."

Garson looked startled, looked around and saw him walking along one of the stone paths that wound through the courtyard garden. She had to admit he looked strange without his suit. Over his shoulder he carried a denim jacket, not for appearance but to hide the holster he wore on his left hip.

He also looked as frazzled as she felt.

"It's hot," he said, dropping onto the bench beside her.

"It's July, Mulder," Garson reminded him. "It's New Mexico. What did you expect?"

"Heat I can get at home. An oven I already have in my apartment." He scratched through his hair and shook his head as though trying to force himself awake.

"It isn't for everybody," Garson admitted, adding without saying so that "every-body" must be crazy if they didn't instantly fall in love with this part of the country. "And remember, you're a mile farther up than you were in Washington. Thinner air. Take it easy for a while, understand? You go shooting off in fourteen directions at once, you're going to drop."

Mulder grunted, then stood again. "Hey, look." He headed for the gate.

"Mulder," Scully called. "We haven't time—"

He turned, grinning, and pointed to a small dust devil spinning lazily in the road. "We used to get these things at home. Leaves, you know?" He moved closer; it was no higher than his shin. "We'd try to get inside." His foot inched toward the dervish's base and apparently broke some unseen barrier. The dust devil fell apart, and Mulder toed the place where it had been.

Scully, who was already feeling the effects of the altitude, let the silence settle for a few seconds before she said, "Mulder, come over here, I think we'd better not waste any more time." She checked her watch; it was just after four. "I suppose it's too late to catch Dr. Rios. What about... Patty? Patty Deven. Is she well enough to talk to us?"

Garson stabbed a thumb at her as Mulder rejoined them. "She always like this?"

"We have three people murdered, Red. The altitude didn't kill them."

The man nodded, accepting the point and the rebuke without taking offense. "The Devens live about a mile down the road. They're fixing to head back to Chicago as soon as this is cleared up. I'll take you over, but I'm telling you now that you won't be welcome."

He was right.

Scully caught the instant hostility as soon as Kurt Deven opened the trailer door and saw who it was. When Garson introduced his companions, the man scowled and told them to wait. Then he closed the door. Hard.

Mulder nodded toward the riverline of cottonwood sixty or seventy yards away. "Down there?"

"Yep. The bank slopes sharp right about where you're looking. It happened a little ways to the right."

Scully shaded her eyes against the low-hanging sun and tried to see it at night, with little but moon and stars for illumination. The trailer wouldn't help; it was too far away, and except for the skeleton of an unfinished house beside it, there were no other homes in the immediate area, even though she saw flagged wooden stakes in the ground, marking other lots soon to be developed. The nearest trailer was a good sixty yards away.

The door opened.

The two men stepped aside as a woman stepped down onto the cinder-block steps. She was short and slight, with straight blonde hair that needed a brushing, and a lost, empty look in her eyes. When she spoke, rage and grief made her hoarse: "She doesn't want to talk to you again, Mr. Garson."

Red told her softly he understood, and apologized for the intrusion. "But I have these folks here, Mrs. Deven. All the way from Washington." He cleared his throat, glanced at the open doorway. "They're experts in this kind of crime. If anyone can catch the—"

"Nobody has," she snapped. "It's been two weeks, and nobody has."

Scully lifted a hand to draw her attention. "Mrs. Deven?"

The woman took her time: "What?"

Scully kept her voice gentle. "Mrs. Deven, I won't lie to you. I won't pretend to know how you feel for your loss, or how your daughter feels. But Agent Mulder and I have done this more times than I ever want to tell you. And if nothing else, I can promise you that we don't quit. We're not perfect, but we do not quit."

Mary Deven's hands pressed lightly to her stomach, eyes narrowed. "Are you promising me you'll catch him?"

"No," Mulder answered, just as gently, just as firmly. "We're only promising you that we won't quit. And if you don't want us to bother you, or your family, you won't have to worry."

Mrs. Deven stared at the trees, blinking rapidly, then not at all. "Just don't take her down there," she said, barely above a whisper. "You take her down there, I'll lose her."

Scully agreed readily, and said nothing when Mulder asked Garson to show him the scene. After all this time, there wouldn't be anything left of real value—Garson and his men and the local police would have raked it over thoroughly. Mulder, however, had a knack for finding things in barren places, a knack she didn't pretend to understand as well as she wanted to.

"Agent Scully?"

Wan, painfully thin, Patty Deven was the mirror image of her mother, right down to the haunted look. A fading bruise spread across her right cheek and temple. Her eyes were too large behind her glasses.

They sat on two lawn chairs. There was no shade, and no offer of a drink.

After a long silence, with the girl staring at the knot of fingers in her lap, Scully leaned forward and said, "What did you see, Patty?" Nothing more.

Mulder stood on the bare ground, checked the branches above him, glanced at the shallow river below. "Here?"

"Just about," Garson said. But "here" was nothing. The ground was too hard for tracks, and with no direct line of sight to the trailer, there was nothing much to work on. He asked Garson to stand approximately where Patty had been, and scowled.

Dark night, thirty or forty feet away, she wouldn't have been able to see much of anything.

Flashes of movement that accompanied her brother's attack and screams.

She saw a ghost because there was nothing true to focus on.

He hunkered down and ran a palm over the ground. "Have you had rain?"

Garson walked back, taking his time. "This is what we call the monsoon season,

Mulder. You wouldn't know to look at it now, but afternoons we get storms in. Big ones. Usually from the west, and they don't fool around." He shrugged as Mulder stood. "Trouble is, rain washes the evidence away, and the ground's like rock again before noon the next day. This is a waste of time."

Maybe, Mulder thought; maybe not.

He walked north along the bank, gaze shifting slowly from side to side. Ahead, the underbrush was thick, still uncleared by the developers. He saw no signs that anyone had broken through, which meant they had either come from down below, or from the far side of the trees.

It was something, and it was nothing.

By the time he reached the other agent, he was scowling again. "Gangs?"

"Some." They headed back to the trailer. "This is no gang hit, though. Knives and guns; nothing like this."

"Cults?"

They left the trees behind, and he felt the temperature already beginning to rise. Scully was still in her lawn chair; she was alone.

"What kind of cults you want, Mulder? We have New Age swamis communing in the desert. We have the Second Coming believers who wander around the mountains and then use their cellulars when they get lost. And we have the flying saucer nuts, who figure Roswell is the key to all intergalactic understanding." A sideways glance Mulder didn't miss. "That's kind of your territory, isn't it?"

The only answer was a noncommittal grunt, and Garson was smart enough to leave it alone.

Scully stood as they approached, a brief shake of her head when he looked her a question. At that moment he couldn't help a yawn, and turned away so the pale face in the trailer window couldn't see him.

He hoped he had been quick enough.

The one thing Mary Deven didn't need now was the sight of an FBI agent yawning at the site of her only son's murder.

Garson saw it, though. "We're going back," he told them both, not giving them an option to refuse. "You two get something to eat and get some sleep, or you're going to be worthless tomorrow."

"Why? What's tomorrow?"

He touched his hat brim. "Tomorrow, my friend, you're going to meet a genuine movie star."

NINE

Mulder couldn't sleep.

After a slow, almost lethargic dinner, he listened as Scully told him about the interview with the girl, which hadn't told her anything new. Patty had seen even less than her statement had implied. Almost as soon as the attack began, the branch club her brother had been holding spiraled out of the dark and struck her on the side of the face. She had fallen, dazed, and in that state thought she might have heard someone whispering, someone else laughing.

But it was all too muddled, and she had passed out shortly afterward. It was her father who had found the body.

"No ghosts, Scully," Mulder had said, walking her back to her room. "We're dealing with people here."

"You sound disappointed."

He hadn't answered then, and he had no answer now as he put on a jacket and left the room, glad now that he had listened to Carson—despite the day's heat, the desert was downright cold at night.

He walked through a short passageway between the rooms and the main building, and paused.

The back was a garden of cacti and now-closed desert flowers set in random circles ringed by stone, as it was in front. Stone paths wound between them and joined at the back to lead to a half-dozen benches that faced the river. Cotton-woods and willows were illuminated by miniature lanterns hanging amid their leaves, leaving patches of lazy shifting light on the ground.

He wasn't sure, but he thought he smelled honeysuckle.

When he was sure he was alone, he sat on one of the benches and watched what little water there was flow past his feet, electric lanterns on metal riverbank poles glowing just enough to turn the dark to gray.

The moon was out.

He shoved his hands into his jacket pockets and watched it for a while, thinking of nothing in particular until a slip of a cloud gave the moon a face.

Patty Deven, or her mother, adrift in a darkness they would never be able to escape. Pale, only shadows for expression, only hints of what used to be behind their smiles.

It was an all too easy, and all too painful, jump from there to his sister, gone too many years now. Taken when she was eight, by someone, or something, hiding behind the glare of a light that even now he couldn't think about without shuddering, or squinting to shut it out.

To try to see what was behind it.

That was the foundation of his pursuit of the truths buried somewhere within the X-Files.

He looked away from the moon and wiped a hand over his face, then absently rubbed the back of his neck.

He would find Samantha, there was no question about it; until then, however, the best he could do would be to find the men who had murdered Patty's brother.

Again his hand passed over his face. When it slipped into its jacket pocket, though, a brief smile was left behind.

"I'm okay," he said, shifting over to make room for Scully. "Just thinking."

"Out here, that'll get you pneumonia."

"Is that a doctor's truth thing?"

She stretched out her legs, folded her hands on her stomach. "No, it's cold, that's what it is. God, Mulder, why can't you ever have a mood someplace warm?"

They said nothing else for a long time, watching the river, listening to the rustle of the trees, once in a while listening to a dog bark or a car roar past the Inn. For a while the garden filled with diners having after-dinner drinks as they strolled among the garden islands, conversation soft, laughter sometimes loud; for a while the evening breeze stopped, and they couldn't hear a thing but their own breathing.

Then Mulder said, "Scully, has it occurred to you that maybe the people who mutilated those cows weren't the ones who killed Patty's brother and that couple?"

A bird sang softly in the cottonwoods.

"No," she said at last. She looked over. "Why?"

"The history, Scully, the history. Animal mutilations of this sort aren't usually tied to murder. Particularly not brutal ones like these. The animals are assaulted, not people."

He watched her carefully as she looked away. He'd only been thinking aloud, but once the thought had been voiced, he had to make sure.

"No," she repeated with a slow shake of her head. "Whatever was used, however it was done, the timing's too close, the similarities too great. From what we've been told." She shifted uneasily. "I'll know more when I speak to the M.E., but…" She shook her head again. "No." A quick smile. "Besides, aren't you the one who told me that there are coincidences, and then there are coincidences? One is real, the other only an illusion?"

He returned the smile. "Yep."

"Okay. Well, this is no real coincidence, Mulder. The brutality itself is a strong indication of that. All we need to do is find the connection."

"Right. All we need to do."

The bird sang again.

"Then think about this, Scully," he said quietly. "Why? What's so damn important out here that both cattle and kids have to die?"

She didn't respond; he hadn't expected her to.

But he had a strong feeling, an unpleasant one, that whatever answer they finally uncovered, it would be one neither of them would like.

In the middle of the desert, they had been dropped into a nightmare.

"I am not crazy!" Mike Ostrand insisted from his hospital bed. He glared at Sheriff Sparrow, who returned the look without expression. "I did not imagine the accident. I did not imagine this goddamn cast on my goddamn arm. I did not imagine my brand-new car flipped over and left me hanging there like a goddamn Peking duck!"

Sparrow was patient.

"Okay." Ostrand shifted uncomfortably, lips pulling away from his teeth in a grimace. "Okay. So I was a little drunk, I admit it. But that's not why I crashed."

"No, you crashed because some kind of mysterious vehicle, so low you couldn't see it out your window, deliberately forced you off the road."

Ostrand looked at him angrily. "That's right."

"And then it tried to kill you when you were hanging from your seatbelt."

The artist shrugged, winced at the pain that exploded in his shoulder, and sighed capitulation. "Okay, okay, so it was a stupid coyote, okay? So I was so damn scared it scared the hell out of me. It would have scared anybody. But it wasn't a coyote that ran me off the damn road!"

"Good." Sparrow nodded sharply. "Now we're getting somewhere." He glanced down at the small notepad he held in his left hand, chewed on the eraser end of his pencil for a moment, and said, "Now, about that invisible vehicle…"

The Coronado Bar was unoriginal in both name and decor. As Bernalillo inexorably changed from an outpost on the Rio Grande into an Albuquerque bedroom community, the Coronado just as stubbornly refused to change with it. A long bar on the right-hand wall, tables and booths everywhere else, and a jukebox that muttered country-western all day long. The TV on the wall in back never played anything but sports, minor league baseball tonight from Southern California. Smoke and liquor in the air, as many cigarette butts on the bare floor as in the aluminum ashtrays. It catered neither to the tourists nor the newcomers, and didn't much care that business didn't boom. It did well enough, which was well enough for its regulars.

Indian Territory was at the back.

Although there were a handful of exceptions, most of the men who drove in from the pueblos stuck to the two last booths and three last tables. There was nothing belligerent about it; it just happened that way. Even the Spanish stayed away.

Especially when the Konochine came to town.

Leon Ciola nursed a long-neck beer in the last booth. He was alone, seated under a wall lamp whose bulb he had unscrewed as soon as he'd taken his seat. He didn't like the light, didn't like the way the Anglos tried not to stare at the web of scars across his face or the scars on his knuckles.

It was better to sit in shadow.

It was also better to face the entrance, so when the man came in, Ciola would see him first and lift a hand in greeting, before a question could be asked or a voice raised. What he didn't need tonight was talk, debate—What's the matter with your people, Leon, don't they believe in the twentieth century? The time for that was past. The others—Nick Lanaya, Dugan Velador, fools like that—they could do their best to keep the talk alive, to deal with Anglo crooks like that Falkner woman and sell the People down the river without an ounce of guilt. Not him. He had plans.

They thought he was beaten. They thought his time away would change him.

He drank, not sipped.

It had.

It had changed him.

It had made him worse.

Just before eleven the man came in, spotted him right away, and dropped heavily into the booth.

Ciola tugged on the beak on his cap, a greeting and an adjustment. "You're late."

"Shit truck wouldn't start. Wasn't for you, I wouldn't make the effort."

Ciola watched him, hiding his distaste by emptying the bottle and waving it over his head, so the waitress, such as she was, would bring him another.

The other man didn't ask for one, and one wasn't offered.

"So?" Leon said.

The man lifted one shoulder. "So they brought in some FBI, straight from Washington. They came in this morning. One man, one woman."

Ciola coughed a laugh. "You're kidding."

"They're supposed to be experts."

"A woman?"

The man nodded, and offered a lopsided grin. "Gets better. They're Anglos."

The empty bottle was taken away, a full one left in its place. The man grabbed it before Ciola did, took a long swallow, and set it down. His fingers stayed around the neck. "Am I worried?"

"No."

"Good." The man stood and hitched up his pants. "I hate being worried. It always pisses me off."

He left without a word to anyone else.

The bartender turned up the baseball game.

Ciola wiped the bottle's mouth with his palm and drank the rest without coming up for air.

When the waitress returned for the empty, he grabbed her wrist, just strongly enough to keep her bent over the table. "*Chica*," he said softly, "what are you doing tonight?"

"Getting a life," she answered, yanking her arm free. "Try it sometime."

He laughed. Not a sound, but he tilted his head back and laughed. Wonderful! She was wonderful! He wiped a tear from his eye and shook his head. Since she didn't want him, he would leave her the biggest tip she had ever had in her miserable life.

And to make it better, he wouldn't even kill her.

\\\\\\\\\\\\\\\\\

Scully massaged the back of her neck. It was hard to keep her eyes open, and she didn't bother to hide a yawn.

"The desert night air," Mulder said. "It s almost too peaceful here."

"I know." She dropped her hand into her lap. "The point is, Mulder, we haven't

enough data yet to show us why they were killed, much less explain the connections in any reasonable fashion. And I don' t think we're going to find them out
here. Not tonight, anyway." She smiled wanly. "I think I'm a little too punchy."

"We both are." He stretched one arm at a time over his head, clasped his hands,
and pushed his palms toward the sky. "I just wish I could see the connections
between a handful of cows, a kid by the river, and a couple in the desert." He
brought his arms down, one hand again moving to his nape.

"Mulder, relax, we just got here, remember? Besides, you have to remember that
the thinner air out here slows down the intellectual process, the result of less
oxygen flowing to the brain."

He grinned and looked at her sideways. "Is that a doctor thing?"

"No, that's a Scully thing." She grinned and pushed off the bench and held out
her hand. When he grabbed it, she pulled him up, turned him around, pushing
him lightly toward the motel. "The doctor thing is, get some sleep, like Red said,
or you'll be useless in the morning."

He nodded as he waved a weary good night over his shoulder, sidestepping a
garden wall just before he tripped over it. Another wave—*I'm okay, I know what I'm
doing*—before he disappeared into the passageway, and she couldn't help wondering
what it was like for him—seeing things other people sometimes couldn't; engaging
in a pursuit with oftentimes terrifying intensity; looking so young and deceptively
guileless that there had been many times when he was severely underestimated.

She wasn't surprised when, passing his room on her way to bed, she saw light
slipping around the edges of the drapes.

Exhausted or not, he would be up most of the night, turning over what he
knew, and setting up what he didn't know so he would know the right questions
to ask, beyond the how and who and why.

She wished him luck.

Right now, she was having difficulty remembering her own name.

She fingered her key out of her pocket, moved on to the next room… and
stopped as she inserted the key in the lock.

You're tired, Dana, that's all.

She looked anyway.

The Inn gates were closed, the lanterns out. Only a faint glow from a nearby
streetlamp reached over the wall.

A man stood at the gate, arms loose at his sides.

She couldn't see his face or his clothes; just his outline.

Tired, she reminded herself, and pushed into the room, flicked on the wall switch, and, as she closed the door, checked the gate again.

He was still there.

Watching.

TEN

M ulder didn't have to be outside to know it was hot and getting hotter, even though it was just past ten. Even with sunglasses, the sun's glare was almost too much, and to stare at the passing scenery too long made it jump and shimmer, showing him things he knew weren't there.

There were no clouds, no signs of rain. It was hard to believe there ever was.

He rode with Scully in the back seat of Sheriff Sparrow's dusty blue-and-white cruiser, Garson up front on the passenger side. It was evident from their conversation that the two men had known each other for a long time, using shorthand gestures and single-word answers, mostly grunts. As far as Mulder could tell, the gist of it was, there had been no further incidents since the death of the boy, except for a drunk driver who claimed to have been forced off the road by an invisible, or incredibly short, vehicle.

"It brings out the nuts, this kind of thing," the sheriff said, lifting his gaze to the rearview mirror. "You find that, too, Agent Mulder?"

He nodded. It was true. Just as it was true that Chuck Sparrow was laying on the western sheriff routine a little thick, constantly hitching his gunbelt, chewing a wad of gum that was supposed to simulate tobacco, getting a deeper drawl in his voice every time he opened his mouth. It wasn't necessarily a bad thing, but it made him wonder why the act at all. Garson would have already filled the man in, and it was the sheriff who had finally asked the FBI for help.

It didn't sit right.

Like not wearing a suit and tie, like wearing running shoes.

He knew Garson was right—wearing his usual clothes out here would have been ludicrous as well as stupid; still, like the sheriff, it didn't sit right.

The Sandias passed them on the right as Interstate 25 left the Albuquerque suburbs behind. And although other ranges broke the horizon, there was nothing out there now but the high desert.

And the sun.

"Cult," Sparrow said then, raising his voice to be heard over the air conditioning.

"What?" Scully, startled out of a reverie, asked him to repeat it.

"Cult. You know… cult. One of them Satanist things, probably. Look hard enough, betcha them poor folks were all involved somehow."

"A seventeen-year-old boy?" Mulder asked skeptically.

"Hey, that ain't no rare thing, you know what I mean? You got your heavy-metal crap with all that subliminal stuff, you got your rap stuff telling kids to kill cops, shit like that… drugs and sex…" He lifted a hand off the wheel, palm up. "What more do you want?"

Mulder saw his eyes in the mirror, watching him, gauging.

"Maybe," he answered reluctantly.

"No maybe about it, son, no maybe about it."

Fifteen miles later, at a speed Mulder thought would soon launch them into orbit, the cruiser slowed, pulled onto the right shoulder, and crossed a narrow wooden bridge. A two-lane paved road led into the desert.

Sparrow pointed with a thumb. "What you got up there, them hills there about ten miles along, is what they call the Konochine Wall." He scratched under his hat. "Kind of like a jagged outline of a lightbulb lying on its side. Fat part, it's pointing toward the Sandias back there to the south. The base part, it crosses the road onto the ranch where we're going. Unless you want to climb the hills, the only way in or out is a gap where the road is."

Mulder watched a barbed-wire fence blur past on his left. Beyond it was desert, and he couldn't imagine how anyone could raise anything out here, much less cattle. When he had asked at breakfast, Garson only told him to hold onto his horses, he didn't want to spoil the surprise.

"Do the Konochine fit in here?" Scully asked. "This case, I mean."

Sparrow shrugged one broad shoulder. "Who the hell knows? Doubt it myself. Their place isn't like the other pueblos, see. It's a res and all, but they don't like tourists, they don't like Anglos, they don't like other Indians…" He laughed. "Hell, I don't think they much like each other a whole hell of a lot." He yanked at an earlobe, then scratched vigorously behind it. "Some of them, mostly the young ones, they've been trying for years to change things. Most of the time it don't work, though, and they leave, don't come back."

"And the ones who do?"

"Well…" He glanced at Garson. "Nick Lanaya, right?"

Garson nodded agreement and half-turned so he wouldn't have to yell. "Nick's a good guy. He went off to college, and came back with enough ideas to fill a canyon. Because of his family, he's on the Tribal Council, so he has to be heard. And he is, believe me. Trouble is, not a lot are listening."

"So why does he stay?"

Garson thought a moment before saying, "Because they're his people."

Sparrow chuckled, sarcasm, not humor. "Doesn't hurt he's making a few bucks, Red."

Garson sighed dramatically, a wink at Mulder to signal what was obviously a long-standing argument. "Nick," he explained, "has a deal with a local woman, an Anglo, Donna Falkner. He brings out some of the crafts the Konochine make, she sells them in town or up in Santa Fe, they each get a cut and the tribe gets the rest. Mostly jewelry," he added. "Once in a while some incredible bowls and ceremonial-style plates, things like that. Every time he brings out a load, he has a fight with the other side, who claim he's selling their heritage down the river."

"And every time he brings back the bucks to the Mesa," Sparrow said sourly, "they line up with their goddamn hands out."

"The mesa?" Scully said.

"Sangre Viento Mesa," Garson explained. "It's in the middle of the reservation. Their homes are at the base, their religious ceremonies are held up top."

"What does that mean, Sangre Viento?"

Garson faced front. "Blood Wind. It means Blood Wind."

Eventually the barbed wire gave way to a short stretch of well-maintained split rail. In its center was an open gate over which was a wide wood arch. Burned into the face was Double-H.

Mulder sat up as Sparrow drove under the arch, onto a hard-ground road. He looked between the men in front and saw what surely had to be a mirage:

A wide expanse of impossibly green grass inside a blinding white fence; a long adobe and Spanish tile ranch house so simple in its design it looked prohibitively expensive; a stable and corral behind and to the left, with a small black horse plodding toward the shade of a tree he couldn't name; a two-car garage behind and to the right, the driveway curving around the fence to join the entrance road in front; *ristras*—strings of dried red chiles—hanging from vigas protruding from the walls beneath a porch that had to be fifty or sixty feet long.

"You want to be a millionaire and live like this, Scully?"

"I wouldn't mind."

Sparrow parked in a cleared patch of ground beside the driveway, took off his hat and slicked his hair back. He opened the door, and paused as he leaned forward to slide out.

"I would appreciate it," he told them, "if you wouldn't bother her too much. She only found the bodies. She didn't see anything else."

From that unsubtle warning, Mulder fully expected a withered and frail woman to greet them, not the beautiful woman who came out of the double front doors and stood on the porch, shading her eyes and smiling.

Scully joined him while Sparrow fumbled with the gate latch, and as they approached the porch, a man and woman stepped out of the house and moved to one side, she in a simple white dress, he in work clothes. Their expressions were anything but friendly.

"Hey, Annie," the sheriff called, and when they were close enough, he made the introductions.

Ann Hatch, Mulder thought as he shook her cool dry hand and looked down into those incredibly green eyes; so this is Ann Hatch.

As she waved them to seats around a wrought-iron table, it was clear Scully liked her at first sight. "You know," she said, accepting a tall glass of lemonade from the woman in white, "this is like finding an oasis, it's so lovely."

Annie's eyes widened in pleasant surprise. "Why, thank you. But it's just my home."

She smiled broadly, and ten minutes later, the three of them were chatting as if they were old friends, long separated but never far from mind. Mulder didn't believe for a minute she was acting.

Another ten minutes passed before he sat back, abruptly sobered when she noted but didn't remark on the holster at his hip. She caught the change in his mood instantly, and took a deep breath.

"You want to know what I saw, and how."

"If you don't mind, Mrs. Hatch."

She rolled her eyes. "Oh, for God's sake, Agent Mulder, please call me Annie. And I don't mind at all." Her gaze shifted to the improbable lawn and the desert beyond it. "They were newlyweds, you know. They were on their honeymoon."

He knew; he had read the report so many times, he could have recited it word for word, footnote for footnote.

Doris and Matt Constella, from Kansas, twenty-five, in Albuquerque only four days, and, from all Garson could figure out, on a wandering drive around the county in a rented van. They had already stopped to visit at least two of the pueblos, and it was there, it was supposed, they had heard about the Konochine. There was no other reason why they'd be on that road. There were no signs, not for the road itself, and not for the ranch.

She explained how she had discovered their bodies, and how she had immediately ridden back to call the sheriff. "Near the gap," she said sadly. "They were right by the gap."

So much for the connection between them and the boy, Mulder thought.

"Mrs. Hatch," Scully began, and cut herself off at the woman's chiding look. "Annie. Have you had any trouble with people from the reservation?"

Annie blinked once, slowly. "No."

She's lying, Mulder thought, and looked to his left when he sensed movement. Nando Quintodo had taken a short step forward, one of his hands fisted at his side. When he saw Mulder look, however, he stopped, his face bland, his hand quickly relaxed.

"Why do you ask?" Annie said.

"It's routine," Mulder answered before Scully, and grinned at her skepticism. "I know, it sounds like a line from a movie, but it's true. We've been told there's some trouble, and…" An apologetic gesture. "We can't afford not to ask."

Scully echoed the procedure, and apologized as she took Annie through her story again. Mulder, meanwhile, stretching as if he were too stiff to sit, rose with a muttered apology and left the table. As soon as he took a step, Quintodo walked away from him, heading for the door.

Mulder spoke his name.

When the man turned, his hand was a fist again.

Mulder leaned against the porch rail and looked out over the lawn. He didn't raise his voice; he knew the man could hear him. "Tourists ever call you Tonto?"

"Not here. No tourists here." Flat, unemotional. Careful.

"But sometimes."

There was a pause.

Mulder waited.

"Yes. In town. Sometimes." Still flat, still unemotional.

Mulder faced him, leaning back against the rail, one hand in his pocket. "You're from…?"

Quintodo's eyes shifted to the table, shifted back. "The Mesa."

"Your wife, too?"

He nodded.

"So tell me, Mr. Quintodo. Why would a woman like that want to lie?"

The sheriff, mumbling something to Annie, stood.

Quintodo saw him, and Mulder couldn't miss the flare of hatred in his eyes.

"Why?" he repeated softly.

But Sparrow was already on his way over, a mirthless grin beneath dark glasses. "Why what?" he asked, rubbing a hand over his chest.

"Why would I want to visit the stable when I don't ride?" Mulder answered. "I'll tell you why—because I'm a city boy, and I'd like to be able to see manure first-hand."

"Very well, Mr. Mulder," Quintodo agreed before the sheriff could say anything. "I will show you everything. Mrs. Hatch, she has a pair of very fine horses. I think you will be impressed. Maybe you will learn something."

He nodded politely to Sparrow and went inside without looking back.

The sheriff hitched up his belt, and spat over the railing. "This is a beautiful place."

"Yes, it is."

"Annie's been alone out here for a long time, you know. Some say too long."

"I wouldn't know, Sheriff."

Sparrow spat again. "Let me give you some advice, Agent Mulder."

"Always ready to listen, Sheriff Sparrow. You're the expert around here, not me."

Sparrow nodded sharply, *damn right.*

"Okay, number one is, Nando there is a Konochine. You know that already, I assume. Don't trust him. He may live out here with Annie, but his heart's still over the Wall."

Mulder said nothing.

"Second thing is…" He stopped. He took off his hat, wiped sweat from his brow with a forearm, and shook his head as he walked back to the table.

Mulder watched him.

The second thing, unspoken, was a threat.

ELEVEN

The stable was gloomy, despite the open door. There were six stalls on either side, but most of them hadn't been used in a long time. A scattering of hay on the floor. Tack hung from pegs on the walls. When Mulder looked outside, all he could see was white light; the corral and the black horse were little more than ghosts.

Quintodo stood beside a chestnut, running a stiff brush over its flank. He hadn't looked up when Mulder walked in, didn't give a sign when Scully followed, unsure why Mulder had asked her to meet him out here.

Quintodo concentrated on his grooming. "You know what *tonto* means, Mr. Mulder?"

"My Spanish is—" A deprecating smile. "Lousy."

"Stupid," the man said, smoothing a palm over the horse's rump. "It means stupid." He reached into his hip pocket and pulled out a lump of sugar, handed it to Scully. "She won't bite. Just keep your hand flat, she won't take your fingers."

Scully offered the treat, and the horse snorted and snapped it up, then nuzzled her for more.

"She's a pig," Quintodo said, with a hint of smile. "She'll eat all you give her, then get sick." A loving pat to the animal's side. "Tonto."

With a look, Scully asked Mulder why they were here; he nodded a *be patient*, and put his back to the door. All he said was, "Why?"

Quintodo worked for several long seconds without speaking, the scrape of the brush the only sound. Then:

"She is one, you know."

Mulder's head tilted slightly.

"Konochine. One of us. Her husband, Mr. Hatch, he met her in Old Town, in Albuquerque. She was fifteen, he was from Los Angeles. I don't know what they call it, looking for places to make a movie."

"Scouting," Scully said.

He nodded. "Yes, gracias. He told her about the movies, about being in them." The smile finally broke. "All hell broke loose on the Mesa. But he was very persuasive, Mr. Hatch was. Very handsome, very kind. Very young and…" He hesitated. "Dreamy. Before we knew it, she was gone. Making movies. Getting married." He looked at Mulder over the horse's back. "They were very happy. Always."

The smile slipped away.

"No children?" Scully asked.

"Not to be."

The horse stamped impatiently, and Quintodo murmured at it before resuming his grooming.

"She is special, Mr. Mulder," he said at last. "She hears the wind."

Scully opened her mouth to question him, and Mulder shook his head quickly.

Quintodo swallowed, second thoughts making him pause.

When he did speak again, he spoke slowly.

"We have priests, you know." The horse stamped again; a fly buzzed in the stifling heat. "Not the Catholic ones, the padres. Konochine got rid of them a long time ago. Our own. Seven, all the time. They... do things for us. *Comprende?* You understand? Today they are all men. It happens. Sometimes there are women, but not now. Priests are not..." He frowned, then scowled when he couldn't find the word. "They live like us, and then they die. When one dies, there is a ceremonial, and the dead one is replaced."

A two-tone whistle outside interrupted him. Mulder heard hoofbeats trot across the corral.

The chestnut didn't move.

"They know their call," Quintodo explained. "That was for Diamond."

"And the ceremonial?" Mulder prodded quietly.

Quintodo lowered his head, thinking.

"There was one now. Like the others, it lasted six days. No one is allowed to see it. But the wind... the wind carries the ceremony to the four corners. Sometimes you can hear it. It talks to itself. It carries the talk from the kiva. The songs. Prayers. Mrs. Hatch..." He inhaled slowly, deeply, and looked up at Mulder. "Sometimes you think you hear voices on the wind, yes? You think it's your imagination, no?" He shook his head. "No. But only some, like the kiva priests, can understand. Mrs. Hatch too can understand. We knew this recently, Silvia and I, we could tell because Mrs. Hatch was very nervous, very..."He gestured helplessly.

"Afraid?" Scully offered.

"I'm not... no. She didn't like what she heard, though." His voice hardened. "Never once since she came back from the movies has she been to the Mesa. Never once. She turned them down, you see. An old man died, and they wanted her to be in his place, and she turned them down. She had a husband, she said, and she had a way of her own. She would not go, and they never talked to her again."

"They don't have to," Mulder said, moving closer to the horse, keeping his voice low. "She hears them on the wind."

Quintodo stared at him, searching for mocking, for sarcasm, and his eyes narrowed when he didn't find it.

"These dead, Mr. Mulder, they didn't start until the ceremonial started."

Scully sidestepped nervously when the chestnut tried to nuzzle her again, upper lip momentarily curled to expose its teeth. "What are you saying, Mr. Quintodo? That these priests killed those people out there? And the cattle? For a… for some kind of—"

"No." He kept his gaze on Mulder. "Six days and six nights they stay in the kiva. Praying with the man who is to join them. Taking visions from the spirits to be sure they have made the right choice, and to show them the way until the next time. When they do all this, soon the wind blows." He made a rapid spinning motion with his free hand. "Whirlwind, Mr. Mulder. You know what I mean?"

Mulder didn't, and the man spat dryly in disgust at himself.

"Sangre Viento, Mr. Mulder. There are some who say they make the Sangre Viento."

A knock on the front door sounded thunderbolt-loud. Donna sat at her desk, a small secretary in the living room, working on the accounts. They added up, but not fast enough. If she was going to leave soon, on her terms, there would have to be more.

She was tempted to ignore whoever it was, pretend she wasn't home, then realized with a roll of her eyes that she could be seen through the room's picture window. With a martyred sigh, she scooped the ledger and papers into a drawer, pushed at her hair, and opened the door.

She couldn't believe it. "What are you doing here? It's practically the middle of the day."

"No. That's the wrong question. The right question is: have you been cheating me?"

A hand shoved her shoulder, hard, forcing her backward.

"Here's another one, *chica*: what do you think they would do if they found out?"

Mulder kept to himself on the way back to the Inn. They had declined Annie's invitation to lunch, promised to return for a nonofficial visit, and had visited the site where the couple had been murdered. It hadn't taken long; there wasn't much left to see, and when Sparrow asked, he only said it was too soon to make any kind of determination.

Once out of the car, Garson promising to see if he could set up an appointment with the hard-to-reach medical examiner, he went straight to the front desk and arranged for a rental car to be delivered that afternoon.

"I don't like being chauffeured around," he explained to Scully, leading her into the restaurant, complaining of imminent starvation. "Especially by him. He figures, but I don' t know how yet."

Scully said that was the easy part. The man was clearly fond of Annie. Just as clearly, he intended, somehow, to make sure she didn't spend the rest of her life living alone.

"He's after her money?"

"I don't know. It's been known to happen. You could see he was protective; he just wasn't loving."

They took a table in the far front corner, Scully facing the white-curtained window directly behind him. They ordered, and he watched her fuss with her silverware, fuss with her napkin before spreading it on her lap.

"What?"

She didn't hide her exasperation. "I know what you're thinking, and I'm not going to let you turn this into something it isn't."

That, he thought sourly, was the problem with working with someone who knew you that well.

Still, there was no harm trying. More than once, she had saved him from making a total fool of himself, determined to keep him at least within screaming distance of reason.

"You heard what he said."

She nodded. "And it might even be possible that that couple, the Constellas, saw something they weren't supposed to. It might even be possible they were killed for it. They wouldn't be the first to die because they'd witnessed a religious event meant to be secret." She held up a knife like a finger. "Possible, I said, Mulder. Possible."

"Okay. Possible." And she smiled.

"Likely?"

He smiled back. "Don't push it. I'm still working on possible."

She started to speak, changed her mind, then changed her mind again. "But what about Paulie Deven? Don't you think it's stretching things a little to assume he saw something, too? Which he would have had to do, if you're going to keep him with the Constellas."

"Which means?"

"Mulder, it means there's no connection between the victims and the ceremony. A horrible coincidence, nothing more."

"And the…" He stumbled several times, making her smile, before he managed, "Sangre Viento?"

He winced when he heard himself; his Spanish was still lousy.

The waiter brought their meal, and he stared at the strips of meat, the vegetables, the salsa in the side dish, practically feeling the heat of the spices without even getting close. He knew he would regret this later, and after his first taste, knew he would have to stock up on a supply of heavy-duty antacids if he wanted to get any sleep. The trouble was, it was so good, there was no way he wouldn't eat it.

Scully, on the other hand, popped a small jalapeno into her mouth, plucked the stem from between her teeth, and said, "Not bad, not bad."

The Sangre Viento aside for the moment, he was pleased to hear that her reaction to Sparrow was the same as his. Yet neither could think of a good reason for the act, nor could they believe the man actually thought he was fooling anyone with it. It was too broad, too born of bad movies and worse television. That led them to wondering, his feelings for Annie aside, if he was somehow involved, or just a lousy cop trying to cover his ass, make them feel sorry for him so whoever he had to answer to wouldn't take his badge.

"A little farfetched," she judged when the table had been cleared and coffee served. "Not that we haven't seen it before."

"This isn't it. I don't know what it is, but this isn't it."

"Neither is that blood wind thing."

He opened his mouth, closed it, picked up a spoon and tapped it lightly against his thigh. "How can you be so sure?" He propped his elbows on the arms of his chair and clasped his hands in front of his mouth. "There are any number of recorded so-called unusual phenomena associated with meetings, especially religious, where the emotional intensity and concentration are abnormally high."

"All of them recorded by the people who were there, not by outside observers."

"They, these priests, were in a kiva. An underground chamber whose only exit and entrance, and source of air, is a single hole in the roof. There may have been herbal drugs, peyote maybe, something like that. Six days and six nights, Scully, and they all focus on a single thing—the man they're investing with their knowledge. Their history. With their power over the people they have to live with." He rocked forward, hands dropping to the table. "Can you imagine what it must be like? Day in and day out? All that energy building up there?"

Scully didn' t answer him for a long time. She sipped her coffee, stared out the window, glanced around the otherwise empty room. She was about to reply when a woman appeared in the archway entrance. Short, stocky, in a severe summer-weight suit; her graying black hair pulled back into a bun. Her left hand held a purse tight to her side.

Mulder watched her hesitate, then march across the room toward them, no nonsense, all business. When she reached the table, she nodded a greeting.

"You are the agents from Washington?"

"Yes," Mulder answered. "And you are…?"

"Dr. Rios. Helen Rios. I performed the autopsies on those poor people."

He stood immediately and offered her a chair while introducing her to Scully. When they were all seated again, he told her he was pleased to see her. Garson wouldn't have to make the appointment after all.

"He wouldn't have made it," the woman said.

"I… what?"

"You read my report?" she asked Scully.

"I did. To be honest, there weren't a lot of—"

"It's wrong."

Scully looked at the table, then back to Dr. Rios. "Excuse me?"

The woman opened her purse and pulled out a folded sheet of paper. "This is what I wrote first. What you read before is what I was told to write."

Mulder couldn't believe it.

Nor could he believe it when Scully opened the paper, skimmed it, and said, "Oh my God."

TWELVE

After signing for the meal, Mulder moved them immediately to his room, a precaution against eyes and ears he couldn't control.

The women sat at a small round table set by the window, covered now by dark green drapes. Mulder sat on the edge of the king-size bed.

There were four lights in the room; every one of them was on.

Dr. Rios wasted no words, or time.

"New Mexico," she said, "has been trying to upgrade its image for years; decades. People still ask if you need a passport to come here. Easterners still look for cowboys and Indians battling it out in the foothills. What the politicians and businessmen do not want most of all are the hints, the stories, the urban legend-style fables that mark the state as a place where UFOs and weird cults are not only welcome, they're encouraged. Leave that kind of nonsense," Rios said, "to Arizona, and good riddance."

Then a case like this falls into their laps.

She tapped the paper she'd taken back from Scully. "Agent Mulder, it's bad enough that these poor people died the way they did. I could tell right away how it really happened, any first-year intern could have figured it out. But for the sake of appearances, because my superiors knew it was bound to hit the papers, I was asked to file a second report. The one the public would know."

It was cool in the room, but she took a handkerchief from her purse and dabbed at her forehead.

Mulder understood the chance she had taken, and the pressure she felt. He, of all people, was no stranger to either.

"I did. For the basest of reasons—I want to keep my job." She smiled grimly across the table at Scully. "I am a woman, a Hispanic woman, in a state where the Anglos and outsiders call the tunes. I am not proud of what I've done, but I make no apologies for it."

Scully kept her expression neutral, and the doctor wiped her brow again. "The official version, Agent Mulder, is that those people were flayed. They weren't."

Mulder lifted an eyebrow. "Skinned?"

"Scoured."

He choked back a laugh of disbelief. "I'm sorry, but I don't understand."

The woman checked her watch. "I have no time. Particles of dirt, pebbles, other debris were found deeply embedded not only in the muscle tissue, but also in their mouths and the back of their throats. Other indications, such as circular striation of the exposed muscles and bone and the cauterization of most of the blood vessels, point to only one conclusion."

"Scoured."

She nodded, and stood. "Like being held up against a high-speed spinning drum covered with coarse sandpaper, Agent Mulder. Or inside a cylinder lined with the same. The only thing I can't explain is the dirt." Another grim smile, another glance at her watch. "Thank you for listening. Please don't tell anyone I have seen you. If you come to my office, if Agent Garson insists we meet, all you will hear is what you've already read in the official report." She tucked the purse under her arm. "By the way, Agent Garson knows the truth, too."

Mulder rose as she left without looking back, and stayed on his feet.

A high-speed drum covered with coarse sandpaper. "Scully—"

"Don't say it."

"But you saw—"

"I saw the pictures, yes. I read the report, yes. But given the time frame we're working with, unless Paulie's father and sister are incredibly off-base with their sense of timing, there's no way it could happen like that."

He looked down at her, pale under the table light. "It happened, Scully. It happened."

She leaned toward him, arms resting on the table. "Then explain it to me. Explain how someone could assemble an apparatus of that size, bring it down to the river without being seen, put the boy in it, kill him, take him out, and get away. Again, without anybody seeing a thing."

"The girl—"

"Saw nothing we can substantiate. Ghosts, Mulder. She said she saw ghosts."

"And whispers," he reminded her. "She also said she heard whispers."

Scully slumped back and shook her head. "What does it mean? I don't get it."

"I don't either." He yanked open the drapes, turned off the lights, and dropped into the chair opposite her. "But so far, everyone who's talked to us has—" He stopped, closed his eyes briefly, then moved to the bed and stared for a moment at the telephone on the night table.

"Mulder?"

"Konochine," he said, and picked up the receiver. "Why do we keep bumping into the Konochine?"

"While you're at it," she said. "Give Garson a call and find out why he's so reluctant to tell us the truth."

Donna looked helplessly at the two dozen cartons stacked in her spare room. They were all ready for shipping, or for hand delivery to area shops. A permanent cold seemed to have attached itself to her spine, to her stomach. She couldn't stop shaking. She had denied cheating anyone, of course, and had even shown him the ledger to prove it. But it had been close. There had been no apology, only a lingering warning look before he left, slamming the door as he went.

She had to get out.

All the potential money in this room wasn't going to do her any good if she wasn't around to spend it.

She looked at her watch. If she hurried, she could clean out the bank account, be packed, and be out of this godforsaken state before midnight. Leave everything behind. It didn't matter. The house, her clothes… none of it mattered. Just take the money and get out.

But first she would have to make a phone call. She couldn't leave without saying goodbye.

\\\\\\\\\\\\\\\\\

Garson wasn't in his office, and no one there knew where he could be found. The secretary thought he might be at the ME's office.

The second call was to information.

When the third was finished, Mulder replaced the receiver and began to wonder.

"What?" Scully asked.

"According to his sister, Paulie picked up a piece of jewelry from one of the local shops. A silver pendant of some kind." Mulder looked up. "She thinks it was Konochine."

"And?"

"And I don't remember seeing it as being with his effects."

"Such as they were," she reminded him.

"Whatever. It wasn't there." He rose, and paced until Scully's warning groan put him back in his chair. "That woman, the one who handles the crafts."

She flipped open a notebook, paged through it, and said, "Falkner."

"You want to take a ride?"

"Mulder—"

"The connection, Scully. You can't deny we have a connection."

The rental car had been delivered, and the clerk at the front desk gave him a map and directions to the address he had found in the telephone book. The parking lot was on the north side of the Inn, through a gated entry in the side wall.

As he slipped behind the wheel, Mulder noted that the car seemed to have every gadget known to Detroit, except perhaps an orbital trajectory tracking system.

It took him a few seconds to get oriented, and a few seconds more before he convinced himself that he wasn't charging headlong into foolishness. The how of the murders was still beyond him, in spite of Dr. Rios's description. Concentrate on the who and the why, however, and the how would come wagging its tail behind them.

He hoped.

As he pulled out onto the street and headed north, Scully inhaled quickly.

"What?" They passed a series of four small stores in a common one-story building. A man stood in front of one of them, not bothering to conceal his interest in the car.

"Last night," she said. "I didn't see him clearly, but there was a man at the gate, watching me."

He checked the rearview mirror.

The man, face hidden by the bill of his cap, still watched.

There was no flip of a mental coin. Mulder swung the wheel around, made a U-turn, made another to pull alongside the stores.

The man hadn't moved.

Scully lowered her window. "Do you want something?" she asked calmly.

Leon Ciola swaggered over and leaned down. "You the feds?"

With one hand still on the wheel, Mulder leaned over, curious about the fine scars that swept across the man's face. "Special Agent Mulder, Special Agent Scully. Who are you?"

"Leon Ciola."

"You've been watching us. Why?"

Ciola spread his arms wide in a mocking bow, smiling impudently. "Always like to know who's in town, *amigos*, that's all. It's very dull around here, you know? Not much to do. The sun's too hot. Not much work for a man like me."

"What is a man like you?" Scully said.

"Ex-con. They didn't tell you that?"

No, Mulder thought; there's a lot they haven't told us.

Then he spotted a faint racial resemblance to Nando Quintodo. "You're from the Mesa?"

Ciola's smile didn't falter. "Very good, *amigo*. Most people think I look Apache." Fingers fluttered across his face. "The scars. They make me look mean."

"Are you?"

The smile vanished. "I'm a son of a bitch, Agent Mulder. A good thing to know."
He's not bragging, Mulder thought; he's not warning, either.

Ciola glanced up and down the street, then placed a hand on the window well.
"Sheriff Sparrow will tell you that I have killed a man. It's true. Maybe more, who
knows? He'll tell you, when he gets around to it, that I probably killed those
stupid tourists. I didn't, Agent Mulder. I have more important things to do."

He tipped his cap to Scully and backed away, interview over.

Mulder nodded to him, straightened, and pulled slowly away from the curb.
The man chilled him. What chilled him more, however, was the fact that Sparrow
hadn't said a word about him. An obvious suspect, a self-confessed killer ex-con,
and the sheriff had, conveniently or otherwise, kept Ciola's name to himself.

"Scully, do you get the feeling we've dropped down the rabbit hole?"

She didn't answer.

A glance at her profile showed him lips so taut they were bloodless.

He didn't question her. Something about the man, something he hadn't caught,
struck a nerve. Sooner or later, she would tell him what it was. As it was, he had
to deal with street signs he could barely read because they were too small, and the
vehicles impatiently lining up behind him because he was driving slow enough to
try to read the damn signs.

The sun didn't help.

It flared off everything, and bleached that which wasn't already bleached.

Everywhere there were signs of a town struggling to find the right way to
grow—obviously new shops, shops that had gone out of business, houses and
buildings in varying stages of construction or repair. It was either very exciting to
live here now, or very frightening.

"There," Scully said.

He turned left, toward the river, and found himself on a street where lots were
large and vacant, spotted only once in a while by small, one-story houses in either
brick or fake adobe. A drab place, made more so by the gardens and large bushes
flowering violent colors. No toys in the driveways. The few cars at the curbs
seemed abandoned.

He parked in front of a ranch house whose front window was buried by a
tangled screen of roses. A Cherokee parked in the pitted drive faced the street. As
they got out, he saw a suitcase by the driver's door.

"Somebody's going on vacation."

"I don't think so," she said, nodding toward the two other suitcases sitting on the stoop. "Not unless she's planning to stay away for six months."

He knocked on the screen door.

No one answered.

He knocked again, and the inner door was opened by a young woman with a briefcase in one hand.

"I don't want any," she said.

Scully held up her ID. "Special Agent Scully, Special Agent Mulder, FBI. Are you Donna Falkner?"

It didn't take any special instinct to realize the woman was afraid. Mulder opened the screen door carefully and said, "We'd just like to talk to you, Ms. Falkner. It won't take a minute, and then you can take your trip."

"How did you know that?" Donna demanded, her voice pitched high enough to crack. Then she followed Mulder's gesture toward the suitcases. "Oh."

"Just a few minutes," Scully assured her.

The woman's shoulders slumped. "Oh, what the hell, why not. How much worse can it get?"

THIRTEEN

The air conditioning had been shut off. The room was stifling. The woman hasn't left yet, Mulder thought, and already the house feels deserted.

Donna grabbed a ladder-back chair from in front of a small desk and turned it around. When she sat, shoulders still slumped, she held the briefcase in her lap, looking as if she wanted to hold it against her chest. Scully took a seat on a two-cushion couch, pen and notebook in hand; Mulder remained standing, leaning a shoulder against the wall just inside the room's entry.

It kept him in partial shadow; it kept the woman in full light.

"So," she said resignedly. "What do you want to know?"

"The Konochine," Mulder told her, and saw her gaze dart in his direction.

"What about them?"

"You sell their jewelry," Scully said, shifting the woman's attention back the other way. "We were told they didn't like the outside world very much."

"Hardly at all," Donna answered. Her shoulders rose a little. "I got chased off the res once, back before I knew what I was doing." She shifted the briefcase to the floor beside her. "See, they're not the only Indians I deal with, but they give me the most trouble. Or did, anyway. There's this man—"

"Nick Lanaya?" Mulder said.

"Yeah. He's one of the out-and-backers. You know, got out, came back? Well, we met at a party once, got to talking—he's very easy to talk to, kind of like a priest, if you know what I mean. Anyway, he knew his people needed money, and after he asked around, he knew I'd be able to get them a fair price for the work."

Scully moved a hand to draw her attention again. "How mad are the ones who don't want outside contact?"

Donna frowned, the understanding of what Scully meant slow in arriving. "Oh. Oh! Hey, not that mad. God, no. You think they killed those poor people?" She dismissed the notion with a wave. "Jesus, no. They talk a lot, yell a lot, but Nick just yells right back. He's—" She stopped, frozen, as though something had just occurred to her. "Tell you, though, the guy you should be talking to is Leon Ciola."

"We've met," Mulder said dryly.

"You're kidding." Her right hand drifted down to brush at the case. "You know he was in the state pen, up by Santa Fe? Killed a man in a bar fight." Her left hand drew a line across her throat. Slowly. "Nearly cut his head off. I don't know how he got out. A good lawyer, I guess."

"Where are you going?" Scully asked.

"Vacation," Donna replied instantly.

"You take more clothes than Scully," Mulder said with a laugh.

"I'll be away for a while."

"Who takes care of the business? Nick?"

She shrugged. "Mostly, yeah."

Scully closed her notebook. "You have no control over what you receive from the Mesa? Or who buys them retail?"

"Nope. Nick chooses the pieces, I choose the shops. After that, it's the guy who has the most money."

Mulder pushed away from the wall. "What if somebody who didn't know any better just drove onto the reservation?"

"Nothing." Donna retrieved her case. "No one would talk to them, probably. Sooner or later, they'd get the hint and leave."

"And if they didn't?"

"You mean like me?" She laughed; it was false. "I'm pushy, Agent Mulder. I pushed too far. Chasing is all that would happen, believe me." She stood and looked none too subtly at the door. "I still say you should check Ciola. He has a knife and…" She shuddered for effect.

Scully rose as well. "Thank you, Ms. Falkner. We appreciate the time."

"No problem." She led them to the stoop. "If you don't mind, though, I have a plane to catch, okay?"

Mulder thanked her again, asked her to call Agent Garson if there was anything else she thought of before she left, and got behind the wheel, cursing himself soundly for forgetting to leave the windows down.

The sun out there, and an oven in here. He set the air conditioning to high and hurry up about it and drove off, taking his time, while Scully watched Donna Falkner in the outside mirror. When they turned the corner, Scully said, "She relaxed very quickly."

"Yeah. Because we didn't ask her about what she thought we would."

"Which was?"

"Scully, if I knew that, I would have asked her."

She grunted disbelief; he knew what she was thinking. There were times when asking questions got you answers, but not necessarily when you wanted them. There were times when it was better to spin a web and see who tried to break free.

Donna was breaking free.

Once she got on that plane, New Mexico would never see her again.

Scully looked over. "How are you going to stop her?"

He gestured toward the backseat, asking her to grab his denim jacket. When she did, his portable phone fell out of the inside pocket.

"Garson?" she said.

"Material witness to an active investigation."

"But she isn't, Mulder."

"No, maybe not. But he can delay her long enough to miss her flight. Maybe discourage her enough to wait until tomorrow."

She called, discovered Garson couldn't be reached, and demanded to speak to an agent on duty. After convincing him they weren't kidding about Falkner, she asked where the Constella van was being held.

"Right here," she said when she hung up. "A lot behind a sheriff's substation."

"Why do you want to see it?"

"You wanted to see Ann Hatch, and look what it got us. I want to see that van."

Sometimes they made her too much like him.

"And what do you mean, I take too many clothes when I go on a trip?"

The substation was little more than a doublewide on cinder blocks, only a sign on the door announcing its function. The parking area in front was only big enough for four vehicles, and the tree that cast a weak shade over the building looked about ready to collapse at any second. Beyond the tree was another lot, fenced in with chain-link and topped with concertina wire. Within were a handful of cars, a pickup, and a van.

Sheriff Sparrow was outside waiting when Mulder pulled in off the street.

"Garson works fast," Scully said when they stopped.

"Your tax dollars at work."

Sparrow waved them over to a padlocked gate in the fence. "Looking for anything in particular?" he asked as the gate swung free and they walked in.

"You never know," Mulder told him.

The van was at the back, dusty enough to ward off the sun. Mulder shaded his eyes and looked through the side and front windows, then asked Sparrow for the key.

"What for?"

"To get inside." He rapped a knuckle against the sliding side door. "You never know."

Sparrow grumbled, complained that he'd left the keys inside, and headed back to the trailer.

"Mulder?"

She was on the passenger side, and he took his time joining her. The heat was brutal, worse than the day before, and he understood now why life was so deliberate in this part of the world. Anything faster than a crawl on a day like today meant sure heatstroke, and a tub packed in ice.

"So?"

She pointed to the side.

He looked and saw the dust; then he saw what lay under the dust.

He used a palm to wipe the metal clean, and yelped when the heat scorched him. "Damn!" He shook his hand, blew on it, and pulled a handkerchief from his pocket.

"Be careful," she said. "It's hot." When he gave her a look, she only shrugged and added, "Your tax dollars at work."

There were two large tinted windows, one in the sliding door, the other at the back. He shook the handkerchief out, then folded it in quarters to form a makeshift dusting pad. Hunkering down, balancing on his toes, he swiped at the dust and dirt first, to knock off what he could before he started rubbing.

"What the hell you looking for?" Sparrow said, tossing the keys to Scully.

"This was a rental," Mulder said without looking up.

"Yep. So?"

"New, then, right?"

"Probably." The sheriff leaned over him, squinting at the panel. "So?"

"So I guess Mr. Constella wasn't much of a driver."

He didn't have to rub. When the area was clear, he rose and took a step back, waiting for Sparrow to comment. He was also waiting to hear why the man hadn't noticed it days ago. Or, if he had, why he hadn't said anything.

From the window to the bottom of the frame, the paint had been scraped off, right down to bare metal. The dust had been thick, the van having sat here for more than a week in the sheriff's custody. A glint of that bare metal was what had caught Scully's attention.

"Well, I'll be damned." Sparrow hitched his belt. "Run up against a stone wall, boulder, something like that, looks like."

"I don't think so." Mulder ran a finger lightly over the surface. "No appreciable indentation, so there was no real collision."

Scully stepped in front of them and peered at it closely, shifted and sighted along the side to the rear bumper. "If there was, it wouldn't be in just this one place." When she straightened, she leaned close to the window. Touched it with a forefinger. Took the handkerchief and wiped the glass clean. "Scrapes here, too."

"Road dirt," Sparrow said. "You get it all the time out here, dust and all, going the speeds you do."

She ignored him for the moment, using the finger to trace the damage's outline, right to the strip above the window. "Whatever it was, it was big. Man-high, at least."

"Like I said, a boulder."

"Come on, Sheriff," Mulder said, having had enough of his forced ignorance. "Scully's right. A collision would have produced damage wider than this, and by the force of it, at the least this window would have been cracked, if not smashed."

He scratched under his jaw, and leaned close again.

"Agent Mulder, this is—"

"Do you have a magnifying glass?"

He heard the man snort his disgust, but the expected argument didn't happen. Sparrow trudged away, muttering about how the damn feds think they know everything, just loudly enough.

Scully unlocked the passenger door and stood back to let the heat out. Then she climbed in and through the two front seats to the back. Mulder couldn't see her until she rapped on the window and beckoned.

He knelt on the passenger seat and leaned over the top. The two rows of bench seats had been taken out, leaving the holding rails behind. The floor and walls were covered with alternating swatches of vivid purple and dull brown carpeting.

"This is a love nest?" he said, wincing at the garish combination.

"Love is blind, Mulder." She was on her knees, poking at a loose section of carpet with her pen.

"In here it would have to be."

"Got it."

She rocked back on her heels and held up the pen. Dangling from it was a length of silver chain. She followed when Mulder backed out, and dropped the chain into his palm. "That's not a store chain. It's handmade." She prodded it with the pen, shifting it as he watched. "I'll bet it's not silver-plated, either."

He brought the palm closer to his eyes.

The links were longer than he would have expected, and not as delicately thin as they first appeared. Neither were they the same length.

She took the chain back, grasping each end between thumb and forefinger. Tugged once. "Strong. You couldn't yank this off someone's neck without sawing halfway through it."

"Konochine."

She gave him a maybe tilt of her head, and headed back to the car to fetch a plastic evidence bag from her purse.

"Bring a couple," he called after her, and glanced at his watch.

Sparrow still hadn't returned; Mulder finally lost the rest of his patience. He marched over to the trailer, yanked open the door, and stepped in. The sheriff was seated behind one of three desks in the room, his feet up, his hat off, a flask at his lips.

He looked startled when he saw Mulder, but he didn't move until he had finished his drink. "It's hot out there," he said.

"It's going to get hotter," Mulder told him, not bothering to suppress his anger. "Give me the glass, then get one of your people ready to take some evidence to Garson's technicians. I'll call him myself to tell him what to look for."

Sparrow glared as he set the flask onto the desk. "I don't believe I heard the magic word, Agent Mulder."

Mulder just looked at him, and "FBI" was all he said.

FOURTEEN

He couldn't see Scully when he returned to the lot, slapping the magnifying glass hard against his leg. He was angry and disappointed, not nearly as much at the sheriff as at himself. Losing control like that, pulling rank, wasn't his style. Working with local law was something he had learned to do years ago, knowing that their assistance was just as vital to investigations as his own federal agents. What he had just done was a violation not only of policy, but his own code.

"Scully?"

It was dumb.

"Hey, Scully!"

It was stupid.

"Over here, Mulder."

But boy, did it feel good.

He found her standing next to what used to be a sleek Jaguar. Now most of its windows were shattered, the windshield web-cracked, the racing-green paint pocked and scored from front to back, and the roof crushed as though someone had dropped a flatcar on it.

"Our drunk driver?" he asked.

"I don't know. I think so. Look at this."

He went around to the side, and saw the same pattern of scouring she had uncovered on the van, only this time it was wider.

"Invisible car," he said.

She lifted a questioning hand. "I give up, Mulder. What's going on?" A closer look at his face. "Never mind. I think I'd rather know what happened in there."

There was no chance to answer. The trailer door slammed gunshot loud, and Sparrow stomped toward them. The way his hand chopped the air, Mulder figured he was having one hell of an argument with himself. By the time he reached them, the argument was over.

He stood with one hand resting on the handle of his holstered gun, while the other folded a stick of gum into his mouth. Then he pulled off his sunglasses by pinching them at the bridge and sliding.

"I'll take the evidence in myself." It wasn't an order, it wasn't a demand. It was an offer of truce.

"That's fine with me, sir," Mulder said, accepting the offer.

"Chuck." The sheriff chewed rapidly.

Mulder grinned. "I don't think so."

"Me neither. My mother hated it. She always said it wasn't the name of anything but chopped meat." He pushed the sunglasses back on. "So, FBI, what's so important you got to rush it into the city?"

While Scully explained about the partial necklace chain, Mulder went back to the van and, with the magnifying glass and the tip of a blade on his Swiss army knife, pried loose samples of debris caught in the deep gouges on the door. He did the same to the car, sealed his findings in the bags, and handed them over.

Uneasy, but more at ease, they walked back to the office, grateful for the cool respite. Scully tagged and numbered the bags. Mulder called Garson's office, told them what to expect and what he wanted done.

"That shouldn't take very long," the secretary said confidently.

"Have you found Agent Garson yet?"

"No sir, I sure haven't."

He gave her his number and instructed her to have Garson call as soon as he came in. When he asked whether Donna Falkner had been intercepted, he was told that she had been, by one of the other agents. Apparently she hadn't been very happy, certainly not when she was brought back to the Silver Avenue office, where she currently was giving a statement.

"A statement? About what?"

"I wouldn't know, sir. I'm only the secretary. They only tell me what I need to know."

Sure, he thought; and all the rest is magic.

He perched on the edge of the nearest empty desk and wiped his brow with a sleeve.

Sparrow was back in his chair. "You reckon it's the Konochine somehow? I figured that, what with you talking to Donna and all."

"I don't see how it can't be, now. There are too many connections."

"A lead, anyway," Scully added.

"Oh boy." The sheriff reached for his flask, changed his mind, and propped his feet up instead. "Trouble is, there's a couple hundred of them. It can't be all—" Suddenly he snapped upright, boots stamping the floor. "Son of a bitch!"

Mulder looked first to Scully before saying, "Leon Ciola."

The sheriff's jaw sagged. "Damn, Mulder, you're good." He drummed his fingers against his cheek thoughtfully, then reached for his phone. "There's somebody you should meet. He'll be able to tell you what you want know about who you need to know about. Lanaya. I already told you about him. Believe it or not, he still lives on the res."

"What about Ciola?"

Sparrow held up a finger as the connection was made, winced as he made arrangements with the dealer to meet at the Inn after dinner that evening, winced again and rubbed his ear as he hung up. "Storm coming," he explained. "Static'll deafen you sometimes."

Thank God, Mulder thought; at least it'll get cooler.

"Ciola," he reminded Sparrow.

"Bastard. Pure and simple bastard. Got sent up for murder, got a lawyer who found a hole and squeezed the son of a bitch through it. There's not much I can do but keep an eye out, and hope he doesn't lose his temper again."

It didn't take special intuition to figure out the man not only hated Ciola, he was afraid of him.

"You thinking he's involved with this?"

"You have to admit, he's a likely candidate."

"Nope, don't think so."

Mulder was surprised, and let the sheriff know it.

"Not his style," Sparrow explained. "He's all intimidation and reputation. The man he killed, it was over quick and dirty. These people… that took patience."

"But not much time, Sheriff," Scully said. "The Deven boy, remember?"

He granted her that reluctantly, but insisted it couldn't have been Ciola. "There's a reason for those people, Agent Scully. We just ain't found it yet. With Leon, there doesn't have to be one."

"Heat of the moment," Mulder suggested.

"Got it in one."

Scully seemed doubtful, but didn't argue.

The sheriff accepted her silence without comment, looked around the station, then carefully locked the plastic bags into an attache case he pulled from a bottom drawer. "Better get going. I want to get back before the storm." He walked to the back and radioed one of his men, telling him where he'd be and for how long; he called a central dispatcher with the same information, for intercepting any calls; he spat his gum into a wastebasket, opened a wardrobe on the far wall, and took down a clean, blocked hat.

When he saw Mulder staring, he pointed to the hat on the desk. "That's my comfort hat, had it for years." He flicked the brim on the one he had on.

"This is my showing-up-in-the-city hat. Pretty dumb, ain't it."

Scully laughed, and Mulder could only nod as Sparrow walked with them to their car.

"Check it out, folks," he said, pointing over the trailer. "Be inside when it happens."

Mulder looked, and couldn't believe that clouds that massive, and that high, could assemble so quickly. Shaped like anvils, boiling at the edges, they had already buried most of the western blue.

"My God, Scully, we're going to drown."

He drove back to the motel as fast as he dared, which still wasn't fast enough for the others on the road. They passed him on the left, on the right, and would have driven over him if the car had been low enough.

"Calm down," Scully said when the engine died. "We've still got some work to do while we wait for Lanaya."

The bone pile stirred as the wind brushed over it, dust in tan clouds passing through ribs and eye sockets, through a gaping hole in one of the skulls.

A scorpion scuttled across the curled horn of a ram.

In the center, using the pelvic bone of a stallion for a temporary stool, a man stirred the loose earth with the point of a knife. Designs were fashioned, and erased; words were written, and vanished. He glanced up only once, to check the storm's approach, returning to his work only when he saw the lightning, and didn't hear the thunder.

It would move fast.

He would move faster.

Donna Falkner slammed into her house, slammed the door shut behind her, flung a suitcase across the living room, and began to scream her outrage. She kicked at the nearest wall, picked up the desk chair and hurled it down the hall; she grabbed the couch cushions and tried to rip them open with her nails, tossed them aside, and dropped to the floor, sobbing.

It wasn't fair.

It wasn't goddamn fair.

All she had to do was get on the goddamn plane, and she was out of here. Gone. Lost in another city, where they never heard of Indians except on TV, never bothered with Southwest crafts except in fancy boutiques that overpriced everything from a wallet to a brooch. Gone. New name, new hair, new everything.

Gone.

Now the FBI wanted her, and *he* wanted her, and there was nothing she could do about it but sit around and wait.

She punched the floor.

She screamed again, cheeks florid, teeth bared.

The sunlight began to dim, and the thorns of the rosebushes began to scratch lightly against the windows.

Suddenly she couldn't breathe, made a double fist with her hands, and pressed it against her chest. Harder. Gulping for air. Rocking on her buttocks until she thought she would faint. Tears streaming down her cheeks, dripping off her chin, coating her lips with the taste of salt.

When the attack passed, she let herself fall backward slowly, seeing nothing but tiny cracks in the plaster ceiling, forming them into images that made her weep again.

The telephone rang.

She wiped her eyes with the backs of her hands and sat up. She had no intention of answering it. Let it ring. If it was those agents who had come to see her, they could just come over on their own. The hell with them. The hell with them all.

When she stood, she swayed; when she walked down the short hall toward the bathroom, she staggered. When she reached the bathroom, she looked at her reflection, gagged… and giggled. Touched the tip of her reflection's nose with a finger and told it there was nothing to worry about, nothing she couldn't handle.

What she would do was, if they wouldn't let her fly, then fuck it, she would drive. By the time they realized she was gone, she would be… gone.

She giggled again.

Gone, but not forgotten.

Gone, and goddamn rich.

Wash up, she ordered; wash up, change your clothes, get the damn money, and be... gone.

What the hell are you so worried about?

She didn't know.

Suddenly, she didn't know.

She hurried into the spare room, squinted through the small window, and figured by the sky she had maybe an hour before the storm arrived. If it arrived. They had a bad habit of being all show and no action sometimes. Not that it mattered. Only a fool would tempt clouds like that on an open road.

Another giggle.

Screw'em.

Now that she wasn't flying, she could load the Cherokee to the gills, take a little inventory to pad the mattress. The not-so-perfect plan, but better than nothing. Nothing would mean sitting around, waiting for things to happen.

She grabbed a carton and headed for the door.

Sand stirred, lifting sluggishly from the ground as if drawn by a weak magnet.

Nearby, a dead leaf quivered.

A twig shifted, rolled an inch, and stopped.

The sand settled a few seconds later.

Nothing moved.

FIFTEEN

T he shower was wonderful.

After crawling around the van and automobile in the sun all that time, Scully was drenched with sweat, caked and streaked with dust, and ready to scream. In spite of the silver chain, in spite of what Mulder had dug from the vehicles' sides, they hadn't accomplished very much.

What frustrated her was a combination of the case itself, which seemed to be going nowhere fast, and the certain knowledge that she had already seen the break point and had missed it. Something small. Something so obvious she had overlooked it. The purloined letter in New Mexico.

The storm didn't help.

The clouds, frightening black and impossibly huge, were still out there, still in the middle distance. If they moved, she couldn't tell. They sat there, not small enough to be lurking, and too large to even be called looming. There was nothing ahead of them but a steady, hot wind.

They were also tired. The mix of altitude and heat had sapped them without their realizing it. When they reached the motel, it was a mutual decision to clean up and rest for an hour, then meet again to see what they could come up with before their meeting with Nick Lanaya.

So she used the shower to make her comfortable again, to drain the afternoon's tension from her shoulders and limbs, and to let her mind roam, seeking pathways and the places where they might possibly join into something concrete she could follow, something hopeful.

When it didn't happen immediately, she was mildly annoyed, but she didn't mind. It would come eventually; of that she was confident.

She took her time dressing, sat on the edge of her bed, and gazed at the window, scowling at the tension she could feel building again. She rolled her shoulders, massaged them one at a time, to get rid of it; it didn't work. She stretched until her joints threatened to pop or separate, deliberately groaning aloud; it didn't work.

Maybe it was just anticipation of the storm.

The clouds must have moved closer while she had been in the bathroom. The sunlight held considerably less glare, a hint of false twilight filtering into the front courtyard. By that part of the bench tree she could see, the wind had died down as well.

It seemed that the outside had decided to do nothing but wait until the storm made up its mind whether to strike or not.

"Damn," she whispered.

No wonder she was still tense. That was exactly what she was doing. Waiting, not acting. Some son of a bitch had butchered three innocent people, and all she could do was sit here like a lump and wait for the damn rain.

She snapped to her feet, grabbed her shoulder bag, decided the hell with the hat, and hurried outside.

No one in the courtyard and, when she couldn't help looking, no one standing at the gate.

The image of Ciola's face so close to her own made her pause and shudder. Those scars, and those dead eyes… she shuddered again and knocked hard on Mulder's door, one heel tapping impatiently. When he answered, naked to the waist and drying his hair with a towel, she said, "Get decent, Mulder. We're going out again."

＼＼＼＼＼＼＼＼＼＼＼＼＼

The sand stirred.
The leaf quivered.

"You're the one who made the connections," Scully said as he pulled on a shirt. "So why wait?"

"Scully, we haven't been here twenty-four hours."

"That doesn't answer my question: Why wait?"

He couldn't think of a good answer, and didn't especially want to, not when she practically sparked with energy like this. It was best, always best, to go along for the ride. Besides, she was right. With too many signs pointing to the Konochine, it only made sense to pay an official visit to the reservation. The only problem was, he thought they ought to have a guide, someone who knew who they should talk to, preferably someone who knew the language.

"The sheriff."

"He's in Albuquerque, remember?"

"Falkner."

"They rode her out on a rail."

She tapped a fingernail on the table. "Lanaya would be perfect, but we don't know how to get in touch with him."

They tried the phone book, but no luck; they tried the sheriff's dispatcher, and had the same result. A call to Falkner brought no answer; Scully let the phone ring twenty times before hanging up in disgust.

Neither one of them even breathed Leon Ciola's name.

He switched on a lamp without thinking. "We could always go out to the ranch," he suggested, not really too happy with the idea.

Neither was Scully, from her reaction. At the moment, however, there was no place else to turn. And, he added, reaching for his gun and holster to clip on his belt, it didn't especially have to be Annie. In fact, it probably shouldn't be, if what the foreman had told them was true. Quintodo himself would do just as well, assuming he was willing. It wasn't a raid; they were simply looking for information.

Which, he thought glumly, they probably wouldn't get anyway. If the Indians wanted as little to do as possible with whites in general, representatives of the government in Washington, especially the law, would no doubt be treated as if they had the plague.

Then he opened the door, took a quick step back, and said, "You have an ark handy?"

The storm had finally reached them.

Scully made a wordless sound of amazement as they watched the rain pound the courtyard in dark and light streaks shot through with silver, pockets of steam rising from the ground in swirling patches that were shredded and whisked away. It was so heavy, they could barely see the wall.

Scully turned on the rest of the lights and rubbed her upper arms. "Close the door, it's cold."

Mulder didn't mind. After walking around in a furnace all day, the sensation was luxurious.

And the rain fascinated him.

"It can't last long," she said, although it sounded like a question.

He had seen downpours before, but this was more than that, this was an outright deluge; it didn't seem possible it could last for more than a few minutes. There couldn't be that much water in the sky.

Ten minutes later he closed the door and shrugged. "I guess we're stuck. Unless you want to try it anyway."

"Out there? In that?"

Looking out the window didn't do any good; the rain smothered it, completely obliterating the outside world.

He wished, however, that the wind would rise. It didn't seem natural, all that rain and no wind to whip it.

Scully moved over to the bed and picked up the receiver. "I'll try Garson again. I'd like to know what he's been doing all day."

He would, too. He had already run through a couple of scenarios, neither of which he liked. He doubted seriously that the man was upset because of their arrival; they were all supposed to be working the same territory no matter what state that territory was in. He also didn't think Garson was part of what they were looking for; it felt wrong. Nothing more; it just felt wrong.

Scully hung up. "Nothing. Sparrow's been there, but there are no results yet."

Rain slapped at the door, a little wind at last.

A constant thudding overhead, like an army marching across the roof.

"Talk to me, Mulder," Scully said then.

He sat at the table, drew invisible patterns on the surface to focus him and, at the same time, to let him think aloud without built-in restrictions.

"It's a cliche," he said slowly, "but maybe it's true here, who knows? What we know for sure is that Paulie and the Constellas had Konochine jewelry. Except for that partial chain you found, it was gone when the bodies were discovered. Destroyed or taken, we don't know yet. But it's gone.

"Maybe this Lanaya brought out the wrong kind. Maybe it has some religious or traditional significance we don't understand yet. Everyone we've talked to has made a big deal of telling us they don't want contact, minimal contact at best. So it's possible that exposing those pieces to the outside could be considered a form of sacrilege. There might be some on the reservation who would do anything to get it back."

"You're right, it is a cliche." She leaned forward and rested her forearms on her thighs. "And don't forget, Lanaya is one of their own. He wouldn't make a mistake like that. Not even a careless one."

"Then maybe it's the very fact that the pieces went out at all."

"He's been doing it for years."

"He's been fighting them for years."

"But he's still been doing it."

Right, he thought; and by now, after all this time, hundreds of people must have Konochine rings and necklaces and who knew what else? Hundreds, at least, but only three had died.

A damp chill filtered into the room.

The light flickered once and settled, startling him into the realization that there was no thunder, no lightning. How could clouds like that, with all that power, not have thunder and lightning?

Scully rose and walked to the bathroom door, walked back and sat again. "I'd still like to know how it was done."

"Scoured. Dr. Rios said scoured."

"How?"

He almost said, "Sentient Brillo," but changed his mind when he saw the *don't you dare, Mulder* look on her face.

Instead, he answered, "I haven't a clue."

"Yes!" She slapped her leg angrily. "Yes, damnit, we *do* have a clue! We just don't know what it is."

There was no response to exasperation like that, so he drew patterns again, over and over, while he listened to the thunder the army made on the roof.

"Sangre Viento," he said at last.

"It has a nice ring, but what does it mean, aside from the translation?"

Patterns; always patterns.

He watched the finger move, trying not to control it consciously. Automatic writing that did nothing but draw senseless patterns.

Thirty minutes after the storm began, he tilted his chair back, reached over and opened the door, squinting against a spray that dropped ice on his cheeks. "This is impossible. When the hell is it going to end?"

And the rain stopped.

He almost toppled backward at the abruptness of the cessation. One second he couldn't see an inch past the tree, the next all there was were glittering droplets falling from the leaves and eaves, and a slow runoff of water along narrow, shallow trenches set along the paths.

He looked at Scully and said, "Am I good, or what?"

\\\\\\\\\\\\\\\\\\

Donna whispered a prayer when the rain finally ended and the sun came out. One more quick turn around the house and a check of the back yard, and she would leave. The Cherokee was packed; she had never unpacked. It had been a stupid idea anyway, thinking she could use the rain for cover. She wouldn't have made it half a mile on the interstate before she would have been forced to pull over. This way she was calmer, and had a clearer head.

She had had time to think.

Now it was time to fish or cut bait.

The bone pile had been touched by only a fringe of the storm, washed clean and gleaming.

The water had been taken by leaves and roots and the porous desert floor; there were no puddles, and there was no wind.

Nevertheless, the sand stirred.

SIXTEEN

Mulder stepped outside and inhaled deeply several times. Too many scents mingled for him to identify, but they were sweet, and he was pleased. He had caught Scully's determination, and with the dust washed away, even the prospects of success seemed more bright.

You're pushing it, he told himself, and didn't much care. It felt pretty good, and he took that where he could get it.

Scully followed, checking to be sure the door locked behind her. A detour to the front desk assured them that the clerk had Mulder's portable phone number and would relay calls or messages as soon as they were received.

Just as they were about to turn away from the desk, Scully gave a nod toward the side entrance. "I think we have company."

A tall man in denim and a ponytail walked toward them, taking off his hat as he approached. "Agent Mulder? Agent Scully?"

Mulder nodded warily.

The man held out his hand. "Nick Lanaya. We were supposed to meet later." He cocked a lean hip as he shifted his weight. "Sorry I'm early, but I took a chance catching you. I was going to stop at a friend's first, but the storm…"

"Actually," Scully said, "your timing is perfect. We were about to drive out to the Mesa."

His eyes widened. "Alone?"

"No. We were hoping someone from the Double-H would go along. But," she added with a smile, "now you're here, which is exactly what we need."

"Damn right about that," he said, matching her with a smile of his own. "Today's Thursday. You go there today, they'll probably shoot you."

"What?" Mulder said.

"Well, not really shoot you, Agent Mulder, but you wouldn't have gotten in. It's a… call it a holy day. Kind of like Sunday, only a little more intense." He used the hat to gesture toward the restaurant. "So what do you say we have something to eat? Chuck said you had a few questions, and I answer better on a full stomach."

Not long after they were at a table, this time near the entrance. Other diners had already begun to arrive, and the room was more lively, more cheerful than last time. The contrast was startling, and it took Mulder a few minutes before he was able to concentrate on what Lanaya told him.

Anecdotes at first, as their meal arrived and they ate, trying to give them a feel for his people. They were conservative, hard-working, and surprisingly, they didn't feel at all oppressed.

"They've been at Sangre Viento since their Time began. No one has ever defeated them in war badly enough to drive them out, although the Apache gave them a hard time for a while, a hundred years or so back, and the white man hasn't seen any need to do anything but leave them pretty much alone." He seemed slightly embarrassed. "To tell you the truth, it makes them kind of smug."

Scully brushed the corner of her mouth with a napkin. "I understand you're an important person there."

Lanaya closed his eyes as he laughed, shook his head and waved his fork. "Lord, no. Important?" He laughed again. "Not the way you mean, no. Some sort of authority figure, a position of power, something like that?"

"Something like that, yes."

"Nope. Sorry. I'm important only in that I keep their contacts with the outside healthy, that's all. They're not stupid, Agent Scully. They don't live primitively; not by their standards, anyway. They just pick and choose what they want from the white man's world, that's all. Some have TV, everybody has a radio. Schooling is important. I'm not the only one who went to college."

"But you went back."

"Yes. Yes, I went back. Often there are ties too strong to be broken." His left hand moved to his chest and away, but not before Mulder spotted a bulge there.

A medicine bag, he thought; he carries his power with him.

"Anyway, what is it, exactly, that you want to know?"

Mulder watched Scully's smile, and hid one of his own. The man was taken with her, and whether he knew it or not, Scully had already gotten more from him than he probably wanted them to know.

They.

He said *they* instead of *we*.

Scully's next question was predictable, and Mulder couldn't help feeling a faint disappointment at the answer.

"No, there's no significance to any of the things I bring out for Donna to sell. Traditional designs, that's all." He chuckled. "Once in a while, the designs are... borrowed, shall we say? The artisans get bored doing the same thing all the time."

"You mean they fake it? Pass their work off as someone else's?"

"I mean they get bored, Agent Scully. What they use, they make their own."

They again.

Mulder began to wonder.

Suddenly the man grunted and clutched at his stomach. Scully was on her feet immediately, but he waved her away. "It's okay," he said, gasping a little, his eyes watering. "Took me by surprise, is all."

Scully stood by him anyway. "What did?"

Lanaya gestured toward his plate. "Ulcer, I think."

"What? You have an ulcer and you eat this stuff?" She rolled her eyes and took her seat. "You're out of your mind."

"Maybe." He took a roll of antacid tablets from his pocket and popped one into his mouth. "No, definitely. But I keep hoping I'll get used to it before I die."

"Don't worry, you won't," she told him. "Because that stuff will end up killing you."

He laughed, and Mulder managed a polite smile in response.

He was getting damn tired of people lying to his face.

\\\\\\\\\\\\\\\\\

There was someone in the backyard.

She heard movement as she dropped her suitcase into the passenger seat, and swore. With hardly any neighbors to speak of, who the hell would be out there? Unless it was a stray cat, or... she glared. Or a goddamn coyote.

She hurried into the house, yanked open a desk drawer, and pulled out a wood-stock .38. She had never given a damn what the cautions were; it was always loaded. A single woman living alone would scarcely have the time to load if someone broke in in the middle of the night.

She hefted it, thumbed off the safety, and marched through the Pullman kitchen to the back door. As far as she could tell, the yard was empty, its grass long since given over to weeds and bare earth.

Still...

A low, constant hissing.

Shit, she thought; she had left the outside faucet on. That's what it was—water spilling onto the weeds beneath the damn faucet. She tried to remember when she last was out here, and couldn't. Good God, it could have been as long as a week, maybe more. Her water bill was going to be—

She laughed and shook her head.

Who cared about a stupid water bill? She wasn't going to be around to pay it anyway. Nevertheless, a twinge of guilt at all that waste made her open the door and step outside, swinging immediately to the right and crouching under the kitchen window. She already had her hand on the faucet when she realized it was dry.

No water.

"What the hell?"

The noise grew louder, and now she heard what she thought was whispering. She rose and turned in the same move.

Too terrified to scream, she managed to fire twice before she was struck and spun away from the house, her arms flailing, her clothes shredded, strips of flesh taken and flung against the wall, her eyes blinded, her lips gone.

When it was over, she remained on her feet for as long as it took for a breeze to touch her.

When she fell, no one heard her.

Lanaya folded his napkin beside his empty plate. "If it's all right with you, I'll pick you up in the morning. The sooner we get there, the sooner we can leave."

Mulder reached for a glass of water. "You don't sound very proud of your home."

"It's for your own good, Agent Mulder. And there's not much to see." He pushed his chair back, but neither Mulder nor Scully moved. "I have to admit, I'm still not convinced you're looking in the right place. Coincidence, that's all it is."

"Maybe. Probably, if you like. But as I already said to someone, we have no choice."

"Sure, no problem. I understand."

Mulder turned around, looking for a waiter to signal so he could get the check. Who he saw was Sheriff Sparrow coming through the front door. By his attitude, the way he snapped a question at the clerk, who had walked over to greet him, it was business. Bad business.

"Scully," he said quietly, and excused himself to hurry into the lobby.

Sparrow brushed the clerk aside with a brusque nod and stared over Mulder's shoulder. "News," he said.

"What?"

"Lanaya been with you all this time?"

Mulder nodded. "What's happened?"

"You already eat?"

"Sheriff, would you mind telling me what's going on?"

Sparrow stared, shook himself without moving a muscle, and blew out a sigh. "Sorry. I didn't mean to snap like that. But I guess you're in luck, Agent Mulder. There's been another one."

Mulder beckoned to Scully automatically as he said, "Who?"

"Donna Falkner."

\\\\\\\\\\\\\\\\\\\

Shots, two, maybe three, the sheriff told them as he sped out of the parking lot. A neighbor went over to complain, couldn't get an answer at the front door and wandered around to the back. As soon as he saw the body, he called the sheriff's office. As soon as the first deputy saw the body, he called the sheriff, knowing the FBI was in on this case.

Several patrol cars were already on the scene when they arrived, and an ambulance backed into the driveway. Yellow crime scene ribbon fluttered around the property. A handful of people stood in the lot across the street.

"How well did you know her?" Mulder asked as Sparrow led them around the garage to the back.

"She was a pain in the ass." A sharp wave. "She was okay, though."

"Did you know she was going on vacation?"

Sparrow stopped and turned at the corner. "Are you crazy? She never went on vacation. Working herself to death is what she was. Wanted to be a goddamn millionaire before she was thirty-five."

Mulder stepped around him and walked slowly through the shin-high weeds. A sheet had been placed over the body. He didn't bother to ask if the ME had been called; this report wouldn't be any different from the others.

Scully brushed by him and knelt beside the sheet. He stood behind her, holding his breath as she pulled on a pair of latex gloves, pinched a corner, and pulled it back.

Mulder looked away.

Scully braced herself on the ground with one hand, and whispered something he couldn't catch. He saw a shudder work its way down her back before she asked if someone had a camera. A deputy appeared at her side, and she directed the lens as she pulled the sheet farther back.

The mutilation here wasn't as complete as the others. There were areas where the skin was raw but still intact, and areas where a gleam of white showed through liquid red. Her face, however, was completely gone, as was most of her hair.

This had not been a swift dying.

While the sheriff barked and grumbled at his men, Mulder began a slow walk around the yard, until he realized that the color near and on the ground was actually bits of flesh. So were the splotches on the wall near an outside spigot. At the foundation just below it, he found the gun, took a pen from his pocket and picked it up through the trigger guard. Two shots, maybe three, the neighbor had said.

At what?

"Scully."

She looked up, a little pale but recovered.

He jerked his head to tell her he would be inside when she was finished, then opened the kitchen door and went in.

It was still hot, no moving air, and no sign that she intended to return from wherever it was she'd been heading. The drawers in the tiny bedroom dresser were empty; there were a few cartons in the spare room, which looked like those he'd seen in the Cherokee outside. Nothing in the medicine cabinet. Papers and some ledgers in the desk; bills paid and unpaid, but no letters.

He didn't realize how much sunlight had slipped away until someone snapped on an overhead light.

It didn't make the place look any better.

When he took another turn around the room, he saw a briefcase against the wall beside the desk. He knelt, lifted it up, and raised an eyebrow in mild surprise. It was heavier than it looked.

When he opened it, he knew why.

"What do you know?" he said softly, closed it again, and snapped the locks. He kept it in his hand as he went through the house again, finding nothing more than tangles of dust in the corners.

Eventually he found himself by the window, staring at Nick Lanaya, who stood by a pickup parked across the street. Funny reaction, he thought as he headed for the door. The man's partner is murdered, and he just stands there.

He moved onto the stoop and waved, but Lanaya didn't see him.

He was too busy talking to Leon Ciola.

SEVENTEEN

"Mulder."

He lifted a hand to his shoulder, bringing Scully out of the house and cautioning her at the same time. He pointed when she stood beside him. "Well, well."

The two men were close together, sideways to the house, every so often glancing down into the truck's bed. Not once did they show any interest in the deputies bustling around the area, or in the police when they arrived, lights spinning. Mulder couldn't tell if they were arguing or not, but they certainly weren't simply passing the time.

He could see Ciola's shark smile; he couldn't read Lanaya's face at all.

Then Ciola jabbed Lanaya's chest with a stiff finger, once, twice, and leaned so close their noses almost touched.

"Do you think we should join them?" Scully asked.

"What, and disturb their grief?" He sidestepped back into the living room. "Look at this, Scully." He set the briefcase on the desk and opened it to show her the packets of money he had found, as many as could be crammed in without bursting the seams.

"A bank is safer." She picked up a packet, another, but there was no sense trying to fix the amount now. Some were in equal amounts, others were mixed. That there was thousands, however, was beyond question. She pulled back her hand and closed the briefcase with a slap. "The same as the others, Mulder." Her gloves had already been stripped off, but she scrubbed her hands anyway. "Not as complete, but the same." She looked at him, almost angry. "I'm going to do this autopsy myself. And this time the report will be right."

"What will it say, Agent Scully?" Nick Lanaya asked from the doorway.

She turned to him. "It will say, once the remains have been confirmed, that Donna Falkner was murdered by person or persons unknown, for one thing. For another, it will say that it appears to be in the same manner of death as the others you've had in this area." She turned away. "You'll have to wait for the rest."

Lanaya sagged against the door frame, head bowed. "I looked in the Cherokee."

Mulder kept the case as he walked over to Lanaya. "She was your partner. Where was she going with all that?"

Lanaya didn't look up. "I would say she was stealing it. According to the markings, they should have been sold months ago." Suddenly he kicked back at the screen door, slamming it against the house. "Goddamnit, Mulder, what the hell was she doing? All the years we worked together—" He kicked the door again and stared blindly into the room.

This time Mulder saw the pain. And something else. Maybe betrayal.

He nudged Lanaya until he went outside, and they walked away from the house, Mulder drawing closer until the man had no conscious choice but to take him to the truck.

The bed was empty, except for a length of tarp folded near the cab.

"I didn't know you knew Leon," Mulder said, careful to keep accusation from his voice.

"There isn't an adult Konochine alive who doesn't know all the others, Agent Mulder. You can hardly avoid it the way we live."

"It seemed a bit more than just casual, from what I saw."

"Personal, okay? It was personal." Lanaya's expression couldn't decide whether to be angry or insulted. "I was with you, remember?" A one-sided, humorless smile flashed on, flashed off. "Just in case you were wondering."

"I wasn't. I have a pretty good short-term memory. Do you happen to know where Mr. Ciola was?"

"Don't know, don't give a shit." Lanaya reached into the bed and picked up a twig with long needles on it. He twirled it between his fingers before flicking it away. "Stupid woman. My God, what… what… " He gave up.

"You were lovers?"

The Indian shrugged, one shoulder. "For a while. A couple of years back. Turned out we wanted to be business partners more, so we stopped."

"That briefcase is filled with money. Would you have any idea where she got it?"

Radio chatter hung over the street.

A cop and a deputy laughed too loudly.

It should be dark, Mulder thought as he waited for an answer, there's too much light here. It should be dark.

"We haven't been doing too well lately, actually," Lanaya finally admitted. He sniffed, rubbed his nose with the back of a hand, and pushed his hat up off his forehead. "About a year ago, she said the usual stuff wasn't working anymore, that we needed a gimmick, something to distinguish our product from all the other Indian stuff getting produced around here." He laughed bitterly. "I got a bad feeling, Agent Mulder. A bad feeling I've been had." Another laugh, and he slapped the truck's side. "Son of a bitch! When they find out about this, I'll never be able to get them to trust me again."

Scully and Sparrow left the house, talking softly.

Lanaya swept a nervous hand back over his hair several times. "Will I... she has no relatives, I mean. Will I have to, you know, identify her?"

"That won't be necessary."

He looked, one eye nearly closed. "That bad?"

Mulder couldn't face him. "There'll have to be the usual tests."

"Tests?" He moved as if to take a run at the house. "Tests? Then how the hell do you know it's her, Mulder? My God, maybe it's someone else, a vagrant or something."

The only thing he could say was, "I know, Mr. Lanaya. I don't want to, but you'll have to trust me on this. I know it's her."

Lanaya made a growling noise in his throat, took a step around the truck, and asked with a look if he was needed. Mulder waved him on, and backed away back when the pickup barreled away, turning the corner without the brake lights flaring.

Mulder watched for a moment, then returned to the front yard, where Scully joined him.

"You all right?" he asked, seeing the expression on her face.

She nodded. "I'm just finding it a little hard to believe, that's all." She glanced toward the house. "Aside from the method, though, it's strange."

"That's not strange enough?"

She almost smiled. "Did you get a good look at the yard?"

"I saw the bare patch where she fell, if that's what you mean."

"Right. But before we leave, take another look. That bare area where the grass and weeds were cut down, that wasn't done by any kind of mower I'm aware of."

"Wait."

She passed a hand over her chin. "What I mean is, where she died isn't where she was first attacked. Whoever killed her… it's as if she was pushed around, and the murderer followed her."

"A force like that, I'm not surprised. When you get into a fight, you hardly ever stick to one place."

"This wasn't like a fistfight, Mulder. She wasn't punched around, falling down and getting up again. From what I can tell, given the… given the positions of the body, and the flesh and bone shards around the yard, she fell only once. When she died."

Mulder swallowed, but said nothing.

"The point is, Mulder—whoever attacked her, with whatever weapon, kept her on her feet."

"But the force it would take to do that much damage…" He gestured toward the house.

"Exactly, Mulder," she said. "Exactly. She should have fallen almost immediately. But she didn't."

That night, after the paperwork was done, interviews completed, and he and Sheriff Sparrow had finished debriefing each other, he returned to the bench in the garden. His room had grown too small, and Scully was transcribing her notes into the computer. Her mind was already on the morning autopsy—a fresh, puzzling corpse to decipher.

Oh God, he thought; you're sick, pal, you're really sick. What you need is a vacation.

He almost laughed.

Right; that's what got me into this in the first place.

The Rio Grande was higher after the downpour, but only slightly, and the ground and paths were completely dry. There were no strolling guests tonight, either; that didn't surprise him. Word was probably out that the killer had struck again. For a night or two, people would stick close to home, the papers would editorialize about the alarming incidence of psychopathic murders in contemporary society, and someone, somewhere, would manage to reap a large or small political harvest.

Which knowledge got him exactly nowhere.

He reached down between his legs and picked up a pebble. He bounced it on his palm a few times before swatting it toward the water.

He did it a second time, swinging a little harder.

He stood for the third one, and hit it with a fist. It stung a knuckle, but he barely felt it. It was the motion that mattered. When he missed the fourth stone, he considered stopping wasting time and going back to the room. That lasted as long as it took him to find it, and miss again.

Now it was a matter of personal honor, and now he couldn't find the damn thing. Not that any of the others he spotted while on his hands and knees wouldn't have worked, but the one he had missed was the one he wanted.

He was nearly stretched out under the bench, feeling like a jackass, when he heard the rustle of something moving through the brush on the riverbank. At first he thought it might be the evening breeze, but listening for a few seconds told him it was too irregular.

Stop and start.

Just out of reach of the tree lamps and the moonlight, and the lamp poles along the bank.

He used the bench to push himself to his feet, staring upriver as he dusted off his knees. That, too, was a waste of time; the lamps in front of him blocked any chance of seeing what lay beyond.

The rustling stopped.

All right, so what do they have around here at night? Dogs, cats, coyotes? After that, he went blank.

When he heard it again, he took a long step off the path and picked up a small rock, aimed, and threw it as hard as he could. The crash of the missile through the brush and weeds was followed by the dull plop of its landing in shallow water. But there was no yelp, no sudden rush of an animal scurrying to get away.

Nothing at all, in fact; nothing at all.

Accepting that as a sign he was in danger of losing it, he flicked one more pebble at the water and started back to his room. He hadn't gone three steps when the noise returned.

Not a rustling now, but a barely audible hissing.

Not stop and start, but continuous and moving; slowly, very slowly.

Common sense and experience ordered him to head immediately for the inside, or, at the very least, get Scully out here with him.

What he did, for no good reason he could think of, was sidestep cautiously off the path, turning his head in short stages to try to pinpoint the source's location, whatever the source was. When he reached the lamp poles, his right hand closed around one as he slipped past, while his left instinctively slipped his gun from its holster.

He wouldn't have done that if he hadn't heard the whispering.

More than one voice, although he couldn't tell how many. Nor could he understand what they were saying. One moment it sounded like muffled laughter, the next like little children exchanging secrets in the dark.

Beyond the last pole, there were still several yards of cleared earth straight ahead, while to the left the ground sloped downward toward the river. He flexed his knees to keep his balance on the slope, to keep from sliding as he moved forward, staring, silently cursing the weak reach of the lamplight. He could barely see the brush, could only just make out a twisted branch above it, no higher than his head.

The noise was on the other side, coming toward him.

Carefully he reached behind him, fumbled for and grabbed the last square pole, a clumsy position until he put most of his weight on his right foot.

The whispering sounded more frantic, quickly blending into what sounded like a low hum.

No animal, he knew; and he couldn't see how it could be people, either. That many would make a different kind of noise, and it certainly would be louder. Which made his drawn weapon a little ludicrous.

If there was nothing to shoot at, why have it out?

But nothing didn't make a noise.

It didn't hiss.

It didn't whisper.

He released the lamp pole and eased forward, keeping low, freezing when he had a sudden image of a woman about to open a door everyone in the theater knew hid the monster. They called her stupid, they yelled at her not to do it, they threw things at the screen to get her attention, but she opened it anyway.

And she was always wrong.

And what, he asked himself, does that make you?

Hissing, climbing to a higher pitch that puzzled him because the pitch was still quite low.

It reminded him of something.

It definitely reminded him of something.

He took a step back, snapping his head around when something splashed to his left. No ripples that he could see, not even when he heard another splash, farther across the water. He could have turned then, but he didn't want to show his back to whatever was out there. He wanted to see it if he could, just in case it came into the open and could see him, too.

Then something struck the pole, taking a chip from the edge.

He didn't wait to see if it had been a shot; he fired one of his own into the dark, whirled and began to run, slipping once on the grass, flinging a hand out to stop him from falling on his chest.

When he reached the bench, he turned, trotting backward, staring at something he could finally see down by the lamps.

He never had a chance to see it clearly.

He heard a voice, heard a popping sound, and all the lamps turned red.

EIGHTEEN

Dugan Velador was tired of being old.

He didn't want to die, that would be a waste of his life. What he wanted, however, was for people to stop coming to him with questions whose answers they already knew if they would only stop to think. What he wanted was a little peace, and he didn't think that was too selfish a wish. Not at his age. Not after all he had done for his people.

He also wanted the killing to stop.

It should have ended the other night, the last night in the kiva.

For as long as he could remember, and for all that he had been taught and told, the last night should have meant the end, for it had always been before.

Not this time.

This time, from what he had heard on the portable radio he kept by his bed, another one had died. A woman. The name was familiar. He couldn't place the face or the occasion of the meeting, so he knew she wasn't Konochine *frastera*, one of those who had left.

Still, the name was familiar, and he worried at it while he ate breakfast, worried at it while, with a sitting blanket over one shoulder, he walked from his place to sleep by the Tribal Center to the Wall that overlooked the road that pointed west. When he was younger, but not young by any calculation, he used to sit there every dawn and stare at the unseen place where he knew Annie lived.

He tried to will her to return.

He prayed for her to leave the ranch and move back to her rightful home.

When that didn't work, he figured he had either really garbled the prayers so badly that the spirits hadn't recognized them, or he wasn't half as strong as he thought he was. Velador was a practical man. When one thing didn't work, there was always something else. If the spirits wouldn't listen, someone else would.

As Nick would say, what the hell.

The only thing he hadn't done, and would not do, was visit her in person. That would insult her, and demean him.

Practical, however, sometimes meant taking a bite out of pride, swallowing it, and hoping it wasn't poison.

He would have to think about it hard today. The killing of the woman he could not remember was too important. Annie would know that; maybe she already did. Maybe she would take a bite, too, and at least meet him halfway.

If she didn't, he'd be sitting in the sun for nothing.

Practical didn't always mean that what he did was smart.

When Mulder opened his eyes, he instantly allowed as how he fully deserved the booming explosion whose echoes rebounded through his skull for what seemed like forever. And when forever arrived, he still had a splitting headache.

At least he was still in his room, or would be as soon as the walls stopped shifting.

Last night, when he'd regained consciousness, he had thought he was in a hospital. A beautiful hospital with soft lights and attractive, natural decorations complete with all the appropriate scents and aromas. The bed was too hard, though, and the air conditioning had been turned up way too high. They hadn't even bothered to cover him with a blanket.

When his vision cleared an eyeblink later, he realized someone had stretched him out on one of the benches in the motel's back garden.

Scully knelt beside him, urging him to stop hiding and come all the way out. When he did, she scolded him for doing whatever he had done to get him clunked like this.

"Clunked?"

He had tried to sit up, but his head wouldn't let him; neither would his stomach. A rolling nausea engulfed him briefly, and he tightened his jaw, clenched his fits until the urge to vomit had passed.

Sparrow leaned into sight then, and between thumb and forefinger held up a

stone that would fit perfectly in his palm. He turned it so Mulder could see the
fresh bloodstain.

"What were you doing, Mulder?" Scully's expression was stern, but her voice
was pure concern.

Again he tried to sit up, and again the dizziness was too strong. He accepted
the order her hand on his shoulder gave him. "Someone was out there." He
pointed vaguely, not sure of the right direction. "Maybe more than one. Definitely
more than one." His eyes closed as he tried to remember.

While he did, the sheriff said, "And they knocked you out with a rock? Agent
Scully said she heard a shot."

Voices had interrupted them, for which he had been grateful. He needed time
for all parts of him to get back together, and when they did, reluctantly, he said,
"No, never mind. I don't think it was a person."

The sheriff grunted. "Then you're the first man on record to get himself beaned
by a coyote."

"Not an animal either."

"He's delirious." Sparrow sounded disgusted. "Such a little scratch, too. I'll be
back in the morning, folks. There's nothing out there, Agent Scully. And if there
was, he's long gone by now. Long gone."

More voices, footsteps, murmuring, then silence.

He opened his eyes.

Scully was still there, patient. "What did you shoot at, Mulder?"

"Little scratch? I thought a boulder hit me."

"Mulder, pay attention. What did you shoot at?"

He hadn't known then, and he didn't know now. Not that he could think very
straight yet anyway, even if he did know. Fingers touched his forehead gingerly,
skated over it until they reached the lump of a square bandage just above his left
temple. He pressed, it protested, and he let the hand fall away.

What the hell was it?

Sleep on it, he ordered, and no one argued.

When he next woke up, the ache had lessened considerably, and he felt well
enough to stumble into the bathroom before his bladder exploded. A double
palmful of water scattered the rest of the cobwebs, allowing him to check his
reflection without wanting to break the mirror.

All in all, he looked a lot better than he felt. The bandage was small, and someone, probably Scully, had already washed the blood from his face. Other than his hair poking out in all directions, he figured he looked pretty human.

A few minutes of washing, holding onto the basin while ripples of nausea and dizziness settled, and getting that hair back into place, and he felt even better. Hungry, even. He was about to give Scully a call to meet him for a late breakfast when he spotted a note taped to the mirror over the low dressing table in the front room. It was a reminder that she had an autopsy to perform, and a warning not to do anything on his own. She hoped to be back by noon, or shortly after.

Taking care to move without jarring anything loose inside his skull, he finished dressing and stepped outside.

The sky was blindingly blue, the sun simply blinding, and the heat hadn't changed, although it might have been, relatively, a bit cooler than yesterday. None of it did his head any good, and he hurried to the restaurant and the safety of the indoors.

A simple breakfast eaten in solitude allowed him to get past the muted throbbing behind his brow, to go over what had happened the night before.

Not that he needed much reminding. The humiliation of the lump was bad enough.

What had happened was, he had ignored all his instincts and had opened that damn door. What had made him do it, he couldn't figure out. It had been more than simple curiosity, and until the end of the episode, he didn't recall feeling all that threatened.

So… why?

He ordered a second tall glass of orange juice and sipped it while he watched the other guests come and go, wind through the courtyard, take pictures of each other beneath the cottonwood. In the white sun they had no idea what he had seen yesterday in that weed-infested yard; or if they did, they weren't going to let it ruin their day. A tale to tell when they got home, nothing more, a whole lot less.

The glass was empty when he remembered something else—that the noise he had heard by the river had reminded him of something. He concentrated, and scowled in defeat when he couldn't give it a name. He did bring back the feeling, however, and it made him put the glass down and take a deep calming breath.

Above and in that hissing was the whispering.

she is special, mr. mulder.

His spine stiffened.

she hears the wind.

He was on his feet before he realized he had even left his seat, and that he hadn't yet received his check. Luckily, the waiter spotted him and came right over. Mulder signed it, added a large tip and an effusive verbal thanks that startled the young man, and did his best not to run from the room to the lobby reception desk. There were no messages from Scully, and none from Sheriff Sparrow, who had said, Mulder recalled, that he would be back sometime this morning to ask some questions about last night.

He wondered if he could convince the man that he hadn't been delirious at all...

The wind.

Not wanting to confine himself to his room again, he strolled deliberately slowly around the courtyard, for all the world like a tourist who couldn't think of a damn thing to do. When he couldn't stand it anymore, he veered into the passageway to the back garden. Except for a woman standing near the center, he was alone.

The wind.

As he passed her, heading for the place where he'd been struck, he heard a noise. A familiar noise. One that made him stop, that made his headache return.

"Are you all right?"

The woman, a short Hispanic woman in a maid's uniform, looked up at him, not really concerned; she was only being polite because she had to. Behind her he saw a wheeled cart stacked with fresh linens and towels.

He nodded, and stared at her hands when the noise started again.

"Hey," she said, both a question and a warning.

"I'm sorry." He added a smile to the apology and moved on, forcing himself not to look back. A moment later he heard the cart's wheels roll quickly across the stone. Obviously she thought he was nuts. Maybe he was. The sound he had just heard was an emery board being drawn across her nail. Almost like sandpaper.

At the bench where he had been last night, he looked toward the spot where he had heard the hissing, the whispers.

He didn't have to go there now to know what he would find, but he went anyway. A justification, a confirmation. He hadn't seen it on the riverbank where Paulie Deven had been killed, but he had seen it yesterday, in Donna Falkner's backyard. He just hadn't known what he had been looking at.

It didn't take long.

At the place where the grass met the underbrush, he stopped and rose up slightly on his toes. The growth wasn't so dense that he couldn't get in there; he didn't need to. He could see well enough from where he stood.

About ten feet away was an open spot, a scar. The branches of the brush at its rim were either snapped off or had their bark worn through. Stretching his neck allowed him a glimpse of the ground, and the debris that covered it.

He grinned.

"Agent Mulder!"

Sheriff Sparrow came into the garden, and Mulder answered him with a gesture that he'd be there in a second. One more scan of the area showed him everything he needed to see, and he rubbed his hands briskly as he returned to the garden path.

"Sheriff, do you think you can get hold of Nick Lanaya?"

"I suppose so. What do you need?"

Scully, he thought as he headed for the sheriff, you're going to hate what I know. You're going to hate it a lot.

NINETEEN

There were no chairs in the lobby. The only place to sit was a thick wood bench beside the fountain. Mulder waited while Sparrow used the desk phone to reach Lanaya, hoping that Scully would return soon. He didn't want to leave without her, but he felt a need to move fast, before someone else died.

After last night, he had more than an unpleasant feeling that he knew who that target was.

Sparrow sat beside him, hat and sunglasses off, rubbing his eyes. "I left a message. There's only a couple of phones out there. Portable jobs like you have. Half the time they're left behind." He leaned back against the fountain's broad lip. "So you want to tell me what's going on, or is this going to be one of those need-to-know bullshit things?"

Mulder shook his head. "No need-to-know, Sheriff. Scully and I are going to need all the help we can get." He checked the time, wondering aloud how long his partner would be.

"She's done, and on her way," the man said wryly.

"How do you know that?"

"I read minds, Mulder." The jerk of a thumb toward the reception desk. "Plus, I called."

Close, Mulder thought; not quite, but close enough.

"Half an hour, maybe a little more." The sheriff rocked to nudge Mulder with a shoulder. "I can't read minds that good."

Mulder debated. No matter how many times he told it, there would be arguments and counter-suggestions, especially from Scully. He decided it would be best to get it out in one session rather than have to keep repeating himself.

It would also give him time to convince himself more thoroughly that he was right.

At his hesitation, the sheriff took off his hat and dropped it beside him on the bench. He took a notepad from his breast pocket, and a pen whose tip had been chewed close to chipping. "Okay. So how about you tell me about last night? You fired a gun, Mulder. FBI or not, that needs some explanation."

Grateful for the change of subject, Mulder complied readily. He took the man through his movements step by step from the time he entered the garden until he had been struck. Sparrow asked few questions. A clarification here, a doubt there. When Mulder was done, the man put the notepad away, fixed the pen to his pocket, and scratched his forehead.

"Basically, what you're telling me is that you shot at a shadow."

"No, Sheriff. I shot at something that was definitely no shadow."

"So what was it?"

Mulder smiled and stood. "Patience is a virtue, Sheriff Sparrow."

"Patience, my friend, is a royal pain in the ass. And you gotta admit, I've been pretty damn patient with you."

Mulder agreed, and decided to take the lawman out back to show him what he had found. Sparrow reminded him that he had already been there, he and his men, but Mulder insisted gently. What he wanted the sheriff to see was something his men, good as they were, probably wouldn't have thought twice about.

"I did the same, Sheriff, the first time I saw it."

They were already at the riverbank when Scully called his name.

He made a silent wish for no surprises, no complications, then looked at the sheriff.

Sparrow was laughing.

"What?"

He pointed at Scully, then reached over and tapped a finger against Mulder's chest. "Couldn't stand it, could you?"

That was the first time Mulder realized that in dressing this morning, he had put on his tie and blue suit. It had been automatic. He had been too busy fighting his headache to think. His hands had grabbed what they knew best.

Scully, too, was the same.

For some reason, even out here, she looked more natural that way.

"Well?" he asked.

Scully greeted the sheriff almost curtly, pushed at her hair to keep the steady breeze from blinding her, and said, "Mulder, I do not want to have to do that again, ever."

"I'd think," Sparrow said, "you'd be used to it by now. Cutting them up, I mean, figuring things out."

"You don't get used to it," she told him. "You just find a way not to let it bother you for a while." She grabbed a folded paper from her shoulder bag, glanced at it, and took a deep breath. "You'll be pleased to know there are no surprises, Mulder. And Dr. Rios was right—it wasn't skinning and it wasn't flaying. Scouring, for the time being, is a pretty damn good word."

"What killed her?"

"Simply? Layman's terms? Shock. If you want the details, we can start with the near-total destruction of a major organ—which is what the skin is—coupled with rapid fluid loss from various sources, including—"

"Never mind," the sheriff interrupted, a queasy look on his face. "I get the picture."

"No," she contradicted. "I don't think you do. Mulder, there were particles of sandy dirt lodged in the sinuses and eye sockets. And in the brain."

"What the hell could do something like that?" Sparrow demanded.

"Force," Mulder answered. "A lot of force." He started for the river. "Which is why I want you to take a look at this."

Scully looked at him quizzically. "What?"

"Just look, Scully. I'll explain on our way to the Mesa."

She didn't argue, but followed the sheriff to the brush at the edge of the grass, where Mulder pointed out the cleared area farther on. It took a while until they found a way through without ripping themselves to shreds, and when they reached the rough circle, he broke off an already damaged twig and held it up.

"The bark," he said. "Torn off."

The ground at their feet was littered with shredded leaves and shards of twigs and branches.

"If I didn't know better," Sparrow said, "I'd say a nut with a weed-whacker got roaring drunk in here."

"There's the same sort of damage done over at Donna Falkner's house," Mulder told them as they made their way back to the garden. "I saw it, but because the yard was so badly kept, it didn't hit me until this morning."

Sparrow told them to meet him in the parking lot; he'd go in to see if Lanaya had been reached. Scully walked with her head down, every few steps shaking her head. Then she stopped Mulder with a touch. "A device, maybe? Maybe the sheriff wasn't so far off with that weed-trimmer idea." She looked away, looked back. "But that doesn't explain the dirt. Just falling wouldn't do it."

"No, you're right."

He started for the car, but she blocked him, a hand briefly on his chest. 'What is it, Mulder? What are you up to?"

"Sangre Viento," he answered. "It's the only thing that makes sense."

"Really?" She glanced over at the sheriff, hurrying toward them. "And you think that makes sense?"

"It does to me."

"Of course it does," she said flatly. "Whatever was I thinking of."

"Nick's waiting at the res," Sparrow said, herding them toward his cruiser. A hard look at Mulder. "We'll ride together, all right? I want to hear this. Just tell me I'm gonna like it."

Mulder couldn't, and by his expression the sheriff knew it. He rolled his eyes in resignation and wondered aloud how Scully put up with it.

"Patience," Mulder said as he slid into the backseat.

"Pain in the ass," the sheriff answered.

"Maybe. But I've gotten used to it."

Scully wasn't amused.

Nick hunkered down beside the old man, hands draped across his knees. "You're going to bake out here, Dugan."

The old man only shrugged.

"The FBI is coming."

"There was a death."

"I know."

"The woman. I think I know her."

Nick shifted uneasily. "Donna Falkner, Dugan. She's… was my partner."

"Ah, yes. I remember her now. She ran pretty good."

Nick couldn't help but smile. "Yes, she did. And she helped us a lot. I hope you remember that, too."

The old man brushed invisible sand from his blanket, the only admission Nick was likely to get.

"There should not have been a killing, Nick."

"Yes. I know that."

"There should not have been any killings." Dugan's head turned stiffly. "The cattle sometimes. I remember a coyote once. But no people, Nick. Never any people before."

Nick nodded earnestly, leaning as close as he could without toppling into the old man's lap. "That's what I've been trying to tell you, Dugan. If we don't do something, the FBI will find out, and we won't be able to stop the news people or the police or anybody from trampling all over the Mesa." He lowered his voice. "But if we stop him now, there'll be nothing to see. Nothing to find."

A breeze stirred the grass.

"Dugan. Father. The Falkner woman won't be the last to die. You know that."

The old man's head bowed, his hands gathering in his lap. "I am hoping for—"

Nick couldn't help himself; he grabbed the man's shoulder harshly. "Damnit, she isn't coming back, Dugan. Annie isn't coming back, and she's not going to help." He felt the shoulder stiffen, and snatched his hand away. "If we're going to make it through this, we have to see that Leon is…"

He didn't finish.

He didn't have to.

All he could do was wait for Velador to make up his mind. As he stood, the old man began a low murmuring, and Nick walked away.

He hadn't gone ten paces when the old man said, "Nick," just loud enough to hear.

He turned to face Dugan's back, and the right hand raised, finger pointing to the sky.

"The FBI."

"What about them?"

"They must be stopped."

The breeze blew.

The sand stirred.

Imagine, Mulder said, a group of men, extremely devout men, confined for so long in a single room. The kiva. Imagine, as he had already mentioned to Scully, the energy they must create and radiate as they perform the rituals required of their faith. Suppose, then, there are moments during that time when the energy can no longer be confined, but its excess escapes through the hole in the ceiling. It can dissipate. Maybe someone nearby feels a little discomfort, but nothing more. They might blame it on the wind.

But suppose, just suppose, it doesn't scatter. Suppose it gathers instead. Suppose it concentrates.

Suppose the earliest Konochine knew this. They would also know that such a concentration would be potentially dangerous. So they come to the valley within the Wall from wherever they had been, and make it their home. It's isolated, protected by both the hills and the mountains, and nobody—not the other tribes, not the Spanish, not the whites—bothers them for very long.

But the energy is the important thing.

What happens to it?

Sangre Viento.

Blood Wind.

Nando making a spinning motion with his hand.

He called it a whirlwind.

Not a tornado dropping from a cloud; an extraordinary dust devil, rising from the ground.

It spins alone in the desert, and when the energy is used, it falls apart, just like disturbing the plane of an ordinary dust devil will cause it to collapse. It's reasonable to suppose, then, that once in a while an animal gets caught in it, and because it spins at such high speeds, far faster than an ordinary dervish, and because it's made up of gritty, sandy earth, leaves, twigs, whatever else is on the ground…

Imagine, he said.

Imagine the power.

TWENTY

He stared at the passing desert, elbow on the armrest, one hand curled lightly across his chin. Now that he had said it aloud, heard his voice, he knew he was right. There was no baroque device a murderer could cart around with him, and there was no group of whip-wielding maniacs.

Sangre Viento was all there was.

And one thing more.

"Mulder," Scully said in that voice he had heard so many times before, "assuming, and only assuming, for the moment that you're right—"

Sheriff Sparrow grumbled a few words, most of which were "bullshit."

Mulder couldn't miss the tone of disappointment and disbelief.

"—what you're talking about is…" She faltered. "Is a form of undirected psychic, for want of a better word, energy. Assuming it's true," she added hastily. "But how does that random activity explain four people dying? It seems to me that where and when they died indicates something else entirely."

"Premeditation," he said, still watching the desert.

"Exactly."

"Oh, sweet Jesus," Sparrow snapped. "Are you telling me there's somebody who can aim this thing? Assuming," he said sarcastically, "you're right." He yanked the cruiser so hard off the interstate, Mulder nearly fell over. "For God's sake, gimme a break."

Unfortunately, Mulder couldn't see any other answer. What he could see, however, was a couple of names who might be interested in such control. The question was, why would they feel the need to kill?

"I mean," the sheriff continued, working himself into a self-righteous rage, "how can a couple of intelligent people like you believe in such crap? Bunch of old Indians sitting around a campfire, shooting cosmic something-or-other at eachother? You been nibbling at some peyote or what?" He slapped the steering wheel hard. "Scully, you're a doctor, for God's sake. You gonna tell me you actually go along with this shit?"

Mulder held his breath.

"Sheriff," she answered in her most official, neutral voice, "I have never known Mulder to be so far off-base that I would dismiss everything he says out of hand."

"Ah… crap."

Thank you, Scully, Mulder thought with a brief smile, I'd rather have a resounding "absolutely and how dare you," but that'll do in a pinch.

On the other hand, the day that "absolutely and how dare you" actually came, it would probably kill him with amazement.

They passed the Double-H, and he wondered if any of this had touched Annie. He wondered what she had heard on the wind. Whatever it was, he didn't believe for a second she was in any way involved.

Suddenly the sheriff braked hard, and Mulder shot his hand out to brace himself against the seatback. In the road ahead, a pickup had been parked across the lane. Nick Lanaya lounged against the bed, arms folded across his chest.

"Stupid bastard," the sheriff muttered. "Has everyone gone nuts on me today?"

They climbed out slowly, Mulder moving around the car to join Scully. As he did, he looked up the boulder-strewn slope on his right and saw a figure sitting near the top, featureless and black against the sky.

"Dugan Velador," Lanaya said, pushing away from the truck. "He's like a priest. One of the six." A tolerant chuckle and a gesture to the hill. "He likes it up there. He says it helps him think."

"But it's so hot" Scully said, astonished. "How does he survive?"

"He's Konochine, Agent Scully. He can pretty much survive anything." He cleared his throat. "So what's up? I got Chuck' s message. What can I do for you?"

The sheriff hitched his belt. "Nick, you ain't gonna—"

"We need to see the reservation, Mr. Lanaya," Mulder said, further cutting the sheriff off by standing half in front of him. "There are some questions we have to ask of the people in charge."

"The Council?"

"Are they the priests?" Scully asked.

Lanaya shrugged. "Mostly, yes. But I don't think they'll talk to you."

Mulder smiled. "That's why you're here. To convince them that cooperation in a murder investigation would be the right thing to do. Maybe save some lives."

Lanaya scuffed the ground with the toe of a boot. "Well, to be honest, Agent Mulder, I'm kind of beat today." A sour look at the sheriff. "I spent most of the morning with a police accountant, going over Donna's ledgers and bank account. It seems she was cheating me more than just a little."

"So I gathered."

"Luckily, most of the money is recoverable, so I won't lose much. But it's the shock, you know what I mean? A lot of years I trusted her, and now I'll never know why she did it."

"Your people trusted her, too," Scully said.

"No." He squinted at the hillside. "No, they trusted me. Like I said, I've got a hell of a lot of damage control ahead of me here. And you coming in like this… it's only going to make things worse."

Mulder walked over to the truck. "You have air conditioning, right?"

Puzzled, Lanaya nodded.

"Good." He opened the passenger door and beckoned to Scully. "Let's go." Expressionless, Scully climbed in first. "We have a job to do. Right, sheriff?"

All Sparrow could do was nod curtly, and Lanaya shrugged an *it's your funeral* before getting in behind the wheel. But his face was hard, and Mulder saw his fingers tremble as they turned the key to fire the engine. Anger, or nerves.

"Ground rules," Lanaya told them as he maneuvered the pickup around. "You don't get out unless I say it's all right. You don't speak to anyone unless I say it's all right, or they speak to you first. And you sure don't go in any building unless I say it's all right. Okay?"

"Drive, Mr. Lanaya," he said. "Neither one of us has all day."

They drove through the gap, the road curving gently to the right. When the hill was finally behind them, Mulder almost asked him to stop. He wasn't quite sure what he had expected, but it wasn't anything like this.

Off the road to the left were small fields filled with crops. Scattered gunmetal pumps resembling steel dinosaurs worked ceaselessly, pumping well water into an effective series of irrigation ditches. He didn't recognize any of the crops except, in the center and by far the largest field, corn.

It was a stark, surreal contrast to the desert land that surrounded it.

On the right, however, was Sangre Viento Mesa.

Lanaya slowed. "The Place, Agent Mulder. You'll see other mesas, but never one like that."

It rose two hundred vertical feet from the desert floor, its sides ridged and furrowed, and stark. Where sunlight washed it, faint red hinted at iron among the dark tans and browns. There was no green at all. There was no plant life that he could see from this distance. On the flat top were outlines of low buildings. Several large birds circled over it. Its shadow seemed everywhere.

At the north base was the pueblo, and again his vague expectations didn't match the reality.

"Your people weren't cliff dwellers," Scully said softly.

"No. No one has ever lived on the Mesa itself." Lanaya looked at her with a faint smile. "Every so often, maybe once a decade, I'm able to bring in an archaeologist or two and some professors who don't believe it. They insist there have to be cave homes there on several levels, with ladders and all the rest. Like at Puye and Mesa Verde. There aren't."

What there were were neat rows of small abobe houses, a single story each. One, apparently, for each family. All the doors and windows Mulder could see were outlined in pale green. As the road curved closer, he saw laundry hanging from lines on poles, orderly streets in a grid, and at the east end, two larger structures which, Lanaya explained, were a storage building for crops and a tribal center. Incongruously, to Mulder, some of the homes sported television and FM antennas; only a few had vehicles parked beside them, and most of them were pickups. He also spotted a corral where several horses munched on hay and swatted flies with their tails, a trio of black-and-white dogs trotting along a street, and a low pen populated by chickens whose plumage was almost garish.

It didn't occur to him to think it odd that he couldn't see any litter.

"Where do they work?" Scully asked, leaning as close to the windshield as she could.

"In the fields, in workshops in the center or in their homes. A few go outside, but not many. The Konochine have no unemployment, if that's what you're wondering. You work to eat. You don't work, you don't eat." Lanaya laughed, but not cheerfully. "I don't know of anyone who has ever chosen to starve."

"And your house?" she asked.

Flatly: "You can't see it from here."

Mulder watched a group of white-clothed children playing in front of a building near the pueblo's middle; another group chased each other through the streets, carrying hoops and switches. "What about Leon Ciola?"

Lanaya forced the truck into a tight U-turn and took a short dirt road that led them to the front of the warehouse and the tribal center. No one looked up as he passed except one small boy, whose eyes grew so wide Mulder had to smile.

When the engine stopped, metal creaking, Lanaya opened his door. "Ciola lives where he wants. I don't follow him around, Agent Mulder. He's… he's having a difficult time fitting back into the life."

Three steps led to double doors in the center.

Lanaya pushed one open and gestured the others in. "You'll have to ask your questions here."

They were in a large meeting hall with exposed thick beams in the low ceiling. Two doors in the side walls and one in back were closed, their frames painted a pale green. The walls were white. The floor was uncovered. The only decoration was on the back wall over the door, a huge woven tapestry with a depiction of the Mesa in the center. Lightning in the sky. Symbols of sun and moon, of birds and animals. No people at all. Nothing he recognized as a language.

"No one knows how old it is," Lanaya said, his voice low. "My grandfather once told me that his grandfather knew an old woman who knew an old woman who helped with the design." He shrugged. "It doesn't matter."

Against the left wall was a long table of Spanish oak, with equally bulky chairs arranged around it. He led them over and bade them sit, Mulder with his back to the wall, Scully opposite him. "You'll want to talk to one of the Council," he said. "Dugan would be the best."

"The man on the hill?" Mulder said.

"Yes. It's time he came in out of the sun anyway. He's going to get heatstroke one of these days. Wait here. Please. It won't take me long."

The echo of his boots on the floor lingered after he had gone. And once gone, there was no other sound. The outside might as well not have existed.

Scully placed her shoulder bag on the table and folded her hands on it. "He's a strange man, Mulder. One minute you think he hates this place, and then he goes all reverent on you."

"He's been outside. How can you not have a conflict?"

She looked doubtful, but she didn't pursue it. Instead, as he expected, she launched into a perfectly reasonable explanation of why, with his belief in the Sangre Viento, he was pushing the limits of her tolerance. While she grudgingly granted him the possibility of undirected psychic energy—a phrase she nearly choked on—she was not about to grant him deliberate control.

"Do you know what that means?"

"Murder," he answered simply.

"Do you want to try to prove that in court? Do you think Skinner will buy it?"

"Right now, I don't care about Skinner. What I care about is who's doing this." He leaned forward on his arms folded on the table. "Scully, four people are dead, there's one agent missing, every connection points here, or to someone here, and unless we catch him, there's going to be more."

She stared at him for a long time.

He held the stare as long as he could, then sighed and looked down at his blurred reflection in the dark polished wood.

"Ciola," she said then.

He looked up without raising his head.

"Leon Ciola." She slipped a sheet of paper from her bag and slid it over. "You were so busy driving Sheriff Sparrow away with your story that I didn't have a chance to tell you." She tapped the paper with a finger. "Preliminary police report on Donna Falkner's house. A lot of prints were lifted. Hers, of course, and Lanaya's, no surprise, he was her partner. And Leon Ciola's." She cocked an eyebrow. "Some of them in the bedroom."

He glanced over the form and resisted the urge to shout.

"It's hard with only that one conversation," she continued, "but I don't get the feeling that she ran that embezzlement scheme on her own. Ciola could have talked her into it. It's been going on for four years. Two of those years were his last two in prison." Another tap on the paper. "She visited him there, Mulder. Often. Evidently she was the reason he lost his temper in the bar."

Mulder rested his chin on his arm. "She gets greedy. He finds out. His infamous temper."

No answer.

He looked up into a disquieting frown.

"We'll assume again, all right? For the sake of argument?"

He nodded.

"Why Paulie Deven? Why the Constellas?"

He had already thought about that; he already had an answer that disturbed him.

"Practice," he said, lowering his gaze to the table. "All they were to him was practice."

She didn't react, didn't speak. She pulled the paper back, turned it around, and skimmed it. Then she put it back into her bag and let her head rest against the chair's high back. Her lips pursed; her eyes followed an unseen trail on the ceiling.

"He's not one of the Council, Mulder. Ciola—"

"Well, well, well, *chica*," Ciola said from the entrance. "Every time I see you, you can't help but speak my name."

TWENTY-ONE

B eyond the cornfield, beyond the last of the water pumps, in the desert, the sand began to stir.

With an exaggerated swagger Ciola crossed the hall, swinging his arms, deliberately cracking his heels against the floor for the gunshot sound. His head was bare, his shirt and jeans looked stiff enough to be new, and his hair had been freed from his ponytail to sway against his back as he moved.

"You like it in here?" he asked, spreading his arms.

Neither Mulder nor Scully answered.

He made a face. "This, you know, is the place where they meet every month. They try to think of a way to banish me, you see?" He laughed and stamped a foot. "I am an embarrassment to them, FBI. I spent a lot of time in the penitentiary, and I think they think this shames them."

He reached the head of the table and dragged the chair back, dropped into it and hooked a leg over the arm.

Scully shifted in her chair to face him, her right arm resting on the table. She said nothing; she only looked.

Ciola gestured toward the entrance. "You're all the talk out there today, Agent Scully, did you know that? It's the red in your hair, I think. I figured you were here to talk to me, is that right? So here I am. So talk."

Scully gave him a little nod. "Where were you yesterday afternoon, Mr. Ciola?"

He shook his head sadly. "You'll have to do better than that. I was telling my parole officer how wonderful it is to be outside again."

"Then how did you know about Donna Falkner? You were there."

"I have a police scanner in my truck." He grinned. "It comes in handy."

"A scanner?" She sounded doubtful.

The grin snapped off. "I'm an Indian, Agent Scully. I'm not a savage."

"You nearly cut a man's head off," Mulder said mildly. "That sounds pretty savage to me."

Ciola only glared at him, a quick glance, before he looked back to Scully. "Anything else?"

"Theft," she said.

The leg slid slowly off the arm. "I kill people, Agent Scully, I don't steal from them. You want a thief, I suggest you have a word with Saint Nick."

"What were you two arguing about? Yesterday. In the street."

"Do you know something, Agent Scully? For the life of me, I can't understand why a woman like you would—"

"Ciola," Mulder said, raising his voice.

The man sighed the sigh of a terribly put-upon man, and looked.

Mulder held up his ID. "Just for the record, the Federal Bureau of Investigation has legal authority on Indian reservations, whether we're asked in or not. That means, Mr. Ciola, that I don't need anyone's permission—not the sheriff's, not your Council's—to bring you in for questioning concerning the murder of Donna Falkner. Or Paulie Deven. Or Matt and Doris Constella." He put the ID back in his pocket. "Why don't you just cut the crap, and answer Agent Scully."

The man looked ready to bolt, and from the corner of her eye, Scully saw Mulder tense for the chase. "He told us it was personal," she said quickly, watching them both relax as if strings had been severed.

"It is."

"How personal?"

"We hate each other, Ms. Scully. I'm an ex-con and he's a saint. I dropped out of high school, he's got degrees up his ass and out his throat." Palms down, he spread his fingers on the table. After a long moment, he said, "How confidential is this? If I tell you something, you put me back in the pen?"

"That depends," Mulder answered.

"On what?"

"On whether I say so," Scully said, holding back a grin at the astonishment on his face.

"Let… let me think about it."

"While you're thinking," Mulder said, "tell me how you managed not to be killed by the Sangre Viento."

Ciola gaped, his left hand moving unconsciously to his cheek to brush over the scars. "How the hell did you know that?"

Mulder didn't answer.

Scully knew, however. Now that she could examine them without fearing a knife in her throat, the pattern across his neck and face was clear; at least, clear enough to anyone who knew about the Wind.

"I had a pony," Ciola said quietly. "When I was very little, a man died, one of the six. During the ceremonial, no one leaves the Mesa, or goes into the desert. It's a foolish chance. Only people like Saint Nick do something dumb like that. I was little, and I was foolish, and I wanted my pony. She had broken out of the corral, and I chased her for nearly an hour.

"I almost had her once, but she bolted. I couldn't figure out why until I turned around, and there it was. Right behind me. I fell over backward into an arroyo, and that's what saved me."

Scully couldn't help it: "You believe in this Blood Wind?"

Ciola's fingers fluttered across his face. "That's a stupid question, *chica*. Do you want a stupid answer?"

"No, just a truthful one."

His eyes widened at her boldness, but one of the front doors opened before he had a chance to say a word. Nick Lanaya walked in, an old man trailing behind, both of them unaware of Ciola until they were halfway across the floor.

Lanaya stopped; the old man didn't. He continued on to the table and took the chair on Scully's right.

"What do you want, Leon?" Nick demanded.

"The FBI calls, I answer." He grinned at Mulder. "It's the law, don't you know that?"

"Get out, Leon. They need you in the warehouse."

"Oh, I don't know. There are many questions left to ask." He looked to Scully for support. "They want to know, for example, about Donna. How we loved, how we fought, how we—"

"*Chinga!*" Lanaya spat, face darkening with rage. "You kill, you dare to come back here as if nothing ever happened, and now you dare to talk—"

"Enough!" Mulder ordered, thumping the table with his fist. "Excuse me," he said to the old man, and turned back to the others. "Mr. Lanaya, for all our sakes, let me or Agent Scully be the ones to decide when Mr. Ciola has told us enough, okay? Mr. Ciola, I take it you're not planning a vacation or anything like that?"

Ciola laughed as he stood. "Don't leave town, eh, *gringo*? Don't worry. I won't. I still have to go to Donna's funeral."

Lanaya grabbed the man's arm as he brushed past him and whispered harshly in his ear. Scully couldn't understand what was said, but it made her wonder when Ciola swallowed heavily and left, nearly at a run. Nick made to follow, but a grunted word from the old man brought him to the table, where he sat in the chair Ciola had just used.

"I'm sorry," he said with a sheepish smile. "The man just drives me crazy." His hand waved in front of his face as if clearing the air of a foul odor. Then he introduced Dugan Velador. "He speaks very good English, so—"

"Have I left, Nick?" Velador asked quietly.

Again Lanaya's face darkened, and he lowered his head and didn't move.

Scully raised an eyebrow to Mulder at the control the old man had, then sat back so she could see both of them at once. She wasn't sure what Mulder wanted her to say, and so deferred to him when he cleared his throat, a signal that he wanted to take charge of the interview for a time.

She hoped, though, that when the Sangre Viento came up, as it surely would, Velador wouldn't be insulted. It would be easy for him to think they were mocking him, or being condescending. And although Nick had warned them of the probability, she was somewhat taken aback when the old man said, "I want you to leave the Mesa now, please. There is nothing here to discuss or tell you."

He stood, the bone necklace he wore rattling softly.

Lanaya stood as well, quickly, but Mulder only clasped his hands on the table and said, "I have reason to believe, Mr. Velador, that someone, probably one of your people, has been using either you, or the six, to establish control of the Sangre Viento." When the old man reached out to grab the edge of the table, Mulder paid him no heed. "If that's true, then this man, sir, has committed four murders, and Agent Scully and I don't intend to leave until we find him, and arrest him."

Well, Scully thought as Velador sank back into his chair, that's certainly being subtle.

\\\\\\\\\\\\\\\\\

A small leaf danced in a circle in the air, several inches above the ground. From a distance it looked like a butterfly searching for a blossom. Seconds later it was joined by another, this one pierced by a cactus needle.

Below them, the sand began to rise.

Mulder hoped neither the old man nor Scully noticed when he released the breath he'd been holding. Sparring with Ciola had been bad enough, but Velador, whose posture and expression told those who saw him he was meek and too dull to be considered, had given him a start as soon as he'd walked in. He may have been behind Lanaya, but he was clearly the leader.

When he sat, nothing about him moved, except for those black eyes.

Mulder had no doubt that in another time, in another culture, Dugan Velador would have been royal.

Right now, a quivering left hand covered the rattlesnake necklace, while the right hand rested on fingertips on the table. He said nothing, and Mulder kept silent. What amazed him, and puzzled him, was that Lanaya hadn't protested either. He, too, sat with one hand against his chest, the other out of sight in his lap.

It was Scully's concern that broke the silence. She leaned toward Velador, a hand out but not touching. "Mr. Velador, are you all right? I'm a doctor, sir, if you need help."

Mulder could almost hear the neck bones creaking as the old man turned his head. "I'm fine, young woman. It seems that we are not as alone as we thought."

An angry look at Lanaya forced Mulder to gesture, to regain the man's attention. "It wasn't Nick who told me, sir. He didn't... he didn't betray a confidence."

"What do you know?"

There was no hesitation; this wasn't the time.

"As much as I'm able without having been in the kiva with you."

"Then you know that what you say can't be true."

Mulder avoided Scully's eyes. "No, sir, I'm afraid I don't know that at all." Although he suspected the old man knew more than he gave away, Mulder told him about the four deaths, described the bodies, and used the same hand motion Nando Quintodo had. "It's the only explanation, sir. Nothing else makes any sense."

That surprised Velador. "You think it makes sense?"

Mulder shrugged—*sure, why not?*

"And you?" he asked Scully gently. "Do you think this makes sense?"

"I think I haven't heard anything else yet that... that covers the situation as well."

He smiled then, a broad smile that nearly broke into a laugh. "You look at things differently than your friend."

"Oh yes," she said. "Oh, yes."

Another look to Lanaya, a curious one, made Mulder frown. What had Lanaya done or said that the old man should be so annoyed?

Suddenly Lanaya bent over in a coughing fit, covering his mouth with a loose fist. "Sorry," he gasped, tears filling his eyes. "Sorry. I—" He waggled his fingers at his throat and coughed again, much harder, more harshly. Finally, when he couldn't stop it, he got up and, behind an apologetic gesture to carry on, left the hall, muttering about finding some water. Mulder could hear the awful hacking until the door swung shut behind him.

"He always gets that way when I embarrass him." Velador smiled mischievously. "One day I will have to beat it out of him. He's too old for that sort of thing."

Mulder straightened.

"Mr. Velador," Scully said, "we were told no one would speak to us. Why did you change your mind? Because of—"

"Sometimes I am not as smart as I think I am, you know. Sometimes, sitting in the sun, there is a buzzing in my head, and I don't hear the words everyone says to me very well. Sometimes the words I say are not the words others hear."

"What did you say?"

"I said the FBI must be stopped."

She tapped a knuckle lightly, thoughtfully, against her lips. "Are you saying that now we're in some kind of danger. Just because of that?"

He nodded, then shook his head. "If what this man says is true, young woman, you're in more danger than you know. But not because of what I said."

"Yes," Mulder said suddenly, getting to his feet. "I'm sorry, sir, but you're wrong." He started around the table. "Scully, we have to leave." He beckoned to her urgently, took her elbow when she stood, and nearly dragged her toward the door. "Mr. Velador, please stay inside. Scully and I aren't the only ones who have to be careful."

The old man didn't move.

The necklace rattled; he hadn't touched it.

Once they were outside, Scully pulled her arm free. "Mulder, what's going on? You're acting like a madman."

"You got it, Scully. You hit it right on the nail."

"Then what's—"

"Look."

He swept his hand through the air. Showing her the empty streets. The shuttered windows. Closed doors. No dogs, no chickens, no horses in the corral.

The pueblo was deserted.

Nothing moved but a single sheet, flapping in the wind.

TWENTY-TWO

Lanaya's pickup was gone.

A curl of brown dust moved down the street, folding in upon itself when the wind began to pick up.

Over the flat roofs, Mulder could see another dust cloud rising and falling like the hump of a lumbering beast, until the wind shoved it against a wall and scattered it.

Scully took a step down, shading her eyes against the sun and blowing grit. A shake of her head when she couldn't find what she was looking for. When she turned toward the Mesa, the wind snapped her hair around her cheeks, momentarily blinding her until she turned again.

"How did they know?" she asked. "It's so fast. How did they know?"

"Someone told them," he answered grimly, and stepped all the way down to the ground. The few vehicles he could see were undoubtedly locked, and he didn't think pounding on doors or windows would get them any help. "We'll have to go back in."

Scully was way ahead of him. She grabbed the large doorknob and tried to turn it over.

It didn't budge.

"Mulder, he's locked us out."

They both tried, and tried using their fists and voices to get the old man to let them in. They stopped when she cursed and massaged her right wrist.

He returned to the street. "Okay, maybe we can find someplace else. A stable or something."

The first place they tried was the warehouse next door, and neither was surprised to find it locked as well. If Ciola is still in there, Mulder thought, he's probably having the time of his life.

They darted across the street and made their way between the two nearest houses to the next street over, saw nothing promising and moved on to the next. By the fourth, he knew they weren't going to find shelter. Not here. And not, he thought as he stared at the Mesa, up there. He didn't know how the Konochine got to the top, but he didn't think they'd take kindly to his trying.

Scully slumped against a house wall out of the direct push of the wind, using a forearm to mop the sweat from her forehead. "Why don't we just wait it out here, whatever it is?"

"We can't, Scully." He stepped away from the house's protection and looked up and down the street. Still nothing. Shutters and doors closed against them. He stretched out a hand and beckoned. "We have to get inside someplace."

"Mulder, it's only a dust storm. We'll need a week of showers when it's over, but it's only a dust storm."

"No. No, it isn't."

And he knew she didn't really believe in the dust storm idea, either. If it were one, they'd be offered shelter somewhere in here; if it were one, the people wouldn't have gone to ground so swiftly. Ciola had told them only a fool stayed outside when the ceremonial was in progress. But since there was no one, not now, they were obviously convinced the Sangre Viento was on its way.

He turned in a slow circle, frustrated, growing angry, beating a hand against his leg while he tried to decide what to do next. Hide, was the obvious answer, but where?

Nowhere.

At least, nowhere in the pueblo.

Apparently Scully had reached the same conclusion. She left the wall's protection and started up the street toward the road, purposeful urgency in her stride. He hesitated before following, hoping she wasn't thinking what he feared she was.

When he caught up, she said, "How far do you think it is?"

Damn, he thought.

"Too far to run. There's got to be someplace closer."

"I have no intention of running, Mulder. At least not yet." She pointed to the fields, and the desert beyond. "If it comes from out there, we'll be able to see it, right?" She gave him a tight smile. "When we see it, then we'll run and see what happens."

"What if it comes from somewhere else?"

"Then we won't have to run, will we."

More leaves, dancing.

When they were close enough, they gave the illusion of a funnel; when they separated they were butterflies again.

Until the sand joined them.

Then they become a cloud.

What Mulder desperately wished he knew, what he couldn't deduce from any of the information he had, was how long it took the whirlwind to form. If it took six men to create one only once in a while over the course of a week, surely a single man, no matter how skilled, couldn't create one with just the snap of a finger.

"Oh God," he whispered as they passed the last house and angled westward toward the road.

Not with the snap of a finger, but after sufficient preparation. Which meant—

Scully, staying on his left, unabashedly using him as a windbreak, picked up the pace as she said, "It's Lanaya, isn't it."

"Yes," he said, more convinced now than he had been that morning.

"Why? Ciola's too obvious?"

"No. Ciola didn't know we were coming today. Lanaya did. He's had time, Scully, to get ready. He took that old man literally. He's going to stop us." He held up a hand before she could interrupt. "He's going to try to stop us, okay?"

She ran a few steps, slowed, ran a few more.

The wind died abruptly.

He couldn't help glancing to the right every few feet, grateful when the fields blocked him, a little apprehensive when he could see all the way to the mountainous horizon. He had no idea what the Wind would look like, or if he'd be able to hear it coming.

He caught up with her when she paused to shake dust from her hair, and grinned when a sudden gust blew it back in her face. "It's a no-win, Scully."

"Tell me about it."

They walked on.

Ahead, above the road, curtains of shimmering heat hung in the air. He took off his tie and jammed it in a pocket. What the hell was he thinking of, wearing a suit on a day like today? And why, he thought further, turning around to walk backward a few steps, didn't he just take his gun, walk up to one of those doors, and threaten to blow the lock off if they didn't let him in?

Because, he answered, they'd probably just shoot back.

Swirls of sandy soil snaked across the blacktop when the wind returned. Rustling made him jump until he realized it was only the corn in its field. A tumbleweed rolled between them, tangling in Scully's feet until she kicked at it savagely and it broke apart, and was blown away.

"Tell me something, Mulder—if this man is so well-liked here, and he can cross successfully between this world and the one out there, why did he do it? Why risk it all?"

They had no water.

His throat was dry, his eyes felt gritty. When he breathed, it was like taking in clouds of fire to his lungs.

They weren't walking nearly as rapidly now.

"He kept saying 'they,'" Mulder answered, licking his lips to moisten them, finally giving it up as futile. "When he gave us that big speech about the Konochine and their dislike of the outside world, he kept saying 'they.'"

He had been one of them until he'd left to go to school. When he came back, he had changed. It was inevitable. And for reasons they might never know, or understand, he hadn't been able to change back, or to adapt as he had adapted to the outside. Mulder suspected it was unfocused anger that forced him to attempt to steal what belonged to the six. They were... Dugan Velador was the wise man, the leader. What he did, what the others did, was accepted without serious question.

How could he not want that respect, too?

What he hadn't understood was that the power the old men had came from the respect they were given, not the other way around.

Lanaya figured, have the power, have the respect. That would make him fully Konochine again.

Scully slowed a little, and he saw how her hair had begun to mat to her neck and scalp. He took off his jacket and slung it over his shoulder, his shirt nearly transparent where the sweat held it against his skin. When he brushed his fingers over his hair, the hair felt hot. He would give a lot right now to look stupid in a hat.

Then he blinked, wiped his face, and blinked again.

The gap in the Wall was only a hundred yards away.

He looked back at the pueblo, and saw nothing move. Dust blew through it, and all he could think was *ghost town*.

The dust devil grew and spun in place.

It was little more than two feet high, wobbling around its axis as if ready to collapse should the wind blow again.

Butterflies and sand.

No sound at all.

Mulder stumbled, and Scully grabbed his arm to steady him. He smiled at her wanly. "Isn't that what I'm supposed to do?"

"Since when did you ever think I was helpless, Mulder?"

Never, he thought; never.

They walked into the gap, and into its shadow which was no shade at all. Ahead, the road rose and fell as if it were a narrow wave, making him rub his eyes until it steadied. In his shoes his feet burned, and his ankles promised spectacular blisters once he took the shoes off.

Something small and dark scuttled across the road.

It was tempting, very tempting, to take his shirt off. The cloth was a weight his shoulders could barely handle. The jacket on his arm already weighed a ton, and he didn't think he'd be able to carry it much longer.

"How did they do it?" Scully asked as they came out of the gap and stopped. She stared across the desert floor. They could see no interstate, no trucks, no cars, no planes overhead. There was nothing but the sky and the mountains. "How did they cross this place without killing themselves?"

"They had water, for one thing," Mulder said sourly.

"It must have been incredible," she said. She laughed. "It must have been a bitch."

He let his knees fold him into a crouch, his jacket slipping to the road. There was too much space here, too much sky; gauging distance accurately was nearly impossible, but he seemed to remember that the ranch house wasn't much more than a mile to his right. If they climbed the fence and angled overland instead of sticking to the road, they might make it faster.

He didn't realize he'd been speaking aloud until Scully said, "What if you twist an ankle?"

"Me? Why me?"

She grinned. "I'm a doctor, I know better."

It was heartening to see the smile; it wasn't good to see how her face had reddened. They were dangerously close to sunstroke; they had to be. And dehydration wasn't all that far behind. If they were going to do it, they'd better do it now.

He rose with a groan, and with a groan leaned over to pick up his jacket.

"Ciola is evil, you know," she said.

He draped the jacket over the barbed wire and held it down while she climbed awkwardly over.

"Lanaya is worse."

He didn't get it. "Why?"

"I can understand Ciola. But it'll take me a long time to understand Nick."

As tall as a man.

And now it began to whisper.

He stumbled over nothing, and commanded his limbs to knock it off. It wasn't as if they were in the middle of the desert, a hundred miles from the nearest civilization. He could already see the fences, could already make out the dim outline of the ranch house. A mile, maybe, he couldn't be sure. But he was acting as though it was ten miles, or more.

Scully sidestepped a prickly pear and nearly walked straight into another. She swiped at it with her suit coat, the move turning her in a circle.

"Do you think Sparrow is in on it?"

"What? Sparrow? No, why?"

"He didn't follow us into the reservation, and he wasn't waiting when we came out."

It was too hot to think straight, but he doubted that Sparrow was anything more than understandably skeptical about the whole thing. He was, no doubt, sitting in his office, drinking from his flask, and trying to figure out how he would charm them, or bully them, into getting some credit for the crime's solution. Even if it meant having to accept some magic.

It began to hiss.

It began to move.

"There!" Scully announced. "There it is."

They stood on the lip of a shallow arroyo, beside a hand-crafted bridge.

"Thank God, you see it too," Mulder said. "I thought it was a mirage."

They crossed the bridge single file. The vivid green of the lawn was visible now, and through the rising ghostly heat he could make out the house, if not its details.

On the other side, Scully leaned over the rail. "I think those holes in the bank down there are rattlesnake dens."

Mulder wasn't listening.

He had stopped to take a breath, a brief rest on his feet. Without much hope, he checked the gap just in case Ciola, or someone, had taken pity on them, and had followed them in a truck. He also checked the top of the hill, just in case the old man was there.

Then he said, "Scully, how fast can you run?"

TWENTY-THREE

t rose out of the arroyo a hundred yards away.

Mulder had expected it to be shaped like a miniature tornado, but it was conical from top to bottom, and cloudy with the debris that whipped around its surface, the source of the hissing it made as it left the dead river and made its way toward them.

Eight feet high; at least four wide in the middle.

Whether it was the force behind it, or the weight of the sand and grit that formed it, it wobbled as it moved, with thin dark bands rippling along its surface, snapping apart and re-forming. Every so often a gap would appear and he could see right through it; then the gap would close, swallowed whole.

Had it arrived an hour or two earlier, he didn't doubt they would have had a chance to make it to the house. Its ground speed was not much greater than that of a leisurely trot. Not now, though; not after so much time in the sun.

They ran over the uneven ground as if palsied, as if drunk, veering wildly away from each other, then having to veer again in order not to collide when they tried to rejoin. Serrated grasses slashed at their ankles; shrub and brush stabbed at their arms and legs.

The sun hadn't gone; it was still there, pressing down.

Something exploded in the dirt to Mulder's left, leaving a geyser of dust to hang in the air.

Scully cried out wordlessly in alarm when the top of a cactus shattered as she passed it.

When a third puff rose from the ground a dozen yards away, he realized it was the heavier material caught in the force of it—pebbles, perhaps large twigs; their own weight would eventually fling them out like grapeshot.

They skidded and slid down a short depression.

Mulder glanced back over his shoulder and saw the whirlwind sweep past a small bush, shredding the branches it touched.

Scully grunted and went to one knee, her left hand crossed over to grip her right shoulder. She'd been hit. Mulder raced over and hauled her to her feet, pushed her on when he was struck behind his right knee. He dropped as she had, then launched himself forward as if from a starting block. His right hand went around her shoulders when he reached her, and they supported each other into another depression, and up again.

The ranch house bobbed not that far ahead.

He could see the white split-rail fence, the grass, and no one on the porch.

They didn't know; they couldn't hear.

"How does it know?" Scully demanded.

It hissed along the ground, moving faster, growing taller.

Growing darker.

Mulder couldn't tell her. He was distracted by the sudden, guttural roar of an engine, searching wildly until he spotted a battered pickup lurch out of a boiling dust cloud to their right.

He was so startled he didn't see the rock until it was too late. His right foot slid over its smooth, flat surface, and he would have gone down had not Scully gripped him tightly and yanked him, still running, back to his feet.

The porch was still empty; what the hell were they doing in there?

Sweat ran into his eyes, blinding him, stinging.

Scully yelled, and he thought for a moment she'd been hit again, and his shoulders automatically hunched in anticipation. When she yelled a second time, he understood; she was trying to get the attention of the house.

It wouldn't do any good.

The hissing was too loud.

Something large snapped not far behind them, like the crack of a huge bullwhip.

The pickup drew closer, jouncing recklessly over the ground, slipping sideways left and right as the driver tried to keep it in line.

Scully finally noticed and waved at it frantically once, but when Mulder tried to steer them toward it, she suddenly shouldered him away. "Him," was all she was able to say.

Nick Lanaya was behind the wheel, and it didn't take long for Mulder to realize that the man wanted to herd them away from the house, to keep them in the open. It was also the answer to Scully's question: since the man hadn't known exactly where they would be, he would have had to keep them in sight once he'd set the Wind in motion.

Someone stepped out onto the porch.

"Almost there," he gasped. "Hang on, we're almost there."

The pickup aimed right for them.

Mulder stubbornly refused to give ground, forcing his concentration on the maddeningly slow approach of the fence and the lawn. It was Scully who threw them aside when the truck roared by, smothering them in a dust cloud that made it impossible for them to breathe.

The Blood Wind swerved.

The hiss deepened to a growling.

He couldn't see anything, but Mulder heard the Wind and urged Scully back to her feet, shoved her ahead of him and pulled out his gun. Not for the Wind, but for the truck, which had swung into a turn so Lanaya could come at them again.

Stalling them.

Dividing their attention between one death and another.

Twenty yards to the fence when Mulder swung his arm around and fired blindly, not expecting to hit anything, just hoping Lanaya would think twice before trying to close again.

The truck didn't stop.

The Wind didn't stop.

Suddenly the ground hardened, and Mulder looked down and realized they had reached the drive.

Scully had already climbed halfway over the fence.

On the porch Nando's wife screamed, and kept on screaming, her hands clutched against her chest.

The pickup charged, and Mulder fired a second time, hitting the windshield on the passenger side, causing Lanaya to swerve, and swerve again to avoid hitting the fence in front.

But the Wind didn't stop.

It hissed across the driveway, forcing him into a move he knew immediately was foolish but was too late to stop—he bolted to his left, away from the house and lawn. But the sight of it so close and the sound of its voice had panicked him, and by the time he was able to think again, Lanaya had turned the truck around.

Scully yelled at him on her knees from the porch, where Nando was now, a rifle in his hands.

The Wind had paused; a stone, a piece of wood, smashed through one of the ranch house windows.

Mulder felt dizzy. The exertion, the heat and the dust, the sound of that thing spinning slowly in place… he took a step back and almost fell, staggered sideways and saw Lanaya in the cab, grinning.

Sangre Viento; it moved.

Nando fired at the truck, and a headlight exploded.

It won't make any difference, Mulder thought, sidling to his left; kill Lanaya, and the Wind will still be there. It has its target now.

He froze.

No; no, it won't.

The Wind brushed against the corner fence post, and sawdust filled the air, some of it showering into the yard, the rest sucked into the spinning.

Lanaya gunned the engine.

Mulder had no choice left but to run straight toward him. If the Wind picked up speed, he would use the truck to stop it; if it didn't, he would stop it anyway.

If he was right.

The Wind moved, and Scully shouted a warning, her own gun out and aiming.

A Wind-whipped stone glanced off Mulder's knee, and he dropped before he knew he'd lost control. He felt the blood before he felt the pain, and the pain stood him up again.

At that moment, both Scully and Nando fired; at that moment, Mulder aimed and fired.

At that moment, Sangre Viento moved, and moved fast.

If I'm right, Mulder thought as he raced as best he could to the truck.

The windshield was pocked with holes and weblike cracks, the engine still ran, and as he grabbed for the door, he saw Nick behind the wheel, his head back, his face covered with running blood.

He saw the whirlwind speeding toward him.

If I'm right, he thought, and yanked the door open, scrambled onto the seat, and reached for Lanaya's throat.

It wasn't hissing now, it was roaring.

He grabbed the rawhide thong around the man's neck and pulled, pulled again as the truck began to rock violently.

Pieces of the windshield began to fall in.

Giving up on the thong, Mulder nearly crawled into the dead man's lap and ripped his shirt open, grabbed the medicine bag and tried to rip it apart. He couldn't, and something slammed into his side, into his shoulder, throwing him against Lanaya's chest and rocking him back.

Metal shrieked.

Glass cracked and shattered.

He held the bag up, as far away as he could, and put a bullet through it, blowing it apart as he threw himself into the well and waited for one of them to die.

TWENTY-FOUR

"They were all acting," Mulder said.

He and Scully sat at the porch table with Annie Hatch, he with a slick glass of iced tea, Scully with a glass of fresh-squeezed lemonade. They had invited themselves out on their last day, because Mulder felt the woman should know.

"Sparrow wanted us to believe he was either dumb as a post or a hick who was only around for comic relief. Ciola was the macho, I-dare-you-to-touch-me man, but he was terrified because he knew what Nick could do." He took a long drink and sighed. "And Nick didn't think we'd believe for a second in the Sangre Viento. We're trained agents, we deal with solid evidence and behavioral science and the magic we can do ourselves in the lab."

"It wasn't magic, Mulder," Scully said.

He smiled at the lawn. "Suit yourself."

Too many parts of him still stung where he had been struck by missiles hurled by the Wind, and his face was still an alarming red from his sunburn. He had also been right about the blisters.

Scully, too, was walking wounded, but over the past two days, neither of them had had much time to think about it while they filled out reports, filled out more reports, and listened as Sheriff Sparrow figured for the papers and local television news that the pickup had slammed into the fence while trying to run Scully and Mulder down.

The Sangre Viento had died when the contents of Nick's bag were scattered by the bullet.

None of the news people heard that story at all.

Annie poured herself another glass. "You know, I don't think any of my movies ever had so much excitement. I'm rather sorry I missed it." Mulder looked at her until she had the grace to blush.

"All right, all right, I was scared out of my mind and hiding in the kitchen. And I'm not sorry at all, are you happy?"

He toasted her with his glass, emptied it and pushed away from the table. They had a late-afternoon flight back to Washington, and driving wasn't going to be all that easy.

Scully finished as well, and as she picked up her bag and stood, he saw genuine reluctance to leave the ranch and Annie.

"Fox?" Annie said.

He didn't correct her.

"What happened to Red?"

"We don't know for sure," Scully answered for them. "We think he was trying to conduct his own investigation. From what the office tells us, he was hardly ever there once we arrived. Sparrow admitted to keeping him informed on the phone, but even he hasn't heard from Agent Garson since the night before we went to the Mesa."

"I think he went there on his own," Mulder said, slipping his sunglasses from his pocket and sliding them on. "I think he'll be found before long, but he won't be alive."

Another actor, he thought; the easterners he couldn't stand had come out to conduct what should have been his investigation, and he had to pretend to like it all the way.

They said their goodbyes, and Mulder, if he hadn't already had the sunburn, would have blushed with pleasure when Annie kissed his cheek and made him promise to come back for a visit before she was too old to enjoy it.

They started for the car, but as Scully slid in behind the wheel, Mulder asked her to wait and hurried back to the porch. Annie leaned over the rail when he crooked a finger.

"What is it now?"

He pulled down his sunglasses. "There's a guy over there," he said, pointing toward the Wall. "He sits on that hill and fries himself practically every day. Maybe you ought to go over there sometime and have a talk with him."

Annie stared. "A talk?"

"It's a thought," he said.

"I'm not going back, Fox, if that's what you're asking."

"I'm not," he said innocently. "But there was this guy they thought was a saint, and he turned out to be a thief and a killer. The kids liked him, I understand."

She didn't respond.

"Besides," he added as he pushed the glasses back up, "who says a saint has to be a man?"

She was still on the porch as they drove toward the main road, and he suspected she would be there for some time to come.

He didn't speak until Scully pulled out onto the interstate. "Amazing, wasn't it? The Sangre Viento, I mean."

She glanced over at him, unsmiling. "I'm working on it, Mulder, I'm working on it."

"Of course you are."

Gradually the desert gave way to the first houses, which multiplied and grew taller, and the interstate grew more crowded. Scully had a silent, close to obscene altercation with a pickup that cut them off, and another with an old tail-fin Cadillac that hadn't yet discovered the speed limit was all the way up to fifty-five.

A mile later, she glanced at him and said, "Do you really think it was power he was after? Because he wasn't really part of that world?"

He didn't answer right away.

"Mulder?"

"Yes," he said at last. "Mostly. Power equals respect is an old lure for those who think they don't have either. Ciola hid in the warehouse because he knew what Nick would do. And—"

"That's not respect, Mulder, it's fear."

"Sometimes people like that don't, or can't, make a distinction." A van passed them, music blaring from its open windows.

"Acceptance," Mulder said then.

"What?"

"Acceptance. Power equals respect equals acceptance."

"Equals fear," she added quietly.

He agreed. He also agreed that murder was seldom as uncomplicated as most would believe. He and Scully could probably talk about it all the way back to Washington, and they still wouldn't have the complete answer.

The only one who did was Nick Lanaya. "Scully," he said while she tried to follow the signs to the airport, "what do you think would happen if, for example, the man who replaces Velador in that circle gets a notion? Like Lanaya did. Lanaya didn't know exactly what went on in the kiva. He made a few guesses, got a few answers from the old man, who didn't know he was giving them, and did the rest on his own.

"What if one of the circle decided to turn mean?"

She didn't answer.

He had no answer.

What he knew was that Nick could possibly have gone on indefinitely, killing those he didn't like, killing those he took a dislike to for no reason at all. He could have, mostly because no one else believed.

He watched the city, the cars, saw an airplane drifting low toward a landing.

Those old men may be wise, but they aren't all old, and none of them is perfect.

Imagine, he thought.

Imagine the power.

RUINS

By Kevin J. Anderson

ONE

Xitaclan ruins, Yucatán, Mexico
Friday, 5:45 P.M.

Even after days of hard excavation, they had barely scratched the surface of the ancient city. But Cassandra Rubicon had already seen enough to know that the ruins held unimaginable secrets about the birth of the Maya empire.

At the far western edge of the Yucatán, where the limestone plateau butted up against volcanic highlands and steamy jungles, the lost city had been hidden by nature for more than a thousand years. The native helpers had called the place Xitaclan, their voices tinged with awe and fear.

Cassandra rolled the word over in her mouth, reveling in the images it evoked of ancient sacrifices, pomp and splendor, blood priests wearing ornaments of jade and green quetzal feathers. *Xitaclan.*

In the late afternoon, she alone worked inside the Pyramid of Kukulkan, shining her flashlight ahead as she crept deeper, exploring. This place was absolutely alive with secrets. In the chalky bitterness of the air, she could taste the mysteries waiting for her to discover them.

Shining her flashlight ahead, Cassandra ran a dusty hand through perspiration-dampened cinnamon hair—the color of cinnamon bark, freshly peeled from the trees, her father always insisted, not the faded reddish-tan powder found on grocery-store spice racks. The color of her eyes hung midway between green and brown, like rich copper-bearing ore.

Outside, her partners in the University of California expedition kept themselves busy with the external excavations, mapping the overall layout of the city, with its ceremonial plaza, temples, and monolithic limestone obelisks—stelae—carved with fearsome images of mythical feathered serpents. They had found a vine-overgrown "ball court" arena, where the ancient Maya had played their bloody sport in which the losers—or winners, depending on some historical interpretations—were sacrificed to the gods.

An archaeological treasure trove, Xitaclan provided far too many ruins even for a large, well-financed crew to explore in anything less than a year. But Cassandra and her four young companions would do their best, for as long as their meager university funding held out.

Numerous moss-covered stelae towered at strategic astronomical points throughout the jungle, while others had toppled; all of them, though, contained rich and exciting glyphs. Christopher Porte, their team's epigrapher, delighted in attempting to translate them, transcribing them into the battered record book he kept in his pack at all times.

The showpiece of Xitaclan, though, was the magnificent stair-stepped Pyramid of Kukulkan that loomed over the center of the city. Though overgrown with weeds and underbrush, it was still beautifully preserved. Its architecture rivaled the great ziggurats at Chichén Itzá, Tikal, and Teotihuacán—but this one stood untouched. The locals' paralyzing superstitions had protected it from prying eyes. Until now.

Topping the pyramid's highest platform stood the many-pillared "Temple of the Feathered Serpent," with its amazing carvings and ornate friezes depicting calendars, myths, history. Cassandra had named the temple herself after noting the dense motifs that showed the wise god Kukulkan and his feathered reptilian companions or guardians—a common symbol of power in the Maya mythos. The intricate bas-reliefs added a new richness to the Quetzalcoatl/Kukulkan legends of the early Central American peoples.

Her team had also found an unfathomably deep cistern behind the pyramid, a natural limestone sinkhole filled with oily black water whose murky depths Cassandra suspected hid many artifacts, relics… and quite probably the bones of sacrificial victims. Such limestone wells, or cenotes, were common in Maya cities of the Yucatán—but this one at Xitaclan had never been ransacked by treasure seekers or explored by archaeologists.

Her team planned to break out the diving equipment within a week, and she herself would descend into the depths—but for now they still had too much initial cataloguing to complete. More breathtaking discoveries, more work—but too little time, and too little money.

For now, she concentrated on exploring inside the pyramid.

If her team didn't do an overwhelming job here on their first visit, someone else in the competitive archaeological community would no doubt return with a larger expedition, better funding, and superior equipment. It could completely overshadow Cassandra's work.

The crews of native workers recruited by her team's local guide—Fernando Victorio Aguilar, a self-styled adventurer and "expediter"—had worked for days already, hacking and chopping at the underbrush, removing mahogany and ceiba trees, slashing ferns with their machetes, uprooting creepers to remove the shroud of time and nature from around Xitaclan.

As soon as they saw the carvings of feathered serpents, though, the native workers had retreated in terror. They whispered to each other fearfully and refused to come closer to the site or to help with cleaning the ruins, even when she offered to increase their meager payment. Finally they fled. And then Aguilar ran off, abandoning her team in the deep jungle.

In her work, Cassandra had always respected native traditions and beliefs—it came with the territory—but her excitement at these discoveries had grown so intense that she found such superstitions frustrating, and her impatience flared up.

The archaeologists continued working on their own. They had supplies for a few weeks and a transmitter to call for help, should they need it. For now, she and the four others enjoyed their solitude.

Today, Kelly Rowan, the team's second archaeologist (and, as of recently, the man with whom she shared her tent) was spending the last hours of daylight on the outside steps of the pyramid, studying the Maya hieroglyphics. Christopher Porte bent beside him with his battered sketchpad, excitedly trying to translate the chiseled glyphs as Kelly used brushes and fine tools to remove debris from the designs.

Cait Barron, the team's historian and photographer, took advantage of the late afternoon light to work on one of her watercolors. Quiet and highly professional, Cait did her official work with the cameras and logbooks in a no-nonsense way. She took rolls of archival photos rapidly and efficiently—but once finished, she preferred using her paints to recreate the spirit of the place.

It was a long-standing tradition of Yucatán explorers to capture the detail their eyes saw, to depict something more than simple, two-dimensional photographic plates could. So far Cait had filled three portfolios with beautiful paintings that evoked the history of the Maya: diptychs pairing images of the ruins as they now appeared and as she imagined the city must have looked during its golden age.

While the team's quiet but frenzied work went on outside, the simmering jungle sounds increased with the fading light. Daytime creatures sought shelter against the darkness, while nocturnal predators awakened and began to search for their meals. Biting flies that swarmed in the day's heat flew off to sleep, while mosquitoes, bloodthirsty in the cooler air of evening, swept out in clouds.

Deep inside the Pyramid of Kukulkan, though, the damp shadows knew no passage of time. Cassandra continued her explorations.

After she and Kelly had worked together to pry open the long-sealed outer door, careful not to damage the masonry or the stone carvings, Cassandra had spent most of her time combing through the rubble inside, cautiously penetrating deeper, picking her way from one intersection to the next. She had spent days working through the chambers and vaults, mapping the incomprehensible passages within the immense stone structure, trying to solve the maze.

She had spent the afternoon inside again, taking only brief breaks to check on Kelly and Christopher, who worked at deciphering the hieroglyphic staircase, and John Forbin, the grad-student architect and engineer who was studying the other half-fallen structures. John's wanderings took him farther into the jungle as he marked the locations of ruins on the wrinkled topographical map he kept with him at all times. Being an engineer, John had no imagination for naming discoveries. John relied on simple numerical designations—Temple XI or Stela 17.

Cassandra glanced at her compass-watch and pushed deeper inside the labyrinth, aiming her high-powered flashlight ahead of her like a weapon. The cold shaft of light raked across rough-hewn limestone blocks and the crude support beams. Stark shadows leaped at her with exaggerated angles every time she shifted the flashlight. She moved cautiously, smelling the moldy air. Something dark skittered into a wide crack in the wall.

Cassandra carried a small microcassette recorder in her hand, as well as a sheet of graph paper on which she kept track of her movements. So far, most tunnels she'd explored had turned into blind alleys that might have been designed to confuse trespassers... or they could have been sealed treasure chambers. Even more exciting—from an archaeologist's point of view—the dead-ends could be sealed-off burial crypts or storage vaults for collected volumes of ancient writings.

If her team could find an intact Maya codex, one of the gloriously illustrated books written on mulberry-bark paper, it would increase knowledge of the Central American empire a hundredfold. Only four Maya codices were known to exist. Most of the others had been destroyed by Spanish missionaries overzealous in their attempts to squash all beliefs but their own. Xitaclan, though, had been abandoned long before the Conquistadors had arrived in the New World.

Cassandra worked now with dust in her hair and powder smeared under her eyes, across her cheeks. Her arms and legs were bone-tired, stiff and sore from too many nights on an uncomfortable bedroll, her skin inflamed from hundreds of insect bites. It had been too long since she'd had either a cold drink or a warm shower.

But the wonders she had already found were worth all those sacrifices. *Archaeology isn't for wimps*, she thought.

Her father always called her beautiful, claiming that she was wasted in the cobwebs of ancient civilizations, but she only laughed at him. Her father was quite a character. It was his own fame as an archaeologist that had driven her into the field in the first place. The great Vladimir Rubicon had gained renown as one of the foremost authorities on Native American cliff dwellings, particularly the once-thriving Anasazi civilization, though he had begun his career studying the Maya.

Cassandra wanted to make her own mark in the field, not just continue her father's work. Her original passion had been geology, analyzing the composition of the terrain beneath the jungles of Central America—but as she continued her studies, she found she knew as much about the ancient Maya as did Kelly, the team's self-proclaimed archaeological expert.

Together, they had made an impressive pair, able to talk the Board of Regents at UC-San Diego into funding their modest expedition to Mexico. The team would be all students, willing to work for the possible credentials and the right to publish striking new research, without being paid more than a starvation-level stipend. It was the bane of academics everywhere.

Luckily, like a surprise gift, they had been blessed with matching funding from the Mexican state of Quintana Roo, in which the ruins of Xitaclan had been found. With the Mexican money Cassandra had been able to obtain the diving equipment, hire the native workers, and pay Fernando Victorio Aguilar... for all the help he'd been. She snorted at the thought.

So far, their expedition had been a success, and it seemed they would all share a page in the history books.

Cassandra worked her way deeper into the temple, dictating a description of her path as she went. She ran her fingers over the stone blocks, and her voice rose and fell—fiery with excitement, then whispering in amazement—recording what she observed. The marvelous constructions within constructions inside the Pyramid of Kukulkan reminded her of a Russian doll—one inside another inside another, each one depleting her stock of adjectives.

Suddenly, in the flashlight beam ahead of her, she saw that the inner walls to her left were of a markedly different color. With a flush of excitement, Cassandra realized she had stumbled upon the inner temple. This must be the original structure on whose foundation the Pyramid of Kukulkan had been erected.

The ancient Maya had often built taller, more impressive temples atop old ruins, because of their belief that certain places concentrated magic as time went by. The glorious ceremonial center of Xitaclan had been the nexus for rituals in this locality. What had long ago begun as an isolated religious center in the thickest jungle had eventually become a magnet for Maya power.

Until the people had abruptly and mysteriously abandoned it… leaving it preserved and empty for her to uncover centuries later.

Forcing herself to speak in a slow, analytical voice, Cassandra pressed the microcassette recorder close to her lips. "The stone blocks here are smoother, more carefully cut. They have a glassy finish, like varnish, as if they were vitrified by intense heat." She caught herself with a smile, realizing she had been studying the stone with a geologist's eye, not an archaeologist's perspective.

She ran her hands along the fused stone surface, and in a breathless voice continued to record her impressions. "Normally I would have expected to see fragments of the whitewash or stucco the Maya used to decorate their temples—but I see no remains of paint, not even any carvings. The walls are completely smooth."

Cassandra followed the inner perimeter. The air inside smelled more and more stagnant; no currents had disturbed it in countless centuries. She sneezed, and the sound echoed explosively throughout the catacombs. Trickles of dust rained down from between ceiling blocks, and she hoped the ancient support beams would hold.

"This is clearly the remains of the first temple," she dictated, "the innermost structure that was once the heart of Xitaclan, the first structure on this site."

Very excited now, Cassandra followed the inward spiral, brushing her fingers against the cool slick surface of the stone. She kept to the new wall—actually, it was the oldest wall—wondering what secrets might be contained at the core of the pyramid.

From all the evidence she had uncovered, Xitaclan's glory was no mere stepping-stone in Maya culture. Tales of the legendary city were so deeply implanted in the psyche of the native people that the locals still talked about the curse and the spirits that clung to the place. Many people had supposedly disappeared in the area, too, but Cassandra put that down to local mythology.

What had caused the ancient Maya to place their hub of religious significance here, in an uninteresting portion of the jungle with no roads or rivers, no copper or gold mines nearby? Why here?

Rubble had fallen across the passage ahead, blocking her way. But Cassandra felt her adrenaline pumping. Now that she had reached the center of the pyramid, she needed to see what lay beyond. It was possible that she stood on the brink of a great discovery—but not unless she could go all the way.

Stuffing the tape recorder into her pocket and the scribbled graph paper inside her shirt, she laid the flashlight down and worked with both hands to pull away fallen limestone bricks from the top of the pile. She ignored the clouds of dust and grit raised by her efforts. She had been dirty before.

Digging bare-handed in the rubble, Cassandra managed to make an opening just wide enough to wriggle her slender body through. She clambered up to the opening and thrust the flashlight forward; then, bumping her head as she strained forward to see, she crawled partway into a new corridor that sloped steeply down.

Ahead, the echoing chamber seemed much larger than the numerous other alcoves she had found in the pyramid, large enough to hold dozens of people. A curved shaft led away from it, a spiral ramp that went even deeper. She played her beam around the new room and nearly dropped the flashlight in her surprise. She had never seen anything like this.

Cassandra's white light reflected off walls made of peeling metallic plates, bent girders, crystalline panels. When she moved the flashlight beam away, portions of the newly exposed interior continued to glow with an eerie, pale afterlight.

From her knowledge of ancient history and culture, these bizarre fixtures seemed impossible to her. The Maya had never been known to use any kind of metal extensively, mainly satisfied with obsidian and flint for their needs. But here, unmistakably, she saw smooth, untarnished metal as if it had been made in modern smelters. It was an unusual alloy—certainly not the crude gold and bronze the ancient Maya had used.

Astonished, she stared for a while, still practically facedown in an opening barely large enough for a badger. She drew out her tape recorder, squirming and wedging herself deeper into the opening so she could hold the flashlight in one hand and the tape recorder near her mouth with the other. She pressed the RECORD button.

"This is amazing," she said, then paused for a long, silent moment as she searched for words. "I'm seeing metal with a silvery consistency, but not dark like tarnished silver. It gleams white—aluminum or platinum? But that can't be, since the ancient Maya culture had no access to those metals."

Cassandra recalled reading how some artifacts recovered from Egyptian tombs had gleamed shiny and new despite being locked away for millennia; yet, once exposed to post-Industrial Age air clogged with sulfur-bearing pollutants, the artifacts had tarnished and deteriorated within weeks. "Note—we must explore this chamber with extreme caution," she said. "It seems to be quite an exceptional find."

She desperately wanted to climb all the way inside, to explore to her heart's content. But common sense warned her not to.

"I have decided not to proceed into the chamber yet," she dictated, struggling to keep the dejection out of her voice. "Nothing must be disturbed until the entire team is here to assist me and provide second opinions on questionable items. I'm going back for Kelly and John. They can help me clear the rubble from this opening and support it with overhead beams. We'll need Cait to photograph the objects in state before anyone else goes inside."

After a long pause, she spoke again. "For the record, let me say that I think this is it… the Big One."

Cassandra switched off the microrecorder, then swallowed hard. After crawling back out, she unenthusiastically brushed herself off, then gave up, leaving the grit and dust. She began to retrace her steps, winding through the labyrinth to reach the exit, forcing herself to be calm. She thought of her wiry old father and imagined how proud he would be to see his daughter making discoveries that rivaled—even overshadowed!—those at the high point of his own career.

She quickened her pace. Her footsteps whispered and echoed through the stone passageways. As she approached the low exit to the pyramid, bright rays from the setting sun shone in her eyes like the light of an oncoming train. She rushed forward and stumbled out of the pyramid into the open air. "Hey, Kelly!" she shouted, "I've found something! You have to get the team, quick. Wait'll you see this!"

No one answered her. She stopped, blinking, and stood outside for a moment in the silence. She held on to the edge of the pyramid doorway for support.

The ruins seemed abandoned again. She heard only the murmur of jungle sounds, nothing else. She looked toward the high levels of the ziggurat, expecting to spot a couple of students on the hieroglyphic stairs… but the pyramid stood deserted.

By now the sunset was fading into dusk, the worst time of the day for visibility, when the shadows took on dim colors. Only a thin curve of the retreating sun remained above the treetops in the west, like an orange beacon backlighting the scene with an incomprehensible glare.

Cassandra saw no one, no members of her team, none of the vanished Indian helpers.

"Kelly, John, Christopher!" she called. "Cait, where are you?"

Shading her eyes, she peered out into the open plaza where Cait had earlier erected an easel for her watercolor work. Now the easel lay smashed on the ground. Cassandra could clearly make out a muddy bootprint stomped across one of the new paintings.

Greatly uneasy now, she again scanned the steep staircase that ran up the outside of the ziggurat. There Christopher and Kelly had painstakingly cleaned the chiseled glyphs and sketched them on pads, translating the chronicle of Xita-clan's mythic history as they went.

No Kelly, no Christopher… not a soul in sight.

Across the plaza where young John Forbin had been studying the collapsed ruins of a minor temple, she spotted his case of equipment, his small wooden stakes and colored ribbons marking line-of-sight intersection points—but found no sign of the grad-student engineer.

"Hey! Kelly? This isn't a damn funny joke," she shouted. Her stomach knotted. She felt utterly isolated, engulfed by the surrounding forest. How could the bustling, verdant jungle be so damned quiet? "Hey!"

She heard movement to the side—footsteps coming around the pyramid from the direction of the deep sacrificial cenote. She heaved a sigh of relief. Here were her friends after all.

But then the shadowy silhouettes of strange men appeared—obviously not any members of her team. In the dim light she could barely discern their features, but she did see without a doubt that they carried guns. Rifles.

The men pointed their weapons at her.

One spoke in heavily accented English. "You will come with us, Señorita."

"Who are you?" Cassandra demanded, the old fire within her flaring up enough to burn away her common sense. She gripped her flashlight as if it were a club. "Where is my team? We're American citizens. How dare you—"

One of the other men jerked up his rifle and fired. The bullet ricocheted off one of the pyramid's stone blocks, barely six inches from her face. A spray of needle-sharp stone fragments peppered her cheek.

With a sharp cry, she ducked backward into the temple, seeking refuge in the ancient darkness. She ran down the long tunnel, hearing loud shouts in Spanish outside. Angry curses. More gunfire. Merciful confusion.

Her heart pounded, but she wasted no mental energy trying to guess who the men could be or what they wanted. She didn't dare think of what they might already have done to Cait, John, Christopher… and Kelly. She would think about that later—if she survived.

She glanced behind her. The men were barely discernible outside the temple. She saw them appear at the doorway, arguing with each other. One figure cuffed another, then raised a fist high in anger. More shouts in Spanish.

Cassandra ran around a sharp corner. Her flashlight beam bobbed ahead of her. She had forgotten to turn it off when she came out of the pyramid. Perhaps the murderous strangers didn't have lights of their own, but they could see the reflection of her beam on the stone walls. She switched off the light and plunged blindly ahead.

More rifle shots rang out behind her. Bullets bounced along the pyramid walls, whining a high-pitched song of death. Regardless of how poorly these men could shoot, a ricochet could still kill her.

Cassandra had no choice but to keep running headlong into the dark, labyrinthine passages, deeper into the barely explored depths. Rounding one comer, and then another, she finally switched her flashlight on again, although she still heard the sounds of clumsy pursuit behind her. Back in the direction of the opening she saw flickering orange lights splashing against the walls, and guessed that the armed men had taken to striking matches and cigarette lighters to find their way after her.

Cassandra had the advantage—for now. She had been down here before, she had a flashlight, and she had a vague idea of where she was going: back toward the center of the pyramid.

But she had no place to go from there.

Going deeper inside would only drive her more firmly into the trap. She had to think, use her wits to outsmart these men, whoever they were. No problem.

She took out the microcassette recorder and rewound it, hoping that her breathlessly dictated directions and notes could help her to retrace her path to the strange chamber that had remained hidden for centuries. Maybe she could hide there until the men gave up looking for her.

Right. No problem.

The strangers might just post a guard at the outer doorway, then return better equipped to hunt her down. They could search relentlessly until they found her and gunned her down in a corner of the ancient ruin. Worse still, they could just lie in wait for her until she staggered out in a few days, nearly mad from hunger and thirst.

She couldn't think about that. Survive for *now*. She kept moving.

Cassandra pressed the PLAY button, listening for directions on her microcassette. She heard only a faintly crackling hiss. Her words had been erased! Something had blanked her tape.

"Dammit!" She groaned and added another item to the list of things she didn't understand but couldn't think about at the moment. Well, the route was fresh enough in her mind that she could find her way without any other assistance.

She had to.

The corridors of the outer pyramid wound downward on a slope, littered with fallen limestone blocks and rough debris. She stumbled, scraped her hands against the rough walls, but kept moving. Moving. She heard another gunshot. Why did they keep wasting ammunition? The men couldn't possibly have a good shot at her. Maybe they were just spooked by the echoes of their own footsteps. Frightened men with guns were the most dangerous kind.

Finally, Cassandra found the smooth, vitrified walls of the inner temple and knew she had nearly reached her destination—though what she intended to do there was another question altogether.

Casting her flashlight beam ahead, she discovered the small opening she had recently excavated. It looked like an open wound....

No. It was an escape hatch.

Gritting her teeth and panting for breath, Cassandra crawled onto the pile of rubble and squirmed into the hole like a snake. Before, the opening had seemed too cramped, too constrictive. But now panic propelled her forward. The rocks scraped her elbows, her shoulders, but she didn't care.

She fought her way over the rubble barricade into the isolated chamber and dropped down. Her feet echoed on the floor—a floor that was inexplicably metallic.

The passageways became oppressively silent again.

Her flashlight beam reflected off polished surfaces, curves, and spheres with a geometrical perfection that should have been far beyond Maya capabilities. The light flickered, as if her batteries were rapidly dying.

Another volley of gunfire echoed through the winding labyrinth far behind, separated from her by walls of stone. Then more shouts came, much louder, possibly nearer—but she couldn't be certain due to the reflective rock of the twisting corridors.

Inside the weird chamber, Cassandra was in totally unexplored territory. She rushed ahead to the final descending passage, the spiral ramp at the exact core of the pyramid. The steep tunnel looked as if it burrowed well beneath ground level. Without pausing to think, she hurried down it, moving farther and farther from her pursuers.

A faint wave of hope splashed across her mind. She wondered if this ramp might lead to some unknown exit from the pyramid, perhaps far down the wall of the limestone sinkhole. Maybe she could get out of this after all!

The sharp crack of a gunshot drove a spike of sound through the echoing rooms. Logically, Cassandra knew the shadowy men couldn't be close. She had to be far ahead of them. She *must* have lost them in the twisting and turning passages, but her fear drove her faster and faster down the sloping ramp… until the passageway opened into a grotto of wonders, glimpsed only briefly.

Glass panels on the walls around her reflected arrays of crystal spheres, gleaming shapes, metal strips laid down in geometric paths along limestone blocks. But she caught only a peripheral blink of everything around her before her flashlight winked out, as if something had consumed its electrical power, sucked its batteries dry, in the same way as her microcassette had been mysteriously erased.

Cassandra swallowed hard, feeling claustrophobic, lost. She staggered forward blindly, sweeping her hands in front of her, searching for a landmark. Her questing hands encountered an opening, a small doorway. She staggered through it, hoping to find some source of light.

A brilliant glare washed around her, and in an instant Cassandra saw that she had crossed into a dead-end room the size of a closet... or a coffin. Blazing illumination flooded from behind smooth, glassy walls.

Too late, Cassandra wondered if this fate might not be worse than the men with guns.

Icy, cold light cascaded over her like liquid, freezing hard—and all of her thoughts ceased.

2

FBI Headquarters, Washington, D.C.
Tuesday, 9:14 A.M.

Every time Special Agent Dana Scully ventured into the bowels of FBI Headquarters to see her partner, Fox Mulder, she felt as if she were doing something illicit—or at least unwise.

She remembered the first time she had come here to Mulder's private sanctum, a fresh young field agent inexplicably assigned to the X-Files. "No one down here but the FBI's most unwanted," he had called by way of introduction. At the time, Agent Mulder had considered her a spy for Bureau higher-ups who did not condone his passionate interest in unexplained phenomena.

Now, after three years of working together, Scully and Mulder had investigated dozens of cases and relied on each other's help more times than they could count. Mulder's belief in the supernatural and extraterrestrials remained unshaken, while Scully remained just as steadfast in her search for rational explanations. Though they frequently did not agree on their conclusions, they performed extraordinarily well as a team.

Scully visited her partner's narrow office often enough that its dreary clutter was etched permanently in her mind. She knew exactly what to expect. This morning the room did not disappoint her.

Debris from his unusual research lay strewn about the office: videotapes, DNA records, medical histories, close-up photos of smallpox scars on withered skin, blurry snapshots that supposedly showed evidence of flying saucers. A hunk of twisted shrapnel, purportedly from a crashed spacecraft found in Wisconsin, rested on one shelf. A dozen unsolved mysteries in open folders waited to be put to rest in the nondescript black file cabinets that contained Mulder's raison d'etre: the X-Files.

She knocked on the frame of the open door and stepped inside, brushing a hand through her red-gold hair. "I'm not sure I have the energy to face this chaos so early in the morning, Mulder," she said.

Mulder swiveled around in his chair, spat out a sunflower seed, and stood up. "Try eating more presweetened breakfast cereal," he said. "That'll give you the energy to face anything." He grinned at her.

She felt uneasy when he grinned like that, because it usually meant he had focused his attention on some new or unorthodox theory… a theory she would most likely have to debunk.

Looking down, she noticed that he had piled his desk with archaeology texts, books on ancient mythology, and detailed maps of Central America. She tried to put all the ingredients together in a flash, because she would have to prepare herself for what her partner would propose for their next investigation.

"Take a look at this, Scully," he said, and held out an object about the size of his fist, intricately carved and polished, made of a buttery, whitish-green stone. "Three guesses."

She took the heavy relic and held it in her hands. The stone's surface was polished so smooth it felt as if it had been oiled. The carving showed a sinuous serpentine form, some kind of viper bristling with large, incongruous feathers. Curved, needle-like fangs protruded from its mouth, giving the creature a ferocious appearance.

The artisan had been a master. The design fit exactly with the irregular contours of the chunk of rock. She ran her fingertip along one of the notches, wondering what sort of test Mulder might be putting her through.

"What do you make of it?" he said.

"I give up." She scrutinized the artifact again, but it remained a mystery. "A Christmas tree ornament?"

"Not even close."

"Okay," she said, taking the question seriously now. "I think I recognize the stone. It's jade, isn't it?"

"Very good, Scully. I didn't know they taught mineralogy in medical school."

"I didn't know they included mineralogy in behavioral psychology courses either," she countered, then turned her attention back to the object. "It looks very old. Some sort of mythological figure, maybe? From the books on your desk, I would guess its origin to be... Aztec?"

"Maya, actually," he said. "Best estimates date this piece of work to be about fifteen hundred years old. The Maya people revered jade. It was a sacred stone to them, used for only the most precious of objects."

"As valuable as gold?" Scully asked, playing along, wondering what he was getting at.

"Much more valuable. The Maya used to wear it around their loins as a cure for colic and other maladies. They even placed a piece of jade in the mouths of dead noblemen, because they believed the stone would serve him as a heart in the afterlife."

"Talk about a heart of stone." She turned the piece over in her hand. "It's obvious they put a great deal of effort and intricacy into the carving."

Mulder nodded, pushing one of the books out of the way so he could rest his elbow on his desk. "And it had to be quite a challenge for the carvers, too. Jadeite is exceptionally hard and dense, and so craftsmen couldn't use their traditional flint or obsidian tools." He reached over to tap a fingernail against the carving in her hands. "Instead, they had to use abrasive powders and disposable tools, dozens of them—wooden saws, bone drills, cords drawn repeatedly across the surface to wear down small grooves. Then they polished the whole piece of jade with gourd or cane fibers. Quite a piece of work."

"Okay, Mulder, so this wasn't a simple figure whittled out of wood for amusement. Somebody really wanted to make this particular object. In that case I take it there's some significance to the special design? A serpent with feathers. Did the Mayans revere snakes?"

"Ah," he said. "Not exactly. You'll notice that's no ordinary snake. It's a famous mythological figure associated with the god Quetzalcoatl. That's what the Aztec called him. The Maya used the name Kukulkan, a god of great wisdom. Some sources say Kukulkan taught the Maya about calendars and astronomy."

He offered her a sunflower seed. She shook her head, so he popped it into his own mouth.

"The Maya astronomer-priests were so precise in their calculations that the accuracy of their 'primitive' calendars wasn't surpassed until this very century. They even built interlocking gear-machines to make their calendar computations based on overlapping cycles out to fifty-two years. Kukulkan must have been an exceptional teacher... or he knew something the rest of the people didn't."

"Their mathematical abilities were extraordinary, too—in fact, they were the only ancient civilization ever to invent the concept of zero. That's important for balancing your checkbook, of course."

"Not my checkbook," she said.

With some effort, Scully found a place to sit down, moving a cardboard box filled with plaster casts of huge footprints. She glanced down at the casts but decided she didn't want to risk asking about them.

"That's all very interesting, Mulder," she said, "but what does a fifteen-hundred-year-old lump of jade in the shape of a feathered serpent have to do with a case? Have people started seeing feathered snakes in their back yards? Or have you discovered some discrepancy in our calendar that can only be explained by ancient Mayan carvings?"

She handed him back the jade sculpture, and he carefully placed it atop his Central America reference works.

"Under normal circumstances it wouldn't have anything to do with one of our cases," he said, "but this particular relic was recently confiscated at the border of the Mexican state of Quintana Roo, down in the Yucatán. The arrested dealer claims that this artifact came from the archaeological dig of a rediscovered Maya city deep in the jungles, a ruin called Xitaclan.

"According to official Mexican reports, there have been numerous unexplained disappearances in the area, dating back decades. And because the area is so primitive and isolated, you can bet plenty more of them have gone entirely undocumented."

"I'm still not sure I see the connection here, Mulder." She waited, casually crossing one leg over the other.

"Most locals won't go near the place, claiming it's cursed, or sacred... depending on which translation you use. Their legends tell of vicious feathered serpents, and the god Kukulkan, and the lost ghosts of sacrificial victims whose blood stained the temple stones."

Scully shifted on the old, government-issue chair. "I doubt that the Bureau would consider sending us to investigate an ancient Maya curse."

"There's more to it than that." His eyes grew bright. "A team of American archaeologists had just begun excavating Xitaclan under the auspices of the University of California, San Diego. According to early reports, this one site is untouched and the key to many mysteries of Maya history. It *could* be the first large-scale construction their civilization attempted. Definitely the site of frequent sacrifices."

He smiled, as if delivering a coup de grace. "Also, my preliminary chemical analysis of this object turned up some interesting anomalies, an odd crystalline structure, unidentifiable impurities that imply that this material did not come from the Yucatán near the ruins…"

She focused on the soft green color of the stone. "You think this thing comes from outer space?"

He shrugged and brushed a pile of damp sunflower-seed shells into his waste-basket, accidentally leaving several behind. "The archaeology team disappeared without a trace a week ago. No signal of distress, no sign of trouble. You and I get to go find them."

"But, Mulder, wouldn't this normally be handled by the Mexican authorities?"

Mulder said, "I also received a call yesterday from the father of Cassandra Rubicon, the young woman who led the UC-San Diego team. It seems her father's an extremely well-known archaeologist himself. He's made a few phone calls, contacted the FBI field office for San Diego. They heard the words 'ancient curse' and 'Maya ruins' and passed the case on to me." Scully met his gaze, and he raised his eyebrows. "I have a meeting with Skinner this afternoon. You and I are going to meet Vladimir Rubicon tomorrow. He's here, in Washington."

Scully glanced at the jade sculpture, at the mythology books, and then at the fascinated expression on Mulder's face. "I don't suppose it'll do me any good to try to talk you out of this?" she asked.

"Won't do you any good at all," he said.

"In that case, I suppose I always wanted to go to Mexico," she answered.

Assistant Director Skinner sat at his desk, ritually tapping his fingertips on the neatly typed forms in front of him. He did not stand when Mulder entered the room.

That's usually a bad sign, Mulder thought. On the other hand, Skinner had thrown him a curve enough times that he decided it would do no good to second-guess him.

The balding man was either a very good friend or the worst kind of enemy. Skinner knew things and passed the information on to Mulder only when he considered it important to do so.

Right now, Mulder needed to stay in Skinner's good graces. He and Scully had to get down to the Yucatán.

Skinner looked at him through wire-rimmed glasses. "I'm not sure you realize just what a sensitive subject you've stepped into, Agent Mulder."

Mulder stood at attention in front of his superior's desk. Keeping his expression neutral, he looked at the framed photographs of the President and the Attorney General on the wall. "I intend to exercise due discretion, sir."

Skinner nodded, showing that he had already considered this. "See that you do. As far as the Bureau is concerned, this is an important missing-persons case, relating to possible crimes committed upon American citizens. I have obtained for you and Agent Scully the status of LEGATS, legal attaches sent out of the country operating for the United States Embassy in Mexico City."

He held up a finger. "But bear in mind how delicate this situation is, given the current economic and political tensions. The Mexican government is always sensitive to intrusions by U.S. officials on its soil. I don't need to remind you about the number of DEA agents who have been assassinated by drug lords in Central America.

"The area you're heading into, in the state of Quintana Roo, is a political hotbed at this time. The local government is particularly vulnerable because of a violent separatist movement that seems to be growing in force, thanks to an unidentified supply of weapons."

"Are you suggesting that the archaeological team might have fallen victim to political unrest?" Mulder said.

"I find that more likely than an ancient Mayan curse," Skinner said. "Or weren't you going to suggest that?"

"Maybe, maybe not," Mulder said. "We have to examine every possibility."

Skinner picked up a set of travel authorizations and expense vouchers. He passed them across the desk, and Mulder took them, noting that all the signature lines had already been filled in.

"I expect you to strictly adhere to protocol, Agent Mulder," Skinner said. "I would urge you in no uncertain terms to hew the line in this investigation."

"Yes, sir."

"If you offend anyone in high places, you'll have more than just the FBI to answer to; you'll have the State Department as well. That is, unless you get yourself thrown into some Mexican jail first."

"I'll try my best to stay clear of that, sir." Mulder took the forms and tucked them under his arm.

"One more thing, Agent Mulder," Skinner said with an unreadable expression. "Have a nice trip."

3

"When all else fails, Special Agent Mulder comes to us for the real answers," said Byers, leaning back in his chair. He straightened his suit and tie, ran a finger across his neat reddish beard, and looked up calmly.

Entering alone, Mulder closed the door behind him in the dim offices of *The Lone Gunman*, a conspiracy exposé publication that purported to know the official truths about a thousand secret plots in which the government was engaged.

Scully had told him once that she considered the oddball characters who produced the magazine to be the most paranoid men she had ever met. But Mulder had found time and again that the esoteric information the three Lone Gunmen had at their fingertips often led in directions that official channels would never have suggested.

"Hi, guys," Mulder said. "Who's taking over the world this week?"

"I think Mulder just likes to keep tabs on us," Langly answered, sauntering across the room with a lazy shuffle that, with a little work, could have been turned into a dance step. Tall and scrawny, inelegantly dressed, he was the type who could easily have fit in with any crowd of computer nerds or roadies for a rock band. "It's for his own protection," he added, adjusting his black-rimmed glasses.

Langly had stringy blond hair that looked as if he washed it in a blender. Mulder had never seen him wear anything other than a ratty tee-shirt, usually advertising some fringe rock group.

"I think he just likes our company," Frohike mumbled, working with several pieces of extremely expensive camera equipment on one of the metal shelves at the rear of the office. In the background, Langly switched on the big reel-to-reel tape recorders, getting their entire conversation down on tape.

"Yeah, you three are just my kind of guys," Mulder said with a disarming smile.

Byers always wore a suit and a tie. He was soft-spoken and intelligent, the kind of son any mother would have been proud to have—if not for his vociferous opposition to various government organizations and his obsession with UFO conspiracies.

Frohike, with glasses, close-cropped hair, and rugged features, didn't look as if he would fit in with *any* social group. He had a long-standing crush on Dana Scully, but basically it was all talk. Mulder suspected Frohike would turn into a jittering mass of nerves if Scully ever consented to go out with him. Nevertheless, Mulder had been deeply touched when the short-statured man had brought flowers to Scully's bedside while she lay in a coma after returning from her abduction.

No identifying sign marked the door to the offices of the Lone Gunmen, and they were not listed in any phone book. The three kept their operation very low-profile. They tape-recorded every incoming phone call and took care to cover their own movements in and around Washington, D.C.

Nondescript, utilitarian shelves held surveillance equipment and computer monitors. Wires snaking out of the wall provided hard links to any number of network servers and databases. Mulder suspected the Lone Gunmen had never been granted official access to many of the systems, but that did not prevent the three from hacking into libraries of information closely held by government organizations and industrial groups.

Most of the chairs in the office were filled with boxes of stuffed manila envelopes, preprinted address labels facedown. Mulder knew the envelopes carried no return addresses.

"Your timing is good, Agent Mulder," Frohike said. "We're about to mail out our new issue. We could use some help dispersing them through a couple dozen mailbox drop points."

"Do I get a sneak preview of the contents?" he said.

Langly popped an old reel-to-reel magnetic tape from one of the recorders, labeled the flat metal canister, and installed a new backup system. "This one's a special issue of *TLG*. Our 'All Elvis' number."

"Elvis?" Mulder said in surprise. "I thought you guys were above all that."

"No conspiracy is beneath us," Byers said proudly.

"I can see that," Mulder answered.

Langly took off his glasses and rubbed them on the tail of his tee-shirt, which advertised a concert tour by the Soup Dragons. He blinked small eyes at Mulder, then put the black-rimmed glasses back on. "You won't believe what we've uncovered, Mulder. You'll have a whole new take on it after reading our historical retrospective. I did most of the research and writing myself on this one.

"We think that Elvis is being positioned as a messiah figure—by powerful persons unknown to us. You can find similar instances all through history. The lost king who reappears after his supposed death to lead his people again. Could be a strong basis for forming an insidious new religion."

"You mean like legends of King Arthur promising to come back from Avalon?" Mulder said. "Or Frederick Barbarossa sleeping in a mountain cave until his beard grows all the way around the table, at which point he'll return to save the Holy Roman Empire?"

Langly frowned. "Those two are misfires, because the messiahs in question never did come back, as promised. However, take Russia, for instance—Tsar Alexander II defeated Napoleon and supposedly died… but for years the peasants told of seeing a wandering beggar or a monk who claimed to be the real Tsar. It was quite a popular legend. And of course there are the Biblical accounts of Jesus Christ dying and coming back to continue leading his disciples.

"We don't need to remind you how many supposed Elvis sightings occur daily. We believe they have been staged, to provide the foundation for a fanatical new cult."

"Everybody wants an encore," Mulder said. He reached for one of the manila envelopes and slid out the issue to study the photo of Elvis on the front cover. He scanned the first article. "So what you're telling me is that somebody is trying to establish the birth of Elvis was in reality the Second Coming."

"You know how gullible people are, Mulder," Frohike said. "Think about it. Some of Elvis's songs have a very New Testament feel to them. 'Love Me Tender,' for instance. Or 'Don't Be Cruel.' Could almost be part of the Sermon on the Mount."

Byers leaned forward. "And if you think about placing it in a modern context, any hit single reaches far more people than the Sermon on the Mount ever did."

"Ah," Mulder said, "so what was Elvis really trying to say with 'Jailhouse Rock' or 'Hound Dog?'"

"Those took a little more work," Langly said. "Our interpretations will be in the next issue. You'll be surprised."

"I already am."

Byers shrugged and shifted in his chair. "We don't make judgment calls, Agent Mulder, we just report the facts. It's up to our readers to draw their own conclusions."

"About you guys, or about the conspiracies you report?"

Frohike pointed a large camera and clicked a picture of Mulder. "For our files," he said.

Mulder held up the newly printed issue. "Can I keep this copy?"

"Yours should be in the mail," Frohike said.

"Why not go ahead and buy an official subscription, Mulder?" Langly suggested. "Put some of your FBI salary to good use."

Byers smiled. "No, for someone of Mulder's stature, we should make sure he gets a comp copy of each issue. Besides, I'd be uncomfortable having his name and address on our mailing list."

"What, you're afraid you couldn't sell the list of addresses to Publishers Clearing House then?"

"Our readers are a certain type of person, Mulder," Byers said. "The type who might not want their names included among others who are also interested in the conspiracies we expose. We take great efforts to ensure that our mailing list can't fall into the wrong hands. Each of the three of us keeps a third of the names in separate electronic files with separate passwords on separate computer systems. We can't access each other's records. We just bring in the mailing labels, already printed."

Frohike said, "We print them out at the copy shop."

"Can't be too careful," Langly said.

"No, you can't," Mulder agreed.

"Well, we have to get started sealing envelopes," Langly said. "We'd be happy to press you into service, Mulder."

Mulder held up his hand. "No, thanks, I just came here for some information, then I'll be on my way."

"And how can we help save innocent citizens from the nefarious workings of the shadow government?" Byers said. "For this afternoon, at least?"

Mulder moved aside one of the boxes of stuffed envelopes and sat down. "What's the buzz you guys hear on Central America, the Yucatán, particularly some new Maya ruins that are being excavated? Xitaclan. I've got a missing archaeology team and a recovered artifact that may be of extraterrestrial origin."

"Let me think," Langly said, tossing his long blond hair. "I majored in archaeology in college."

Byers looked at him skeptically. "I thought you majored in political science."

Frohike squinted through his glasses. "You told me it was electronics engineering."

Langly shrugged. "So, I had a lot of varied interests."

Byers grew serious, looking back at Mulder. "Central America? I hear a lot of unconfirmed rumors about events in the area. There's been a separatist movement brewing in one of the states in the Yucatán. It's called *Liberación Quintana Roo*. The violence seems to be escalating—car bombs, threatening letters—and of course, you know about the U.S. military complex supplying arms at an exorbitant price to the freedom fighters."

"Why would they do that?" Mulder said.

"To create political instability. It's a game to them," Byers said, passion flickering behind his normally calm eyes. "And don't forget about some of the more powerful drug lords in the area who have become arms merchants themselves. Buying up technology. Serious stuff that we never would have dreamed about a decade ago."

"I dreamed about it," Frohike said.

"And how does this tie in with your particular interest, Mulder?" Langly asked.

"As I said, an American archaeological team disappeared there a week ago. They had unearthed new artifacts in the ruins—artifacts that are now turning up on the black market. The locals won't go near the place. Apparently there's a long-standing curse on the city. It was abandoned a thousand years ago, and now I've been hearing talk about the revenge of Kukulkan and his ferocious guardian feathered serpents."

"Knowing you, Mulder, I'm surprised you're not out chasing ancient astronauts," Langly said.

"I'm keeping an open mind," he answered. "There are plenty of mysteries connected with Maya culture and history, but I'm not necessarily ready to adopt any of them yet. With ancient astronauts and the Maya curse... not to mention the drug lords and military operations and revolutionary movements Byers was talking about, the Yucatán really sounds like a happenin' place."

"So are you and the lovely Agent Scully going down to investigate?" Frohike said, sounding hopeful.

"Yeah, we leave for Cancún tomorrow."

"Our tax dollars at work," Langly snorted.

"I'd love to see Agent Scully with a healthy tropical tan," Frohike said.

"Down, Frohike," Mulder said.

Mulder turned to leave. It was late in the afternoon, and traffic on the Beltway would be horrendous. He thought he might go back to the office and do more research. "Thanks for the information."

As he stood by the door, Byers called after him, standing up and straightening his tie. "Agent Mulder," he said, "if you do find anything interesting, be sure to let us know. For our files."

"I'll see what I can do," Mulder said.

4

Private villa of Xavier Salida,
Quintana Roo, Mexico
Tuesday, 5:01 P.M.

The old Mexican police cruiser with official state markings rolled along the tree-lined driveway, working its way uphill. The walled fortress of one of Quintana Roo's most powerful drug lords stood like a citadel in the dense forest.

The car rode low on the damp driveway made of packed limestone gravel. Blue-gray exhaust belched in oily clouds from its tailpipe. The police car had been painted recently, but unevenly, so that it did not look as new as it should have.

In the front passenger seat reclined Fernando Victorio Aguilar, feigning a calm and ease that he had learned always helped him to do better business. He rubbed his fingers along his slick cheeks. He had shaved only an hour before, and he loved the delicious, glassy-smooth feel of his skin. The sharp but pleasant scent of his cologne filled the car, masking other less pleasant aromas that Carlos Barreio, the chief of Quintana Roo's state police, had collected during his daily work.

Barreio drove slowly, easing around muddy puddles in the driveway. He wore his clean police uniform as if he were a military general, pleased with his position and flaunting it in a way he thought was subtle. Aguilar didn't find many things about Barreio to be subtle.

In the back seat rode young Pepe Candelaria, Aguilar's assistant, a steadfast young Indian who felt compelled to do everything Aguilar told him. Pepe sat protectively beside the precious object packed in its crate as if he were a common criminal under arrest in the back of Barreio's police cruiser.

While Aguilar and Pepe might have deserved to be arrested under the national system of laws, they both knew beyond the shadow of a doubt that Police Chief Barreio would never take them into custody. He had too much to lose.

The cruiser pulled to a stop outside the ornate, imposing wrought-iron gates that closed the access way through a stone wall. Barreio rolled down his window, grunting as he turned the door crank. He waved at the heavily armed private guard, who recognized him immediately.

Aguilar stared out the windshield, gazing appreciatively at the thick wall that surrounded Xavier Salida's huge fortress. Slabs of stone covered with ornate glyphs, Maya writing and sculptures, designs of jaguars and feathered serpents, images of priests wearing quetzal-feather headdresses and loincloths studded with beaten gold plates. Some of the carved panels were genuine, uprooted from forgotten and overgrown ruins out in the jungle. Others were clever forgeries Aguilar had commissioned.

Xavier Salida never knew the difference. The drug lord was a self-deluded, if powerful, fool.

"Tiene una cita, Señor Barreio?" the guard said in rapid Spanish. Do you have an appointment?

Carlos Barreio frowned. A heavy mustache rode on his upper lip like luggage, and his dark hair was slicked back under his police cap. His hair was thinning, receding with a pronounced widow's peak, but the bill of his official cap covered those details.

"I shouldn't need an appointment," Barreio boomed. "Excellency Salida has told me I'm always welcome in his home."

Aguilar leaned across to the driver's side, eager to divert an annoying and time-wasting confrontation. "We have another one of the ancient treasures Excellency Salida so fervently desires," he said out the window. "You know how much he enjoys them—but this item is even more precious than most."

He tossed a meaningful glance to the back seat, where the crate remained covered, hiding its contents. Whip-thin Pepe Candelaria slid a protective arm over its top.

"What is it?" the guard asked.

"It is for Excellency Salida's eyes only. He would be very upset if his guards were to get a look at the merchandise before he has a chance to assess its value." Aguilar tugged on his floppy ocelot-skin hat and flashed a hopeful smile.

The guard fidgeted, shifted his rifle from one shoulder to the other, and finally opened the wrought-iron gate, swinging the barricade inward so Barreio could drive the police cruiser through.

The police chief parked the car in the broad, flagstoned turnabout inside the walled courtyard. Dogs barked and howled from their kennels: Salida kept half a dozen purebred Dobermans, which he used for intimidation whenever necessary. Imported peacocks strutted around the grounds, clustering near the cool mist of a fountain that splashed into the hazy air.

Aguilar turned to look at both the driver and the passenger in the back seat. "This is a complex deal, so let me do the talking. When we meet with Salida, I'll handle the negotiations. Since this object is rare and unusual, we have no way of determining its true value."

"Just get the most you can," Barreio growled. "Weapons cost money, and *Liberación Quintana Roo* needs them."

"Yes, yes, your precious revolutionaries." Aguilar smoothed down the front of his khaki vest and then adjusted his spotted hat, making certain that his long dark hair was still in its neat ponytail that hung beneath the ocelot skin. Then he looked up at the broad expanse of Salida's whitewashed adobe villa.

It had taken a great deal of effort to smuggle Xitaclan artifacts from under the watchful eyes of the American archaeology team—but now that had all been taken care of. The foreigners would cause no further problems. This particular artifact was one of the last large relics taken from the pyramid, a "chamber of wonders" the Indian had called it in an awed voice… just before he had disappeared back into the jungles, never revealing where he had discovered the treasures.

But now his people had the run of Xitaclan again and plenty of freedom to explore… and exploit. For all of them who had risked so much, the time had come to reap the rewards.

Aguilar and Barreio got out of the car, while Pepe hauled the crate containing the artifact with him, lurching awkwardly under its bulk. The mysterious object was surprisingly lightweight for its size, but the young man had short arms and legs. Neither Aguilar nor Barreio offered to help.

Salida's second-floor balconies were decked with flowers, splashes of color that trickled between the railings and across the clean adobe surface. A hammock hung on one small balcony. Wicker chairs sat empty on another.

A guard at the door came forward , also armed with a shoulder rifle. "Hola!" Aguilar said, flashing his well-practiced smile. "We are here to see Excellency Salida."

"I'm afraid he is not having a good day," the guard said. "If you see him, you must accept the risk of upsetting him."

"He will see us," Aguilar said, again smiling. "If you wish to improve his day, you'll let him see what we've brought for him, eh?"

The guard looked at the box and stiffened, instantly suspicious. Before the man could ask, Aguilar said, "Another prize for your master. Even more breathtaking than the feathered serpent statue we delivered. And you know how highly he prized that carving."

Outside in the courtyard one of the peacock males set up a racket, a raucous squawking that sounded like a chicken being slowly crushed by a cement truck. Aguilar looked around and saw the large bird spread its amazing plumage. It sat on top of a tall stela, a stone pillar carved on all sides with Maya glyphs and pictures surrounding a ferocious-looking jaguar head.

The stela was ten feet tall and weighed many tons. It had begun to tilt, though Salida's landscaper had anchored it firmly in the ground. Dozens of sweating workers had labored for hours to bring the artifact in secret up the gravel driveway and into the drug lord's fenced courtyard.

The peacock squawked again, flaunting its feathers. Aguilar considered yanking them out, one by one.

The guard ushered them inside to a cool hallway and then up a curving grand staircase to the second level, where Xavier Salida kept his offices and his private withdrawing rooms. Sunlight drifted in through narrow windows, glistening on dust motes that fell through the air.

Their footsteps echoed with a hollow sound. The house seemed silent and sleepy… until they reached the second level. They could already hear Salida shouting as they approached down the hallway.

The guard looked wryly at the three visitors. "I told you, Señor Salida is not having a good day. One of our small cargo planes was shot down near here. We lost a pilot as well as many, many kilograms of product."

"I had nothing to do with this," Barreio said, suddenly defensive. "DEA?"

The guard looked back at the police chief. "Señor Salida has his own suspects."

They approached the largest withdrawing room, where two ornately carved mahogany doors stood mostly closed, leaving a gap of only a few inches between them. The drug lord's shouts carried through, only slightly muffled.

"Grobe! It must be Pieter Grobe. No one else would have the audacity!" Salida paused for a moment as if listening. "I'm not afraid of escalating our rivalry," he said. "We must take out twice as much in retaliation—but make no comment, no threats. Just do it." He slammed the phone down with an echoing clang, and silence fell on the rooms like a smotherer's pillow.

Aguilar swallowed, adjusted his floppy cap, and made to step forward. By smiling and taking the initiative, he hoped he could cheer the drug lord. The guard remained in place, blocking their way, his rifle on his shoulder. He shook his head in warning. "Not yet. It is not wise."

A moment later the strains of an opera emerged from a large stereo system inside the room. A shrieking soprano voice that sounded, if anything, worse than the peacock's cries outside in the courtyard, sang of some unimaginable human misery in a language Aguilar could not comprehend.

He knew the drug lord couldn't understand the words either, but Salida loved to put on airs, to wear the mask of cultured enlightenment. The opera went on for five nearly unbearable minutes, and then it was abruptly switched off to be replaced by a much more relaxing classical piece with orchestral instruments playing rich and complex melodies.

Hearing the change in music, the guard nodded and gestured for them to enter. He pulled open the heavy mahogany door on the right side.

Aguilar and Carlos Barreio entered side by side, but Aguilar knew that he had the upper hand. Behind them, Pepe struggled to carry the crate containing the precious and exotic artifact.

Xavier Salida turned to look at them, folding his hands in front of him and smiling a patient smile with a warmth that looked almost genuine. Aguilar was amazed at how rapidly the drug lord had transformed his mood from the shouting fury they had heard only moments before.

"Greetings, my friends," Salida said. His clothes were fine, his shirt made of white silk, his pants precisely tailored. He wore a nice vest with a gold watch chain dangling from its pocket.

Aguilar nodded and took off his ocelot-skin cap, holding it in front of him in the posture of a supplicant. "We are pleased you would see us, Excellency," he said. "We have another fine artifact to show you. Something so marvelous you have never seen anything like it."

Salida chuckled. "Fernando Victorio Aguilar, you say that every time you bring something to my home."

Aguilar smiled. "And aren't I usually correct? Don't you usually buy what I offer you, eh?" He gestured for Pepe to come forward and set the crate down on a glass table near the drug lord's desk.

Carlos Barreio stood at attention, trying to look imposing in his police uniform, while Aguilar glanced around the room: the familiar collection of fine art prints, professionally matted with heavy gilt-covered frames, the Maya sculptures on pedestals, some examples of pre-Colombian art in glass cases, others sitting on windowsills. Salida showcased the ones he liked the most, since he had no idea which were truly valuable and which were merely gaudy trinkets. A wine rack filled with the most expensive wines sat in one corner of the room.

Aguilar knew that although Xavier Salida flaunted his wealth and power, the drug lord had been illiterate until he became wealthy and powerful. The story was told of how he had brought in a tutor to teach him to read. The man had done a good enough job at it, but unfortunately the hapless tutor, after consuming too much tequila in a local cantina, had joked about the drug lord's lack of education... and so Salida had had him removed.

There had been a succession of other tutors who had taught Salida courses in art and music appreciation, transforming him into a fine upstanding citizen. He ate his expensive Sevruga caviar. He drank his fine wines. He played his old music on the newest stereo systems. And he pretended to know what he was doing when he collected expensive art objects.

Aguilar had taken advantage of this, fawning on him, playing on the drug lord's lack of expertise. Rather than admit he didn't know what he was doing, Xavier Salida nearly always bought the objects Aguilar offered.

But this time the prize was indeed something special. No question about it.

Pepe stood back from the glass table, sweating, swallowing, shuffling his feet. He wiped his palms on his pants, and waited for further instructions.

The drug lord gestured to the crate. "Well, go on, Fernando—open it, let me see what you have found this time."

Aguilar impatiently turned to Pepe, waving his hands. The young helper went to the crate and dug his nails in so that he could pry the tacks free. The lid popped open. He lifted aside the packing material, then carefully withdrew the magical artifact. Aguilar smiled magnanimously.

The drug lord caught his breath and stepped forward, compelled and fascinated. Aguilar's heart pounded. This was exactly the reaction he had hoped for.

Pepe set the object on the table and stepped back, wiping his sweaty hands on his pants again. The artifact was a completely transparent rectangular box a little more than a foot on each side. It gleamed with prismatic colors in the light, as if the workings inside were really sheets of thin diamond plating.

The components within were strange and exotic, interlocked components, connections made of glass fibers, glinting crystals. Aguilar thought it looked like the world's most complicated clock, made entirely of lead crystal. Tiny holes had been drilled in the side of the clear case. Other movable squares marked the corners and part of the top. Etched symbols not unlike some of the incomprehensible Maya glyphs marked portions of the clear glass faces. None of it made sense at all.

"What is it?" Salida said, touching its side and withdrawing his fingers quickly, as if burned. "It's cold! Even in this heat it's cold."

"This object is a great mystery, Excellency," Aguilar said. "I have never seen such an artifact before, even with all my archaeological expertise." In fact, Aguilar had very little archaeological expertise… though it was true enough that he had never encountered such an item before. Xitaclan was home to many unusual things.

The drug lord leaned toward the strange object, his mouth partly open. "Where did it come from?" He was entranced—and Aguilar knew the deal was assured. A high-priced deal.

"This artifact came from a secret new dig called Xitaclan, a pristine site. We are in the process of removing many of the most valuable pieces now. Before long, though, I am certain a new archaeological team will arrive to remove more of the objects."

Carlos Barreio's face became stormy. "They want to steal them from Quintana Roo," he said, "and take them from the land where they belong." Aguilar hoped the police chief wouldn't get distracted and plunge into one of his interminable political lectures.

"Yes, but we will 'preserve' what we can before that happens, eh?" Aguilar said, smiling. "And you, of course, are one of our foremost citizens, Excellency Salida."

Fernando Victorio Aguilar had grown up on the streets of Merida. His mother was a prostitute. While he was still young, she had taught him how to steal so they could live in relative comfort. But he had quickly learned that stealing was stealing, whether he stole a piece of fruit from the market or a Mercedes-Benz car. His philosophy, he had said with a laugh one night while sharing a bottle of mescal, was that if you are going to steal a mango, you may as well steal a diamond watch from a tourist and use the money to buy yourself a lifetime supply of mangoes. Stealing was stealing. Why not take the best?

Despite his upbringing, though, Aguilar had always felt uncomfortable about the thievery. He allowed himself a touch of guilt after seeing the anger, grief, and fear on the faces of the tourists he mugged and the shopkeepers from whom he stole.

But Aguilar had discovered to his delight that stealing expensive artifacts was a completely different prospect. That was stealing from people who didn't care, people who were long dead. He could make more money at it, and it wasn't as risky as robbing a tourist in Cancún.

Unless, of course, a meddling American archaeology team happened to be in the wrong place at the wrong time....

When Xavier Salida offered to buy the relic, his opening price was already far more than Aguilar had hoped to get. Carlos Barreio could barely restrain himself, but Aguilar still managed to increase the offer by another fifteen percent.

When the guard led them back out to the parked police cruiser, everyone was happy. The drug lord had brightened visibly after acquiring his new objet d'art, while Aguilar and Barreio were more than satisfied with the agreed-upon price.

The police chief drove his cruiser back out through the wrought-iron gate and down the long gravel drive. When they reached the dirt road at the bottom of the hill, Aguilar ordered Barreio to stop the car. He turned to talk to his young helper in the back seat.

"You'll get out here, Pepe. I want you to return to Xitaclan right away. You saw how much money we earned for this one artifact. There must be more. I trust no one but you. See what you can find at the ruins—and hurry."

Pepe climbed uneasily out of the rear passenger door. He reached under the seat to retrieve an old machete he frequently carried with him. "But... you want me to walk there?"

Aguilar scowled. "You can get there in a day. Two days if you're slow. Hitch a ride for part of the way, but hurry! Or are you afraid? There's a big bonus in it for you."

Pepe swallowed, then shook his head. "I will do as you ask, Señor Aguilar."

"You know where to find me," Aguilar said. He reached into his case and drew out a stack of pesos. "Here, this is for your family," he said. "There will be much more, but you shouldn't carry it all alone. Tell your lovely mother and your sisters hello for me. Perhaps I'll come and visit them again sometime soon."

Pepe stammered his own promises, then fled into the jungle beside the road. Aguilar tugged his floppy-brimmed ocelot hat hard against his head again, then loosened his ponytail, letting his dark hair fall free. He lounged back in the police car's seat, immensely pleased with himself. He might even reward himself with another shave.

"Off to Cancún," Aguilar said. "Let's spend some of our money, eh?"

Carlos Barreio wore a hard, satisfied grin on his face. "Spend your own share," he said.

"I intend to," Aguilar answered, and they drove off down the narrow dirt road through the thick trees.

5

Museum of Natural History, Washington, D.C.
Wednesday, 10:49 A.M.

The stone jaguar stared at the spectators with eyes that were disks of polished green jade. Fangs of sharp flint were embedded in its open mouth; the scarlet paint on its stylized body of sinuous curves had weathered and faded over the centuries. A placard identified the statue as a relic from the tomb of a Maya high king in the city of Uxmal.

"Reminds me of a cat my neighbors used to have," Mulder said.

A crowd of third grade schoolchildren led by a harried-looking teacher bustled through the Pre-Colombian Treasures exhibit room, yelling and playing tag despite the teacher's strenuous efforts to keep them quiet and respectful.

Mannequins dressed in bright feathered headdresses and ritual loincloths stood in front of colorful backdrop paintings that showed squarish ziggurats and the encroaching jungle. In another mural, Spanish Conquistadors arriving from the eastern sea looked like spacemen in their gleaming silvery armor.

Speakers mounted within the dioramas pounded out tinny recorded drumbeats, flute calls, and Indian chanting, as well as the sounds of jungle birds and insects. Tinted lights simulated Central American sunsets.

In the middle of the exhibit hall a carved limestone stela—or at least the plaster reproduction of one—towered nearly to the ceiling rafters. Bright spotlights shone down on the high-relief glyphs and exotic carvings that depicted the Maya calendar and astronomical markings.

Scully bent over to scrutinize a strange stone sculpture within a rectangular Plexiglas case: a squatting scarecrowish figurine with a long chin and hooked nose, wearing what appeared to be a charcoal brazier on his head. Scully glanced at her watch, then at her partner, and raised her eyebrows.

"Archaeologists deal with centuries at a time," Mulder said. "You can't expect a guy like this to even notice if he's five minutes late for a meeting."

As if on cue, a thin weathered man appeared behind them, peering over Scully's shoulder to look at the sculpture of the hooked-nose man. "Uh, that's Xiuhtecuhtli, the Maya fire god. He is one of the oldest deities in the New World."

The man's wide, strikingly blue eyes carried an owlish expression of unintentional surprise, as if he was on the verge of knowing what to say but hadn't yet figured out how to articulate it. A pair of reading glasses dangled from a chain around his neck. He continued his lecture.

"This fellow was the lord of passing time. Ceremonies in his name were particularly important at the peak of a fifty-two-year cycle. On that night the Maya would put out their fires in the entire city, making it dark and cold. Then the high priest would kindle a brand-new blaze." The old man's eyebrows went up, and his thin lips curled in a devilish smile. "That special fire was kindled on a prisoner's breast. The victim was tied to an altar, and the fire blazed, consuming his still-beating heart. The Maya believed that the ceremony kept time moving forward."

"Of course," Scully said.

The man extended his hand. "You must be the FBI agents. Uh, I'm Vladimir Rubicon. Sorry I'm late."

Mulder shook the proffered hand, finding the old archaeologist's grip strong and firm, as if from a lifetime of moving heavy stone blocks. "I'm Special Agent Fox Mulder. This is my partner, Dana Scully."

Scully shook his hand, while Mulder studied Rubicon's demeanor and the details of his features. The old archaeologist had a narrow chin accentuated by a thin goatee. Unkempt hair hung long about his ears, its whiteness tinged with brownish yellow where blond had not yet turned entirely gray; it looked as if he had spilled coffee in his hair and beard.

"Uh, I thank you for meeting with me." He fidgeted nervously, as if he didn't know how to come to his point. "If there's anything you can do to help find my daughter Cassandra and bring her back, I would be forever in your debt."

"We'll do our best, Mr. Rubicon," Scully said.

He gestured toward the exhibit, looking tired, and sad, and worried. He seemed to be avoiding a conversation he dreaded. "I volunteer at the museum in the afternoons, since my course load is light this semester. I don't really have time for it, but it's an investment in our future to keep new students interested in archaeology. It's the only way we old diggers can maintain job security." He forced a laugh, and Mulder got the sense it was a joke he used often.

"We'll need to find out more information about your daughter, Dr. Rubicon," Mulder said. "Can you tell us what exactly she had discovered at this new site? What was she looking for, in particular?"

"Of course. Uh, let's see…" Rubicon's eyes widened again. "Xitaclan is a magnificent city, judging from the photographs Cassandra sent up. The find of the decade for pre-Colombian artifacts. I wish I could have been there."

"If it was such an important find, Dr. Rubicon, why was such a small team assigned to it?" Scully asked. "The UC-San Diego expedition doesn't appear to have been terribly well equipped or funded."

Rubicon sighed. "Agent Scully, you overestimate the importance universities place on unlocking the past. Would it surprise you to learn that there are an estimated one thousand sites still unexcavated in the Yucatán, Guatemala, and Honduras? That area of the world was the center of Maya culture where, uh, the greatest cities of the New World were built.

"Think of the Yucatán as ancient Greece, but barely scratched, abandoned in place. In Greece the land has been exploited for thousands of years. Old-hat stuff. In much of Central America, though, the jungle still reigns supreme. The encroaching rain forest has swallowed up all the old cities like a protective blanket, covering them from the eyes of man."

Mulder cleared his throat. "Dr. Rubicon, I understand that the Indians in the area have some strange legends and superstitions about the old abandoned city. I've heard talk about Maya curses and supernatural warnings. Do you think it's possible that your daughter in her excavations has perhaps discovered something… unusual? Something that might have gotten her into trouble? Are you aware of the numerous reports of missing persons in that area of the Yucatán?"

Scully sighed and kept her comments to herself, but Mulder looked at the old archaeologist with intense interest.

Vladimir Rubicon swallowed, but raised his chin, as if searching for strength. "I am fully aware of the numerous disappearances—and it terrifies me that my Cassandra has fallen prey to some awful fate. I have seen many strange things in this world, Agent Mulder, but, uh, I'm more inclined to believe Cassandra ran afoul of black market artifact smugglers. There's quite a brisk trade in selling off antiquities to private owners. Since my daughter and her team were uncovering an unexploited archaeological site, I think it would have drawn the black marketeers like parasites."

He scratched his goatee and looked at Mulder with a concerned expression. "I'm more afraid of men with guns than I am of any myth."

Near the Conquistador mural, one of the children on the field trip pushed open a side door marked "Emergency Exit Only," setting off the fire alarm. The teacher hurriedly dragged the wailing boy away as sirens screeched through the room.

The other children scurried like panicked chicks around a mother hen. A security guard came running.

"Sometimes I think it would be more peaceful for an old archaeologist to be back out in the field again," Vladimir Rubicon said, toying with the glasses hanging around his neck. He forced a smile, turning first to Scully, then to Mulder. "So, uh, when do we leave? How soon can we expect to be at Xitaclan? I'm anxious to find my daughter."

"We?" Scully said.

Mulder put a hand on her arm. "I've already cleared it, Scully. He's an expert in the geographical area, as well as the field in which Cassandra was working. He knows Maya ruins as well as any guide we could find."

"I've got money saved. I'll pay my own way." Rubicon's bright blue eyes took on a desperate look. "Can you really feel what I've felt since Cassandra's disappearance... not knowing whether she's alive or dead, where she might be?"

Mulder looked at Scully, who was staring back at him. Suddenly it became clear to her how much her partner empathized with the old man and his search for his lost daughter. Years ago, Mulder too had lost someone very close....

Mulder swallowed. "Yes, Dr. Rubicon," he said. "You may not believe me, but I can understand exactly what you're going through."

6

Miami International Airport, Florida
Thursday, 1:49 P.M.

Vladimir Rubicon made a fuss, insisting that it would be no trouble, no trouble, as he graciously offered to take the center seat between Mulder and Scully. His form was lanky, but he seemed good at folding it up to fit into tight places. Probably, Mulder thought, because of an early career filled with squeezing through tight openings, sleeping in cramped tents, or huddling under trees in the rain while he worked in the field as an archaeologist.

As passengers filed onto the airplane, Mulder took the window seat as usual, hoping to catch a glimpse of something interesting outside. He scanned the rows of other passengers on the specially chartered flight and saw shimmering rows of blue-white hair and musty suit jackets that had been out of style for so long they were bound to come back in fashion any day now.

But instead of being primly nervous elderly people who sat quietly in their seats as if waiting for church services to begin, this group of retirees was as rowdy as kids on a school bus. Each one wore a self-adhesive "Hi! My Name Is:" tag.

Thinking back on all the cases he and his partner had worked on together, Mulder leaned over to the aisle seat to speak to her. "Scully, I'm not sure we've ever encountered a situation as frightening as a senior citizens chartered flight to Cancún." He buckled his seatbelt, ready for a wild ride.

After they were airborne, the flight took them away from Florida's clear and sunny skies, past the Keys, heading southwest across the Caribbean toward a horizon decorated with cloud cover over the Yucatán. Scully sat back and closed her eyes, snatching a moment of quiet relaxation.

Mulder remembered their very first case, flying out to Oregon to look into the mysterious deaths of high school students who, Mulder was convinced, had been abducted by aliens. During their flight, the plane had lurched and lost altitude. He had remained confident and calm, while Scully gripped the arms of her seat.

Sandwiched between them, Vladimir Rubicon slid his half-glasses onto his nose and squinted at a notepad. He scribbled names, places, people he remembered from previous expeditions. "It's been a long time since I've worked down in Central America, but Maya work is one of the cornerstones of my career," he said. "Perhaps some of my old contacts will be able to help us get out to Xitaclan. Uh, it's not on any map, you know."

"Tell me a little bit about your former work, Dr. Rubicon," Scully said. "Anything I would have heard of? I'm afraid I'm not as familiar with archaeology as I'd like to be."

The old archaeologist smiled at her and tugged at his yellow-gray goatee. "Those words are music to an old man's ears, my dear Agent Scully!

"My primary research interest lies in the American Southwest, particularly the Four Corners area of northern Arizona, New Mexico, southern Utah, and Colorado. The pueblo-building Indians there had a spectacular culture, which still remains quite a mystery." His half-glasses slid down his nose, and he nudged them back into place.

"Like the Maya, the Anasazi Indians had a vibrant and thriving civilization along with other cliff dwellers in the Southwest—but they inexplicably dwindled from a thriving, burgeoning culture to become pueblo ghost towns. Other groups around the area had extensive trade—the Sinagua, the Hohokam, the Mogollon—and left behind significant ruins you can see in many national monuments, especially Mesa Verde and Canyon de Chelly.

"I made my own fame—if you can call it that—unearthing and reconstructing sites in northern Arizona around Wupatki and Sunset Crater. Most of the tourists in that part of the country just head out to the Grand Canyon and ignore all the historical areas… which is good news for us archaeologists, since tourists tend to have sticky fingers, wandering off with fragments and souvenirs." He cleared his throat.

"I was personally fascinated by Sunset Crater, a large volcano near Flagstaff. Sunset Crater erupted in the winter of 1064 and virtually wiped out the bustling Anasazi civilization, knocking it to its knees—sort of like Pompeii. Their culture never fully recovered, and when extreme droughts ruined all their crops another century later… well, that was all she wrote for the Anasazi. If memory serves me correctly, I believe the place was finally turned into a national monument because some Hollywood filmmaker wanted to fill the crater with dynamite and blow it up for a movie."

Scully folded down her tray table as the flight attendant came by with a cart of beverages.

"The Native Americans scattered around the Southwest after Sunset Crater erupted nine hundred years ago… but on the positive side, the volcanic ash made the surrounding area much more fertile for the farmers. Until the drought came, at least."

As Mulder had dreaded would happen, once the pilot turned off the seatbelt light, the senior citizens tour group got up and began to exchange seats, gossiping, walking up and down the aisles, waiting in long lines at the coffin-sized lavatories.

To his horror, some vile ringleader got it into her head to start singing "family favorites"—and to his even greater surprise, most of the passengers actually knew all the verses to "Camptown Races" and "Moon River."

Vladimir Rubicon had to shout to be heard over the singing. "My little girl Cassandra accompanied me on some of my later digs. Her mother left us when she was ten, didn't want to deal with a crazy man who spent his time digging in the dirt in uncivilized portions of the world, playing with bones and reassembling broken pots. But Cassandra was just as fascinated as I was. She went with me happily. I suppose that's what sparked her desire to follow in my footsteps."

Rubicon swallowed and removed his half-glasses. "Now I'll feel guilty if something terrible has happened to her. She focused more on Central American civilizations, following the Aztec and Olmec and Toltec southward as they swept into Mexico, one culture overtaking and adopting the best parts of another. I never could tell whether Cassandra was doing it for the love of the work itself, or if she was trying to impress me and make me proud of her… or if she just wanted to compete with her old man. I hope I get the chance to find out."

Mulder frowned solemnly, but said nothing.

About an hour into the flight, the senior citizens performed an act that Mulder considered tantamount to a highjacking. One old man wearing a golfing cap stood up at the flight attendants' station and commandeered the telephone handset used for the plane-wide intercom.

"Welcome, everybody, to Viva Sunset Tours!" the grinning man said with a tip of his golf cap. "This is your entertainment director, Roland—are we having fun yet?"

The senior citizens let out a loud cheer that rattled the inner hull of the plane. Someone whooped, while other scattered individuals made rude catcalls.

"Think of it as a second childhood," Scully murmured. Mulder just shook his head.

Then Entertainment Director Roland announced that the flight crew had graciously agreed to allow them to use the intercom so they could spend the remaining hour of their flight playing a few rounds of Bingo.

Mulder felt his stomach sink. Looking amused, the long-suffering flight attendants marched down the aisles, handing out stubby golf pencils and index cards printed with numbers.

Entertainment Director Roland seemed to be having the time of his life.

After a while, the intercom chatter ceased being entirely annoying and became instead a background drone, easy to ignore… except when a plump old woman literally leaped out of her seat, waving her card and yelling "Bingo! Bingo!" as if she were being mugged.

Mulder stared out the window, seeing nothing but the blue ocean and tattered white clouds. "I wonder if we're anywhere near the Bermuda Triangle," he muttered, then smiled to show he had just been joking.

If Scully had been sitting next to him, she might have elbowed him in the ribs.

Vladimir Rubicon munched on one of the bags of pretzels the flight attendant had distributed, sipped from his paper cup of coffee, and cleared his throat, turning to get Mulder's attention.

"Agent Mulder," he said, his words difficult to decipher above the roaring background noise of coach class, "you seem to carry a deep sadness yourself. A lost loved one? You still wear the pain like an albatross around your neck."

"The Rime of the Ancient FBI Agent," Mulder said. But the humor didn't work, and he looked seriously into Vladimir Rubicon's cornflower-blue eyes. "Yes, I lost someone." He didn't elaborate.

Rubicon placed a strong, blunt-fingered hand on Mulder's arm. To his credit, the archaeologist did not probe any further. Mulder was reluctant to describe his memories about the bright light, the alien abduction, how his sister had floated up in the air, drifting out the window as he glimpsed the spindly, otherworldly silhouette that beckoned from the glowing doorway.

Mulder had buried those thoughts himself for a long time and had only reconstructed them through intense sessions of regressive hypnosis. Scully suspected that Mulder's memory of the event might be unreliable, that the hypnosis sessions had only reinforced images he himself wanted to believe.

But Mulder had to trust his memory. He had nothing else to go by—except for his faith that Samantha must be alive and that he would find her again some day.

"It's the not knowing that's the worst," Rubicon said, interrupting his thoughts. "Waiting and waiting, hearing nothing."

Someone else in the back squealed "Bingo!" and Entertainment Director Roland set to work, meticulously checking the numbers off. Apparently the winner of each game received a free tropical drink at their tour group's resort in Cancún.

Mulder fervently hoped that the entire group would board a double-decker luxury bus and drive off to a hotel—any hotel—far from where he, Scully, and Rubicon had made reservations.

Finally, the plane began its gradual descent, and Mulder could see the distant coastline of the Yucatán Peninsula, a curve that sliced across the azure waters of the Caribbean.

"At least you can do something to find your daughter," Mulder said to Rubicon. "You have a starting place."

Rubicon nodded and folded his notepaper, tucking it into his pocket. "Traveling again feels good—to get out and around, I mean," he said. "It's been a long time since I did, uh, field work. I had thought my days of Indiana Jones excitement were long gone."

He shook his head, looking very tired, very sad. "I've wasted far too much time teaching, lecturing about artifacts that somebody else discovered and brought to a museum. I've been reduced to an old fart who lives on his lost glory, doing nothing but puttering around." He said the word with derision. "I just wish it hadn't taken such an extreme event to wake me up."

Scully leaned over. "We'll do everything in our power to find your daughter, Dr. Rubicon. We'll find the truth."

7

Yucatán jungle, near Xitaclan
Thursday evening

The jungle at night held a thousand noises, a thousand shadows, a thousand threats….

The big silvery coin of the moon cast its watery light like rain, barely penetrating the clenched fists of branches above. Pepe Candelaria felt as if he had been transported into another universe, all alone.

He stopped to get his bearings. He could see the stars, but was barely able to discern the trampled path through the underbrush. Even without the path, though, he knew his way back to the Xitaclan ruins. His unerring sense of direction was an innate skill, common among his Indian ancestors.

Thorn bushes snatched at his pale cotton sleeves like desperate beggars, holding him back. With his father's machete, he hacked them away and moved onward.

He felt greatly honored that his friend and employer Fernando Victorio Aguilar had such confidence in him. Pepe was Fernando's most trusted guide and helper—although such an exclusive level of trust often meant Pepe had to accomplish his tasks without the luxury of assistance. Sometimes it seemed that his work could not be done by one man, that Fernando was taking advantage of him, pushing him too far—but Pepe could not refuse. Fernando paid him well enough.

Pepe Candelaria had four sisters, a fat mother, and a dead father. On his deathbed, sweating and moaning from a fever that coursed like lava just beneath his skin, Pepe's father had made him promise to take care of the family.

And now Pepe's mother and sisters took him at his word….

He ducked under a low-hanging tangle of gnarled branches. As he jiggled the twigs, something small and many-legged dropped down on his shoulder. Pepe briskly swiped it away without taking the time to identify the creature. In the jungle, spider and insect bites were often poisonous, or at least painful.

The moon continued to rise, but shed little light through the gauze of high clouds moving swiftly across the sky. If he was lucky, and worked hard, he might be able to get back home before dawn.

Pepe followed his instinct through the forest, making his way along the old paths, the uncharted roads used for centuries by descendants of the Maya and Toltec who had made their civilization here, before losing it to the Spaniards.

Unfortunately, all the customary roads led away from the sacred site of Xitaclan, and Pepe had to chop his own path with the machete. He wished he had taken the time to sharpen the blade.

His father had died from an infected wound, a sting from a deadly fire-colored scorpion. Father Ronald at the mission had called it the will of God, while Pepe's weeping mother had pronounced it to be a curse from Tlazolteotl, the goddess of forbidden loves, an indication that her husband had been unfaithful to her.

Because of this, Pepe's mother had refused to stay in the same room with her husband as he died—and then, according to tradition, she had demanded that he be buried beneath the dirt floor of their home. Then the family had no choice but to abandon their small dwelling… and Pepe was forced to secure a new house for them.

Building a new home had merely been the first of the new financial burdens Pepe had endured. Now, to atone for his father's disgrace and fulfill his own grief-driven promise, the family counted on Pepe to take care of everything.

And he did. He had to. But it wasn't easy.

The money he received from Fernando Victorio Aguilar kept them all fed, kept the new home repaired, and had even allowed him to buy his little sister Carmen a parrot. She adored the bird and had taught it to say his own name, much to his delight… except when it squawked "Pepe! Pepe!" in the middle of the night.

A palm tree scraped dry fronds together with a sound like a rattlesnake. Now, as he fought the dangling vines, Pepe longed to hear the parrot, longed to hear his sisters breathing softly in sleep and his mother's deep snores. But he had to get to Xitaclan first, in order to keep his friend Fernando happy.

He understood the task well enough. So long as Excellency Xavier Salida was interested and anxious to buy, Fernando must have more artifacts from the ancient ruins. Fernando needed Pepe to help him take advantage of the timing.

The ancient city was deserted, the American archaeological team now gone. He was particularly glad that the foreigners no longer rooted around in the ruins— Fernando couldn't allow outsiders to make off with more of his treasures, while

Pepe just didn't want them touching the precious objects, cataloguing them, analyzing the pieces as amusing debris from a lost civilization. At least Fernando's customers prized the treasures for what they were.

Without Fernando's help, Pepe's family would certainly have starved. His sisters would have been forced to work the streets of Mérida as prostitutes, even little Carmen. He himself might have become enslaved in the marijuana fields of Xavier Salida or Pieter Grobe or one of the other drug lords. Recovering precious Maya artifacts from long-abandoned ruins seemed safer, more honorable.

Pepe's mother adored Fernando, flirted with him, praised his cologne and his ocelot-skin hat. She claimed that Fernando's patronage had come to her son as a gift from the gods, or God, depending on whether she was thinking of the old images or the Catholic religion at the time. Pepe didn't complain—he would accept such luck, whatever its source.

In their church gatherings on Sundays, when the entire village came together to celebrate Mass, Pepe was entertained by some of the fanciful tales Father Ronald told from the Bible, but he doubted their relevance to his life here. Singing angels and white-robed saints might have been fine for people living comfortable lives and attending air-conditioned churches, but here in the thick jungle, in the primeval womb of the Earth, the older… more primal beliefs seemed to hold a greater credence.

Especially at times such as now.

A branch cracked overhead, settling into other twigs. Leaves whispered together as something moved unseen across the treetops… a snake, a monkey, a jaguar.

Pepe splashed across a narrow stream, placing it in his mental map of the area, knowing indisputably where he was, how close he had come to his destination. Xitaclan lay just up ahead.

In a thicket of fragrant hibiscus shrubs on the bank of the stream, the underbrush rustled. Something heavy splashed into the water. He recognized the reptilian eyes, the sleek form of a night-hunting cayman—large, and hungry, judging from the ripples that arrowed through the water toward him. Pepe quickly slogged through the mud, climbing the bank and rushing into the underbrush to get safely away from the crocodile-like creature.

Above, he heard more movement, crashing branches, falling leaves. He hoped it wasn't a night-prowling cat, ready to drop down on him to rip him apart with curved claws and powerful feline muscles—then he heard the scolding of a group of awakened monkeys, disturbed by his flight from the cayman. He sighed, feeling a shiver tingle through him. The old religion had revered jaguars, but he would not have felt blessed to encounter one of the jungle panthers alone in the night.

For centuries, the Catholic priests had done their best to squash continued practice of the old beliefs. In the village Father Ronald railed with stories of hell-fire and eternal damnation whenever he found evidence of ritually shed blood, of scars from self-scourging, even missing fingers or toes cut off with razor-sharp obsidian knives in personal mutilation.

The villagers apologized, did their penance, behaved with meek shame in front of the priests... but altered none of their thinking. Their hearts had not changed since the coming of the Spaniards five hundred years earlier. Sometimes pure sacrificial blood washed away stains the frequent jungle rains could never obliterate.

Pepe remembered quite vividly, while his father lay dying of the scorpion sting, his mother kneeling outside the door of their hut. She drew a thorny vine through her mouth, ripping her tongue open so that she could spit bright, fresh lifeblood onto the earth in her own sacrifice.

The sacrifice had not worked, though. Pepe wondered if the old gods had demanded more blood than she was willing to give.

In the golden past, the Maya gods had feasted on blood, on hearts torn out of willing victims, on sacrificed prisoners hurled to their deaths into the sacred limestone wells beside the great temples.

Now only ruins and artifacts remained of all that glory. Perhaps the gods had tired of blood after all....

Finally, after another hour of trying to slip like a thief through the jungle's night, Pepe arrived at the forgotten metropolis of Xitaclan.

Parting the wide, slick leaves of a banana tree, he gazed into the moonlit clearing, the rough hummocks of fallen temples, the sculpture-laden walls showing the hook-nosed masks of the rain god Chac, the numerous feathered serpent motifs now defaced by moss and vines, the impressive Pyramid of Kukulkan tall in the night, but smothered with vegetation.

Some of the thick trees had been chopped down and hauled away as the archaeological team had worked on their initial excavations, clearing the site of the densest foliage to remove the blanket of undergrowth deposited by undisturbed time. The trenches and shorn tree stumps stood like raw wounds in the earth.

The American team had been gone for only days, but the jungle had already begun to reclaim its territory.

In the center of Xitaclan's plaza, the stepped pyramid dominated the scene. The regularly spaced platforms had partially crumbled on one side, huge blocks tugged free by the strength of roots and vines. But at the ziggurat's apex the temple to Kukulkan, the god of wisdom, flanked by his feathered serpent guardians, remained intact.

Pepe would have to go inside the pyramid, rummage around the narrow passages until he found a few more alcoves containing jade artifacts, intact pots, glyph-painted tiles. Fernando Aguilar would make up a fanciful story or legend for whatever Pepe found, increasing its potential worth. Pepe had merely to bring back the treasures, for which he received his share of the money.

With a lightness to his step, he started forward into the plaza clearing—then Pepe looked up as he noticed a flash of movement, mysterious independent shadows gliding down the pyramid's crumbling steps, like hot oil trickling across water.

He held still, but the shadows kept moving... toward him.

Above, the branches rustled again with a slithering sound. On the ground, the tall feathery ferns waved as something large crawled through the leafy underbrush.

Narrowing his eyes, Pepe flicked his gaze from side to side. Smearing cold perspiration away from his face, he held up the gleaming arc of his father's machete, ready to fight an attacking jaguar or wild boar. He drew a long breath, his senses fully alert, then took another step away from the trees, glancing up to make certain that no huge predator could drop down on him from above.

The moon slipped behind a cloud, hiding its weak but comforting light. Pepe froze, listening—and the jungle seemed to become alive with movement, creatures slipping toward him with imperfect silence. In the renewed darkness, he saw a faint glow limning the edge of the Pyramid of Kukulkan, like a luminous mist that seemed to rise from the dark mouth of the cenote well.

Swallowing hard, Pepe stepped away from the dangling branches of a tall chicle tree, wishing he knew where he could find shelter. He was far from any village, from any help. Could he hide inside the pyramid or one of the other temples? In the debris-littered ball court where Maya athletes had played a violent sport in front of cheering crowds? Should he run back into the forest, away from Xitaclan? Pepe didn't know where to go.

With daybreak, the low jungle would be a much safer place. But not now, not at night. Never at night—he should have known.

Then he saw two long, supple forms coming over the piled rocks, the stone blocks of another fallen temple covered by moss and time. The creatures glided with reptilian, liquid motions mixed with a bird-like grace, jerky yet somehow delicate movements: the two shadows he had seen descending the steep pyramid steps. He found it entirely unlike the ominous, sluggish advance of the scaly cayman he had seen in the jungle stream.

At the edge of the ball court stood a glyph-adorned stela, a stone monolith used by the Maya to record their calendar, their conquests, their religion. A third shadow separated from the side of the stela, slithering toward him.

Pepe slashed his father's machete in the air, hoping the threat would frighten the creatures off. Instead, they came at him faster.

The high, thin clouds drifted apart, and the moonlight returned, spilling details into the murk of the excavated plaza. Pepe's heart pounded, and he gasped his amazement in the ancient language his mother and father had spoken. In the plaza before him, he saw monsters that emerged from the myths and legends he had heard since he was a boy.

The feathered serpents moved with the speed of dancing lightning—larger than crocodiles but with a power and intelligence that surpassed any other predator. They came at him from three sides, stalking, confident.

"Kukulkan!" he cried. "Kukulkan, protect me!"

The three feathered serpents hissed with the sound of water spattered on fire. They reared up, flashing long fangs as sharp as any sacrificial knife.

With bright clarity Pepe knew what he had to do.

In awe even greater than his terror, Pepe used the edge of his machete to slash open his arm, feeling the warm gush of blood, yet experiencing no pain whatso-ever. He extended his arm, offering them his blood as a sacrifice, hoping to appease the benevolent Kukulkan's servants with what he knew of the ancient rituals, the old religion.

But instead of satisfying them, the scent of the fresh warm wetness drove the creatures into a frenzy. The feathered serpents charged toward him with the sound of rushing water, crackling leaves. In the moonlight, feathered scales gleamed… bright teeth… long claws from vestigial limbs.

Tonight, Pepe thought, the old gods would get their sacrifice. His machete dropped to the dirt. The feathered serpents fell upon him.

8

Cancún, Mexico
Thursday, 4:21 P.M.

With some amusement, Scully watched Mulder heave a sigh of relief as the crowd of partying senior citizens filed off the chartered airplane and ambled toward the baggage claim area and customs station in the Cancún airport. They waited by a row of stations where uniformed men took their tourist cards and stamped their passports, before turning them loose to retrieve their luggage.

The man at the counter stamped Mulder's passport and handed it back. "If I ever start wearing plaid pants, promise me you'll stop me before I buy a ticket for the Love Boat," Rubicon said, as if forcing a joke. "I'm never going to retire."

Dozens of people hawking tour packages swarmed among the tourists, stuffing brochures into every empty hand. After conquering their luggage, the senior citizens tour group descended upon the bus aisle outside and climbed aboard their specially chartered Luxury Coach like lost chickens being rounded up and ushered back to the coop. Young men—certainly not airport employees—bustled about to help with the baggage, hoping for a tip.

Scully led the way through immigration to the baggage pickup area where they grabbed their luggage, passed through customs without incident, and went to find the courtesy van that would take them to their hotel. Though neither she nor Mulder spoke Spanish, nearly all signs and shops around them catered to English speakers. The moment any one of them looked confused, two or three Mexicans appeared, smiling warmly and offering their assistance. Rubicon made a show of employing his linguistic abilities to get directions and exchange their money. The old archaeologist seemed delighted to be useful as part of the expedition.

On the way to the Caribbean Shores hotel, they rode in the small van with a newlywed couple who were entirely preoccupied with each other. The driver played brassy disco music on the car stereo; he hummed along, tapping his fingertips on the steering wheel, the dashboard, or his leg.

Mulder sat next to Scully, flipping through a handful of colorful brochures the various tour representatives had forced upon him. "Listen to this, Scully," he said. "Welcome to Cancún, 'where the beautiful turquoise Caribbean Sea caresses the silky sand beaches.' The waters are 'filled with romantic coral reefs or mysterious and exciting sunken Spanish galleons.' Somebody must have a good thesaurus to concoct those descriptions."

"Sounds charming," she said, looking out the window at the bright sun, the vibrant colors. Thick trees lined both sides of the road. "At least this is better than an Arctic research station or an Arkansas chicken-processing plant."

He flipped through other pamphlets, including a map of the hotel zone, a narrow spit of land between the Caribbean Sea and Nichupte Lagoon. Bright letters proclaimed, "Nearly every room with an ocean view!"

Rubicon sat with his duffel across his bony knees. He seemed either to be listening to the disco music or preoccupied with his own thoughts. His blue eyes blinked rapidly against a sheen of dampness. Scully's heart went out to him.

The van driver honked his horn and muttered curses in Spanish as he swerved to avoid an ersatz old-fashioned motorized buggy that took up more than its lane in the road down into the hotel zone. The laughing American driver of the buggy waved and then honked his horn in return, a loud cartoonish *ahooogah*. The driver of the van forced a smile at the tourists and waved back, then cursed again under his breath.

In the back of the van, the newlywed couple giggled and continued kissing.

Rubicon held on to the half-glasses hanging from a chain on his neck and turned to Mulder. "One of the hotels even brags about the golf course they designed so that the ninth hole is constructed around the ruins of a small Maya temple." His astonished-looking eyes now carried a look of weariness and dismay.

"It's sad that they should be allowed to do that," he said. "They've exploited their history and culture, cheapened it. You should see the Hollywood-style extravaganza at Chichén Itzá. They charge a lot of money for their 'spectacular temple show' with lights and sounds, multicolored spotlights blazing across the pyramids every night, cheesy folk dances by professional actors wearing plastic feathered capes and gaudy costumes. The drumbeats pound out through stereo systems."

The scorn in the old archaeologist's voice surprised Scully. Rubicon gave a defeated sigh. "The Spanish Conquistadors were only the first devastating invasion of the Yucatán—next came the tourists." He forced a smile. "At least some of the tourism income goes toward funding restoration of the archaeological sites… like Xitaclan."

Their stucco-faced hotel boasted modern construction with a pseudo-Aztec design, gleaming windows, sun decks with palm-thatched umbrellas, and direct beach access. The curling waves were as jewel-tone blue and the sand as powdery white as the brochures had promised. They sent their bags off with the bellman while Mulder and Scully waited in line to check in.

Rubicon murmured to himself, taking out his handwritten notes, anxious to make phone calls and track down potential guides for their expedition deep into the jungles. He did not want to waste a moment in the search for his daughter. The old archaeologist wandered around the lobby, looking at cast-plaster jaguar sculptures, bogus bas-reliefs, and stylized Maya glyphs.

"Welcome to the Caribbean Shores Resort!" The desk clerk handed them room keys and cheerily began his memorized spiel of the evening's planned events. "Señorita, you cannot pass up your chance to go on a fun-filled party boat for an evening dinner cruise." He waggled his eyebrows.

Scully shook her head politely. "No, thank you. We're here for business, not pleasure."

"Ah, but there is always time for pleasure," he said. "We have a fine selection of lobster cruises or disco boats, even an adventure with the real pirates of the Caribbean." He continued to sound hopeful.

"Thank you, but I still have to say no." Scully took the keys and turned away.

The clerk called after them one last time. "Señor, surely you cannot pass up our famous limbo party tonight."

Mulder took Scully's arm and leaned close, whispering in her ear, "The limbo could qualify as calisthenics for the Bureau's physical fitness requirement."

Scully glanced over at the old archaeologist. "Let's hold off on the vacation until we find Cassandra Rubicon."

After showering and changing, they met in one of the hotel restaurants for dinner. The maitre d' showed Mulder and Scully to a table with a centerpiece of tropical flowers that showered the air with heady perfume. While the waiter held the chair for Scully, Mulder sat down. He glanced at his watch, knowing that Rubicon would join them at any moment.

Mulder had dressed down in a comfortable cotton shirt and slacks, leaving his usual suit and tie behind. Scully finally noticed his change of outfit and raised her eyebrows, hiding a small smile. "I see you're already getting into the casual Mexican spirit," she said.

"It's the Caribbean," he answered. "We're supposed to be undercover, so we ought to look like tourists, not FBI agents."

Unbidden, another server brought them each a lime-laden margarita, the glass rims crusted with salt. Scully settled down to study the menu, a mouthwatering list of local fare—fresh lobster, lemon-and-cilantro grouper, chicken with spicy chocolate molé sauce. Mulder sipped his margarita, smiled, then took another drink. "Love those ancient Mayan beverages," he said.

Scully set her menu down. "I called the consulate to check in. The Bureau has filed all the appropriate clearances and notified local law enforcement, but apparently they weren't too helpful. So the next step is up to us."

"As soon as we figure out what the next step is," Mulder said. "I think we can rent a car and drive toward the area where the team disappeared. Maybe we can find a guide to take us through the jungles."

Before Rubicon even arrived, the waiter came by to take their order. Mulder was famished after eating only snacks on the charter plane from Miami. He chose chicken cooked with bananas and a side dish of lime-and-chile-pepper soup, while Scully ordered fish marinated in annato-seed sauce and baked in banana leaves—supposedly a Yucatán specialty.

Scully opened her briefcase and drew out a folder. "I've been going over the background information we have on the members of the archaeological expedition," she said, "the other missing American citizens. You never know where we might find a lead."

She spread the folder and took out several dossiers on the UC-San Diego grad students, along with photographs. She held up the first one. "In addition to Cassandra Rubicon, another archaeologist was instrumental in getting this team put together: Kelly Rowan, twenty-six years old, six feet two inches, athletic, an honor student with a specialty in pre-Colombian art. According to his course advisors he had nearly finished writing a thesis that traced the connections in Central American mythologies between key stories of the Mayans, Olmecs, Toltecs, and Aztecs." She passed the paper over to Mulder, and he picked it up to study it.

"John Forbin, the youngest of the group, twenty-three, first-year graduate student. Apparently he planned to be an architect and structural engineer. According to this, he was chiefly interested in primitive methods of large-scale construction, such as the Central American pyramids. It seems likely that Cassandra Rubicon took him along to suggest methods for restoring the fallen buildings." She passed the paper over.

"Next, Christopher Porte, from all reports a well-respected... *epigrapher*. Are you familiar with that term?"

"Just from what I've read recently," Mulder answered. "It's someone who special-izes in translating codes and glyphs. Much of the Maya written language is still unknown and is very context sensitive."

"So they brought Christopher along to translate any hieroglyphics they found," Scully said, then shuffled to the last piece of paper. "And finally, Caitlin Barron, their historian and photographer. Also an aspiring artist. It says here Ms. Barron has even held a few minor exhibitions of her watercolor work in one of San Diego's student art galleries."

She handed Mulder the photographs, and he glanced at each one in turn. Then, checking his watch again, Mulder scanned the room just in time to see Rubicon at the entrance to the dining room, newly shaven and dressed in an evening jacket. Most of the other patrons of the restaurant wore shorts, sandals, and loud shirts. Mulder held up a hand to catch his attention, and the old archaeologist came over, walking as if already exhausted.

The waiter hovered beside Rubicon as he took the empty seat at the table. He ignored the margarita the waiter placed at his right elbow.

"No luck," Rubicon said. "I've called all the contacts I still have. Of course, some of them in the outlying areas don't have ready access to telephone service, but the ones in Cancún and Mérida were unavailable. One is retired. I tried to talk him into accompanying me for one last field expedition, uh, until I found out he's confined to a wheelchair. Another of my old friends—a man who saved my life during an expedition in 1981—has been killed in some sort of drug-related shooting. I set his wife to weeping when I asked for him." Rubicon cleared his throat. "I had no luck reaching the three others."

"Well," Mulder said, "we may be forced to rely on our own ingenuity to find someone who can take us to the site. It's a long drive just to get to the right geographical area."

Rubicon slouched back in his chair and pushed the menu aside. "There's one other possibility," he said. "In the last postcard I received from Cassandra, she mentioned a man who had helped her. A local named Fernando Victorio Aguilar. I have tracked down someone with that name and left a message, uh, that we are interested in being guided into the jungles. The man who answered the telephone seemed to think Señor Aguilar might be willing to help us. If so, I hope we can connect with him either tonight or tomorrow."

He threaded his fingers together and squeezed his hands as if trying to massage arthritis out of his knuckles. "Sitting around at some glitzy tourist resort makes me feel so helpless… so guilty, not knowing what my Cassandra could be going through at this very moment."

Mulder's and Scully's meals came, breaking the mood. Rubicon quickly chose a selection of his own from the menu and sent the waiter off.

Looking at the forlorn expression on the old man's face, Mulder remembered the days after Samantha had disappeared. Though he had teased her mercilessly—as any brother teases a sister—he had longed for her, desperately trying to think of what he could do to help, how he could find her. He took it as his personal responsibility, since he had been with her when she disappeared. If only he had done something different on that night. If only he had faced the bright light….

As a twelve-year-old boy he had limited resources but endless drive, a drive that had stayed with him all his life. He remembered riding his bike around the hometown neighborhood of Chilmark, Massachusetts—population 650—ringing doorbells, asking everyone if they had seen Samantha. He knew deep in his heart, though, that no simple explanation could possibly account for what he had seen.

He had worked for days, making "Missing" posters that described his sister, begging for information as if he were putting up notices for a lost dog. And that had been in the days before accessible photocopy machines, so he had hand-written each one individually with a black marker, the pungent fumes of the solvent drifting up into his nose and making him sniffle even more than he already had for his lost sister. He had taped up his paper notices on store windows, tacked them to utility poles and bus stop signs.

But no one had ever called except to offer sympathy.

His mother had been devastated by her grief, incoherent with tears, while his father remained stony and stoic through it all. Possibly, Mulder now knew, because his father had had some dark knowledge about what had really happened. His father had been given some warning, had known something regarding Samantha's danger—and he had done nothing.

For years now Mulder had seen an echo of Samantha in every little dark-haired girl. She had disappeared long before the days of the "Have You Seen Me?" pictures of missing children on milk cartons or bulk-mail flyers. All Mulder's efforts to put up posters or knock on doors had ultimately been useless, helping not in the least. But he'd felt he had to do something. It had been his mission.

Now he watched Vladimir Rubicon going through a similar process, coming to the Yucatán, calling his old contacts, insisting on accompanying the FBI agents on their investigation.

"We'll find her," Mulder said, reaching across the table, forcing confidence into his voice. In the back of his mind he again saw an image of his sister being dragged off into the light.

Mulder looked into Rubicon's eyes. "We'll find her."

But he wasn't sure to whom exactly he was making his promise.

9

Caribbean Shores Resort, Cancún
Thursday, 9:11 P.M.

Scully had just settled in for the evening, satisfied from a delicious meal and finally comfortable after removing her shoes and pantyhose. Knowing the lack of amenities and jungle hardships they were bound to encounter in the coming days en route to Xitaclan, she planned to get a good rest.

Her hotel room displayed a colorful, if typical, painting of a sunrise over the Caribbean, complete with calm surf and silhouetted palm fronds. Her private balcony looked out over the powdery white beach and the ocean. She smelled the evening salty breeze, listened to the rumble of the waves, and watched couples stroll along the sand beneath bright electric torches posted above the tide line. The thought of swimming and relaxing sounded wonderful—but she reminded herself that they were here on a case.

With a weary sigh, Scully flopped back onto the bed without turning down the sheets, hoping that the moment of peace would last for more than two minutes.

The pounding on her door was sharp and strident, like cannon blasts from a warring Spanish galleon.

She hadn't ordered room service, and she became instantly on guard as she got up off the bed. The pounding didn't stop. "All right, coming," Scully called out in a voice devoid of enthusiasm.

She glanced over at the half-open connecting door to Mulder's room, feeling a cold chill—the insistent thudding knock was not the polite request for attention that room service would ever use. This pounding sounded bold and impatient. Cautious, she picked up her own weapon from the courtesy table.

Upon opening the door she found a barrel-chested man clad in a police chief's uniform, his hairy-knuckled fist raised to continue the insistent knocking. Before she could blink back her surprise enough to speak, the man planted his foot in the door to prevent her from shutting it in his face.

"I came as soon as I learned of your arrival," the man said beneath a thick black mustache. "You are FBI Agent Scully—and the other one's Mulder." His police cap rested firmly on his head, and sweat glistened on his cheeks. His shoulders were broad, his chest wide, his arms muscular, as if he juggled bags of cement mix for exercise.

"Excuse me?" Scully said, making sure he saw her 9-mm pistol. "Who are you, sir?"

He waited for her to invite him into her room, ignoring the weapon. "I'm Chief Carlos Barreio of the Quintana Roo Police Force. I am sorry I could not meet you at the airport. Please pardon my rudeness. I have many cases, but few men."

"We were told you had been contacted," Scully said, "but that you offered no help in our investigation."

The connecting door opened, and Mulder stepped into her room, his hair tousled, his shirt untucked and hastily buttoned. She noticed that he had missed his buttonholes by one, but at least he had taken a moment to tug his shoulder holster in place.

Seeing the burly policeman, Mulder said, "We sure must have upset that hotel desk clerk by not going on one of his disco cruises."

"With your heavy case load, we're glad to focus our own efforts on this particular investigation," Scully said, straightening her blouse and running her hands down her skirt and hips. Despite his outwardly polite manner, she sensed an antagonism buried deep within him. "We have obtained all the proper clearances and authorizations."

"Yes, I cannot spare the manpower," Barreio said. "You understand." His complexion was ruddy, his face calm, but his posture remained stiff and on guard. He removed his cap, and she noted that his thinning hair had been slicked into a pronounced widow's peak. "I'm afraid I have little to report on the disappearance of the American archaeological expedition."

Scully, trying to remain polite, said, "We have a long-standing tradition of cooperation with local law-enforcement agencies, Mr. Barreio. We both have the same goal, after all—to find our missing people. We are anxious to proceed and happy to add our expertise to your own."

Barreio, his eyes still cold, said, "Of course I will cooperate. I have been informed by the Federal Bureau of Investigation satellite office in Mexico City that you two have been assigned here as legal attaches. Your inspector in charge at the Office of Liaison and International Affairs has graciously requested that I provide you with copies of all information I have currently compiled. My own superiors have passed along this request."

"Thank you, Mr. Barreio," Scully said, still cautious, still sensing his antagonism. "Please be assured that we are not trying to infringe upon your jurisdiction. The State of Quintana Roo is the area in which the crime was committed—"

"Alleged crime," Barreio interrupted, letting his composure slip. "Allegedly committed,

"Allegedly committed," Scully conceded. "You have jurisdiction. Mexico is a sovereign country. As agents of the Federal Bureau of Investigation, my partner Mulder and I are empowered only to offer our assistance."

Mulder cleared his throat. "However, we do have the right to investigate crimes perpetrated upon American citizens." With one hand he smoothed his hair back, standing beside his partner. "The FBI has as its mandate investigations into terrorism, arms dealing, drug trafficking—as well as possible kidnapping of American citizens. Until we know additional information about Cassandra Rubicon and her companions, we must operate under the assumption that someone may intend to hold them as potential hostages."

"Hostages!" Barreio smiled. "I'm sorry, Agent Mulder, but I think it's more likely they just got lost out in the jungle."

"I hope that proves to be the case," Scully said, keeping herself between Mulder and the burly police officer.

Outside, an imperious-looking room-service waiter strode down the hall carrying a tray loaded with fruit-garnished tropical drinks that looked like Dr. Jekyll's chemistry experiments gone awry. As he walked past, the man studiously ignored the conversation taking place in the doorway of Scully's room.

Barreio sighed, shaking his head slightly. "You'll forgive me if I don't entirely trust the FBI." Barreio's eyebrows bunched like black caterpillars on his forehead. "My former counterpart in Mexico City—Arturo Durazo—was the target of one of your sting operations. He's now rotting in an American jail."

Scully frowned. The name was completely unfamiliar to her.

"The FBI claimed Durazo was selling millions of dollars of drugs to the United States," Barreio said. "They lured him outside our borders to the Caribbean island of Aruba, where they could 'legally' arrest him—he was never extradited, as far as I know. It was a setup."

Scully tossed her red-gold hair, looking calmly at the police chief. "I assure you, Mr. Barreio, we have no interest in the police force in your state or its internal activities. We're only looking for our missing citizens."

Two men hurried down the hall, and Scully looked past the police chief to see Vladimir Rubicon, his yellow-white hair unkempt, his reading glasses landed haphazardly on his sharp nose. He hustled along, leading another man who was deeply tanned and wiry, with long hair bundled in a ponytail under a floppy wide-brimmed hat made from the skin of a spotted cat. The long-haired man reeked of aftershave.

"Agent Scully! Guess who I found," Rubicon called, then stopped upon seeing the police chief. "Excuse me. Is anything wrong?"

Barreio looked at the two men, his eyes blinking in recognition as he saw the man with the floppy spotted hat. "Señor Aguilar," Barreio said, "are these people part of an expedition you are mounting?"

"Yes, yes indeed," the other man—Aguilar—said. "I have just entered into arrangements with this gentleman here. Quite satisfactory arrangements. Dr. Rubicon is a most eminent archaeologist. Carlos, you should be impressed to have a man of his stature come to Quintana Roo! Perhaps you will be pleased to receive positive international publicity instead of those unpleasant stories about revolutionary activities and illicit arms sales, eh?" Aguilar's voice carried a barely hidden threat. Barreio bristled, his skin darkening.

Scully looked over at Dr. Rubicon, who was flushed with excitement. Grinning, he paid little attention to the uniformed police chief.

"Agent Scully, Agent Mulder," he said, popping his head into her room. He swept his hand in a welcoming gesture to the man behind him. "Allow me to introduce Fernando Victorio Aguilar. He's the person I was, uh, trying to contact… a—what did you call yourself?—an expediter, yes, that's it, a man who can promptly arrange for helpers and guides and equipment to take us out to the site of Xitaclan. My daughter was indeed in touch with him, and he helped put together her party originally, though he hasn't seen her since she departed. He can take us out there."

"That should help our case," Scully said, then she turned with forced pleasantness to the police chief. "I believe Mr. Barreio here was about to offer us the maps and notes from his ongoing investigation, everything he has compiled so far about the missing team members." She raised her eyebrows. "Isn't that correct, Chief Barreio?"

The ruddy-faced man frowned, as if he had just remembered an important detail. "If you are about to mount an expedition, have you obtained the proper permits, the entrance passes, the work release forms? Have you paid your appropriate state fees?"

"I was just about to take care of all that," Fernando Aguilar interrupted. "Carlos, you know you can trust me." The man removed his floppy hat and looked from Scully to Mulder, back to Vladimir Rubicon. "In order to make certain portions of our expedition move more smoothly through political channels, we require clearances and taxes and fees. An unfortunate complication, but it cannot be helped."

"How much will all that cost?" Scully asked, immediately suspicious.

"It varies," Aguilar said, "but a thousand American dollars should allow us the complete freedom for our expedition to depart as early as tomorrow morning, eh?"

"Tomorrow! That's wonderful!" Rubicon said, rubbing his hands together in delight.

"A thousand dollars?" Mulder said. He looked over at her. "Is your per diem higher than mine, Scully?"

"The Federal Bureau of Investigation does not engage in bribery," Scully said, her voice firm.

Rubicon seemed exasperated and impatient. "Nonsense," he said to Scully, "you don't understand how things are done."

He untucked his shirt and withdrew his own money belt. Yanking out a wad of hundred-dollar bills, he counted out ten and stuffed them into Aguilar's outstretched palm. He looked back at the FBI agents. "Sometimes you have to make concessions, and I don't want to get into a bureaucratic head-butting contest for weeks while my Cassandra remains lost."

Aguilar nodded deeply, hiding a grin, as if he had just stumbled upon an unexpectedly easy mark. "It will be a pleasure doing business with you, Señor Rubicon," he said. He pocketed two of the hundred-dollar bills and extended the remaining eight to Barreio, who snatched them quickly, scowling at Mulder and Scully.

"That'll be enough for the standard government fees," he said. "I'll contact the office and see if it is possible to copy our case files for you by morning. Check at the hotel desk. I make no promises. I have such limited help in my offices." The police chief turned and marched off down the hall, turning the corner toward the elevators, where he deftly sidestepped another room-service waiter bearing drinks served inside hollowed pineapples and coconuts.

Vladimir Rubicon stood in the hall outside Scully's door, flushed with the urgency of his mood. Fernando Aguilar placed the spotted hat back on his head and extended a hand. "I'm very pleased to meet you, Señorita Scully." He nodded to Mulder. "We'll be seeing much more of each other in the coming days."

He released her hand and stepped back, bowing his head. "Be sure to get a good night's rest, and take the time to enjoy a relaxing bath. I assure you, your accommodations for the next few nights will be much less... comfortable."

10

Private villa of Xavier Salida, Quintana Roo
Thursday, 10:17 P.M.

The fire crackled in the hearth, burning hot as it consumed the aromatic wood, sending curls of perfumed smoke into the upstairs drawing room. Xavier Salida stood in front of the blaze, his hands clasped behind his back as he drew deeply of the bay and nutmeg scent, the peppery oils that made the smoke heady, almost a drug by itself.

He turned away from the warmth and went over to the thermostat on his wall, turning up the air conditioning so he could enjoy his fire, yet keep the room from getting unpleasantly warm. There weren't many things in life that one could enjoy both ways. But Salida had reached the point where he could do anything he wanted.

From the rack of brass-handled fireplace implements, he selected the cast-iron poker and jabbed the flaming wood, watching the sparks fly. He liked to play with fire.

Salida stepped back and strutted around the room with the poker as if it were a walking stick, practicing his moves, reveling in his personal grace—though newly acquired, he expected the grace would remain with him for the rest of his life. Education and culture were an investment, an intangible wealth that went beyond mere baubles and art objects.

Salida went over to the stereo system on the wall and casually flipped through his collection of phonograph records, LPs of the best classical music, performances memorable as well as pleasing to the discerning ear. He selected a symphony by the great Salieri, an obscure eighteenth-century composer. The man's very obscurity meant his works must be rare and therefore precious.

As the bold overlapping strains of violins overwhelmed the old album's scratchiness, Salida went over to the bottle on the table, twisted off the cork with his fingers, and poured himself another glass of the purplish red wine, a 1992 Merlot. It was well aged and smooth, he thought, not as young as some of the Cabernet Sauvignon he had in the wine cellar. He had been told this label was from one of the best California vineyards. He held up the glass, swirled it, and allowed the firelight to shine through its rich garnet color.

Salida stepped out to his open balcony, taking a deep breath of the moist night air. The hammock hung, suggesting thoughts of lazier days, relaxing afternoons… but this past week had been very difficult. A thousand stressful challenges, each one dealt with decisively.

As he gazed beyond where the lights shone, he saw the monolithic silhouette of the ancient Maya stela in the middle of his courtyard. Starlight trickled down on the prized monument, and he could make out the lumpy form of that damned male peacock perched on top.

A foolish peacock. Much like his rival, Pieter Grobe, a showy, blustering man who was ultimately insignificant… just an amusing piece of coloration.

Salida had attempted to get even with the Belgian expatriate, requiring revenge for Grobe's ill-advised tactic of shooting down one of Salida's private courier planes. Salida had demanded that his men eliminate one of Grobe's planes in retaliation, but that had not proved possible.

Grobe had tightened his own security procedures, allowing no vulnerabilities around his own aircraft—and so Salida had had no choice but to take an alternative vengeance. Not as full of finesse, but ultimately as satisfying: a large truck filled with fuel oil had "accidentally" exploded in the middle of one of Grobe's marijuana fields. The resulting fire and caustic smoke had damaged a great portion of the crop.

With the score evened again, Salida had no desire to escalate events into a full-scale war. He suspected that Grobe was just bored and needed to blow off pressure every once in a while. Done is done.

Now he could relax and enjoy life, culture, the finer things. As the symphonic strains of Salieri's first movement built to its crescendo, Xavier Salida walked back into his withdrawing room.

He took another sip of the wine, rolling the taste in his mouth, identifying the nuances he had been taught about. He sniffed the "bouquet," judging the "dryness," appreciating the "finish."

In private, however, Salida allowed himself to long for the days when he could sit back with his local compadres, drink too much tequila, laugh out loud, and sing raucous songs. That was in the past... he was beyond such things now. He had become a powerful man.

He paused to inspect his magnificent private collection of historical artifacts, pre-Colombian objects any museum would have been proud to own. But these items would never appear in any dusty display cases, because they belonged to him and him alone.

He saw the delicate, translucent green sculptures of jade, the writhing, other-worldly forms of the feathered serpent companions of Kukulkan, a small stone figure of the great god of wisdom himself. Salida collected pots and carvings from all Central American peoples, the Toltec, the Olmec, as well as the Maya, and later the Aztec. He made a point of glancing at the engraved label on each artifact, refreshing his memory to make sure that he recalled every name and every detail exactly. It wouldn't do to embarrass himself in polite conversation by not knowing the items in his own collection!

Finally, like a boy creeping forward at dawn on Christmas morning, Salida went over to his new prize, the amazing crystalline artifact Fernando Victorio Aguilar had brought to him from the ruins of Xitaclan. He already knew he must place this item in a protective glass case, displaying it but never allowing other visitors or any of the servants to touch it. It must be valuable

Setting his glass of wine next to the shimmering transparent box, Salida reached out with both hands, one on either side, gently touching its slick, cold surface with his manicured fingertips.

Because of all the distractions and headaches caused by Pieter Grobe, he had not been able to spare the time to admire his new prize for the past two days— but now he would reward himself. With Grobe appropriately punished, and the rest of Salida's operation running smoothly, now he could stare at the strange Maya box with a childlike sense of wonder. His fingers touched some of the finely detailed glyphs that had been etched into its diamond-hard surface. He touched one of the sliding squares, and it moved as if gliding on a pool of oil.

The relic hummed.

Startled, Salida drew away, felt the deep cold tingling on his fingertips. But then he bent over again, pressing his hands, feeling the faint vibrations within the arti-fact. The inner tremors seemed to be gaining strength, building in power.

Salida laughed in amazement. In the back of his head, somewhere beyond the range of his hearing, he sensed a high-pitched sound, a throbbing noise that eluded him as he tried to concentrate on it.

Outside, in the fenced-in kennels, his prized Dobermans set up a howl in unison, barking and baying. The peacocks in the courtyard squawked and shrieked.

Salida hurried over to the balcony and looked out. One of the guards had switched on the mercury lamp to spill white light out into the courtyard. Two other guards strode out with rifles leveled at the shadows. Salida scanned the area within his walled enclosure, expecting to see the flitting shadow of a jaguar or an ocelot, some nighttime predator that had dared to cross the fence for a meal of peacock. The dogs continued to bark—but Salida saw nothing.

"Silencio!" he hollered out into the night, and then turned back to the drawing room—astonished to see that the crystalline ancient box now glowed with a silvery light.

As he bent over the shimmering box, the humming turned into a clear vibration. The diamond-like walls throbbed and pulsed. The bone chilling cold had vanished from the oily surface, which now radiated a prickling warmth, a sunny richness that flowed through him like melting butter.

Salida pressed some of the glyphs, trying to stop the frenzied activity—but instead he saw the tiny jewel-like components inside the glass case whir to life.

It seemed to him more amazing to know that this artifact had been constructed by the ancient Maya at the dawn of history. They had used gears and primitive machinery to develop their calendars… but this device seemed amazingly sophisticated, even for modern construction, without any recognizable gears, levers, buttons….

At the core of the gadget, light began to grow, cold yet searingly bright… as if a pool of mercury had flared into incandescence.

Salida stepped back, now frightened and anxious. What had Aguilar given him? What had he done? How could he stop it?

Outside, the dogs and the peacocks set up such a racket, it sounded as if they were being flayed alive.

The light within the crystalline object became blinding, reaching an unimaginable peak. The last thing Salida could make out was his glass of wine rattling next to the artifact.

The dark red liquid rolled in a furious boil.

Then the light reached its critical point and leaped to another level. Its intensity increased a thousandfold. The heat and energy washed over Salida so rapidly he never had time to register the immense explosion... or even a second of pain.

11

Cancún
Friday, 8:05 A.M.

Gentle white clouds rode high against the sunshine, and the sea gleamed as turquoise as a Beverly Hills swimming pool. Tour groups flocked out of the hotels along the thin strip of land between the ocean and the lagoon, waiting in court-yards and traffic turnarounds to catch scheduled buses departing for the famous Maya ruins at Chichén Itzá, Tulum, Xcaret, and Xel-Há.

Marble fountains filled with Mexican coins sprayed next to the lobby courtyard of the Caribbean Shores Resort. A battered Jeep bearing three people approached, swerving around old taxicabs, vans, and the diesel-belching tour buses before it pulled up to the hotel entrance. The driver blared the horn, waved his hand, and honked again impatiently, offending the white-uniformed bellmen who stood in the open doorway. They scowled down at the Jeep, but the driver pulled closer to the curb, parked, and honked again, ignoring the stares from the staff.

Waiting just inside the lobby next to other tourists ready to go on day trips, Mulder grabbed his duffel and turned to Scully. "I'll bet that's our ride."

She set down her Styrofoam cup of coffee next to a sand-filled ashtray and picked up her own bag. "I was afraid of that."

Vladimir Rubicon followed with his backpack and his own duffel, flushed and eager. "I'm sure everyone else enjoys their vacation here in glitzy Cancún—but to me this just isn't, uh... isn't the Yucatán. Might as well be Honolulu."

Inside the Jeep, Scully recognized Fernando Victorio Aguilar by his floppy ocelot-skin cap and his long dark ponytail. Aguilar waved at them, flashing white teeth in a grin. "Buenos días, amigos!"

Mulder took Scully's bag and threw it with his own in the back, while Rubicon stuffed his personal equipment in the crowded compartment. Two dark-haired, brown-skinned young men rode in the vehicle with Aguilar, ready to help. Rubicon took the strangers in stride and crowded into the back seat. Mulder slid in beside him.

Aguilar patted the passenger seat for Scully. "For you, Señorita—beside me, where it is safer, eh?" He turned around, looking at Mulder and Rubicon. "Are you ready to be off? You are properly dressed, ready for the jungles?"

Rubicon fingered his thin goatee. "They're prepared enough," he said. Mulder leaned forward. "I even brought my hiking boots and bug repellent."

Scully looked over at her partner in the back seat. "Yes, the essentials."

The lanky "expediter" looked freshly shaved, his cheeks and chin glassy smooth. Scully could smell his aftershave. He rubbed his fingers along his face. "It will take many hours to get to where we must leave the roads and brave the jungle."

"And who are our new companions?" Mulder asked, gesturing to the other two squashed with him and Rubicon in the back of the Jeep.

"Helpers," Aguilar said. "One will drive the Jeep back, while the other will accompany us into the jungle. He's worked with me before on such expeditions."

"Only one helper?" Rubicon said, leaning forward. "I expected we'd require, uh, much more assistance, more supplies. I paid—"

Aguilar cut him off with a nonchalant wave. "I already have guides and workers waiting for us at the rendezvous point with supplies, Señor. No need to shuttle them all down to the end of the Yucatán."

Aguilar tugged the brim of his cap and shifted the Jeep into gear, roaring off and squealing around a lumbering tour bus that tried to pull out at the same time. Scully squeezed her eyes shut, but Aguilar honked the horn and wrestled the Jeep to the left, running two wheels onto the damp grass before he screeched around the bus and increased acceleration toward the main road.

Aguilar took the Jeep southwestward, toiling through the crowded hotel zone and following the coastal highway, whipping around curves, dodging buses, mopeds, bicycles ridden by careful but unhurried people.

They passed weed-overgrown ruins beside the road, small temples and eroded limestone pillars, some covered with illegible graffiti, none highlighted in any way, not even so much as a roadside marker. The jungle had swallowed them up. Scully found it amazing that artifacts a thousand years old weren't treated with more reverence.

The drive continued, with Aguilar paying more attention to Scully than to the road. He roared along like a madman or a professional, depending on how much credit she wanted to give him. Aguilar managed to cover as many miles in an hour as a scheduled tour bus would do in three.

At first they followed the coast, heading southwest on Mexico 307, passing the popular seaside ruins of Tulum, then continuing inland, past small, poor towns bearing names such as Chunyaxché, Uh-May, Limónes, and Cafetal filled with tiny white-washed homes, log shacks, gas stations, and supermarkets the size of Scully's kitchen.

Scully unfolded a tattered, grease-stained roadmap she found jammed between the dashboard and windshield. With a sinking heart, she saw that no roads, not even dirt tracks, marked the area where they were headed. She hoped it was a misprint, or an old map.

The low jungle sprawled out endlessly on either side of the highway. Women walked on the wide, powdered-limestone shoulder wearing brightly embroidered white cotton dresses, the traditional garment that Vladimir Rubicon identified as a *huipil*.

As they continued inland, the curves got sharper, and the flatlands gradually gave way to hills. Mulder pointed out small white crosses and fresh-cut flowers beside the road at certain points. He raised his voice to be heard above the wind rattling through the flimsy windows of the battered vehicle. "Mr. Aguilar, what are those for?" he said. "Religious sites? Roadside shrines?"

Aguilar laughed. "No, those mark locations where loved ones died in traffic mishaps."

"There seem to be quite a lot of them," Scully pointed out.

"Yes," Aguilar said with a snort, "most other drivers are quite inept."

"I can see that," Scully agreed, looking directly at him.

From the back Mulder sat forward . "We'd better take particular care around those two-shrine curves."

After eating an early lunch at a roadside cantina that was little more than a table and an awning, they set off again, driving at breakneck speed for two more hours. Scully found herself feeling queasy and roadsick, especially after the stuffed chiles she had eaten. The café's menu had been quite limited, though Mulder had enjoyed the fresh, thick tortillas and the chicken stew.

"How much farther?" Scully asked Aguilar in the middle of the afternoon. She eyed the thickening gray clouds.

He squinted through the windshield and flicked on the wipers to smear smashed bugs across his view. He peered intently, looking alongside the road, but remained silent for a long moment. "Right here," he finally said and slammed on the brakes.

Aguilar pulled off the side of the road onto the powdery white shoulder, where a little mud track emerged from the thick jungle. The Jeep slewed from one side to another, fishtailing across traffic. Behind them a bus blatted its horn and casually passed them in the opposite lane without bothering to look for oncoming vehicles.

Aguilar climbed out to stand beside the groaning vehicle, while Mulder popped the back door, stretching his legs. Scully emerged, drawing deep breaths of the humid air filled with the damp aromas of the surrounding rain forest.

Overhead, the morning's cottony clouds had metamorphosed into thicker cumulus clouds, the kind likely to become thunderheads before long. Scanning the low jungle they were about to enter, though, she wasn't sure if rainfall could even penetrate the thick vines, weeds, and undergrowth.

The other two passengers in the back seat climbed out the driver's side of the Jeep and opened the rear, hauling out Mulder and Scully's bags. They handed the backpack to Vladimir Rubicon, who bent over, massaging his stiff, bony knees. Mulder looked at the tall grass, thick vines, palms, creepers, an impenetrable mass of foliage. "You've got to be kidding," he said.

Fernando Aguilar laughed and then sniffed. He rubbed his cheeks, where stubble had already begun to bristle. "Well, amigo, if the Xitaclan ruins were right beside a four-lane highway, it wouldn't exactly be an untouched and unexploited archaeological site, eh?"

"He's got a point," Rubicon said.

As Aguilar spoke, a group of dark-skinned, dark-haired men suddenly appeared out of the jungle, as if from a cheap movie special effect. Scully saw a clear difference in these people from the Mexicans she had encountered in Cancún. They were shorter, not well nourished or well clothed: descendants of the ancient Maya, who lived far from the cities, no doubt in small, unmapped villages.

"Ah, here is the rest of our crew, ready to work," Aguilar said. He gestured for the other Indians to take the supplies and the backpacks, while Aguilar himself removed several canvas bags from the Jeep. "Our tents," he said.

Mulder stood with his hands on his hips, scrutinizing the jungle, sniffing the humid air. "It's not just a job, Scully—it's an adventure." Mosquitoes flew around his face.

When the Jeep was completely empty, Aguilar pounded on the hood to signal that he was ready for the replacement driver to go. One of the dark-haired young men scrambled into the driver's seat without saying a word. He simply grabbed the shift lever and roared off, swerving the Jeep back onto the road without pausing to look for traffic. With a belch of oily exhaust, he proceeded down the highway.

"Let us be off, amigos," Aguilar said. "Onward, to adventure!"

Scully took a deep breath and adjusted the laces on her boots. Together, the group plunged into the jungle.

Slogging through the underbrush, fighting with both hands against the branches and weeds and creepers and vines, Scully soon longed to be back in the Jeep, no matter how bad Fernando Aguilar's driving.

The Indians ahead of them were a flurry of activity, hacking away the most obtrusive debris with stained machetes, grunting with the effort but making no complaint. Beautiful hibiscus and other tropical flowers splashed rainbow colors on either side of the path. Water stood in puddles on the rocky ground. Thin mahogany trees with twisted trunks and smooth bark protruded in every direction, swallowed by thorny shrubs and flowering weeds. Ferns brushed Scully's legs, sprinkling droplets of water from frequent rainstorms.

They paused to rest beside a tall gray-barked "chewing gum," or chicle tree, its trunk slashed and scarred from the sap the locals had harvested over the years. Scully noticed that their helpers chewed diligently on wads of chicle sap. Aguilar allowed them to stop for only a few minutes, then they trudged on, wielding their machetes.

Before long Scully was hot and sweaty and miserable. She had half a mind to write the manufacturer of their commercial bug repellent to complain about its ineffectiveness. It had been late afternoon before they even started on the path, which allowed them no more than four hours of hiking before they would have to stop and set up camp.

Scully asked about it, and Aguilar simply laughed. He patted her on the back, and his touch made her uncomfortable. "I am trying to ease you into the long march, Señorita," he said. "It would be impossible to reach Xitaclan within a day, so this way we take the drive and several hours walk, then we camp. After a good night's sleep, we press on tomorrow, refreshed and ready to conquer the distance, eh? By midafternoon on the next day, we should reach the ruins. From there, perhaps, you will find your missing friends. Maybe their radio is just broken."

"Maybe," Scully said doubtfully.

The heat was incredible, the air moist and thick like a steam room. Her hair hung in stringy wet strands, clinging to the sides of her face. Dirt and smashed bugs covered her skin.

Overhead, howler monkeys chattered and shrieked, charging through the treetops. They leaped from branch to branch, creating an incredible chaos. Parrots screamed rough-throated calls, while jewel-toned hummingbirds flitted silently in front of her eyes. But Scully concentrated only on plodding along, avoiding the murky puddles and limestone outcroppings, stomping down the undergrowth.

"I'll make you a deal, Scully," Mulder said, wiping perspiration from his forehead. He looked as miserable as she did. "I'll be Stanley and you be Livingstone, okay?"

Vladimir Rubicon trooped along without complaining. "We've only traveled two hours off the road," he said, "and look where we are! See how easily there could be immense ruins yet undiscovered in the Yucatán? Once the people abandoned them, the jungle rapidly covered them up—and they live only in, uh, local legends."

"But Xitaclan was special?" Mulder asked. "More than just another set of ruins?"

Rubicon drew a deep breath and paused to lean against a mahogany tree. "My Cassandra thought so. It existed for a long time, from pre-Golden Age through the Toltec influence and later human sacrifices."

Through her own misery and weariness and sticky perspiration, Scully looked in the archaeologist's intense blue eyes—to her surprise she saw that the old man did not look at all uncomfortable in the jungle. He seemed more alive and animated than she had seen him since the first day back in the pre-Colombian exhibit in Washington, D.C. Doing field work, the old archaeologist seemed in his element, on his way to rescue his daughter and also to explore uncatalogued Maya ruins.

When the shadows grew long in the jungle, Aguilar's native workers proved their worth yet again. They labored quietly and vigorously to set up camp, selecting a low clearing near a spring. They hacked away shrubs and weeds to open a sleeping space, then set up the tents where Mulder, Scully, Rubicon, and Aguilar would spend the night, while they themselves found other places to camp, presumably in the trees nearby. Scully watched the Indians moving with precision, using few words, as if they had done the task many times before.

Rubicon pressed Aguilar for more information about when he had accompanied Cassandra and her team out to the ruins, two weeks earlier.

"Yes!" the guide said. "I brought them out here—but because they intended to stay for many weeks doing their excavating, I left and went back to Cancún. I am a civilized man, eh? I have work to do."

"But she was fine when you left her?" Rubicon asked again.

"Ah, yes," Aguilar said, his eyes shining. "More than fine. She took great pleasure in encountering the ruins. She seemed very excited."

"I look forward to seeing them myself," Rubicon said.

"Day after tomorrow," Aguilar answered, nodding enthusiastically.

They sat down on fallen trees and rocks to eat a cold dinner of rolled tortillas, chunks of cheese, and fresh unidentifiable fruit the native guides had harvested out in the jungle. Scully drank from her canteen and ate her meal, slowly relishing the taste, happy for the opportunity just to sit down.

Mulder shooed gnats away from his red banana. He spoke to Scully around a mouthful of fruit. "Quite a bit different from last night's four-star restaurant." He stood up and went into her tent, where the bags had been stowed, rustling around in the packs and clothes.

Scully finished her own meal and sat back, drawing a deep breath. Her legs throbbed with weariness from fighting her way along each step of the path.

Mulder came out of the tent, holding something behind his back. "When I was doing preliminary research on this case, I remembered the story about Tlazolteotl." He glanced at the old archaeologist. "Am I pronouncing it correctly? Sounds like I'm swallowing a turtle."

Rubicon laughed. "Ah, the goddess of guilty loves."

"Yeah, that's the one," Mulder said. "A guy named Jappan wanted to become a favorite of the gods—sort of a midlife crisis. So he left his loving wife and all his possessions to become a hermit. He climbed a high rock in the desert, spending all his time at religious devotions." Mulder looked around at the jungle. "Though where he found a desert around here, I'm not sure.

"Naturally, the gods couldn't turn down a challenge like that, so they tempted him with beautiful women—but he refused to yield. Then Tlazolteotl, the goddess of guilty loves, appeared to him as a real knockout. She said she was so impressed with Jappan's virtue that she just wanted to console him. She talked him into coming down from his rock, whereupon she successfully seduced him—much to the delight of the other gods, who had been just waiting for him to slip up.

"The gods punished Jappan for his indiscretion by changing him into a scorpion. From shame at his failure, Jappan hid under the stone where he had fallen from grace. But the gods wanted to rub it in, so they brought Jappan's wife to the stone, told her everything about his downfall, and turned her into a scorpion, too."

He smiled wistfully at Scully, still hiding something behind his back. "But it's a romantic story after all. Jappan's wife, as a scorpion, ran under the rock to join her husband, where they had lots of little baby scorpions."

Vladimir Rubicon looked up at him, smiling. "Wonderful, Agent Mulder. You should, uh, volunteer to work at the museum, just like I do."

Scully shifted her position on the fallen tree, then brushed crumbs from her khaki vest. "Interesting, Mulder—but why tell that story now?"

He brought his hand from behind his back, holding out the ugly smashed remnants of an immense black scorpion, its many-jointed legs dangling in jagged directions. "Because I found this under your pillow."

12

Yucatán jungle
Saturday, early morning, exact time unknown

As they prepared to break camp in the morning, Mulder noticed that his watch had stopped. His first automatic thought was that sometime in the night their group had experienced an unexplained alien encounter. Then he realized that the time stoppage probably had more to do with the jungle muck than any extraterrestrial phenomena.

Shucking his outer layer of wet and dirty clothes, he pulled on another set that would get just as filthy during the day's trek. Mulder decided to wear his New York Knicks tee-shirt, the one with the torn sleeve, since it didn't matter if it stained or tattered further.

Scully emerged from her tent, slapping at bug bites, her eyes droopy and half-closed from too little sleep.

"Good morning, Sunshine," Mulder said.

"I'm considering being reassigned to the Records Section,"she said, yawning and stretching. "At least those people have a clean, dry office and a vending machine down the hall."

She took a drink from her canteen, then dribbled water in the palm of her hand, splashing it on her face, rubbing it across her eyes. She blinked until her eyes cleared up, then waved away a cloud of mosquitoes. "I never truly appreciated the wonders of a bug-free work environment."

Fernando Aguilar stood by a tree, staring into a small shaving mirror. He held a straight razor in one hand. His ocelot-skin cap dangled from a broken branch within arm's reach. He turned around to grin at them, his cheeks soaped up. "Buenos días, amigos," he said, then went back to stroking his cheeks with the blade, his eyes half closed with pleasure. "Nothing like a good shave in the morning to make one feel clean and ready for the day, eh?"

He flicked soapy stubble off the razor's end with the precision of a professional knife thrower, splattering a white pattern across the ferns. "A secret, Señor Mulder: I mix my soap with bug repellent. It seems to help."

"Maybe I'll try that," Mulder said, rubbing the stubble on his chin. "Which way to the nearest shower?"

Aguilar laughed, a loud, thin sound that reminded Mulder of the squabbling cries of howler monkeys that had kept him awake through the night.

The local workers took down the camp, rolling up clothes and supplies into duffel bags, knocking down the tents and folding them into compact packages. They moved with remarkable speed, packed up and ready to go in no time.

Vladimir Rubicon bustled about, pacing impatiently as he munched from a small bag of raisins. "Shouldn't we be off soon?" Mulder saw bloodshot patterns around the old archaeologist's bright blue eyes and knew that Rubicon hadn't slept well, though he was apparently accustomed to such conditions.

Aguilar finished shaving and wiped his now-glistening face with a bandanna, which he tucked into his pocket. He spun the ocelot-skin cap on one finger, showing off, then settled it firmly on his head. "You are right, Señor Rubicon—we should be off to find your daughter. It's a long walk yet, but if we keep up a good pace, we can reach Xitaclan before nightfall tomorrow."

They set off again through the jungle. The quiet and solemn locals took the lead, hacking with their machetes, with Aguilar right behind to guide them.

A flock of butterflies, a cloud of bright color and fluttering wings, burst from a clear pool beside a fallen tree. They looked like a spray of jewels flashing into the air, as bright as the numerous brilliant orchids that dotted the trees around them.

Snakes dangled from branches, looking at them with cold eyes. Mulder wished he had taken more time to study the poisonous species in Central America. For safety reasons, he chose to avoid all the snakes.

They had been on their way for no more than an hour before rain began to sheet down, warm and oddly oily. Rivulets trickled and pattered like streams from the scooped banana leaves, washing away spiders, insects, and caterpillars from above. The wet air seemed ready to burst with its newly released lush scents.

Aguilar pinched the brim of his spotted hat so the water ran off in a spout. His wet ponytail dangled like a limp rag between his shoulder blades. He flashed a grin at Mulder. "You asked for the showers, Señor. It seems we have found them, eh?"

Wet leaves, moss, and rotted vegetation clung to them. Mulder looked at Scully and Rubicon, whose clothes were spattered with green streaks, brown smears of mud, and clinging yellowed fern leaves. "We've certainly managed to camouflage ourselves," he said.

"Is that what we were trying to do?" Scully answered, brushing her khaki pants. Ever-present mosquitoes swarmed around her face.

"I certainly wouldn't be inspired to build towering temples and pyramids in an environment like this," Mulder said. "It's amazing to me that the Maya could have created such an enormous civilization here."

"At least the temples would have been dry inside," Scully said, flinging water from her hair.

Rubicon's face showed a dreamy look. "Human ingenuity always surprises us when we look back through history. It would be so wonderful just to have five minutes in the past to ask, 'Why did you do this?' But we have to make do with tiny clues. An archaeologist must be like a detective—uh, an FBI agent of the past, to unravel mysteries where the suspects and the victims turned to dust a thousand years before any of us were born."

"I was impressed with the scientific and astronomical achievements the Maya made," Mulder said, "though some people think their civilization may have had some help."

"Help?" Rubicon asked, distractedly pushing a leafy frond away from his face. "Uh, what kind of help do you mean?"

Mulder took a deep breath. "According to Maya legend, their gods told them the Earth was round—quite an observation from a primitive people. They apparently knew of the planets Uranus and Neptune, which weren't discovered by Western astronomers until around the nineteenth century. Must have had great eyesight, considering they had no telescopes.

"The Maya also determined the Earth's year to within *one five-thousandth* of its actual value, and they knew the exact length of the Venusian year. They calculated other astronomical cycles out to a span of about sixty-four million years."

"Yes, the Maya were fascinated by time," Rubicon said, not rising to the bait. "Obsessed with it."

"Mulder," Scully said, "you're not going to suggest—"

He swatted away a biting fly. "If you look at some of their carvings, Scully, you'll see figures that are unmistakable—a towering form sitting in what has to be a control chair, just like an astronaut in the shuttle cockpit. Fire and smoke trail from the vehicle."

Amused, Rubicon countered with a story of his own. "Ah, yes. 'Chariots of the Gods.' Interesting speculations. I'm required to know all such tales and legends. Some of the stories are, uh, quite amazing. This is one of my favorites—you know that Quetzalcoatl, or Kukulkan as the Maya called him, was the god of knowledge and wisdom?"

"Yes," Mulder said, "he supposedly came down from the stars."

"Uh, supposedly," Rubicon said. "Now, Kukulkan's enemy was Tezcatlipoca, whose mission in life was to sow discord." Rubicon slipped his glasses on his nose, though they were perfectly useless in the jungle rain. It seemed to be a habit of his, a required action for the telling of a story.

"Tezcatlipoca came to an important festival disguised as a handsome man and called attention to himself by dancing and singing a magic song. The people were so captivated that a multitude began imitating his dance—uh, sort of like the Pied Piper. He led them all onto a bridge, which collapsed under their weight. Many people were hurled into the river far below, where they were changed into stones."

Rubicon grinned. "In another city Tezcatlipoca appeared with a puppet magically dancing on his hand. In their wonder to see this miracle, the people crowded so close that many of them suffocated. Then, pretending to be dejected at the pain and grief he had caused, Tezcatlipoca insisted that the people should stone him to death because of the harm he had done. So they did.

"But as Tezcatlipoca's corpse rotted, it gave off such a dreadful stench that many died from smelling it. At last, in sort of a commando mission, a series of brave heroes, one after another, succeeded in dragging the body out of town, like a relay race with a stinking cadaver, until finally their city was free of the pestilence."

They continued to slog along through the jungle. Rubicon shrugged his bony shoulders. "They're all just legends anyway," he said. "It's up to us to listen to the stories and learn what we can from them. I'm not going to tell you which to believe."

"Everybody else seems to," Mulder said quietly, but he did not bring up the subject of ancient astronauts again that day.

13

The Pentagon, Arlington, Virginia
Saturday, 1:03 P.M.

Striding down the corridor of the East Wing of the Pentagon, Major Willis Jakes fell into his typical routine of spotting landmarks, memorizing the route so he could trace his path back under any circumstances.

Normally he would have noted a broken tree, a rock outcropping, or a gully in the barren highlands of Afghanistan, tromping through the fever-infested swamps of Southeast Asia, slipping into Kurdish territory in the northern mountains of Iran. Now, though, instead of wearing a camouflage outfit or a survival suit bristling with small weapons and resources, Major Jakes sported his full military dress uniform, neatly pressed and smelling of laundry detergent.

Despite the amenities of civilization, he felt less comfortable this way.

The halls of the Pentagon provided as difficult a challenge as any highland wilderness, though, because each corridor in the labyrinthine headquarters was symmetric and unmemorable. The giant building's geometric shape made it easy to become disoriented and lost. One could emerge from a familiar-looking doorway out to a parking lot… only to find oneself on the wrong side of the immense fortress.

But Major Jakes did not find it an insurmountable tactical obstacle. He looked at the succession of office doors, most of them closed, the interior lights shut off. On Saturday the Pentagon offices closed down, the civil servants and military personnel sent home for their routine weekend activities. Normal civilians worked their regular forty-hour weeks, filling out the appropriate forms, passing them from office to office for the appropriate stamps, signatures, and file copies.

But for a career officer like Major Willis Jakes, the civilian timeclock meant nothing. He did not punch in or punch out when he went to work. His services were available on demand, all day long, all year long, whenever duty might call. He took his vacation and his relaxation time when circumstances permitted. He would have had it no other way.

The fact that he had been called here on a Saturday for a high-level briefing meant that an important mission must be in the works. Before long, Jakes would find himself in some other far-flung corner of the world, performing another series of tasks clearly defined by his superiors. Serving rules he had sworn by, the major unquestioningly took actions his country would almost certainly deny.

Jakes was tall and lean, clean-shaven, his skin the color of mahogany from deep Egyptian blood. His features were angular and Semitic, never rounded and soft.

Jakes followed the office numbers to the end of the corridor and turned left, passing door after door until he reached another darkened room, nondescript, closed—apparently as vacant as the other rooms. He did not hesitate, did not double-check the number. He knew he was right.

He precisely rapped three times on the wire-reinforced glass window. The name on the door said "A. G. Pym, Narratives and Records." In the regular day-to-day activities of the Pentagon, Major Jakes doubted other workers ever called to visit the office of Mr. Pym.

The door opened from inside, and a man in a dark suit stood back in the shadows. Jakes stepped into the dim room. His expression remained stony, emotionless—but his mind spun at hyperspeed, seeing details, sensing options, scanning for threats.

"Identify yourself," the suited man said, his voice disembodied in the shadows.

"Major Willis Jakes," he answered.

"Yes, Major," the shadowy man answered, remaining out of sight. He extended his hand, holding a silver key. "Use this to unlock that door in the rear of the office," he said. "Take the key and close the door behind you. It will lock by itself. The others are waiting for you. The briefing is about to begin."

Major Jakes didn't thank him, simply followed the instructions, opening the back door to find a half-lit conference room. Banks of fluorescent lights alternately flickered white or remained dark. At one end of the wall hung a white projection screen.

Three men dressed in suits and ties sat in chairs, while another man fiddled with the carousel of a slide projector. Major Jakes had never seen any of the men before, nor did he expect ever to see them again.

A man in a charcoal-gray suit with wire-rimmed glasses said, "Welcome, Major Jakes. Right on time. Would you care for some coffee?" He gestured to an urn in the back of the room.

"No, sir," Jakes said.

Another man with a maroon tie and a jowly face said, "We have some Danishes, if you'd like those."

"No, thank you," Jakes answered the man.

"Okay, we're ready, then." A young man fiddled with the projector. A glare of yellow-gold light splashed in a square across the screen, unfocused.

While curiosity was not part of his duty, sharp attention to details and an unfailing memory remained crucial to his work.

The last man, who had steel-gray hair and a white dress shirt, leaned back in his chair, rumpling the brown suit jacket draped behind him. "Show the first slide," he said.

"Major Jakes, please pay attention," said the man with the maroon tie. "All of these details may be important."

The slide-projector operator focused quickly to show a satellite image of a dense jungle, in the middle of which a circular area had been absolutely flattened, a crater excavated with almost perfect symmetry. The ground around it looked like slag, glassy and molten, as if someone had stubbed out a gigantic cigarette there.

"This used to be a private ranch in Mexico. Do you have any idea what might have caused this, Major Jakes?" the man in the charcoal suit asked.

"A daisy cutter?" Jakes suggested, citing one of the fragmentation bombs used to knock down trees in the jungles for the purpose of clearing helicopter landing pads. "Or a napalm burst?"

"Neither," said the man with steel-gray hair. "The scale is half a kilometer in diameter. Our seismic sensors revealed a sharp pulse, and our distant radiation detectors pinpointed a significant rise in residual radioactivity."

Major Jakes perked up. "Are you suggesting this is the result of a small nuclear strike?"

"We can think of no other explanation," the second man said, straightening his maroon tie. "A tactical nuclear device, such as an atomic artillery shell, could provide such a precise yield. This type of ordnance was recently developed by our nation and, we presume, by the Soviets, in the final years of the Cold War."

"But who could have used such a weapon in Central America, sir? What would have been the provocation?"

The man with steel-gray hair, who seemed to be the leader of the meeting, laced his fingers behind his head and leaned back against his suit jacket. "There is no small amount of political turmoil in this portion of the Yucatán. We know of numerous terrorist acts, minor squabbles with a small group of militant separatists—but we feel that an action such as this would be beyond their meager capabilities. There are also many rival drug lords in the area whose tactic of choice has been to eliminate their rivals through the use of assassination—car bombs and the like."

"This is no car bomb, sir," Major Jakes pointed out.

"Indeed not," said the man in the charcoal suit. "Next slide, please."

The slide-projector operator clicked to a higher-resolution image that showed the trees knocked down, the edge of the crater almost perfectly circular, as if a fireball had arisen so quickly that it vaporized the forest, turned the ground to glass, and then faded before the surrounding forest fires could propagate.

"Our working assumption is that at least one and possibly many more of these tactical nuclear warheads have trickled out following the collapse of the former Soviet Union. In the chaos of the breakup of the socialist republics, many of the sovereign states laid claim to the nuclear stockpiles left behind by the central Communist government. Many of those warheads have been... misplaced. That ordnance has been on the open market for international thugs and terrorists. It's the only thing we know of that could have come close to that kind of high-energy devastation. Such a device could have come from Cuba, for instance, across the Caribbean Sea to the Yucatán Peninsula, and from there to the drug lords in this area of Mexico."

"So, you suspect this may only be the first strike. There could be more."

"It's a possibility," said the man with steel-gray hair. "If other such weapons exist."

The next slide displayed a map of the Yucatán showing the states of Quintana Roo, Yucatán, and Campeche, as well as the small Central American countries of Belize, Honduras, El Salvador, and Guatemala.

"We need you to take a team in and find the source of these weapons, then confiscate or destroy them. We cannot allow nuclear terrorists to run free, even if they are just murdering each other."

The man with the maroon tie smiled, and his jowls jiggled. "It sets a bad example."

"My usual commandos?" Jakes said.

"Whatever you desire is at your disposal, Major Jakes," said the man with steel-gray hair. "We know our investment in your efforts will be worth every penny."

"Or every peso," said the slide-projector operator.

The others ignored the joke.

"I presume this will be a covert insertion, a search and destroy mission? But how am I to locate the target? What intelligence do we have that there are additional tactical warheads?"

"We have a strong suspicion," said the man in the charcoal suit. "There seems to be a military base located in one of the more isolated portions of the Yucatán. We've picked up a powerful transmission, encoded with an encryption scheme unlike any we have ever seen before. The signal suddenly appeared a little more than a week ago, so powerful it could not be hidden. We suspect the transmitter indicates a secret military base there."

"Does the target correspond to any known location?" Major Jakes said, leaning forward, drinking in the image on the screen.

The slide-projector operator clicked to the next image—a high-resolution satellite photograph with the lines and contours of a map overlaid upon it.

"It is apparently the site of isolated Mayan ruins. When we cross-referenced our records with those of the State Department, we found that a team of American archaeologists disappeared there at about the same time the signal began, and only a few days before this detonation occurred.

"We suspect our enemies have taken over the ruins as their own secret military base. As no ransom demands or hostage threats have been forthcoming, the status of our American citizens remains unknown… and, for the purposes of your mission, low priority."

"I understand," Major Jakes said. He squinted to see the site on the map. He saw nothing that even remotely resembled a road anywhere in the vicinity.

The slide-projector operator twisted the focusing ring around the lens to bring the photo into crystal clarity.

"Xitaclan," Major Jakes muttered, reading the label.

At least it sounded better than the cold mountains of Afghanistan.

14

Xitaclan ruins
Sunday, 4:23 P.M.

The diligent trailblazers began to mutter quickly and quietly among themselves in their own language, excited or uneasy—Scully couldn't tell which. For the past two days her entire energy had been focused on taking step after step, proceeding deeper into the jungle… farther from civilization, comfort, and safety.

Fernando Aguilar picked up his pace. "Come quickly, amigos," he said and spread ferns aside. He leaned against a tall ceiba tree and gestured. "Behold— Xitaclan!"

Sweaty and exhausted, Mulder stood beside Scully, his eyes suddenly bright with interest. Vladimir Rubicon sprang forward with renewed energy, as if he had been jump-started.

Catching her breath, Scully shaded her eyes and looked out at the ancient, decaying city that might have cost the lives of Cassandra Rubicon and her team. Gray clouds hung in the sky, casting the site in a cool gloom, but the broken edifices still towered like hulking shapes in a storm.

The shadow of the vast ancient city could be easily seen, like an afterimage on the eyes. In the center of a broad plaza, spindly trees pushed up through cracks in the flagstones. A towering, stair-stepped pyramid dominated the abandoned metropolis, overgrown with vines. Smaller shrines and elaborately decorated stelae lay collapsed, unable to withstand time and natural forces. Intricately carved glyphs poked out from the moss and vines.

"This is astounding," Rubicon said, pushing past Fernando Aguilar. He stepped out into the broad plaza, scratching his yellow-white goatee. "Look at the size of the place. Imagine the number of people who came here." He turned to look at Scully, then Mulder, desperate to explain.

"Maya slash-and-burn agriculture never could have supported a large population center like this. Most major cities such as Tikal or Chichén Itzá were probably inhabited only during, uh, religious ceremonies, ball games, and seasonal sacrifices. For the rest of the year, the cities were abandoned, left to the jungle until it was time for the next festival."

"Sounds like an Olympic village," Mulder said. He and Scully came out to stand next to the old archaeologist, while the native guides hung back, talking nervously with Aguilar in some Indian dialect.

"You said ball games, Dr. Rubicon?" Scully asked. "You mean they had spectator sports?"

"There, I believe, was their stadium." He gestured across the clearing at a broad sunken space walled in with carved bricks. "The Maya played, uh, sort of a cross between soccer and basketball. They hit a hard rubber ball with their hips, thighs, and shoulders—they were not allowed to touch it with their hands. The object was to knock it through an upright stone ring on the wall."

"Cheerleaders, pennants, and everything," Mulder said.

"The losers of the tournament were usually sacrificed to the gods," Rubicon continued, "their heads cut off, their hearts cut out, their blood spilled on the ground."

"I suppose you couldn't say it was an honor just to make the playoffs," Mulder said.

A deeply troubled look crossed Rubicon's face as he walked forward, turning from side to side. He tugged at his grimy goatee, leaving a mud-streaked finger-print across his chin. "I don't see much sign of Cassandra and her team here, no ambitious excavation work." He looked around, but the jungle seemed very vast, very oppressive. "I suppose I should give up hope that her problem was some-thing so innocuous as a broken radio transmitter."

Scully indicated where the trees and underbrush had been hacked away. Piles of discarded branches and uprooted creepers lay in a mound half burned, as if some of the missing team had tried to make a bonfire to get rid of the debris… or to send some kind of desperate signal.

"They were here not long ago," she pointed out. "I would imagine all scars of their work would be obliterated and swallowed up by new growth within a month."

Aguilar said, grinning at them, "Perhaps they got lost in the jungle. Maybe jaguars ate them, eh?"

"You're not being helpful," Scully chided him.

"Cassandra's team would have been more careful than that," Rubicon said, as if trying to convince himself. "Unlike the old days of amateur diggers coming on a lark, professional archaeologists must proceed with caution, prying up every stone, uncovering the fine details."

He blinked his blue eyes, staring at the weathered stone structures. "Some of the worst amateurs thought they were doing good for history. They came to the old temples at the turn of the century, shoveled away the fallen blocks from walls, and dumped all the discarded potsherds and glyph stones down into mounds of rubble-things we now call GOK piles, for God Only Knows… because God only knows what's in them."

They stepped cautiously, tiptoeing and whispering, as if afraid they might offend the ancient ghosts of Xitaclan. The limestone paving bricks formed a once-level surface to the plaza, but now the flagstones had been buckled and hummocked by protruding roots.

Rubicon said, his voice hoarse and husky, "I can imagine why Cassandra was so excited here. This is an archaeologist's dream come true—all the stages in Maya history. Everything we see is a new discovery. Every place we visit, every new glyph we find is something never before catalogued. Any one relic could be the long-awaited Rosetta stone for Maya writing. It could be the secret to why this great people abandoned their cities and vanished centuries ago… uh, so long as other people don't ransack it for souvenirs before the scientific teams finish their work."

With her imagination Scully erased the green tufts of the lush overgrowth. Few outsiders had ever seen this place or known of its existence. "Xitaclan must have been a breathtaking spot."

Standing like gateposts, two impressive stelae displayed rows of incomprehensible Mayan writing, calendrical symbols; a great coiled snake bristling with feathers, wrapped around each obelisk. She recalled the feathered serpent symbol on the jade artifact Mulder had shown her.

"Is that supposed to be Kukulkan?" Scully said, indicating the sculpture. "The feathered serpent?"

Rubicon studied the stelae, slipping his half-glasses on his nose while the chain dangled on his neck. "Yes, and very vividly rendered, too. This one seems larger and more fearsome—as realistic as some of those jaguar statues on exhibit back in my museum. Uh, quite unlike the stylized glyphs and symbolic drawings we normally see on Maya stelae. Most interesting."

"Almost as if the sculpture was drawn from life," Mulder suggested. Scully gave him a look, and he offered a faint smile in return.

"The afternoon light is already fading," Aguilar said. "Perhaps we should make a quick inspection of the site and then set up our camp, eh? Tomorrow you can begin your real work."

"Yes, that's a good idea," Rubicon admitted. He seemed torn between his dejection at not finding his daughter there waiting for him... and his other goal of studying this marvelous uncatalogued site.

"It is quite a treat to see a place like this before it is defaced by tourists. The most famous ruins have been corrupted by thousands of visitors who know nothing about history and come there only because a colorful brochure tells them to." He placed his hands on his hips. "Once a new site is opened up, somebody usually manages to destroy it before long."

The four of them went through the plaza alongside the ball court, and then skirted the spectacular central pyramid. The underbrush had been cleared away from two sides, and Scully spotted a narrow entrance passage at the ziggurat's bottom level that had been forced open—a doorway leading into the dark catacombs of the ancient monolithic structure.

"Looks like someone went exploring," Scully said.

Mulder went ahead of them, around the path at the base of the pyramid, and then called for them to come. She found him standing at the rim of a circular well at least thirty feet across that plunged down into the limestone as if it had been drilled there by a giant rig.

"A cenote," Rubicon said. "A sacred well. It's a very deep limestone sinkhole. They're, uh, scattered all over the Yucatán Peninsula. Perhaps that explains one reason why Xitaclan was built at this location."

Scully stepped up to a crumbling platform that must have been like a gang-plank over the edge of the deep hole. They stood at the edge, and Scully peered over to see a mirror-smooth pool of murky green water. The depths seemed fathomless. Stained limestone outcroppings ridged the cenote walls like the turns of a screw. Mulder tossed a pebble into the water, watching the ripples spread out like shock waves.

"These natural sinkholes were considered to be sacred wells, water from the gods rising from the earth," Rubicon said. "You can be sure this one contains a treasure trove of relics and bones."

"Bones?" Scully asked. "From people that fell in?"

"Uh, were thrown in," Rubicon said. "The cenotes were sacrificial wells. Perhaps they would club the victims to death, or just tie them up and weight them down so the bodies would sink.

"Other times, for special sacrifices, the victim was chosen as much as a year in advance. He led a life of pleasures and indulgence, food and women and fine clothes—until the day when he was drugged and led to the edge of the cenote, then thrown into the sacred waters."

"I thought the Maya were primarily a peaceful people," Scully said.

"That's an old belief, a false story promulgated by an archaeologist who admired the Maya beyond all common sense—and so he slanted his findings to downplay the bloodshed evident in the writings and carvings."

"An archaeological spin doctor," Mulder said.

"The Maya culture was quite violent, shedding a great deal of blood, especially in later periods, due to Toltec influences. They considered it beautiful to scarify themselves, to hack off fingers and toes in self-mutilation ceremonies.

"In fact, the most bloodthirsty cult belonged to the god Tlaloc, whose priests would prepare for great festivals by approaching mothers to buy their young children. At a great ceremony the children were boiled alive, then eaten with great pomp and splendor. The priests took special delight if the infants cried or wailed while they were tortured to death, uh, because they thought the tears promised a year of plentiful rain."

Scully shuddered as she stood on the edge of the sinkhole, looking down into the murky cenote, thinking of all the secrets the bottom of that deep, dark well might hold.

"I'm sure nobody practices that religion anymore, though," Rubicon said, as if that might comfort her. He brushed his hands on his pants. "There's nothing you need to worry about. I'm sure it has nothing to do with all those missing-person rumors... or Cassandra."

Scully nodded noncommittally. Yes, here they were, isolated, two days from the nearest major road, at an abandoned site of ancient ruins where the Maya had performed countless blood sacrifices. A place where an entire team of American archaeologists recently disappeared....

Of course, she thought. She had nothing to worry about.

15

Xitaclan ruins
Sunday, 6:38 P.M.

Standing near the broken-brick sacrificial platform at the edge of the limestone sinkhole, Mulder stared downward, feeling the depths beckon him. The air smelled sour and mildewy, hinting of decay. He wondered what secrets lay beneath the murky waters, how deep the well went, how many skeletons it held in its gullet.

A tingle traveled up his spine, a brooding uneasiness—but he could not pinpoint its source. The colored rays of the setting sun and the dim amber light cast long shadows. Mulder thought he saw dark shapes swirling like oil in the cenote, and he felt a slight tremble beneath his feet... a vibration as if from deeply buried engines, generators entombed beneath the earth. He thought of H. G. Wells's novel, *The Time Machine*, the evil Morlocks laboring in subterranean tunnels, working their machines... hungry for the flesh of surface dwellers.

The water in the cenote began to stir and froth. Suddenly large bubbles belched to the surface, each as wide as a barrel, spewing gas from the depths.

"What's going on?" Scully said.

Mulder backed away from the rough edge as the vibration grew stronger beneath his feet. A wave of stench struck him, sour and sulfurous like a thousand rotten eggs made into a giant omelet. He covered his nose, choking. Scully, who was accustomed to smelling cadavers and decay under even the most horrendous autopsy circumstances, wrinkled her nose and gasped.

"What a stink!" Fernando Aguilar said.

"Maybe it's the legendary corpse of Tezcatlipoca," Vladimir Rubicon suggested, unbothered by the event. "That's a stench bad enough to kill off half the population."

Scully took a cautious sniff and shook her head. "No, that's sulfur—sulfur dioxide, I think. It's a volcanic gas."

"Maybe we should talk about this a little farther from the edge," Mulder said.

The four of them hurried back around to the front of the large pyramid. "My knees are still shaking," Scully said. "Wait, that's not my knees—it's the ground. It hasn't stopped."

Mulder saw the trees swaying, the ground jumping and bucking. In the back of his skull, in the rumbling subsonic range below his ability to hear, he experienced a loud tremor… growing in power as a deep subsurface event gained strength.

Aguilar's hand-picked Indian guides stood next to the half-erected tents, talking quickly among themselves. One stocky man fled into the forest, shouting back at the others.

"I wonder what their problem is?" Mulder said. "Haven't they ever experienced angry gods before?"

"That's seismic activity," Rubicon said, his voice sounding out-of-place, analytical. "Uh, how can there be earthquakes, volcanic action? The Yucatán Peninsula is a high, stable, limestone plateau—it is geologically impossible to have volcanic activity here."

Seemingly to disprove him, the ground shuddered as if someone had struck it with a giant sledgehammer. Plaza flagstones bucked. A group of spindly mahogany trees beside an old temple tipped, their roots pulling out of the wet powdery ground like a dirt-encrusted mat of tentacles.

One of the ancient, half-fallen facades collapsed the rest of the way with an explosion of crumbling stone blocks. Bricks from the sides of the stair-stepped pyramid popped loose and pattered down, bouncing, gaining speed.

At the edge of the jungle, the stressed ground split apart like a newly broken scab, bleeding foul gases from beneath the earth's surface. Mulder grabbed Scully's arm to help her keep her balance.

"We better get away from these large structures," Scully said. "One of them could collapse and bury us."

Together they helped the old archaeologist stagger out into the middle of the open plaza while the ground swayed and shook beneath them. The trees thrashed about like gnashing teeth.

From his vantage Mulder could see the ziggurat rocking from side to side like a Chicago skyscraper in a windstorm. He grabbed Scully's shoulder. "Better hang on!"

But then, before the quake seemed ready to reach its peak, the tremors subsided, dampening to a faint vibration that might well have just been Mulder's nerves misfiring with fear.

Rubicon smeared his goatee flat, occupying his shaking hands with some nervous gesture. "Uh, I could be wrong about that seismic stability," he said.

Aguilar pointed to the half-fallen tents and the scattered supplies. The campsite lay empty, abandoned. "It looks like we have lost our assistants for now," he said, his face ashen. He fumbled in his vest pocket to find cigarette papers and tobacco.

"They'll be back tomorrow, amigos. They are good workers. But we are on our own to prepare this evening's dinner and to recover from our adventure, eh?" He forced a laugh, which made Mulder feel decidedly uneasy.

Rubicon found an awkward seat on one of the upraised flagstones. He hung his head. "One of the reasons this area interested Cassandra was because of its, uh, very localized and unusual geological instability. Her first love was geology, you know. My little girl collecting rocks, studying how they were made, igneous, metamorphic, and sedimentary. She had a large collection, knew them all, labeled them all.

"Then Cassandra allowed her interests to shift to digging not just for the rocks themselves but for what lay hidden in them—the marks of human impact and the history trapped between layers of deposited sediment and dust. She seemed very excited about certain seismic readings she had obtained in this area—just as excited as she was about leading the first team out to Xitaclan."

The old archaeologist shook his head. "But it still seems impossible such violent activity would occur here." He gestured toward the tall central pyramid, where a few loose pebbles continued to rain down the exaggerated steps. "You can see that the area is thoroughly stable—if seismic tremors occurred frequently, these ruins would have been leveled centuries ago. The mere fact that Xitaclan remains standing provides incontrovertible evidence that this land is phenomenally stable."

"It didn't feel stable a moment ago, Señor," Aguilar said, standing with his feet braced far apart, as if he expected the ground to begin rocking and shaking again at any moment. He finally succeeded in rolling and lighting his cigarette.

Mulder sifted through the scattered information he kept stored in his brain, the enormous amounts of trivia and tidbits gleaned from encyclopedias and reports he had studied over the years. He always tried to remember items that had the slightest unexplained or mysterious flavor to them.

"Most of the major volcanoes in Central America are in the highlands of Mexico, right down the backbone of the country—but volcanoes are unusual things. One called Parícutin suddenly appeared in 1943… right in the middle of a Mexican cornfield that was as flat as a tortilla. A farmer was out plowing his field when the ground began to smoke and shake. For nine years afterward the volcano continued growing, dumping over a billion tons of lava and ash. It buried two entire towns."

"Mulder, are you saying a volcano just sprang up in the middle of nowhere?" Scully asked.

Mulder nodded. "And as it grew, Parícutin was watched by geologists from around the world. Within the first twenty-four hours, the volcano had made a twenty-five-foot-tall cinder cone. In eight months it grew to about fifteen hundred feet… quite a vigorous little event. In all, Parícutin covered about seven square miles of the surrounding area with lava and volcanic ash. Its maximum height topped nine thousand feet—and that was only half a century ago. No telling what else might just pop out of the ground."

He looked from Scully over to Rubicon and then to Fernando Aguilar. "I'd sleep lightly tonight and be ready to make a run for the jungle if a volcano starts erupting underneath our feet."

"An excellent suggestion, Señor," Aguilar said, puffing on his newly rolled cigarette.

But Scully looked at Mulder with concern, and he knew what she must be thinking, because he was bothered by the same question. What large energy release, what sharp aftershock could have triggered the burst of volcanic activity around Xitaclan? And why now?

Something had happened here. Mulder didn't know if it had anything to do with the disappearance of Cassandra Rubicon's team, or if it was just a coincidence.

He believed in many unlikely things… but Mulder had a difficult time believing in coincidences.

16

Home of Pieter Grobe, Quintana Roo
Sunday, 4:30 P.M.

Removing his policeman's cap at the doorway to the castle-like fortress of Pieter Grobe, Carlos Barreio waited while the guard made a telephone call to his master. Barreio used the meaty palm of his right hand to slick back his thinning dark hair, then brushed his thick black mustache in place. He felt like a supplicant at the gate of a powerful baron, but he would swallow his pride if need be—for the freedom of his land.

In his scuffed leather satchel he held carefully wrapped pieces of Maya jade, ancient relics scavenged from the lesser temples around the Xitaclan site. He had never before tried to sell historical items on his own, and he did not know what price such jade carvings should fetch—but he needed the money... and the *Liberación Quintana Roo* movement needed the weapons and the supplies it would buy.

Aguilar's unreliable assistant Pepe Candelaria had never returned from his mission the week before. The wiry little man seemed to have abandoned his mother and sisters, running off somewhere without ever delivering more treasures from Xitaclan, as he'd been instructed to do. Barreio could not tolerate any additional delay, so he had taken the remaining small pieces he kept in his possession, and decided to do with them whatever he could.

Fernando Victorio Aguilar excelled in selecting discerning customers for the most expensive sculptures, but Aguilar did not sell the art objects frequently enough, and Barreio had his own needs. Besides, now with the recent death—no, the complete obliteration—of Xavier Salida, Barreio had to find new customers, even if it meant cultivating them himself.

The guard hung up the black telephone and grunted, unlatching the steel-reinforced wooden door that led into the limestone block walls of Pieter Grobe's home—it looked more like a fortress than even some of the largest Maya ruins.

"Master Grobe will see you for fifteen minutes," the guard said. "I am to accompany you."

Barreio cleared his throat and nodded. "Thank you." He brushed down the front of his white uniform, still holding his policeman's cap in one sweaty hand. It seemed deeply ironic for him to be waiting at the pleasure of a drug lord when Barreio was one of the men ostensibly in charge of law enforcement in the state of

Quintana Roo, under corrupt Mexican law.

But Barreio understood the games he had to play in order to accomplish his main goal. The descendants of the Maya had long memories. They had waited for centuries to be free again, able to recreate their lost golden age.

Freedom and independence. The people of Quintana Roo would thank him for it, once the turmoil and bloodshed and political upheaval had faded into memory. After all, during the great Mexican Revolution of 1910, wasn't it true that one in every eight citizens had been killed? All those martyrs had paid the price for freedom—and oftentimes that price was high indeed.

When the guard slammed the massive front door behind them, the echoing boom sounded like a cannon shot on the Spanish Main.

Inside, Grobe's fortress looked even more Germanic and imposing, smelling of wood smoke from poorly ventilated fires and mildew in the stone cracks. Ceiling fans twirled from rafters above. The hall arches and narrow windows let in only fragments of light. Shafts of afternoon sun played across the tiled floors, illuminating faded tapestries on the walls. The room felt clammy, heavily air conditioned, cold as a tomb.

Barreio felt the guard walking close beside him, shouldering his automatic rifle. The Belgian expatriate certainly acted paranoid—and with good cause, since rival drug lords killed each other off so frequently that Barreio's police forces had little time to investigate their criminal activities.

Surprisingly, the guard had allowed him to keep his police-issue revolver in its side holster; Barreio decided that must reflect on the guard's confidence and skill, an utter certainty that the automatic rifle would cut him down much faster than Barreio could ever draw and fire his pistol. He hoped he would never have to test that assumption.

The police chief walked along, holding the satchel of jade artifacts in one hand, his cap in the other, wondering if the clock on his fifteen-minute audience had begun ticking when he entered the door of the fortress, or if he would be able to talk for the full time once he actually met the drug lord face-to-face.

The burly guard led him through the main fortress and out to a screened-in back porch, a lavish patio area that contained a kidney-shaped in-ground Jacuzzi. Doors led off to other rooms, perhaps a sauna, perhaps a shower.

Pieter Grobe sat alone in a canvas chair, reveling in the silence, listening to the fine buzz of the jungle outside the walls of his home. He played no music, listened to no distractions.

Barreio stood at the entrance to the patio, waiting to be noticed. A black telephone rested on a round glass table beside Grobe's chair. A transparent pitcher sat looking cool and refreshing, filled with a pale green liquid and garnished with round slices of lime; the pitcher gleamed with droplets of perspiration. Like nylon cobwebs, a protective covering of mosquito netting draped the windows, the chairs, and a rocking swing that hung from chains.

Grobe himself, thin and scarecrowish, sat within one such cocoon of netting. He held a long black cigarette holder with a smoldering, pungent clove cigarette. Grobe took a long puff, exhaled bluish-gray smoke. His hand slipped out between the folds of mosquito netting, reaching toward the table. He grasped the handle of the pitcher and poured a long, languid stream of limeade into a glass. He curled his skeletal hand around the glass and drew it inside the mosquito webbing.

Unable to contain his impatience, Barreio cleared his throat—earning himself a sharp glare from the guard.

Pieter Grobe sighed and then turned from his contemplation, showing a gaunt face seamed with deep lines. His chocolate-brown hair was thick and carefully styled, laced with frosty wings at his temples. Droplets of perspiration stood out on his cheeks and forehead; he looked sticky and uncomfortable in a baggy, cream-colored cotton suit.

"Yes, Señor Barreio?" he said. "Your fifteen minutes have begun. What is it you wish to discuss with me?" The Belgian drug lord's voice was quiet, patient, and firm. Barreio already knew that Grobe spoke excellent English and Spanish without the slightest trace of an accent—a skill that not many diplomats ever acquired with such precision.

"I have some items I was hoping might interest you, Excellency," Barreio said. He drew a deep breath, swelling his already broad chest as he stepped forward to another low table and set the leather satchel down before placing his policeman's cap beside it. The guard stiffened, ready for treachery.

"Don't overreact, Juan," Grobe said, not even looking at the guard. "Let us observe with an open mind what has compelled our friend the police chief to visit us."

"Jade sculptures, Excellency," Barreio said, "priceless Maya artifacts. If you agree to purchase them, they will never become lost in museums, where they would be squandered for the benefit of the public, their true artistic value lost."

Barreio opened the satchel and withdrew the pieces of Xitaclan sculpture. "Instead, these items will be yours to enjoy in private, as you wish."

Each artifact showed the predominant feathered serpent motif, fanciful draw-ings of plumed reptilian forms with long fangs and round intelligent eyes, legendary creatures the Maya had worshipped in times long past.

Grobe leaned forward, pushing his gaunt face against the mosquito netting that surrounded his chair. He stubbed out his clove cigarette and exhaled again. In the thick smoke Barreio could smell a pungent sweet burning scent, not entirely unlike marijuana.

"And what makes you think I am the slightest bit interested in purchasing contraband antiquities, Señor Police Chief Barreio?" Grobe said. "Is this perhaps a… 'sting operation,' as the Americans call it? Are you trying to tempt me into an illegal act, so that you can arrest me red-handed?"

Barreio stood back, appalled. "That would be the height of folly, Excellency Grobe," he said.

"Yes," the Belgian agreed, "yes, it would."

Barreio continued. "The state of Quintana Roo operates on nuances of power. I know my place in this society, Excellency, and I also know yours. I would never attempt something so foolish."

He swallowed. "If I might add, we have seen the results of tangling with you, Excellency. I myself have been to the devastated ruins of Xavier Salida's villa. It is inconceivable to me exactly what you did to retaliate against him, but the threat of your supreme power is absolutely clear, and I have no intention of crossing you."

Grobe actually laughed, a long, dry series of chuckles that might have been misinterpreted as a cough. "I am glad you fear me so, Señor Barreio. It is true that the… squabbles between myself and Xavier Salida had escalated over the past few weeks. But I assure you I had nothing to do with the devastation that occurred at his household. I wish wholeheartedly that I knew how to create such destruction, because then all of my rivals would fear me as much as you do."

Barreio reeled, off-balance with the information. If not Grobe, then who had destroyed Salida? Who had that kind of power in all of Mexico?

The Belgian continued. "I have been given to understand that you and that parasite Fernando Aguilar had also sold artifacts to Salida—ancient Maya artifacts from a newly excavated ruin called… "Grobe placed a slender finger to his lips as he searched for the name. "Xitaclan, I believe. Many of my Indian servants, including our friend Juan here"—with a gaze cast over his shoulder, he indicated the rigid guard, who still had not lowered his rifle—"believe that such items are cursed and should never have been taken from their resting place. The gods are angered and will exact their vengeance.

"Xavier Salida has already paid for the indiscretion of stealing those antiquities. Now, I trust these jade artifacts you intend to sell to me are also from Xitaclan? Señor Barreio, I have no wish to incur the wrath of the ancient gods."

Barreio forced a laugh and shifted uneasily, toying with one of the jade feathered serpent carvings. His mind whirled as he tried to think of another tack, a new way to open negotiations.

He had to sell some of this jade. He had to raise money. He had already donated what cash he could spare from his salary, but it was difficult for him to work as the police chief and also to hide his real passion—the fight for the independence of Quintana Roo.

It seemed only fitting to use the fallen glory of the Maya, the people who had created civilization in this corner of the Yucatán. Their precious artifacts would finance the struggle for freedom, help Barreio and his group of revolutionaries to conquer a new and independent land, help them win their struggle against the corrupt, bankrupt central government of Mexico. If they succeeded, *Liberación Quintana Roo* would proclaim a new homeland where the glory of the lost Maya could rise again.

"You must be joking, Excellency," he said. "Such superstitions! Surely a sophisticated European like yourself places no stock in ancient curses?" He raised his dark eyebrows. His thick mustache bristled, tickling his nose.

Grobe took another patient drink of limeade, glanced at his wristwatch, then blew out a long sigh before he answered. "My own feelings are irrelevant in this situation, Señor Police Chief Barreio. If the locals believe the artifacts are cursed, then I am unable to get anyone to work for me. My household servants are afraid. They disappear in the night, and I have a terrible time finding others to replace them. The quality of my life diminishes."

He tapped his empty cigarette holder on the edge of his chair. "I enjoy my lifestyle as it is, without further complications. I don't even want to consider the possibility that certain followers of the ancient Maya religion might try to get their revenge on me if I were to flaunt these old artifacts."

Grobe leaned forward, finally thrusting his narrow, well-lined face out of the protective netting. His brown eyes bored into Barreio. "With all of my money, I can install defenses against attacks from rival drug producers—but a suicidal religious fanatic is a threat against which few people can defend."

He slipped the netting back around him again and glanced at his watch. "Your time is up, Señor Barreio. I'm sorry we could not accommodate your needs."

Deciding against further negotiation, which would at this point sound like pleading or wheedling, Barreio returned the items to their case and snapped shut the leather satchel. He placed his cap back on his head and, shoulders slumping, he turned to the door that led into the thick-walled fortress.

The Belgian drug lord called after him, "Wait a moment, Señor Barreio."

Barreio spun around, his heart beating fast, hoping that Grobe had been only toying with him, searching for a better deal. But then the Belgian said, "Let me offer you something else of value. I have no interest in your relics, but I will give you this information for free—for now. I'll trust you to remember me if anything else should come up where you might repay me in kind."

"What is it, Excellency?" Barreio said.

The Belgian removed the stub of the cigarette from his holder, fished in his suit pocket for a dark brown box, and inserted a new clove cigarette. He lit it, but let it smolder for a few seconds as he answered.

"I have learned through international sources that a covert U.S. military team is coming to infiltrate Quintana Roo. It is a search-and-destroy mission. The commandos intend to find some weapons cache or military stronghold deep in the jungles. Perhaps you know about it? Perhaps it has something to do with the guerrilla revolutionary group known as *Liberación Quintana Roo*?" He smiled thinly. "Since you are the police chief in these parts, I thought you might wish to be informed of this development."

Barreio froze, feeling the color drain from his face. A knot of ice in his stomach made him desperately uneasy, while at the same time a flush of anger surged through his veins. "The U.S. military is coming here—in secret? How dare they! Under what pretext?"

"The commando team is landing across the border in Belize, I believe. With a little snooping around I'm sure you can get more detailed information."

"Thank you," Barreio said, stunned and startled. "Thank you, Excellency."

The jade relics nearly forgotten, the leather satchel heavy in his numb hand, Barreio stumbled behind the footsteps of the guard.

His mind spun, no longer worried about the short-term solution of raising money by selling artifacts, but wondering what the U.S. military had discovered, what they could be up to—and if his own plans for state independence might be threatened.

17

Xitaclan ruins
Sunday, 8:17 P.M.

Hours after the bizarre volcanic tremors, the ground had settled back down to relative peace. The noxious sulfurous odors had cleared from the air, to be replaced by the heady scents of the jungle: the perfumes of flowers, the sharp spice of decaying mulch, and the crackling resin of dry branches consumed in their campfire.

Fernando Victorio Aguilar came up to them, smiling, a loose satchel dangling at his side. "Instead of your American junk food, I have secured a repast from the arms of the forest." He reached inside to withdraw a handful of bulbous mushrooms mottled with gray-green. He brushed loose strands of moss and leaf debris from their caps. "We shall roast these to start—delicious mushrooms, eh? They taste like nuts when they've been cooked."

Mulder's stomach growled, but Scully shifted uneasily. "These are safe to eat?"

Aguilar nodded vigorously. "These are local delicacies, used in many traditional Maya dishes."

Rubicon reached out to take one of the mushrooms from Aguilar's hand, holding it close to the firelight. Blinking his surprised-looking blue eyes, he hauled up his reading glasses and set them on his perspiration-slick nose. "Yes, I've eaten these before," he said. "Delicious." He skewered the mushroom on a twig next to the fire and held it in the flames, roasting it like a campfire marshmallow.

"At least he didn't bring us beetle grubs to eat," Mulder said. Other bugs swarmed around the firelight.

"Yes, grubs!" Aguilar said, clapping his hands in surprise. "I can go find grubs—there are many delicious kinds! Or, if you would like a true feast, I could shoot us a monkey."

"No thanks," Scully said.

"A little different from dinner last night," Mulder said.

Darkness surrounded them like an oppressive blanket. Their crackling campfire stood as an island of warm light in the middle of the Xitaclan plaza. In other circumstances, Mulder might have suggested they all begin a chorus of "Row, Row, Row Your Boat." But not here, not now.

Bats flew about, swooping silently through the air, their high-pitched chirps beyond the edge of human hearing, though Mulder could feel the sounds in the fillings of his teeth. Large night moths flew in graceful spirals, pale splashes against the darkness. Farther out in the jungle they could see the eyes of predators flickering with reflected gleams.

Scully plucked one of the mushrooms from her stick, looked at it smoking in her fingers, and popped it into her mouth. She chewed, about to comment on its taste, when suddenly a bat swooped in front of her face, chomping one of the large moths. The bat swooped off before she could do anything but reel backward, startled.

When Mulder commented about the Indians who had fled from the rumbling eruptions and now refused to come closer to the ruins, Aguilar snorted. "They are superstitious cowards," he said. "Their respect for their religion outweighs their common sense. They claim this place still holds the spirits of their ancestors sacrificed to appease the gods, not to mention the old gods themselves."

Rubicon stared into the shadows, listening to the buzz of insects, the symphony of night birds, the dance of predator and prey. He wore a pinched, concerned look on his narrow face. Mulder knew the old archaeologist must be imagining his daughter lost and alone in the deep jungle filled with stalking jaguars and poisonous snakes... or murderous treasure-seekers.

Mulder cocked his head as he heard something large stirring in the trees, saw the thick ferns swaying as an unseen creature moved through the undergrowth outside the edge of firelight. The others didn't notice the disturbance.

"Things haven't changed so much in a century," Rubicon muttered, far away in his thoughts. "When I think of Cassandra and her team exploring here, I can't help but remember some of the first amateur archaeologists in this region. They suffered hardships unlike any we are likely to encounter."

Rubicon settled the reading glasses on his nose. Story time, Mulder thought.

"Two of the first white men to explore the Maya ruins were Stephens and Catherwood. They were veteran travelers, confident they could make their way through any rough country.

"They had read some obscure books that mentioned great cities buried in the rain forest, uh, 'ruined and desolate without a name'—I think those were the exact words... I've read their travel diaries.

"Stephens and Catherwood went into the rain forests of Honduras in 1839. After days of trudging through the jungle, they finally reached the ruins of Copán, where they encountered fallen buildings, stone staircases covered with vines or trees. Stephens and Catherwood knew nothing of Maya history, and when they asked the local Indians who had built the ruins, the Indians simply shrugged.

"These two gentlemen returned to Central America on several trips, visiting dozens of ruined cities. Together they published bestselling accounts of their adventures, Stephens with his eloquent journals, Catherwood with his beautiful illustrations. Their books ignited a huge interest in archaeology—uh, for better or worse.

"But it didn't come easy—especially not for Catherwood. He seemed to be under a curse. He contracted malaria and suffered from the recurring fever. He went lame from swollen and infected insect bites. His left arm became almost paralyzed. He had to be carried on the shoulders of Indians, since he was unable to walk.

"But he did recover and made his way back to set up his paintings in New York. Then a fire broke out, and one of their greatest exhibitions was destroyed. Catherwood's drawings as well as spectacular artifacts brought back from Maya country."

Scully shook her head. "What a loss."

Rubicon stared into the campfire. "Years later, when Catherwood was on his way back to the States from yet another expedition, he drowned at sea when his ship collided with another. Bad luck, or a Maya curse-depends on what you believe."

Squatting by himself, Aguilar chewed on something that seemed inordinately crunchy. Mulder caught a glimpse of flailing black legs as the guide popped another morsel into his mouth.

"A good story, Señor," Aguilar said around a mouthful. "But the curse was not strong enough to stop the flood of white adventurers such as yourself, eh?"

"Or my daughter," Rubicon said.

Scully stood up to stretch, brushing her legs. "Well, we should go to bed and try to get some sleep," she said. "Any minute now you'll start telling ghost stories just to give us the creeps."

"Good idea," Rubicon said. "We'll want to get up at dawn so we can start our detailed investigations, search for traces of my daughter."

Mulder said dryly, "I guess the story about teenagers necking on Lover's Lane will have to wait for another night."

Mulder woke in the middle of the night to the sound of rustling and creeping noises. Close, too close. He blinked, then sat up, listening intently.

He definitely heard something moving outside across the plaza... perhaps a large predator stalking them, searching for easy prey. The flimsy fabric walls of his tent seemed weak and unprotective.

He leaned forward cautiously, parting the folds of mosquito netting to reach the opening flap of the tent. He accidentally rustled the cloth and froze, listening intently—but he did not hear the sound outside again.

He pictured some large carnivorous monster from the jungle, a prehistoric denizen lost in time, sniffing the air, looking toward the sound he had made. Swallowing, Mulder gradually eased his tent flap open, pushing his head out into the open night air.

The bright gibbous moon had just begun to rise like a half-closed eye, spilling pale watery light across the treetops as thick clouds scudded across the sky.

The tents had been erected next to one of the weathered stelae around which the feathered serpent wrapped itself like a vicious protector. The tall stela tilted at a slight angle, its shadow blurred and indistinct on the buckled flagstones of the plaza.

Out in the jungle the line of skeletal trees and tangled blackness seemed quiet and still. This late in the core of night, even the nocturnal creatures hung back, waiting.

Mulder heard the rustling sound again, a rattling growl. He scanned the darkness, trying to find its source, but he saw nothing, only shadows, no movement. He waited, breathing shallowly, his attention entirely focused.

Finally, just when he had convinced himself that he had heard nothing more than his overactive imagination, Mulder caught a writhing flash, something stirring in the moonlight at the edge of the jungle.

He turned, trying to see clearly in the uncertain illumination. In the tall, matted trees and the dangling creepers, he spotted a huge serpentine body moving sinuously, slithering, plowing its way through the underbrush with incredible stealth.

He gasped—and the thing turned toward him. He saw a flash of flaming eyes, a glint of impossibly long scales—feathery scales, like cloth mirrors overlapping, reflecting a dazzling sequence of moon images back at him.

Then, with a flick of its lissome body, the thing vanished into the midnight shadows. Mulder saw no further sign of it, though he waited for many minutes. Once, he thought he heard a cracking branch deep in the jungle—but that could have been from anything.

Eventually he went back to bed, crawling inside his tent and replaying the scene over and over in his mind. He needed to understand just what—if anything—he had seen.

Sleep was a long time coming for him.

18

Xitaclan ruins
Monday, dawn

The local helpers returned at daybreak, just as Fernando Aguilar had predicted. The guide sat over the cooling campfire, smoking one of his hand-rolled cigarettes, scowling at the Indians who crept into the plaza, heads down as if in embarrassment.

Mulder crawled out of his tent, watching the locals, who looked for all the world like a blue-collar crew showing up for the morning shift. Vladimir Rubicon was already up, scrutinizing the nearest feathered serpent stela, using a pocketknife to pry loose lumps of moss to get a better look at the glyphs.

"Ah, Agent Mulder, you're up!" Rubicon said. "Today we're sure to find some sign of what my daughter and her team were doing. She must have uncovered a secret in these ruins. If we can find the same secret, we'll discover why her team vanished."

Hearing their voices, Scully also crawled out of her tent. "Good morning. Mulder, are you cooking breakfast?"

"Just cereal and milk for me, thanks," he replied.

Aguilar tossed away the stub of his vile-smelling cigarette. He looked freshly shaved. Seeing his employers awake and about, Aguilar turned to berate the Indians in a language Mulder couldn't understand, his voice filled with disgust.

"What's he saying?" Scully asked. "What did they do?"

Vladimir Rubicon listened a moment before shaking his head. "It must be a Maya language derivative. Many of the locals still speak the old tongue." He shrugged. "Uh, I suspect they didn't do anything wrong, other than running off into the night. Aguilar's just trying to impress us with his authority."

"I had a boss like that once," Mulder said.

Aguilar came over, grinning at them as if he had just learned what they were getting him for his birthday. "Good morning, amigos," he said. "Today we shall discover the mysteries of lost Xitaclan, eh? We shall learn what happened to the lovely Señorita Rubicon and her companions."

"Have you asked the locals?" Scully said, gesturing to the Indians who appeared appropriately cowed after the long string of beratements.

Aguilar said, "They claim the spirit of this place has taken Señorita Rubicon. The old gods are hungry for blood after so many years. That is why the natives camp away from the ruins. They are not civilized people, like you and I. They don't even try to pretend."

"But did any of these workers remain to assist the archaeologists?" Scully said, her voice harder, pressing for an answer. "Somebody must know."

"Señorita Scully, I guided the archaeology team to Xitaclan, for which they paid me a lot of American money—and I am very grateful. These Indians, descendants of the Maya, say there were many loud noises, strange activities, after I had left. Señorita Rubicon and her friends laughed at them for their foolishness, but the Maya helpers all ran to safety. Now they say the gods have shown who is foolish and who is wise."

"Sort of like failing a supernatural IQ test," Mulder muttered.

Aguilar rummaged around in his pocket for paper and tobacco to fashion himself another cigarette. A beautiful green-feathered bird flitted across the plaza from one tall tree to another, singing out a thin musical call. The Indians stopped their work, pointing up and chattering to each other in amazement.

"Look, the quetzal bird," Aguilar said, nodding. He took off his ocelot-skin hat to shade his eyes in the slanted morning light. "Very precious. The Maya used quetzal feathers for many of their ceremonial dresses."

Rubicon frowned and looked around as if he might see some sign of his daughter, while Mulder turned back to Aguilar, exasperated. "Do they know what happened to Cassandra, or not?"

Aguilar shrugged. "All I know is that Señorita Rubicon was safe and quite happy with the work awaiting her when I left her to return to Cancún."

"Let's get busy looking for her, then," Scully said.

"These ruins may extend for a mile or so," Rubicon said, stretching out his arm, "with separate sites or temple buildings blocked off from each other by the dense trees and vegetation."

"Tell the locals what we're searching for," Scully suggested. "Maybe they can help us comb the site."

Aguilar passed on the information, and the Indians dispersed to the jungle, diligently scouring the fallen ruins, talking excitedly with each other. Some looked uneasy, some confused, others eager, as they undertook the exploration.

Scully, Mulder, and Rubicon wandered around Xitaclan, walking the length of the overgrown ball court, poking in alcoves and niches, searching for clues, bodies—or even a note explaining that Cassandra and her companions had gone off to get groceries.

Scully said, "Their team consisted of an engineer, two archaeologists, a hiero-glyphics expert, and a photographer. No real survival expert in the bunch." She scanned the clotted trees, low palms, the dense vegetation hanging from the branches. The sun lit everything like a spotlight.

"Even if all the helpers ran off, like they did last night, I still can't imagine Cassandra's team trying to make their own way through the jungle. We just completed our own hike to get here," she said. "I wouldn't want to do that without a guide."

"Cassandra was good at survival," Rubicon said. "She had topographical maps and plenty of common sense."

Scully lowered her voice. "I studied the maps myself last night, and I'm not certain our friend Aguilar brought us on the most straightforward path. I think he might have been delaying us for some reason."

"I don't trust him either," Mulder said, "but he seems more like an obnoxious used-car salesman than an outright criminal."

"Remember, this is a rough country, Agent Mulder," Rubicon said. "However, if the Maya helpers had indeed abandoned Cassandra and her friends, it would be only a matter of time before she was forced to take some drastic action. They'd have to find their way back to civilization somehow."

"So Aguilar dropped them off, leaving his Indian helpers here… and then the Indians could have abandoned the team," Scully said. "Maybe another ground tremor?"

Rubicon nodded, blinking repeatedly in the bright sunlight. "I hope that's what happened."

"With no more supplies," Scully pointed out, "Cassandra would have had no choice but to fight her way through the jungles."

"But would they all have gone together?" Mulder asked. He ran his fingers along the glyph-carved wall blocks of the ball court. Something small and fast skittered into a shadowy crack. "It would make sense that, say, two of the team members would go to get help while the rest remained here."

"You saw how difficult the jungles were, Mulder," Scully said. "Maybe she thought it was their best bet not to separate."

"It still doesn't sound right," Mulder said.

Rubicon shook his head. His white-blond hair clung to his skull, cemented by perspiration. "For myself, I hope that story is true, because then there's still hope for my little girl."

From not far off in the jungle, they heard a shout of excitement. One of the Indians called over and over. "Let's go," Mulder said, running. "They've found something."

Vladimir Rubicon puffed and wheezed, keeping up with them as they stepped over fallen trees, climbed rocks, splashed through streams. Once Mulder startled a large animal that bounded off into the ferns and shrubs. He couldn't see what it was, but he felt a sudden cold sensation, a lump in his throat. Perhaps he would get a better look at one of those slithering creatures he had half-imagined in the moonlight the night before. Could it be the basis for certain Maya myths, monstrous predators responsible for the numerous disappearances over the years... including Cassandra Rubicon's?

Before long, they came upon a small temple barely the size of a tool shed. Though ancient and overgrown, it seemed sturdy enough. Much of the under-brush had been cleared away, the creepers pulled down to expose stone walls, a low-ceilinged interior.

Near the opening, one of the Maya helpers stood looking cowed while Fernando Aguilar snapped at him, his face stormy and livid—but the moment Aguilar saw the approaching Americans, his expression transformed miraculously. He swept off his spotted hat. "Look what we have found, amigos!" he said. "Equipment stored by Señorita Rubicon's team!"

In the temple shadows, a pile of crates huddled under a tarp. Like a matador taunting a bull, Aguilar grabbed the corner of the tarp and yanked it off to reveal the cache of supplies.

"Señorita Rubicon's team must have left these crates here protected from wild animals. Though the other equipment has vanished, these items appear to have been untouched. What a lucky find for us."

"But why would she leave all this here?" Scully said quietly.

"Look, food supplies and the radio transmitter," Aguilar said. "This large box has something else inside it." Aguilar bent down to scrutinize the crate. He gestured for one of the Indians to help him pry open the top.

"Mulder," Scully kept her voice low, "do you know what this means? Cassandra couldn't have gone off in search of supplies. There's enough food here for weeks, and the team could have used the transmitter to call for help any time."

Vladimir Rubicon eagerly bent forward to inspect the large crate, shouldering aside the Indian and using his big-knuckled fingers to pull open the top of the crate while Aguilar stepped back to observe.

Scully watched, surprised to see the contents. "It's an underwater suit and air hoses," she said, puzzled. "Was Cassandra intending to explore the cenote?"

"That makes good archaeological sense," Rubicon said, nodding vigorously. "In those deep wells artifacts are preserved for centuries and centuries. Yes, she would have wanted to go down there, my Cassandra—just like Thompson."

Scully swatted away a stinging fly. "Who was Thompson? I don't recall any member of their team with that name."

Startled from his concentration, Rubicon looked up from the weather-stained crates. "Who? Oh, Thompson—no, I meant Edward Thompson, the last of the great amateur archaeologists here in the Yucatán. He spent years studying the cenote at Chichén Itzá, where he found the single greatest treasure trove of Maya artifacts ever recovered."

Skeptically, Mulder held up the diving suit's limp sleeve of rubberized canvas fabric. "He dove down into a deep sacrificial well like the one out there?" He gestured back toward the main plaza and the tall pyramid.

Rubicon shook his head. "Uh, not at first. He spent years dredging, dropping a cast-iron bucket down to the bottom, scooping up loads of muck, and sifting through it by hand. He recovered bones and cloth and jade, several intact skulls—one of which had been used as a ceremonial censer and still smelled of perfume.

"But after a while, Thompson decided that the clumsy dredge couldn't do as good a job as a diver working hands-on. He had planned for that possibility when he launched his original expedition, buying the equipment, acquiring training. He taught his four Indian helpers how to operate the air pumps, the winches."

Rubicon looked down at the diving suit his daughter had intended to wear, and seemed to suppress a shudder. "When Thompson went under the cenote, the solemn Indians waved goodbye to him, confident they'd never see him again. In his own words, he sank 'like a bag of lead,' thirty feet down into water so dark that even his flashlight couldn't penetrate it. At the bottom he felt around in the mud to find artifacts—coins, jade, sculptures, rubber objects.

"But despite his armored diving suit, Thompson sustained severe ear damage from his dives. The locals looked on him with awe from that point on—he was the only living person ever to have gone into the sacred cenote and survive."

Scully nodded. "And you think your daughter intended to follow in his footsteps, exploring the Xitaclan cenote."

Mulder pawed around the equipment packed into the crates. "Doesn't look like she had a chance to use the suit, though," he said. "The manufacturer's warranty sticker is still on it."

"She was interrupted before she could complete her investigations," Rubicon said.

Mulder saw Fernando Aguilar flash a final angry glance at the Indian, who turned away, his shoulders slumped.

"Yes, but interrupted by what?" Mulder said.

\\\\\\\\\\\\\\\\\\\

Together, they climbed the steps of the central Pyramid of Kukulkan. Panting in the humid air, they exerted themselves up the steep incline and the narrow and uneven limestone stairs.

"Careful," Mulder said seriously. "It's not very stable."

Rubicon bent to inspect the weathered stairs themselves, pointing out carvings that had been picked clean, the moss removed, the dirt and limestone powder brushed away from the cracks.

"See, Cassandra's team has cleaned the first twelve steps. If I could read these glyphs, we could learn why the Maya built Xitaclan, what made this place such a sacred site." He stood up, pressing a hand against his lower back. "But I'm not an expert in this form. Few people are. Maya glyphs are among the most difficult of all mankind's written languages to decipher. That's why Cassandra brought her own special epigrapher with her team."

"Yes," Scully said, "Christopher Porte."

Rubicon shrugged. "I understand he was quite skilled."

"Let's see what's on the top of the pyramid," Mulder said, and trudged higher up the steep incline.

"Probably an open-air temple," Rubicon answered. "The high priest would stand on the platform and face the rising sun before he made his sacrifices."

At the top, Mulder stopped, placed his hands on his hips, and drew a deep breath as he took in the spectacular view.

The Central American jungle spread out like a flat carpet as far as he could see, trees laden with vines, everything a lush, lush green. Stone temple ruins in the distance poked up through the foliage like giant tombstones.

"The past is strong in this place," Rubicon muttered.

Mulder could imagine the Maya priests feeling godlike, standing so close to heaven under the pounding morning sun. The crowds would have waited in the plaza below, congregating after their labors out in the forest where they slashed and burned to plant crops of maize and beans and peppers. The priest stood here at the top, perhaps with his drugged or bound sacrificial victim, ready to shed blood to honor the gods.

Mulder's runaway imagination was jarred when old Vladimir Rubicon cupped his hands around his mouth and shouted "Cassandra!" into the jungle. His words echoed across the landscape, startling birds from the treetops. "Cassandra!" he bellowed again.

Rubicon looked around, listening, waiting. Mulder and Scully stood next to the archaeologist, holding their breath. The old man had tears in his eyes. "I had to try," he said, shrugging his bony shoulders.

Then, looking embarrassed, Rubicon turned to the tall temple pillars and the flat platform. Mulder saw elaborate stone designs chiseled into the limestone, flecks of paint still visible in the protected crevices and crannies.

The builders of Xitaclan had repeated the feathered serpent motif again and again, creating conflicting impressions of fear and protection, power and subservience. Other drawings showed a tall man, faceless, with some strange body armor or a suit, flames flowing from behind him. A rounded covering on his head that looked unmistakably like a…

"Doesn't that figure remind you of something, Scully?" he asked.

She crossed her arms over her chest, then shook her head. "You're not going to connect ancient astronauts with a missing-persons case, are you, Mulder?"

"Just looking at the evidence with my own eyes," he said quietly. "Maybe Cassandra found some information that others wanted to keep hidden."

"That is Kukulkan," Rubicon said, not hearing Mulder as he pointed to other images that showed a strangely shaped ship, coiled designs that may well have been pieces of machinery or equipment. "Very powerful and very wise, he brought knowledge down from the sky. He stole fire from the gods and delivered it to the people."

Mulder looked at Scully, raising his eyebrows. "Just a myth," she said.

Rubicon put his half-glasses on his nose; then, realizing how useless the gesture was, slipped them back off again to let them dangle at his throat. "God of wind, the master of life, Kukulkan brought civilization to the Maya people at the beginning of time. He invented metallurgy. He was the patron of every art."

"A Renaissance kind of guy," Mulder said.

"Kukulkan ruled for many centuries until eventually his enemy Tezcatlipoca drove him out—uh, the guy whose corpse gave off such a smell. Kukulkan had to return to his homeland, so he burned his own houses, which were built of silver and shells, and then set sail to the east on the sea. Kukulkan disappeared, promising he would return to the people one day."

Mulder felt the excitement beating in his heart. "Houses built of silver and shells" could have meant metal and glass; adding all the fire imagery, he pictured a rocket or a spaceship.

"The Maya people were so convinced by their legend," Rubicon continued, shading his eyes to look toward the horizon, "that they stationed sentries to watch the east coast, uh, waiting for Kukulkan. When the Spaniards came in their tall galleons, wearing bright metal breastplates, the Maya were convinced Kukulkan had returned."

"Men in silver suits could easily be confused for spacemen," he said.

"You're welcome to your opinion, Mulder," she said. "I know it's no use trying to talk you out of it. But we've still got a missing archaeology team to find. What do Maya gods and ancient astronauts have to do with our case?"

"Nothing, I'm sure, Scully," Mulder said in a voice that said exactly the opposite. He kept his smile to himself. "Nothing at all."

19

Xitaclan ruins
Monday, 3:10 P .M.

On their way back down the steep stairs on the opposite side of the pyramid, where the steps were more uneven and crumbling, Scully watched as Rubicon pointed out where someone with a clumsy pickaxe and chisel had broken free ornate carvings, alcoves perhaps containing jade artifacts and other valuable objects.

Rubicon, his temper rising, said in disgust, "These artifacts are probably for sale on the black market in Cancún or Mexico City to self-styled pre-Columbian art collectors, or just people who want to own something so no one else may have it. Cassandra may have run into some of these thieves."

"But this area is so isolated," Scully said, following him down the last few steps of the central pyramid. They walked across the flagstoned plaza. "How would the artifacts be distributed? There would have to be some kind of network in place."

"I wouldn't put it past men like him," Rubicon said, gesturing with a sharp elbow toward Fernando Victorio Aguilar, who bustled up to them, tossing aside the remains of another hand-rolled cigarette.

"Did you find anything up there, amigos?" he said, pandering.

A deeply offended anger burned behind Rubicon's blue eyes. "We'll complete our initial inspection of the area today, but if we haven't uncovered any sign of them by tomorrow morning, we should use Cassandra's transmitter and contact the Mexican officials, request immediate assistance. They can send their own inspectors and security forces. National forces, not locals—the locals are probably in on any black-market trade." He scowled. "Many artifacts have already been illegally removed."

Aguilar looked at him, his expression a combination of miffed annoyance and wounded pride. "What you see could have been caused by treasure seekers from long ago, Señor Rubicon. Xitaclan has been unprotected for a long, long time."

Rubicon glared at him. "Mr. Aguilar, anyone with eyes can see the fresh scars. I know these items have been removed very recently, uh, within months, probably weeks."

Aguilar crossed his tanned arms over his chest, pursing his lips. "Then perhaps your daughter's archaeology team removed the most valuable pieces for their own profit, eh? They work for museums back in America, do they not?"

Rubicon leaned closer to Aguilar, thrusting his lower lip out so that his yellow-gray goatee bristled. "My Cassandra and all of her team members would never do such a thing," he said. "They know the value of historical artifacts, especially artifacts that must remain in place for further study."

"I sense that you do not trust me, Señor Rubicon," Aguilar said, tugging on his hat. His voice held a conciliatory tone. "But we must work together, eh? We are isolated here at Xitaclan. We must make the best of it and not become enemies. It could be dangerous if we fail to work as a team."

Scully headed back to their campsite as the discussion between Rubicon and the long-haired Mexican guide became more heated. She removed her pack and dropped it beside the tent. Though it was broad daylight, the entire crew of Maya helpers had once again vanished into the jungles, nowhere to be seen. It made her feel strangely uneasy.

Scully stopped by the nearer of the two tall stelae, elaborately carved with feathered serpents. She examined the eroded carving in the bright daylight, noticing a change in the dull weathered limestone—bright red splattered the carvings, dollops of thick crimson-like paint that dripped from the fangs of one of the largest feathered serpents. She leaned forward, curious and revolted at the same time.

Someone had rubbed blood inside the stone mouth of the feathered serpent, as if giving the carving a taste… a fresh sacrifice. She followed the trail of blood droplets down the tall pillar to the buckled flagstones at its base.

"Mulder!" she cried.

Her partner came running with an alarmed expression on his face. Rubicon and Aguilar stood frozen, their faces flushed from their argument, looking to see what had interrupted them.

Scully indicated the bright red streaks on the stela… and then gestured to the severed human finger that lay in a pool of congealing blood on the flagstone.

Mulder bent down to look at the amputated finger. The expression of disgust flickered for only an instant on his placid face.

Aguilar and Rubicon finally came up and stared down without words at the blood, the severed digit. "It looks fresh," Scully said. "No more than an hour or so."

Mulder touched the tacky blood. "Just barely starting to dry. It must have happened while we were up on the pyramid. I didn't hear any screams, though. Aguilar, you were down here."

"No, I was out in the jungle." He shook his head in dismay and took off his ocelot-skin hat, as if in reverence for a dead friend. "I was afraid of this, very afraid." He lowered his voice, looking around furtively. He narrowed his eyes, as if concerned the Indians might be watching from the fringes of the jungle, spying on their potential victims. "Yes, very afraid."

Aguilar walked around the stela, as if searching for other evidence. "The Maya religion is very ancient. Their rituals were celebrated for a thousand years before white explorers ever came to our shores, and they became much more violent when they mixed with the Toltec. People don't forget their beliefs so easily, eh?"

"Wait a minute," Scully said. "Are you saying that some of the Maya descendants still practice the old religion? Cutting out hearts and throwing people into sacrificial wells?"

Scully felt a sense of dread as she began to piece together a scenario that even Mulder would believe—how Cassandra Rubicon and her team had become victims in a bloodthirsty sacrificial ritual.

Rubicon said, "Well, some of the people still remember the ancient Toltec chants and observe the festivals, though most have been Christianized… or at least civilized. Some few, though, continue to practice the bloodwork and self-mutilation. Especially out here, away from the cities."

"Self-mutilation?" Mulder said. "You mean one of those Indians cut off his own finger?"

Rubicon nodded, touching the pattern of blood on the limestone pillar. "Probably with an obsidian knife."

Scully tried to imagine the religious fervor required to take a splintered stone knife and hack away a finger, sawing through sinew and bone without making so much as a cry of pain.

Rubicon seemed more detached, as if the possibility of his daughter and her companions becoming a blood sacrifice had not yet occurred to him.

"The Maya and Toltec rituals shed a great deal of blood, both their own and that of prisoners and victims. At the holiest of festivals, the high king would take a stingray spine and reach under his loincloth to pierce his own foreskin."

Scully saw Mulder swallow hard. "Ouch."

"Blood is a very powerful force," Aguilar agreed.

"The blood that flowed out dribbled across long strips of mulberry-bark paper, tracing patterns of red droplets. Some of the priests could divine the future from these patterns." Rubicon looked up at the sky. "Afterward, the strips of blood-spattered paper were rolled up and burned so that the sacred smoke could send messages to the gods."

Scully looked grimly at the fresh blood. "If one of those Indians just chopped off his finger with a stone knife," she said, "he requires medical attention. With this kind of crude amputation, the man could easily get gangrene, especially in a tropical climate such as this."

Aguilar found a bent and mangled cigarette in his pocket and tugged it out, sticking it between his lips without lighting it. "You will not find him, Señorita, never," he said. "The man would have run away, far from Xitaclan. He has made his sacrifice to the guardians of Kukulkan—but now that we know his true religion, we will not see him again. The Maya people here have a long memory. They are still deathly afraid of the white man and persecution. They remember one of the first white governors here, a man named Father Diego de Landa. A butcher."

Rubicon grunted in agreement, his face showing an expression of distaste. "He was a Franciscan friar, and under his guidance temples were torn down, shrines smashed. Anyone caught worshipping an idol was whipped, their joints stretched with pulleys, boiling water poured on their skin.

Aguilar nodded eagerly, as if glad to have the old archaeologist back on his side again. "Sí, Father de Landa found Indians who could still read old writings, and he attempted to translate the hieroglyphics. But to him it was all against the Christian Word of God, eh? Cursed. When they showed him a cache of thirty books bound in jaguar skin, many filled with serpent drawings, he decided they contained falsehoods of the devil. So he burned them all."

Rubicon looked pained just to hear of the loss. "De Landa tortured five thousand Maya, killing nearly two hundred of them before he was summoned back to Spain for his excesses. While he awaited trial, he composed a long treatise detailing everything he had learned."

"And was he convicted for his appalling behavior?" Scully asked.

Aguilar raised his eyebrows and barked a laugh. "No, Señorita! He was sent back to the Yucatán—as a bishop this time!"

Rubicon looked contemplative as he knelt in front of the bloodstained stela. Scully bent over to pick up the severed finger. It still felt faintly warm and rubbery. The thickened blood at the end did not drip off. She saw the ragged stump, where the stone knife had hacked through the flesh and bone.

If some of these people still practiced their violent religion, she wondered what other… sacrifices they might have made.

20

Yucatán jungle, Belize border
Tuesday, 0215 military time

The jungle was the enemy, an obstacle, an object to be defeated—and Major Willis Jakes had no doubt that his hand-picked squadron would succeed in conquering it. That was their mission, and that was what they would do.

The ten members of his covert infiltration squad wore jungle camouflage uniforms and night-vision goggles. After being landed in secret on an uninhabited shore at the northern border of Belize, they had struck off overland through the jungles in a pair of all-terrain vehicles.

The most difficult part had been immediately upon landing, dumped off at the edge of the bay, Bahía Chetumal, crossing a few night-deserted roads and the bridge over the narrow Laguna de Bacalor, and then plunging into the trackless Quintana Roo wilderness.

Negotiating a path through the rain forest, they followed a digitized map, choosing a course that avoided even meagerly inhabited areas as they made a beeline for their destination. Much of the area showed no sign of human settlement, no roads or villages whatsoever… just the way the major preferred it.

Jakes's team had to maintain a good pace to put them well past all roads and the populated coastal areas before daybreak. They could not afford to rest but had to proceed, always bearing in mind that they must reach their target—the source of the high-power encrypted signal—sometime during the following night. Under cover of darkness, they hoped to accomplish their mission. Before they could go home, the secret military base must be completely destroyed.

Their narrow-bodied all-terrain vehicles chewed up the offending tangles of foliage, crushing an obvious path through the forest… but in a place where no one would ever look. Even if anyone spotted Major Jakes's team, the commandos would be long gone before any organized response could find them. The heavily inflated, armored wheels of the ATV trampled the undergrowth, each axle pivoting on its own gimbal to allow the utmost flexibility in negotiating the terrain.

Half of Jakes's team rode in the vehicles, while the other half strode briskly behind, keeping up the pace across the newly cleared path. Every hour, they would switch, so that the first group of riders walked and the hikers rode. He had learned through experience that this was the most efficient way to bring his team overland under cover, without requiring bureaucratic permission or right of clearance from any foreign government. This covert operation did not officially exist… any more than did the secret weapons cache or the undocumented military base deep in the Yucatán jungles.

Major Jakes didn't worry about the implications of such things. His orders were straightforward… not simple by any means, but at least clear-cut. He didn't ask questions unless they pertained to the mission, and his team members asked for even fewer details than he did. They knew better.

Intensified by the night-vision goggles in front of his eyes, greenish residual light made the landscape look alien and surreal. Major Jakes knew how to handle it. He and his team had infiltrated and destroyed many other illegal installations that technically did not exist. Certainly, they existed no longer.

He rode in the lead all-terrain vehicle. Beside him his driver, a first lieutenant, moved along at the best speed he could manage. The driver shone a bright mercury spotlight in front of them, always keeping his eyes open for insurmountable obstacles. So far, they had managed to minimize their backtracking and continue on a very satisfying forward pace.

Get it right the first time, his father had always said—and young Willis Jakes had learned to follow that credo. He could think of few things worse than being forced to repeat a chore, or homework, while his father paced in the background, a stern taskmaster and absolutely unforgiving.

"The world is never forgiving," he had told his son. "Best you learn that early in life." Jakes had spent hours upon hours standing motionless against a wall, contemplating his grades or his test scores. He had learned how to focus utterly on a goal… how to get it right the first time.

The spotlight gleamed across the leaves of the jungle, which swayed in unfelt breezes as if the forest itself were alive. Suddenly Jakes saw two piercingly bright coins, the eyes of a predator, above head level in the trees.

The first lieutenant swept the spotlight up to catch the movement, and a sleek spotted cat bounded away from one branch to another. Jakes knew that his other nine soldiers had automatically flinched for their weapons, prepared to shoot the large cat. But the jaguar showed no stomach for fighting and fled into the darkness.

They rode in silence, rocking and bucking, the vehicle lurching over fallen trees and rocks, yet maintaining its balance. Major Jakes and the other riders struggled to keep hold of their seats. His ribs ached, and his stomach gurgled. He didn't find the rough ride more comfortable than walking, but it did allow some muscles to rest while taxing others.

On one mission in southern Bosnia, he had added a new member to his team, a radio operator who seemed to consider it part of his job as a communications specialist to talk all the time. Jakes and his team preferred the silence, focusing their efforts on attuning all reflexes and all senses to maximum performance—but the new communications specialist wanted to chat about his family, about his high school, about books he had read, about the weather.

Major Jakes knew the young man wouldn't work out from the beginning. He had already decided to request a replacement, but the new radio operator had been shot by sniper fire while retreating from a microwave-relay substation the commando team had just destroyed.

The mission itself had never been mentioned in any newspaper or on any TV network. As far as the boy's parents knew, he had died in a freak training accident in Alabama, during specialized exercises. Luckily, the boy's parents had been members of the "Stars and Stripes, God, and Apple Pie" party and had never even considered asking for an investigation or bringing a wrongful-death lawsuit that would have required even more complicated coverups....

Now, journeying into the jungles, the other members rode in silence, as usual, contemplating the Xitaclan mission, going over the details step by step. They were professionals, and Jakes knew he could count on them.

Behind him, the explosives expert grunted and sighed as he pressed his hands together in an endless ritual of isometric exercises to keep himself in shape. Major Jakes did not question his actions, because the man had always performed impeccably.

Jakes checked his watch, then called for a brief halt. "Time to switch crews," he said. "But first let's triangulate on the signal and verify its position."

In the front of the second all-terrain vehicle, the new communications officer flipped up a flatscreen grid. He extended antennas from the sides of the ATV and adjusted frequencies until he picked up the pulsing message that even the Pentagon's best decryption experts found incomprehensible.

The signal pulsed loud and clear, like a subsonic jackhammer broadcast in all directions far and wide. Major Jakes couldn't comprehend who might be its intended listener, or who had sent it. It sounded like a foghorn, a warning... perhaps even an SOS. But what could that mean? So far, no one had bothered to reply to it.

"We are on course, Major," the communications specialist said. "The signal is loud and strong, and its position has not changed. According to my estimate on this topo map, we've already passed fifteen kilometers beyond Mexico Highway 307."

"Good," Major Jakes said, "we're ahead of schedule then. That should give us a leg up on dawn." He climbed down and stretched his legs, brushing his camouflage pants. "All aboard, Crew Two."

The second shift came aboard while he, the first lieutenant, and the other three men went to follow the two vehicles. The new drivers started up immediately and forged ahead.

Major Jakes trudged along, securing his rifle across his shoulder, holding it ready to be used in an instant. No hesitation. No contemplation. He and his team were the Good Guys, and they had been given orders to take out the Bad Guys. No sweat, no regrets.

He didn't know if the stakes were high enough that his actions might save the world… but someday that could well happen. Major Jakes treated every mission as if it could be The One.

He thought of all the James Bond movies he had seen, the banal secret agent adventures that were so preposterous and yet so uninteresting compared to his own missions. Each one of those movies featured a megalomaniacal mad genius bent on world domination; each one included a bizarre, high-tech fortress isolated in the wilderness.

As Jakes and his team tunneled deeper into the Yucatán forest, homing in on the ominous signal, he pondered what sort of crazed genius might have selected the vast Central American jungles to hide his stronghold. Why would anyone choose to erect a super-secret base in an ancient Maya ruin?

No matter. His team would destroy Xitaclan—and any people they found there—then they would return home. Major Jakes did not think beyond that.

They marched mile after mile, deeper into the jungles. With every step the source of the mysterious signal grew louder.

21

Xitaclan ruins
Tuesday, 7:04 A.M.

After another sweaty night filled with biting insects and unexplainable noises, Scully woke up and lay on her bedroll, trying to decide whether to rest for a few more minutes, or to get up and face the day.

In the light that filtered through her tent, Scully inspected the day's assortment of itching red insect bites, swellings, and skin rashes. From her small kit, she took out a tube of cream and rubbed a dab on the worst spots, then crawled to the flap and thrust her head into the hazy morning light.

The camp was quiet and brooding, as if holding its breath. Inside its ring of stones, the campfire had burned down to cold, gray-white ash. She stood up, hearing Mulder rustle inside his tent, but she stopped short when she turned to Vladimir Rubicon's tent.

It had collapsed in the night, fallen in on itself… as if some giant beast had stomped it flat.

Uneasy, she looked around, shading her eyes from the morning's slanted glare.

The hazy mist added a soft focus to everything, feathering the air. She saw no sign of the old archaeologist, nor of Fernando Victorio Aguilar, nor any of their Indian helpers.

She called out, "Hello, Dr. Rubicon?" She waited for an answer, then shouted his name again.

Mulder climbed out of his tent, stretching.

"Dr. Rubicon seems to be gone," Scully said. "Look, something's happened to his tent. Did you hear anything last night?"

Mulder immediately grew concerned. "Maybe he's just off looking for his daughter. Getting a head start."

Scully cupped her hands around her mouth and shouted again. "Dr. Rubicon!"

Out in the jungle birds squawked, angry at the disturbance. Scully and Mulder heard crackling branches at the edge of the trees. They both turned uneasily, waiting to see what might emerge from the swaying ferns.

Fernando Aguilar led a group of his Indian helpers. They all grinned, immensely pleased with themselves. Between them they carried a dead jaguar trussed on a branch pole, as if they had walked out of an old cartoon about big game hunters.

"See what we have caught!" Aguilar said. "This beast was prowling around the campsite last night, but our friends shot it with their arrows. Jaguar pelts are very valuable." Aguilar raised his eyebrows. "It's a good thing he wasn't hungry enough to come looking for us, eh?"

"Well, maybe he was," Mulder said. "We can't find Dr. Rubicon." He indicated the collapsed tent.

"Are you certain he isn't just out exploring?" Aguilar said. "I have been with my friends here since sunup."

"Dr. Rubicon could be looking around some of the other structures we missed yesterday," Scully admitted, "but he doesn't answer my calls."

"Then we must look for him, Señorita," Aguilar said. "But I'm sure he is all right. We already killed the jaguar, eh?"

The locals held up their pole triumphantly. The spotted cat lolled, bloody from dozens of small arrow wounds.

Aguilar kept his attention focused on the dead jaguar. "We'll be busy dressing and skinning this cat," he said. "You go ahead and search for Dr. Rubicon."

"Let's go, Mulder," Scully said.

Mulder nodded seriously. "Can't blame the good doctor for not wanting to waste

a moment. Let's split up," he said. "Do a broad, rapid sweep until we find him. I'll
go inside the big pyramid. I know Dr. Rubicon wanted to poke around in there."

"Agreed. I'll climb to the top temple and have a look around again. Maybe I can
spot him from up there."

Behind them, in front of the pair of feathered serpent stelae—Scully wondered
if the jaguar hunters had chosen that spot for some religious purpose—the locals
took out black obsidian knives, while Aguilar removed a wicked-looking hunting
blade. Together, they bent over and set to work flaying the dead cat.

Scully climbed the steep hieroglyphic staircase at the side of the pyramid. Her
arms and legs ached from the physical activity of the last few days, but she
ascended the crumbling narrow steps one at a time, leaning forward and using
her hands for support, as if scaling a cliff. She tried to imagine how the heavily
robed priests could have been graceful as they ascended to the upper temple to
perform their ancient rituals.

People would have gathered around the base of the plaza chanting, beating on
tortoise-shell drums with deer antlers, wearing colorful finery decked with
feathers of tropical birds, carved jade ornaments. When she reached the temple
pillars at the top of the ziggurat, Scully saw where royal spectators could watch
and perhaps share in the bloodletting. Due to the steepness of the pyramid, the
details of the sacrifices would not have been visible to the general audience
below—only the blood, the raised hands, the murder....

She shook her head to clear the vision, remembering what Dr. Rubicon had
muttered as he stared in awe around the Xitaclan site. *The past is strong in this place.*

Scully shaded her eyes and looked around. "Dr. Rubicon!" she shouted. Her
voice rang out like an ancient priest's chant, summoning the gods. She looked at
the bas-reliefs around her, the stylized images of the god Kukulkan, designs and
incomprehensible diagrams that Mulder insisted were blueprints of ancient spacecraft.

"Dr. Rubicon!" she repeated, still scanning the surrounding jungle. Below in the
courtyard she saw a splash of red as the Indians and Aguilar skinned the jaguar.
Three of the wiry men carried the raw and dripping carcass into the jungle. She
wondered if they intended to eat the meat.

With a shudder Scully thought of the mysterious Indian who, in his superstitious fervor, had hacked off a finger with one of his obsidian knives—and another
image came to the forefront of her mind unbidden: some of these natives in a

jungle thicket hacking out the raw red heart of the spotted cat and sharing it among themselves, eating the bloody flesh of their great jungle spirit.

She shook her head. She felt very alone and exposed, vulnerable atop the tall pyramid.

Giving up on finding any sign of the lone old man snooping in the jungles, Scully turned, looking closer to the great pyramid. She squinted, unwilling to call out again, remembering the old archaeologist's own shout for his daughter as he waited and watched for her in vain. Cassandra Rubicon hadn't responded to the call either.

Scully was about to give up when she went to the edge and looked down, away from the plaza. Then she caught her breath.

Mulder poked his head inside the dank opening of the pyramid, peering into the shadows. He noted prybar marks where Cassandra Rubicon and her helpers had broken open the ancient edifice. No doubt they had been careful, but smashing through sealed stone blocks required a certain amount of brute force.

He switched on his flashlight, and the brilliant beam stabbed into the unknown like a javelin, penetrating the mysterious blackness in the labyrinth built by Maya slaves. The flashlight comforted him, heavy in his hand. He was glad he had changed the batteries not long ago.

Though the tall pyramid had lasted for well over a thousand years, the interior did not appear sturdy enough to reassure Mulder—especially after the tremors their first night at Xitaclan. The hand-chiseled limestone blocks had begun to crumble at the edges, surfaces flaked by ravenous lichens and mosses.

His footsteps echoed on the stone floor. He shone the flashlight down, looking at the dust and powder to see scuffed footprints—Mulder couldn't tell if the shoeprints matched any member of Cassandra's team, or black-market grave robbers, or if they had been left by the old archaeologist just that morning.

"Hello, Dr. Rubicon—are you in there?" Mulder said, flaring his flashlight in different directions. His words reflected back at him with a resonating quality, a bell-like sharpness.

Mulder proceeded deeper into the pyramid, casting a glance over his shoulder to see the dwindling daylight from the opening. He wished he had brought bread crumbs to leave a trail… or at least sunflower seeds.

Water dripped from somewhere. Out of the corner of his eye he thought he saw movement—but when he flashed his light in that direction and saw the sharp shadows jumping, he knew it had only been an optical illusion. The darkness and the leaden air felt oppressive.

Thankful he wasn't claustrophobic, he rubbed the back of his hand along the tip of his nose. The temperature had dropped, as if some force gradually drank all the heat from the air. It had been at least a dozen centuries since the interior of this temple had been open to the sunshine. Playing his flashlight ahead, he saw that the ceiling had been supported by wooden beams, rough-hewn tree trunks recently placed there, no doubt by Cassandra's assistants. She must have been desperate to explore inside, he thought, excavating deeper and deeper into the pyramid, trying to unlock its secrets.

"Hey, Dr. Rubicon," he said again, in a normal voice this time, afraid of the machine-gun echoes. He looked down at his feet, at the dusty floor, untraveled—but then he saw a pair of footprints made by smaller shoes, definitely not old Dr. Rubicon's, apparently a woman's. Excitement beat in his heart. Cassandra had been here!

He proceeded cautiously now, intrigued on several different levels. His spatial perception suggested that he was approaching the heart of the pyramid. He was winding deeper, perhaps even underground.

The inner walls looked different now, unlike the corridors he had just passed through, which were made of simple blocks hewn from limestone. Those on his left were dark and unusually slick and smooth, as if they had been partially melted. This wall composition implied something new and unusual—of a different nature than the rest of the ancient structure.

Touching the slick glassy surface, he walked on. Up ahead, fallen rubble blocked off the corridor, a partially collapsed ceiling that sealed the passage leading directly into the pyramid's center. Mulder stopped short, thinking he had taken a wrong turn. Neither Vladimir nor Cassandra Rubicon could have proceeded any farther than this—but then he saw an opening dug through the fallen rock, a narrow window that only a very slender or very desperate person might wriggle through.

He crept to the edge, feeling as if he were intruding upon something. The temple around him swallowed all sound and heat. Mulder's light stabbed into the shadowy opening.

He raised himself up on the pile of rubble, pushing the flashlight ahead of him to look in. "Cassandra Rubicon?" he called, feeling foolish. "Are you in there?"

He was amazed at what he saw in the hidden chamber. His light played across smooth walls, reflected metal, curved objects made of glass or crystal. The eeriness and completely unexpected condition of the inner chamber made him pause with a thrill of discovery.

What had Cassandra thought when she first spotted this surprising change in architecture? As visions of Kukulkan danced in his head, Mulder tried to peer deeper, but his flashlight began to flicker. He rattled it to keep the batteries in contact, the beam steady.

He would return to this spot and explore, as soon as they found Dr. Rubicon, Mulder thought. Maybe the old archaeologist could provide an explanation. It would take some work, though, to clear away an opening large enough for someone to get inside without tearing his clothes or losing some skin.

Mulder heard a distant voice, and froze. The words bounced through the winding passages of the temple. He didn't have time to marvel at the acoustics as he recognized the faint sounds of Scully calling his name.

Her voice carried an urgency that made him snap into action, sliding back down from the rockfall and racing along the passages, taking the turns from memory. He shone his flashlight ahead of him—the batteries seemed to be working fine, now that he had moved away from the heart of the pyramid.

She called again and again. He heard the strain in her voice, and he raced faster. "Mulder, I found him! Mulder!" Her words rang between the stone walls, and finally he saw the light ahead, Scully standing at the opening, a humanoid silhouette surrounded by glare.

He burst out into the daylight, panting, his heart pounding.

She looked devastated. "Over here," she said.

He was breathing too hard to ask her questions, but simply followed. She hurried around the base of the pyramid, through the narrow jungle path. They reached the fallen-brick platform where sacrifices had once been performed at the edge of the deep circular well.

Mulder stopped short and looked down at the murky, unfathomably deep water. Scully stood next to him, swallowing hard, saying nothing.

There, like a doll that had been twisted and broken and then cast aside, floated the body of Vladimir Rubicon, facedown in the sacrificial cenote.

22

Xitaclan ruins
Tuesday, 11:14 A.M.

They anchored ropes to sturdy trees near the rim of the cenote, then dropped the cables down into the water. Everyone stood brooding, like spectators at the scene of a car accident, stunned by the discovery of the old man's body.

Fernando Aguilar offered the assistance of the Indian workers, suggesting that some of the wiry and muscular locals could easily scramble down the rope and retrieve Vladimir Rubicon. But Mulder refused. This was something he had to do himself.

Without a word, Scully helped to lash a rope harness under his arms and around his shoulders; she tugged the knots, checking that they were secure. Gripping the rope, Mulder eased himself over the rim and started down the rough side of the limestone sinkhole. Surrounding ledges made the wall itself lumpy and rugged, as if it had been chewed out of the rock with a giant drill bit. Mulder drifted away from the ledges and dangled as the Indians lowered him.

On the rim above, Fernando Aguilar stood close to Scully, bellowing instructions, berating the Indians when they did not move exactly as he said, though the helpers seemed to know what they were doing and paid no attention to Aguilar's specific commands.

Upon hearing the news of the archaeologist's death, the long-haired guide and expediter had reacted with shock and horror. "The old man must have wandered out in the middle of the night," Aguilar said. "The edge is abrupt here—he must have fallen in—and it is a long drop. I am sorry for his misfortune."

Mulder and Scully had looked knowingly at each other, but neither chose to challenge their guide's interpretation, at least not openly… at least not yet.

Mulder reached the level of the placid water. He could smell the dankness, the sour algae and a taint of trapped vapors from the abortive volcanic outburst the first night they had arrived at Xitaclan. His feet dangled below, just touching the water.

Immediately beneath him floated Vladimir Rubicon, his drenched shirt clinging to his bony back, his shoulder blades protruding. The old man's blond-gray head was twisted at an odd angle, his neck obviously broken—but had it been broken by the fall itself, or from a direct physical assault? Rubicon's arms and legs dangled unseen in the deep dark water.

Mulder gritted his teeth and held his breath as the Indians dropped him the last few feet. He plunged into the water, getting completely soaked. The rope harness held up most of his weight, and he managed to swim. He stroked with his hands and feet, pulling himself over to Rubicon's drifting body. The second rope tugged at him as he stretched it.

"Be careful, Mulder," Scully called, and he wondered what she might be warning him about.

"That's foremost on my mind," he said. The water felt thick, almost gelatinous, warm with the jungle heat, and yet tingling against his skin. He hoped the sacrificial pool wasn't infested with leeches, or some worse form of tropical life.

He looked down to where the water swallowed up his feet and his lower body. He could see nothing. Mulder couldn't tell what might lurk in the depths of the cenote beyond the range of sunlight. He thought of old Lovecraftian stories where ancient monsters from beyond time and space—feathered serpents, perhaps?—swam in the dark ooze, waiting to devour unwary innocents.

He thought he felt a ripple below his feet, and he jerked his leg away. Rubicon's body bobbed in the water, jiggling from some unseen disturbance. Mulder swallowed hard, looking down, but still he saw nothing.

"Just my imagination," he muttered to himself, knowing he did have a very good imagination.

He disengaged the second rope from around his chest and tugged for more slack. Above, the Indians obliged. Aguilar waved at him in encouragement.

Mulder draped the loose rope over his shoulder, wet and slick. Touching the old man's waterlogged shirt, he pulled Rubicon's limp body toward him in the water, then worked the end of the rope around the bony chest. He felt as if he were embracing the archaeologist.

"Goodbye, Vladimir Rubicon," he said, securing the knot. "Now at least your search can stop." He tugged on the rope, then shouted up, "Okay, pull him out!" His voice bounced around the wall of the sinkhole.

The ropes tightened as the Indians worked and heaved up above. Even Aguilar pitched in. The ropes strained, tugging Rubicon's body free of the water as if the cenote only reluctantly gave up its new prize—leaving Mulder alone in the water. He hoped that whatever gods still lived in Xitaclan didn't want to make it an even trade, Rubicon's body for his.

The old archaeologist rose up like a soggy scarecrow. Water trickled off his arms and legs. His blunt, big-knuckled fingers hung clenched like claws, and his head lolled to one side. His goatee was scraggly, wet, and clumped with green algae from the surface of the deep well.

Mulder swallowed and waited, treading water in the cenote as the wet corpse was hauled up to the rim of the well like a load of loose construction material. The helpers seemed decidedly uneasy to be so near the dead man.

Mulder watched them swing the body over the lip of the limestone well, then drag it onto the dry ground. Scully helped, leaving Mulder alone for a moment.

The water around him seemed cold, like cadaverous hands feeling his arms and legs, tugging on his wet clothes. Mulder decided not to wait any longer and swam to the steep limestone inner wall, beginning to ascend the corkscrew ledges without any assistance at all.

He had made it halfway up before Aguilar and the Indians got around to taking up the slack on the rope and helping him the rest of the way to the top.

Dripping wet and cold even in the Central American heat, Mulder finally looked back down from the rim of the cenote, staring into the dark water. The sacrificial well seemed undisturbed, placid, infinitely deep… and still hungry.

Back in the plaza by the remains of their camp, Mulder raised his voice, trying to get through to Fernando Aguilar and losing patience. "No more excuses, Aguilar! I want to get that radio transmitter up and running now. We know where it is, so stop stalling. Dr. Rubicon intended to send a message this morning, and now it's even more urgent."

Aguilar finally conceded and smiled at him, backing away. "Of course, Señor Mulder, that is a very good idea. In light of this tragedy, we cannot handle the situation alone, eh? It is good that we give up our search for Señorita Rubicon and her team. Yes, I will go get the transmitter."

Looking relieved to get away from Mulder, Aguilar sped off to the old cache of the UC-San Diego team's equipment, which had been untouched since its discovery the day before.

Mulder didn't tell him, though, that he had no intention of abandoning his efforts to find Cassandra.

Scully had laid out the body of Dr. Rubicon on the flagstones and began checking him over, trying to glean scraps of information from the condition of the cadaver. "I'm not going to need an autopsy bay to determine what killed him, Mulder," she said.

She ran her hands over the old man's neck, feeling his large Adam's apple, then she unbuttoned his shirt to check his clammy chest, his rubbery arms.

The others had fled, not wanting to be around the corpse while she worked with it. For the moment, Mulder didn't mind the solitude. The jungle isolation and their untrustworthy companions were making him more and more uneasy.

Scully pushed down on Rubicon's chest, feeling his rib cage, cocking her head to listen as she expelled air from his dead lungs. She looked up at Mulder, her eyes wide and concerned. "Well, he didn't drown—that much is for certain."

Mulder looked hard at her. She felt delicately around Rubicon's neck. "Several of his vertebrae are broken."

She rolled him over, exposing a livid spot at the base of his neck, turned purplish from the skin's immersion in the cold water. "I'm also convinced this injury wasn't caused by a simple fall," she said. "Dr. Rubicon didn't trip over the edge and drop into the water. I think Aguilar wants us to believe he died by accident—but the evidence shows Rubicon was struck hard from behind. Something crushed his neck. My guess is that Dr. Rubicon was dead before he was thrown into the cenote."

"Aguilar didn't want him to make his transmission this morning," Mulder pointed out. "Maybe that argument yesterday was more serious than I thought. What's he hiding?"

Scully said, "Don't forget that Aguilar led Cassandra Rubicon's team to this site in the first place—and now they're all missing. I think we have to presume them dead."

"Do you believe he intends to kill us?" Mulder realized that was an absolutely serious question, no paranoid fantasy at all. "He holds all the advantages here."

"We've still got our handguns, if it comes to that." Her shoulders slumped. "Look, Aguilar knows we're federal agents. He knows how the United States comes charging in if something happens to their own agents—remember when those DEA undercover officers were murdered here in Mexico? I don't think he'd be foolish enough to bring that upon himself. He can still write off Rubicon's death as an accident, unless we prove otherwise—but he couldn't explain away all of our deaths as accidental."

Mulder looked furtively around the plaza, seeing Aguilar and his ever-present Indian companions finally marching back out of the jungle. They carried a crate of equipment with them. The expression on Aguilar's face did not give Mulder a warm fuzzy feeling.

"Aguilar might realize the consequences," Mulder said, "but what if it's not him after all? What if these locals themselves are making sacrifices, like our friend Lefty who cut off his finger yesterday?"

Scully looked grim. "In that case, I can believe they wouldn't be overly concerned about U.S. government intervention."

Fernando Aguilar hurried up to them while the Indians hung back, afraid of Rubicon's body spreadeagled on the flagstones. "Señor Mulder," he said, "I have bad news. The transmitter is broken."

Mulder said, "How could it be broken? We just took it out of the box yesterday."

Aguilar shrugged, taking off his spotted hat. "The weather, the rain, the conditions here…" He held out the transmitter, and Mulder noticed that the back plate was loose, bent out of its groove. The inner workings were muddy and corroded.

"Water has gotten in, or insects," Aguilar said. "Who can tell, eh? The transmitter has been in that old temple, unattended ever since the first team got to Xitaclan. We are unable to contact outside help."

"That's a tragedy," Mulder said, then muttered, "and also quite convenient."

Scully shot him a look, and he knew that the two of them would have to play their cards carefully. If he stretched his imagination to the limits of credibility, he could believe in the accidental destruction of the transmitter, or he could believe in the accidental death of Rubicon, or in the accidental disappearance of Cassandra and the other archaeologists.

But he couldn't take it all together.

Scully said with forced brightness, "We'll just have to make the best of it, then, won't we, Mulder?"

He knew that she, too, felt trapped in the wilderness, with no contact from the outside… and the only people around them a potentially murderous crew who had no qualms about eliminating any inconveniences they might encounter.

23

Xitaclan ruins
Tuesday, 2 :45 P.M.

Scully felt the weight of the rubberized canvas diving suit on her shoulders, a heavy alien skin that muffled her movements and insulated her body. Here out on dry land, stumbling across the weathered promenade toward the sacrificial well, the suit felt incredibly unwieldy and clumsy. The weights at her waist clanked together. She hoped that once she descended into the water, the suit would become an advantage instead of a hindrance.

Mulder stood back and looked at her, his hands on his hips, eyebrows raised. "That's quite a fashion statement, Scully."

She tugged at the thick fabric folds, adjusting the diving suit as she stood on the edge of the cenote. She felt an eerie sense of displacement. The suit had been purchased for Cassandra Rubicon to use during her own searches for ancient artifacts and the answers to Maya mysteries.

Now Scully was the only one who could fit into the suit—and her personal search was for something much more sinister, something much more recent.

After finding the body of Vladimir Rubicon, her dread had grown. She had little doubt that the five members of the UC-San Diego research team floated below the surface of the sacrificial well, waterlogged, decaying. If she did indeed find the archaeologist's daughter, beaten like her father, her only consolation was that Dr. Rubicon himself would not be around to witness the grim conclusion to their investigation.

Mulder held the heavy insulated helmet in his hands. "And now to complete the ensemble," he said, "your lovely hat."

Even fresh out of the crate, it seemed an old suit, bargain basement. Scully hoped the equipment had been checked out and proven functional. Like many research expeditions, the UC-San Diego team had operated on a tight budget, forced to cut corners wherever they could. According to paperwork tacked inside the crate, translated by Fernando Aguilar, the suit had been donated by the Mexican government as part of its joint financing of the Xitaclan expedition.

As Scully lowered the heavy helmet over her reddish-gold hair, Mulder's expression became serious. "Are you ready for this, Scully?"

"It's part of the job, Mulder," she said. "This is our case, and somebody has to go down and look." She lowered her voice. "Just keep your weapon handy. You'll be alone up here on the rim, and I'll be alone down there. Not a strategically advantageous situation."

Mulder had kept his 9-mm Sig Sauer close at his side ever since discovering the old archaeologist's "accidental death"—but the Indians far outnumbered them, and they had shown no qualms about getting hurt, if they intended to make another blood sacrifice.

Even if Mulder and Scully encountered no violence, they remained at the mercy of Fernando Aguilar to get them back out of this jungle.

Not a strategically advantageous situation, she thought again.

Scully secured the heavy diving helmet, locking it to the collar attachment rings. Inside, her breath echoed like a breeze through a cave. She swallowed heavily.

Mulder helped her check the air connections on the back of her suit, long rubber-wrapped tubes like garden hoses that dangled from her back. A small generator would pump and circulate air into her helmet, though it looked barely large enough to power a portable hair dryer.

Aguilar and the Indians stood around the equipment, watching her with a curiosity mixed with anxiety. Scully glanced at them uneasily, but saw no one with missing fingers or a bandaged hand.

"I do not see what you expect to accomplish down there, Señorita," Aguilar said again, his arms crossed over his khaki vest. "We are in a terrible situation here and should leave as soon as possible."

Aguilar gestured to the Indians, speaking quietly, though Scully doubted any of them could speak English. "My associates are very distressed about the prospect of disturbing the sacred cenote. It is cursed from the victims sacrificed there. They say the ancient gods have taken their revenge on the old man—and if we continue to disturb them, the gods will attack us as well."

"Just like they attacked the members of the archaeology team?" Mulder suggested.

Aguilar tightened his ocelot-skin hat, letting his dark ponytail dangle behind him. "Perhaps there is a reason why Xitaclan remained deserted for so many centuries, Señor Mulder."

"I'm going down," Scully said firmly, her voice sounding hollow through the open faceplate. "We have an obligation to investigate if it helps us find our people. The cenote is the most obvious place we haven't searched, especially in light of finding Dr. Rubicon." She checked the weights at her waist, the utility flashlight hanging from her belt. "While I respect their religious beliefs, your 'associates' need to respect international law, Mr. Aguilar."

Scully sealed the faceplate and then gestured for Mulder to switch on the air generator. A whining, puttering sound throbbed into the jungle like noise from miniature construction machinery. She breathed deeply, smelled the stale air, sour from sealants and old rubber. When she felt a faint breeze stir around her face, she knew the air had begun to flow.

She gestured for them to help her descend into the cenote, hoping that the generator and the suit would last long enough for her to look around under the water. The Indians gazed at her solemnly, as if bidding her a final farewell.

Gripping the same ropes Mulder had used to walk/climb down the rugged limestone walls, Scully made her way one laborious step at a time. Her tedious descent took her many minutes, and the suit seemed as heavy as a truck on her back—but when she reached the edge of the deceptively placid pool, she found herself reluctant to plunge in.

She did not dwell on her irrational fears, but let loose of the wall. Scully plunged into the water, sinking like Thompson's proverbial bag of lead due to the weights around her waist.

The murk swallowed her up like syrup, a primordial ooze that embraced her. Water engulfed her enclosed helmet. The fabric of the suit pressed against her arms and legs, squeezing her intimately as she dropped deeper and deeper. The depths and the opaque water smothered the light, blinding her for a moment.

A fizz of bubbles curled around the seals in her rubber-lined suit. Scully breathed again, double-checking, verifying that no water seemed to be leaking in and that her vital air supply continued pumping through the hoses. Gradually, her confidence grew.

Under the tug of gravity, she continued to sink toward the bottom... if the cenote had a bottom.

As her eyes adjusted, the water around her became murky and greenish, like wan sunlight filtered through thick smoked-glass panes. She moved her hands and legs experimentally, floundering in the water. Disoriented, she felt only that she continued to go deeper. Deeper.

The pressure around her became heavier, and her ears sensed the strain, the water like a vise squeezing her helmet. She thought again of Dr. Rubicon's story of how Thompson had sustained permanent ear damage from a faulty suit during his descent into the Chichén Itzá cenote.

She forced those thoughts away and tried to look around, turning her head in the confining helmet. She continued to drop, meter after meter. She couldn't imagine how deep this well was. Surely, she had already gone below the thirty-foot depth of the Chichén Itzá well.

The circle of light above had dwindled to only a faint, faint reflection of the bright Mexican sky. Her breathing echoed around her ears like distant surf, and she could barely feel the exchange of air through the hoses.

She heaved another breath and could smell the stink of the old tubes, the residual chemicals like the whiff of a long-dead cadaver. The suit seemed terribly hot and stuffy, the helmet claustrophobic.

Her vision swam for a moment, and she became dizzy trying to inhale another breath, then she calmed herself. Her problem had been only imaginary; she had begun to hyperventilate.

Scully noticed a faint lambent glow deep below her, much farther than she wanted to descend—a blue-white light that seemed to seep from the bottom of the sacrificial well, a glowing mist that oozed from the porous limestone itself.

As her eyes adjusted, Scully saw there could be no mistake—the haze of illumination pulsed and throbbed as if sending some sort of signal, a flashed SOS beacon, but at much slower intervals.

The faint light below seemed cold and unearthly. Her skin crawled even as she chastised herself for being foolishly spooked. It was the type of irrational nervousness brought about by telling horror stories around a campfire. Mulder would have loved it.

Her partner might have suggested the light was from a cluster of ghosts, remnants of Maya sacrificial victims. Scully's scientific mind postulated a colony of phosphorescent algae or anaerobic microorganisms living off the limestone far below, shedding faint, heatless light into their surroundings. Vengeful ghosts or extraterrestrials—she knew that couldn't be true.

She realized her descent had slowed, her belt-weights reaching equilibrium with the natural buoyancy of her body and the suit, counteracting her ability to sink. She hung in the water like a suspended anchor, feeling the pressure of the depths around her, but imagining herself to be weightless.

Scully fumbled at her wide belt, reaching for the utility flashlight. She unclipped it, fastened the chain around her wrist for safety, and gripped its handle for comfort.

Swallowing away her uneasiness, Scully switched on the dazzling beam, which stabbed through the murk like a snowplow through a blizzard. Kicking her booted feet, she turned in the thick sluggish water, looking around.

And came face to face with a corpse.

A bloated body hung in the water not three feet from her, arms spread, eye sockets open, flesh tattered and leprous after being gnawed by small fishes. The mouth hung wide, and tiny minnows darted out from between his jaws.

Scully gasped. A huge outburst of bubbles squeezed from seams in her suit as she jerked. In reflex, her hand released its grip on the heavy utility light, and the beam plunged downward, pointing deep below.

She scrambled desperately for the light, suddenly realizing her mistake. The flashlight dangled and stopped, bobbing up and down—then she remembered she had tethered it to her wrist.

Her heart pounded. Scully grabbed the flashlight and pointed the beam back up, studying the corpse that had terrified her.

It was a man, his dark hair drifting about in clumps. Rocks hung from cords tied to his waist. He had been killed and thrown into the cenote. Recently.

She felt the hot air booming in her helmet now, though an incredible cold seeped through the canvas fabric of her suit from the water around her.

Scully swung her flashlight like a lighthouse beam, sweeping through the undisturbed depths of the cenote. She did not linger on the corpse in front of her, but searched through the depths.

The flashlight beam played across other stick-like silhouettes floating like smashed, waterlogged insects, sunk beneath the water.

She had discovered the missing team of American archaeologists.

24

Xitaclan ruins
Tuesday, 4:16 P.M.

The flagstone plaza was littered with bodies.

Since the Indians had refused to help retrieve the bloated corpses from the cenote, it had taken Scully and Mulder hours to hoist the dead figures up to the top of the sinkhole, one at a time.

While still deep in the stygian well, Scully had used her utility knife to saw through the cords holding the stones that weighted the corpses, and the water-logged cadavers had slowly drifted up to the surface.

Standing on the rim, watching anxiously for his partner, Mulder had been shocked to see one swollen form drift up to the top of the cenote, then another and another, while Scully remained deep below, breathing through her air hoses. Finally, she too came back to daylight, opening the faceplate of her helmet and drawing huge breaths of the humid air before proceeding with the most unpleasant part of the task.

As they had dragged the dripping, stinking bodies up and out of the water, sprawling them on dry ground, Fernando Victorio Aguilar had stood by, looking extremely agitated and queasy. Mulder had kept his FBI standard-issue handgun in plain sight. Finally, the guide had grudgingly assisted him with the ropes, helping to haul Scully back up the limestone wall.

Panting, her nerves jangled, she had shucked out of the cumbersome suit, standing in her sweat-dampened shorts and blouse, then stared down at the most difficult part of the work. Four bodies, and plenty of questions.

Aguilar had stammered, staring down at the gray-green, shriveled skin on all the cadavers lying on the packed ground next to the brick sacrificial platform. The distorted, half-decomposed features of the research team stared back up at him with empty, accusing eye sockets. His Adam's apple bobbed up and down, and he rubbed his cheeks as if he needed a shave.

"Just help us get them to the plaza," Scully had said. "They can't walk by themselves."

When they had finally taken the soggy, stinking bodies around the tall pyramid and to the open plaza near their camp, Aguilar continued to look furtively around, swallowing repeatedly as if to prevent himself from vomiting. Finally, he cleared his throat and excused himself. "I'm afraid I am going to be sick if I remain here any longer," he said, stumbling backward. "That foul stench…"

The entire crew of Indians had already fled into the jungle with so much wailing and shrieking Scully doubted they would ever return. She wondered if the Indians had a village nearby, or if they had just found a place to huddle under the overspreading trees… where they could tell each other superstitious stories and cut off their own fingers.

"Go see if you can find our cheerleading squad, Aguilar," Mulder said to the retreating guide. "We'll need those helpers to get out of here. Now that we've found our missing people, we can go."

"Yes, Señor," Aguilar said. "I will be back as soon as I can, and, uh…" He shuffled his feet. "Congratulations on finding your people… though you have my sorrow it had to turn out like this, eh? Just like the old man." He scuttled off, disappearing into a fern-lined path, his dark ponytail bobbing.

Mulder fidgeted in the late afternoon light, gazing at the silent temples and over-grown ruins, listening to the brooding sounds in the jungle. He kept an eye out for anything suspicious, while Scully devoted her attention to the four wet corpses that lay beside Vladimir Rubicon's. Next to the bloated new bodies, the old archae-ologist seemed like a contented retiree who had died peacefully in his sleep.

"Since we have such a limited pool of possibilities," Scully said, "it'll be fairly easy to identify the four bodies," she said, her voice droning, businesslike because she had no choice.

She had taken the dossiers from her pack inside the tent and looked at the sheets of paper, the photographs: smiling pictures of ambitious young grad students eager to make names for themselves in an obscure field. The team had gone off on an innocent adventure to the Yucatán, expecting that their future would hold guest spots on talk shows or slide presentations in academic venues around the country.

Instead they had found only death.

Scully glanced at the photos, the identifying information. She studied the hair color, the height, the general bone structure. After advanced bloating from prolonged submersion and the onset of decay, their handsome facial features were unrecognizable.

"This dark-haired one is Kelly Rowan," Scully said. "He was the tallest of the group, the secondary leader, easy to identify."

Mulder knelt down beside her. "This should have been one of his most glorious accomplishments," he said, looking down at the young man's destroyed features. "Dr. Rubicon said he was a talented scholar with a great potential for archaeology, a good partner for Cassandra."

Scully did not dwell on the subject. In times like this, when performing autop-sies and identifying corpses, she found it best to lock away the part of her mind that considered these figures… these objects… to be actual people. For now she had to be professional, despite the primitive conditions.

"The second man is John Forbin," Scully said, moving on to the next corpse. "He was the youngest of the lot—you can see it on him. In his first year of grad-uate school. An architect with a specialty in large, ancient structures."

Mulder shook his head. "He must have felt like a kid in a candy store here, all these untouched temples to study."

Scully pressed on with the identification tasks. "This young woman is obvi-ously Cait Barron, the photographer and artist. She liked to paint watercolors more than she liked to take photographs. Her hair color and body weight are all wrong for her to be Cassandra."

Mulder nodded. Scully drew a deep breath, forcing herself to shut out the smell. She frequently rubbed camphor ointment under her nostrils to mask the stench during an autopsy, but here in the jungle she had to rough it.

"And that leaves this one to be Christopher Porte, the expert on Maya hiero-glyphics," she said. "What did you call it, an epigrapher?"

Mulder nodded. "Not too many people have that knowledge, and now the field has one less." He cocked his ear, as if he had heard something, pausing…

A sudden noise made him spin around quickly, his hand on his pistol—but it turned out to be only a group of squabbling birds in the overhanging vines. Looking sheepish, he turned back to Scully.

"So what did happen to Cassandra Rubicon? Are you sure you didn't find her body down there under the water? It was dark, and cold—"

"I searched, Mulder. All these others were clustered together, weighted and hanging at the same depth. Believe me, I spent a lot more time than I wanted to beneath the surface with this group of corpses." She nodded to the bodies. "But there just wasn't anyone else. Unless something happened to place her in a different spot, Cassandra's body wasn't down there."

"So we've solved one mystery, and now we're left with another that could be just as difficult."

Scully felt hot and sweaty and dirty. The cloying putrescence of the water-logged corpses clung to everything, a sweet nauseating odor that clawed its way through her nose and mouth to lodge permanently in her lungs. She desperately wanted a shower or a hot bath, anything to feel clean again. A swim in the cenote just wouldn't do it.

But she still hadn't finished her task. Afterward, she might treat herself to a quick sponge bath.

"Let's see if we can determine anything about the cause of death from the condi-tion of the bodies," Scully said. She used her knife to cut away the clothes, exposing the torsos of each of the victims.

"It's been too long to determine if they'd merely drowned," she said, "because the air would have outgassed from their bodies, and their lungs would have filled up with water anyway."

She moved John Forbin's head from side to side, seeing the neck move, but not too flexibly. "Unlike Dr. Rubicon," she said, "the neck hasn't been broken."

She rolled Cait Barron over and looked at the grayish-white skin on her back. Two circular puckered holes marked the base of the young woman's lower back.

"Bullet wounds," Scully said, raising her eyebrows. "I'll bet they were all shot before being thrown in." She shook her head, lost in thought.

"But where was Cassandra during all this?" Mulder asked, pacing on the flag-stones. "She's still missing."

"Yes, we can keep our hopes up," Scully said. She examined each of the bodies. All four had been shot... most of them low in the back, in a paralyzing but not fatal blow. The similar placement of the wounds could not be accidental. The victims had been thrown into the sacrificial well while still alive.

"We have some very bad people here, Mulder," Scully said. Mulder frowned. "After seeing the severed finger and the blood sacrifice, and watching how super-stitious these locals are, it seems that the violent old religion is really still preva-lent. The Indians could have been the ones who performed these sacrifices, murdering convenient strangers.

"I read that the old tribes would take prisoners to slaughter in front of the gods, cutting out their enemies' hearts rather than killing their own people." He turned to look up at the central Pyramid of Kukulkan looming in the center of the plaza.

"Their hearts weren't cut out, Mulder. These people were shot."

Mulder shrugged. "Tossing victims into the sacred cenote was another perfectly legitimate way to appease the gods. If the Indians paralyzed the archaeology team before hurling them in, the sacrifices would still have been living and breathing— appropriate offerings."

Scully stood up, feeling her knees ache. She wiped her hands on her already stained slacks. "Mulder, remember that these people were shot with guns, not attacked with primitive obsidian knives. It doesn't seem their style."

"Maybe they're modernizing their religion."

Mulder actually took out his pistol this time and held it as he continued to scan the jungle warily. "This is their backyard, Scully, and there's a lot of them. Why do I feel very much like another convenient sacrifice... say, like a turkey feels around Thanksgiving time?"

Scully moved next to him, closer than she needed to. They looked out at the wilderness, the only human beings in sight. Even with Mulder next to her, she felt very, very alone.

25

Xitaclan ruins
Tuesday, 11:17 P.M.

Full darkness had fallen, leaving them in the company of only the late-rising moon and their laughably small campfire. The looming darkness of the surrounding jungle threatened to swallow them up. Mulder felt very small and very vulnerable in the vastness of the wilderness.

Staring into the fire, Scully said, "Remember when I told you that Mexico sounded better than an Arctic research station or a chicken-processing plant in Arkansas?"

"Yes."

"I think I've changed my mind."

In light of the unspoken threat from the Maya sacrificial cult, or treacherous Aguilar, or whoever else was responsible for the numerous murders, the two agents had decided to take turns at watch throughout the night. But neither Mulder nor Scully felt the least bit interested in sleep.

Mulder sat on the flagstones watching the campfire, looking up at the moon, and listening to the songs of jungle insects. The smoke from damp, moss-covered wood curled around his nose, thick and pungent, a relief after the underlying stench of decay that arose from the corpses. He cradled his 9-mm pistol in his lap, fully attentive, alert.

Though night had fallen hours before, Scully had crawled out of her tent to sit up beside him. "We could heat some water," she suggested, "have coffee or tea. Seems appropriate for a night around the campfire."

Mulder turned to smile at her. "Did we bring any hot cocoa mix, the kind with the little marshmallows?"

"I think Aguilar took that with him."

Mulder stared out into the surrounding trees, seeing the silver dapple of moon-light. The Indians had not returned, nor—disturbingly—had Aguilar. Mulder wasn't sure if that was a good thing, or if he wanted the others to come back and lead him and Scully back to civilization.

Meanwhile, their only companions in the camp were the lumpy forms of the five corpses spread out not far from the tents, blanketed by a stained tarp Mulder had recovered from the team's supply cache. Mulder kept glancing over at the shapes, unable to dispel images of the bloated, waterlogged forms of the four archaeology team members and the bony body of Vladimir Rubicon, whose open blue eyes had looked surprised even in death.

He looked over at Scully. They were both grimy and dirt-streaked—they hadn't showered for days. Their hair hung in unkempt tangles from the sweat and humidity. He was glad to be there with her, rather than anyone else in the world.

"Scully," he said, his voice quiet and serious, "with the… unorthodox explanations I often find when studying the evidence, I know you're always skeptical— but every time you're at least fair to me. You respect my opinion, even when you don't agree with it." He looked at his hands. "I don't know if I've ever told you, but I really appreciate that."

She looked at him and smiled. "You've told me, Mulder. Maybe not in words… but you've told me."

He swallowed, then brought up the subject he had been avoiding. "I know you're probably not going to believe this either, blaming it on a trick of the moonlight or my own grogginess from lack of sleep—but two nights ago I heard noises out in the jungle. I poked my head out to investigate, and I saw something moving, a large creature that wasn't like anything I've ever seen before. Well, that's not completely true… I've seen it many times before but not in real life."

"Mulder, what are you talking about?" she said.

Out in the jungle they heard other sounds, rustling noises, something large coming closer. Mulder perked up his ears and felt his blood run cold.

"I think I saw… one of those feathered serpents. Just like that statue." He indicated the coiled snake engraved in the limestone column of the stela in the plaza. "It was larger than a crocodile, and it moved with such grace. Ah, Scully, you should have seen it. It reminded me of a dragon."

"Mulder, that feathered serpent is a mythological creature," she said, automatically falling back into her role as skeptic. "What you saw must have been inspired by looking at Maya carvings for days and all the research you've been doing into pre-Colombian legends. You probably spotted a cayman—those are large reptiles found in these jungles. When you saw it move, your imagination could have added other details you wanted to see."

"That's possible, Scully," he admitted, shifting the pistol in his lap from one hand to the other. He heard more branches cracking, additional movement in the jungle, creeping closer to them.

He spoke more rapidly. "On the other hand, look at the sheer number of feathered serpent images throughout the Maya artifacts, at all different sites... here at Xitaclan in particular. It's such an odd thing. A snake with feathers? What could have inspired such a myth if the Indians of the Yucatán hadn't seen such a creature with their own eyes? It could even be an explanation for the prevalent myths worldwide of dragons and reptilian worms."

His words picked up speed as he followed his imagination. "Does it seem likely to you that dozens of cultures around the world would create an image so precisely similar? Think of the drawings you've seen of Chinese dragons. They weren't called feathered serpents, but they had the same configuration. Long feathery scales and a sinuous body."

Out in the jungle the crashing, lumbering sounds became louder and louder. Some creature unmistakably was making its way toward Xitaclan as if drawn to a magnet. As the noise grew, it sounded as if many large creatures were converging on the plaza itself. Mulder raised his pistol.

"Listen to that, Scully. I hope we don't get a chance to meet one of my imaginary feathered serpents face-to-face," he said.

The sounds continued to increase. Trees bent, cracked, and fell over; ferns swayed. Scully cocked her ear and turned her head toward Mulder. They huddled around the campfire, both of them with their weapons in hand, ready to make a last stand, if necessary.

But Scully suddenly became more curious than frightened. "Wait—Mulder, that's a mechanical noise," she said.

As soon as she spoke, Mulder realized that the growling, grinding sound he heard was indeed an engine noise, the crunching of tires, and the humming of generators.

Then, with a blinding roar, stars exploded in the sky, brilliant white glares like aerial combat. Fireworks shot into the air and burst like a white chrysanthemum.

"Those are phosphorous flares," Mulder said. "Military issue."

Under the glare of the scalding white light, two lumbering all-terrain vehicles smashed through the fallen underbrush and rolled up onto the flagstones of the Xitaclan plaza. Behind the ATVs, dark figures wearing camouflage outfits scrambled out of the jungle. They crept low, holding their rifles, snapping abbreviated instructions to each other as they rushed into position like army ants swarming to a new nest.

"What's going on here?" Scully said, looking both alarmed and perplexed at her partner.

"I guess it's not a good idea for us to run for it."

Scully instantly assessed the weaponry, the soldiers, the vehicles. The hulking all-terrain vehicles rolled to a stop, crunching the weathered flagstones beneath them, smashing upthrust tree roots. The camouflaged commandos ran about, intent on their mission—and Mulder realized with surprise that the terse phrases they snapped back and forth at each other were in English, not Spanish.

On first sight he had imagined a Central American guerrilla army, but though he saw no markings on their uniforms or on their vehicles, he knew he had found a different answer.

"Those are Americans," he said. "U.S. military. Some sort of commando operation."

Mulder and Scully sat frozen next to their little campfire, hands raised, pistols in nonaggressive positions. The commando squad ran up and surrounded the two, pointing rifles at them.

"I knew I should have paid that parking ticket," Mulder muttered.

While two of the soldiers aimed rifle barrels directly at their chests, another man crept forward and cautiously removed Mulder and Scully's weapons, holding them at arm's length, as if the small 9-mm pistols were poisonous spiders.

The phosphorous flares had gradually faded out. Several of the camouflaged commandos rigged up brilliant arc lights, flooding the plaza with a harsh glare.

A slender, dark-skinned man marched up to Mulder and Scully, clearly in command of the operation. He had high cheekbones, an aquiline nose, generous lips, and a pointed chin. His eyes were narrow and as dark as obsidian. On his shoulders he wore the maple-leaf-cluster insignia of a major.

"*Habla Espanol?*" the major demanded. "*Que pasa?*" Scully leaned forward. "We speak English," she said. "We are Americans, special agents of the Federal Bureau of Investigation."

The commandos stopped and looked at each other. The major stood rigid. "What are you doing here?" he said. "On foreign soil?"

"We could ask you the same question," Mulder said.

"My partner and I are here on a case involving missing U.S. citizens." Scully reached into her pocket. The soldiers tensed, but she moved slowly enough. "I'm going for my ID," she said and carefully withdrew her badge and photo identification card.

Mulder looked at her, amazed that even here in the jungle she still kept her ID in her shirt pocket.

"We are legal attaches, LEGATS, to the U.S. Consulate," she said. "Our assign-ment here in Quintana Roo is to search for a missing archaeological team."

"Major Jakes, over here!" shouted two soldiers who had been exploring the open plaza area. They held back the tarp that had been covering the five bodies beside the feathered serpent stela. "Casualties, sir." The major turned to look, saw the corpses.

Mulder shrugged. "Well, actually we've already found most of the missing team," he said.

Major Jakes gazed around the ruins and the plaza. Seeing no one other than the two agents, he raised his voice to issue orders to his soldiers. "Continue securing the site. This isn't what we expected to find, but we still have our orders. We must complete the mission, destroy this command outpost, and be gone before morning."

"While you're at it, do you suppose you could give us a lift out of here?" Mulder said. "If you have room in the back seat of one of those ATVs, I mean?"

"If the parameters of the mission allow it," Jakes said, his voice entirely deadpan. He bent over to study Scully's ID. "My men are not here in any official capacity, and we are under orders to respond with full denial."

"We've heard that before," Mulder said.

"We can operate under those conditions," Scully answered more firmly, "if that is the requirement for getting us out of here. What is your mission, Major?"

"To destroy this military site," he said matter-of-factly. "Eliminate the source of a strange encrypted transmission."

"*This* is a military site?" Mulder said in astonishment. He spread his hands to indicate the crumbling pyramid, the weathered stelae, the fallen temples. "These are ancient Maya ruins, abandoned for a thousand years. You can see that with your own eyes. My partner and I have been here searching for days, and we haven't found the slightest evidence of high technology or stored weapons. This place has no military significance whatsoever."

Then, as if specifically to contradict him, a rain of automatic-weapon fire showered from the shadows of the jungle, pelting the commando team.

26

Xitaclan ruins
Wednesday, 12:26 A.M.

As the sharp, high-pitched shots rang out with a sound like a chainsaw, Scully ducked reflexively.

Mulder tackled her, knocking her down beside the meager shelter of their low tents.

Her face pressed against the cold flagstones, Scully could see winking flashes of fire as hidden snipers continued the attack.

Major Jakes and his commando squad exploded into motion, their own response as fast as a swarm of angry wasps. "Get to cover, everyone!" Jakes shouted. "Fire at will!"

"Of course, I could be wrong about this place having no military significance," Mulder said, breathing hard, close to Scully's ear. "Are you hurt?"

"No," she said, panting. "Thanks, Mulder."

Though Scully could not determine where the shots came from, the American commandos responded with an impressive display of firepower, the quantity of bullets sufficient to make up for their lack of a precise target.

One of the soldiers next to her spun around as if from an invisible force, and he sprawled on the broken flagstones. The young first lieutenant gasped and choked as bright arterial blood spilled from both the entry and exit wound in his rib cage. Scully could see at a glance that the young man had received a mortal injury.

Return gunfire rang out from the jungle snipers. A bright puff of splintered stone blossomed on the limestone stela nearest their tent, making a gouge across the feathered serpent carving still smeared with rusty brown splotches from the previous day's blood sacrifice.

The soldiers sprinted back toward the two armored all-terrain vehicles. One man ducked behind the limestone stela, another flattened himself behind the low, tarpaulin-covered corpses on the flagstones.

"Who's firing at us?" Scully demanded when she had caught her breath.

The American commando squad continued blasting the trees, but they had only a slim hope of actually striking one of the shadowy enemies. Someone unseen screamed in pain, then renewed gunfire drowned out all other sounds. A lucky shot from the jungle shattered one of the portable arc lights the commandos had erected.

A deep voice bellowed out of the jungle, using no loudspeaker, but with enough strength to penetrate the chaos. His crisp Mexican accent sliced through the night. "American invaders!" the man shouted. "You are illegally in the sovereign state of Quintana Roo. Your defiance of our laws and our borders is against all international treaties."

As they both remained low to the ground, trying to remain minimal targets, Scully looked over at Mulder. She recognized the voice. "That's the police chief,

Carlos Barreio!" Bullets sang low over their heads. "But why is the chief of state police firing at us in the middle of the night? In the middle of the jungle? This isn't a law-enforcement raid."

Mulder raised his eyebrows. "It seems Chief Barreio has gone out for some extracurricular activities."

One of Major Jakes's soldiers launched another garish phosphorous flare into the sky, where it burned white-hot, splashing a glare down upon the field that caused more confusion than illumination.

"Identify yourself!" Major Jakes shouted, crouching beside Mulder and Scully in the illusionary shelter of the tent. "We have superior firepower."

More shots spat from the trees, tearing holes through the fabric of the tent. Jakes ducked sideways, collapsing on top of Mulder and Scully. A furrow of blood appeared at his shoulder-merely a flesh wound, nothing serious. Major Jakes didn't even seem to notice.

"This is an act of war," Barreio shouted back. "You invaders have brought contraband arms into our land." The gunfire dwindled as the guerrillas' leader spoke, with only a few sharp sounds peppering a flare-lit night. "We have no choice but to protect our culture. We cannot allow military intruders from the United States to walk off with our national treasures."

"But we're not here to steal artifacts," Major Jakes muttered to himself, shaking his head. "We're just here to blow up the pyramid."

Mulder rose to an elbow and looked over at the major. "Well then, if it's all just one big misunderstanding, maybe we can shake hands with him and talk about this?"

Major Jakes didn't appear to hear. "It all makes sense now," he said. "These are freedom fighters, members of the violent revolutionary front in the Yucatán— *Liberación Quintana Roo*. They want to make their own little country and secede from the Mexican nation, regardless of what the rest of the Yucatán population wants. They don't have many weapons, nor do they have any moral compunctions."

Mulder looked at him coldly. "Unlike you and your men."

Major Jakes returned the gaze, his expression blank, completely without anger. "Correct, Agent Mulder."

"Throw down your weapons and surrender!" Barreio continued to bellow. "You will be arrested, charged as illegal aliens, and punished accordingly… unless your country chooses to extradite you."

Major Jakes's nostrils flared. Since this was not an official mission, Scully knew the government would deny its existence and write off the commando squad. Jakes and his men would be abandoned to whatever kangaroo court or dim torture chambers the guerrilla group chose.

"My men will never surrender," Major Jakes shouted back, and more gunfire rang out. "Not to cowardly snipers, and not to terrorists."

"I always wanted to be in a real Mexican standoff," Mulder said.

Scully knew that the covert American commando group might be able to outgun and outfight the *Liberación Quintana Roo* rebels in a standing battle—but they could not escape or retreat with so many snipers hidden in the jungles. They were trapped at Xitaclan.

The phosphorous flare fizzled and faded out, and the second arc light shattered, plunging the site back into a darkness broken only by occasional gunfire and afterimages on Scully's eyes.

"You two will stay next to me," Major Jakes said. "I realize you are both noncombatants—though I'm not sure there's a satisfactory way to resolve this."

"Then could we have our weapons back, sir?" Mulder asked. "Since it's already come down to a fight."

"No, Agent Mulder. I don't believe that would be in your best interests." Major Jakes turned his night-vision goggles toward the forest.

As she lay on the flagstones, wincing every time bullets whined over her head, Scully felt the ground tremble, building to a vigorous vibration, as if even more heavy machinery were rolling toward them—then she realized that this tremor originated from deeper within the earth. Another rumbling came, a quaking, as volcanic pressure built up beneath the limestone crust.

"Scully, hang on," Mulder said. He grabbed her arm, though Major Jakes and his men did not understand what was happening.

The ground bucked and shook as seismic forces writhed beneath them. The great pyramid of Xitaclan rattled and trembled. Blocks of loosened stone tumbled down the steep steps. From the jungle, some of the snipers wailed in terror, while Jakes's commandos scrambled about in equal confusion.

The more distant of the plaza's two feathered serpent stelae groaned, then toppled over onto the flagstones. The ancient obelisk crumbled into broken rubble. The trees danced and waved.

Steam blasted from small openings in the plaza flagstones. Little fumaroles split through the ground, releasing tremendous pressure.

"Come on, Scully, let's get out of here!" Mulder shouted, tugging at her arm. "We can run—use this as a diversion, get to shelter." He stood and staggered away, the ground leaping like a carnival ride beneath his feet.

Scully rose to join him, but Major Jakes stood next to her, blocking the way. "Not so fast, you two. You're staying here."

Angry shouts rang out from the forest, and Scully could hear trees toppling, uprooted by the tremors. She tried to stare down Major Jakes as he held his weapon at her, and she knew from the expression in his eyes that she couldn't flee. Mulder had already crossed half of the plaza, ducking and weaving, trying to get to the cover of one of the low temple ruins. Mulder turned back to her, an anguished expression on his face. He paused as if he meant to come running back, to surrender to Jakes in order to stay beside her.

"Just go, Mulder!" she said. "Get out of here!"

He took that to heart and put on more speed, dashing toward the cover of the pyramid's lower platform. Gunfire splattered against the uneven flagstones near his heels, bullets ricocheting into the night—she couldn't tell if the shots had come from the guerrillas in the jungle or from Major Jakes's commandos.

The ground lurched with one titanic jolt, and Scully heard a sound like muscles tearing, as if the ground below were giving birth. A giant pillar of steam exploded from behind the Pyramid of Kukulkan, water boiling away and draining into the ground.

She realized the steam explosion came from the cenote—a crack in the earth had split the bottom of the intensely deep well, dumping water into a volcanic cauldron.

Scully caught only a glimpse of her partner's silhouette, but she knew with a dismay that made her chest ache that Mulder was running straight toward it, as if drawn.

27

Xitaclan ruins
Wednesday, 1:31 A.M.

By the time Mulder reached meager cover, the ground had stopped swaying and hiccoughing beneath his feet. A few snipers took potshots at him, but most of them seemed concerned more with their own safety. Before the gunfire could pick up again, he took advantage of the stunned motionlessness around the ruins and ran on, taking shelter at the edge of the immense pyramid.

He felt dismayed at leaving Scully behind, a prisoner of—or perhaps "under the protection of"—Major Jakes and his commando squad. But she had told him to run, told him to get away. Her last words piercing through the volcanic tremors had cut him free, as if a leash holding him back had suddenly snapped. If he could solve the mystery, find the answers that Barreio's guerrillas and the American soldiers both wanted, perhaps he could use it to gain Scully's freedom.

Now he plunged in a single direction, for better or worse. He knew that he, one man—unarmed, since Jakes had relieved him of even his handgun—could do little against two opposing military forces. Mulder hoped to approach the problem from a different direction, finding an unexpected solution from left field. He needed to discover the secret of the great pyramid of Xitaclan. What had Cassandra Rubicon found there?

The abortive eruption and tremors had failed to produce gushing lava and ash, but as Mulder staggered toward the abrupt edge of the sacrificial sinkhole, he came to a quick stop—and stared down, awestruck.

Somewhere deep in the basement of the Earth the ground had cracked, splitting open the bottom of the sacrificial well. The limestone sinkhole had dumped its contents into a smoldering pit of volcanic heat—all the cold, quiet water of the cenote, the still depths that had cradled the sunken bodies of Cassandra Rubicon's team as well as the broken old archaeologist himself. As he ran, Mulder had watched the mushroom cloud of stinking steam pour into the sky as if from a boiler explosion....

Now the sinkhole lay empty, dripping and crackling, like a dry, wide-open mouth. Its limestone walls remained slick and lumpy. Steam still curled up with a sour biting stench of volcanic gases.

Mulder looked down into the gasping cenote, a pit into hell like the legendary entrance into Hades from Greek mythology. Deep below, he saw a faint glow. The haze of illumination was unlike firelight, unlike the smoldering glare of volcanic heat. This seemed more of a cold glow, a shimmer that throbbed and pulsed like a beacon shouting silently into the bottomless shaft.

Scully had told him she'd seen a similar unsettling glow during her diving expedition, like distant heat lightning, far below the depth where she had discovered the bodies of the research team. Phosphorescent algae growing far from the touch of sunlight, she had speculated. As Mulder stared at the faint haze, watching the flickering light, he could not accept his partner's scientific explanation. This rising and falling glitter seemed too orderly, too regular, a pattern… some kind of a signal.

He thought of the major's claim that the Xitaclan ruins were the source of some mysterious encrypted signal, a transmission whose code the U.S. military presumably could not break… But what if the transmission was not encrypted or-encoded in any way, but simply in a language that Major Jakes could not understand, that no human had ever learned?

Vladimir Rubicon had gently chided Mulder for his imaginative interpretation of the carvings atop the temple… for his explanation that the wise god Kukulkan, who had come in a silver ship trailing fire, might have been an ancient astronaut, an extraterrestrial come to Earth at the dawn of human civilization. But now, observing the eerie glow deep down in the drained cenote, Mulder felt certain this must be some kind of SOS beacon.

Mulder saw the tangled ropes still lashed to the gnarled trees, dangling along the side of the now-empty sacrificial well. He stared down at the steep curving limestone walls. With the knobs and handholds and sloping ledges, plus the support of the old ropes, he could make the descent. Probably.

The glow called to him. He had to go down there. No question about it.

He grasped the ropes, wet and warm and slick in his palm. They must have been cooked like vegetables in the noxious vapors that had boiled up out of the sacrificial well—but the cables appeared undamaged. They would hold his weight… he hoped.

He tugged, securing the knots firmly above, and lowered himself backward over the edge, digging the heels of his shoes into the damp limestone. As he expected, he found sufficient lumps and footholds to assist his descent—but the drop seemed impossibly far down.

Straining his arm muscles, Mulder picked up speed as he gained confidence, making his way from ledge to ledge, working himself downward. He grasped the rough rope, but frequently used it only as a crutch and not for actual support.

Mulder's head began to spin from the foul odors hissing up from below like the fetid breath of a dragon. He couldn't imagine how deep the sinkhole actually went. Luckily, the beckoning glow did not arise from the absolute depths, but only partially down.

Razor-sharp cracks of gunfire rang out across the air again. Mulder froze, plastering himself in the darkness under an overhang as the blasts reverberated in the hollow chamber of the cenote, but he realized that no one had shot at him intentionally. The fighting had started again, now that the hidden assailants had recovered from their fear and confusion after the violent tremors.

"Guess I better pick up the pace," he muttered. He wasn't going to let anything as trivial as a minor Central American revolution distract him from learning what he needed to know.

Mulder dropped down to another ledge, and the color of the limestone changed from faded white to a darker, browner shade, stained with slimy residue. He was now below what had been the surface of the water.

Another shot rang out far above, and he heard thin voices in Spanish or the back-of-the-throat Maya derivative the local Indians had spoken. He wondered if Fernando Aguilar and his native helpers had returned, bumbling into the conflict… or perhaps Aguilar was somehow in league with Barreio and his *Liberación Quintana Roo* movement.

He and Scully now had another set of murder suspects. Evidently, Barreio's group of violent rebels might have chosen to assassinate a team of American archaeologists defiling their national treasures. The price of revolution.

But… if Mulder's suspicions about the fantastic origin of this ancient Maya city proved to be true, then the relics of Xitaclan belonged to no nation on Earth.

It had always bothered him—why had the Maya people abandoned this lush, isolated site, and so many of their grand cities? Why had they built Xitaclan here at all, far from trade routes or rivers or roads? What had fostered the birth of their entire great empire? Why did the Maya develop such an interest in astronomical knowledge, calendrical cycles, planetary orbits?

The Maya had been obsessed with time and the stars, the passage of the Earth around the sun. They had kept meticulous track of days and months, like a child crossing off dates on his calendar in the month before a birthday.

He had a feeling all the answers lay below, in the light.

Underneath the water's former surface, the cenote's ledges and outcroppings were thicker, knobbier, unweathered. He climbed down, his heart beating faster, his curiosity burning.

Then he ran out of rope.

Mulder looked at the frayed end, the long dangling strands that clung to the cenote wall, all the way to the rim above. He had no choice but to continue downward, unaided.

The glow grew brighter around him now, colder. He sweated from the thick volcanic heat, the leftover steam, the sauna of vapors around him in the empty cenote pit. But the light grew whitish-blue and cold, pulsing through the surrounding rock. The walls seemed barely able to contain the energy seeping out.

Finally, working his way the rest of the distance, his fingers clenching slippery handholds and knobby outcroppings of limestone, Mulder arrived panting at a wide ledge, an arched opening… exposing a smooth rectangle of metal.

More gunfire rang out in the night, but Mulder didn't hear it.

The alloy frame was encrusted and corroded, but remarkably clean after centuries of submersion in the cold cenote waters. The shape and appearance of the portal was unmistakable, and Mulder reached out to touch it, his fingers trembling.

The exposed opening was clearly some kind of door.

The door to a ship.

28

Xitaclan ruins
Wednesday, 2:15 A.M.

The ancient metallic hatch opened with a drawn-out hissing breath of equalizing air pressure—a sound, Mulder suspected, similar to what a feathered serpent might make just before it attacked…

Despite his desperate curiosity, Mulder turned away and held his breath, afraid of what toxins he might inhale inside the newly opened chamber. In other investigations he had been overcome after catching a whiff of the noxious blood from decomposing alien figures. Whatever lay beneath the Xitaclan ruins had been entombed for centuries, and he had no way of knowing just what might lie inside this long-abandoned… craft?

His eyes stung from the fumes still rising from volcanic cracks in the unseen floor of the cenote. He hoped the ground didn't spasm again anytime soon.

But hearing the faint popcorn sound of gunfire above even louder than the dripping echoes trickling down the curved limestone walls, Mulder knew he could not spare any time or energy to worry about his own safety. He had to get his answers, and then get back to Scully.

For that, he needed to go inside.

He planted his foot one step through the doorway, feeling the solidity of the floor.

The entrance corridor was smooth-walled and womb-like, the walls a polished metallic substance that absorbed the light and reflected it back. Mulder could not see any source to the glare. It was a blinding harshness, clearly designed, he thought, for eyes adapted to the light of a different sun.

The Maya had never been skilled metalsmiths, had no smelting capabilities to create the materials he saw around him. He proceeded farther down the corridor, as if drawn. The walls hummed with a high-pitched throbbing sensation, like alien music. He felt it deeply within his bones, his teeth, the back of his skull. Mulder wanted to tell someone, share his amazement. But that had to wait until he escaped again.

He recalled a far more mundane scenario out at the jogging track near FBI Headquarters, when he had finished a long, exhilarating run, the second time he had encountered the man he came to call "Deep Throat." When Mulder had questioned him about alien visitations, hard evidence of conspiracies locked away in secret government vaults, Deep Throat had given his usual answers that weren't answers.

"They're here, aren't they?" Mulder had said, sweating from his run, demanding to know.

With his calm, unassuming smile and his knowing voice, Deep Throat had raised his eyebrows. "Mr. Mulder, they've been here for a long, long time."

But could it have been as long as thousands of years?

Now Mulder stepped deeper down the armored corridor, exploring the remains of what must be an ancient derelict, the ship of an alien visitor who had landed—perhaps crashed—in the Yucatán Peninsula centuries and centuries before, here at the birthplace of the Maya civilization.

"Talk about illegal aliens," Mulder muttered.

The winding passages opened up, revealing dark, half-collapsed chambers, what had been other metal-walled rooms. Where corroded alloy plates had tumbled to the floor, the holes had been repaired with pieces of carved stone. Little of the original ship itself remained, barely a metal framework patched up with limestone blocks.

Mulder imagined Maya priests entering the "sacred" pyramid long after the alien visitors had vanished, still attempting to be caretakers but not knowing how. Generations and generations of awestruck visitors would have worn the floor smooth.

Perhaps the missing equipment and girders had been cannibalized from the main structure to be used in other Maya temples… or perhaps they had been stripped and destroyed by treasure seekers… or cast away by religious zealots such as Father Diego de Landa.

A sense of wonder engulfed him, coursed through his veins as he continued to explore. Never before had he seen such overwhelming evidence, such incredible remains of an extraterrestrial construction.

The corridors in the derelict ship reflected the same blueprint that Mulder had encountered while moving through the labyrinth of the pyramid above in his search for Vladimir Rubicon the day before. Up there, Mulder had explored the dark tunnels until stopped by the strange sealed passage. Perhaps, he thought, it was an upper entrance to the entombed ship.

Mulder wondered if the craft itself had crashed, plowing a crater in the middle of the jungle. When the local, uncivilized people had come to investigate, Kukulkan, the "wise god from the stars," had taught them immense knowledge, fostering the birth of a great civilization.

He ran his fingers along the gaps in the metallic walls, touching the polished limestone. More than anything, he wished Vladimir Rubicon could have lived long enough to see this.

Over the millennia the Maya—or later treasure seekers—had stripped the derelict to the bone, leaving only this skeleton of the original ship. But it was enough. Mulder knew this proof could not be denied.

If only he could bring Scully down here, where she could see.

With a pang he hoped she was still all right, that Major Jakes had at least protected her against a resurgence of the guerrillas, as a hostage if nothing else.

If only he and Scully could get out of here alive. She had told him once before, during their frantic escape from the radio telescope at Arecibo, Puerto Rico, "Evidence is worthless if you're dead."

He came to an ascending, spiraling ramp, and followed the bright, pulsing glow steeply upward. He had no idea how deep underground he still was.

His amazement doubled when he reached the next level. He had arrived at the chamber from which the glowing beacon emanated. He had to shield his eyes from the light, which burned so brightly that his skull hurt. *This must be the control bridge*, he thought. He slowly scanned the entire room.

The entire chamber remained virtually intact, its oddly complex protrusions—machinery?—apparently functional. Mulder instantly realized that this place must have held enormous religious significance for the Maya.

Suddenly Mulder saw something that made him freeze, his stomach tightening. One of the chambers was filled with a strange translucent substance, an ethereal gel that held a shadow, an outline—a silhouetted humanoid figure, poised motionless in the far doorway, arms outstretched, legs partially apart. The silhouette looked slender, skeletal, distorted by the engulfing murk.

Drawn like a moth to a flame, Mulder staggered across the sloping deck of the bridge to reach the narrow chamber—and he saw then that the silhouetted figure surrounded by the gelatinous substance was that of a young woman with long hair and human features.

Mulder hesitated. The rational part of his mind knew it couldn't be his sister. It couldn't be her.

As he stood before the outline, blinking and squinting in the bright light all around him, he studied the woman who hung frozen in place, trapped like an insect in amber....

As he strained to make out the details, Mulder saw that her face seemed surprised, her mouth partly opened, her eyes wide, as if she had been suddenly captured there like a photographic image. The gelatin grew clearer, as if stirred by unseen currents of energy. He noted her green-brown eyes, her petite figure that looked as if it could well have fit inside the diving suit Scully had used. Flowing cinnamon-colored hair, a spray of fresh red scratches on one cheek.

Of all the wonders that Mulder had seen and found inside the derelict ship, he was most surprised by this one.

After their days of searching, he had finally found Cassandra Rubicon.

29

Xitaclan ruins
Wednesday, 2:33 A.M.

Major Jakes ordered Scully to get down, and she had no choice but to obey.

He bellowed orders for his forces to launch their all-out counterstrike. Random sniper fire from the jungle shot out one more hastily erected arc light, but dazzling phosphorous flares lit the sky to compensate, creating a strobelight effect that accentuated the explosions and gunfire.

From the weapons supplies inside one of the armored all-terrain vehicles, two soldiers set up a small rocket battery and then a grenade launcher. Scully covered her ears as the commandos began to wreak Armageddon on the dense jungle.

Startled gunfire rang out from the scattered *Liberación Quintana Roo* freedom fighters. But as trees erupted into gouts of fire and detonations thundered through the underbrush, Scully heard more wild outcries, panicked shouts, and screams of pain.

A salvo of automatic-weapon fire chattered back out of the trees. Two of Major Jakes's commandos were hurled to the ground, torn apart by heavy caliber bullets. One moaned, one didn't.

"Stay under cover!" Major Jakes shouted, with a firm hand pressing Scully down beside the pathetic shelter of the low tents.

The surrounding jungle began to burn. Another commando took the place of the fallen soldier at the rocket launcher and shot four tiny missiles toward the heart of the hidden gunfire. The detonations sounded louder than the recent volcanic tremors.

The sniper fire trailed off again. Over the crackle of flames in the smothering underbrush, Scully could hear receding shouts under cover of the mahogany trees and creeper-entangled jungle. The flares in the sky cast a parade of shadows.

One of the grime-smeared, breathless young commandos came running up, squatting as he scurried for cover. From the soft, rounded features of his face, Scully couldn't imagine that the soldier was more than twenty, but his eyes were flinty and hard, aged well beyond his years.

"The enemy seems to be falling back, sir," the young soldier said. "Temporarily, at least."

Major Jakes nodded. "Superior firepower is always enough to intimidate upstart forces. I want you to run and get a damage assessment."

"I can give you a preliminary, sir," the soldier said. "At least four men down, three fatally, one… well, it still looks pretty bad, Major."

Jakes looked deeply stunned, as if the wind had been knocked out of him, then he drew a deep breath, the nostrils of his aquiline nose flaring wide. "Six left," he said.

Another soldier came up, bleeding from the right side of his rib cage; he didn't allow the injury to slow him down. "The guerrilla force has disappeared into the trees, sir," he said. "We suspect they're regrouping for another assault."

"They know they can't outgun us," Jakes said. "But they can wait us out."

"Do you request that we go out on a hunting expedition, Major?" the soldier asked, distractedly squeezing his side to stanch the blood flow.

Major Jakes shook his head. "Any word on their leader? The man issuing demands?"

"Preliminary only, sir," the soldier said. He pulled his hand away from the wound on his side, flexing his sticky fingers. Scully could see a gouge of ripped flesh, cauterized from the heat of a passing bullet. The soldier looked at the wet sparkle of blood on his palm, then nonchalantly wiped his hand on the leg of his camouflaged pants as if getting rid of a squashed bug.

"The leader has also run for cover, we believe. Unfortunately, we must presume he is not injured. He was last seen making a break for the main citadel in the ruins, there." The soldier gestured toward the Pyramid of Kukulkan. "Perhaps that's some sort of rebel stronghold or additional weapons stockpile. Clearly our primary target."

"This is an archaeological site, not a military target," Scully said, forcing herself to her knees and pushing away from Jakes. It infuriated her to see the death and injuries, the wanton destruction caused by both Barreio's freedom fighters and Major Jakes's commandos. "It's just an ancient Mayan ruin, can't you see? Nothing more!"

"All evidence to the contrary." Major Jakes looked at her, his face stony. "If Xita-clan is merely a site of historical interest, then why is this gang of rebels defending it with lethal force?" He turned to the injured soldier, who stood waiting for further orders. "Proceed with the objectives of the mission. I want two mortar launchers set up and ready to go within ten minutes."

"Yes, sir," the man said, then ran off, ducking low and weaving for cover across the battered plaza despite the lack of gunfire.

"By what right do you come in here and attack a sovereign country and destroy a site of priceless archaeological value?" Scully demanded. "These ruins are thousands of years old, never before studied by science or historians. You have no proof that this is some weapons stockpile or revolutionary base."

Major Jakes withdrew her confiscated badge and ID wallet from the generous pocket of his camouflaged pants, scrutinized her identification again, and handed the wallet back to her. "Very well, Special Agent Scully of the Federal Bureau of Investigation," he said. "Let me show you my evidence. Since you are already inside the security restrictions of this mission, you're bound by the legalities and classification of what you've seen."

"I have a security clearance, and I know how to keep my mouth shut," Scully said. "But I don't have any answers. Yet."

"Come with me, please," he said, "over to the lead vehicle." Without waiting for her, he ducked and ran toward the ATVs. Scully scrambled after him, imitating his evasive pattern as she remembered the training she had undergone at Quantico. She found it amazing how the presence of danger sharpened her memory.

But this operation was different from a simple suspect shoot-out: Xitaclan had become the site of an all-out war. Luckily, though, the offensive sniper fire did not ring out again, and the two of them reached the large-wheeled vehicle without incident.

From a sealed compartment, Major Jakes removed a thin dossier packet: pictures and files printed out on flimsy, water-soluble paper. With strong hands, he pulled out two curling black-and-white satellite photographs. They were blurred, as if they had been faxed several times.

"This photograph shows what remains of the stronghold of a major Central American drug lord, Xavier Salida," Jakes said. "Heavily guarded and well provisioned with weapons. We've known about his illegal activities for some time. The Drug Enforcement Agency has worked with the local Mexican police in an attempt to set him up—but Salida was untouchable. Too many corrupt politicians in his pocket. That's always the problem with the drug lords out here."

"If you worked with local police like Carlos Barreio, I can see why," Scully said sourly. She bent closer to study the satellite photograph. "So why am I looking at a crater? Did your team take him out because you couldn't extradite him legally? Is this what you intend to do here at Xitaclan? Leave a big crater?"

"No," Jakes said, not the least bit offended. Even the close firefight seemed not to rattle him. The small injury to his shoulder had stopped bleeding. "We had nothing to do with this event.

"The crater radius and the condition of the surface, as well as concurrent seismic evidence and a faint atmospheric flash detected by one of our side-looking horizon satellites, allows us to draw only one conclusion: without question, this is the result of a tactical nuclear strike."

"You mean somebody lobbed an atomic bomb at a Mexican drug lord?" Scully said in disbelief.

"That's what the evidence conclusively proves, Agent Scully. Nothing else could have released this much heat and energy in a single burst."

"But how?" Scully asked. "Where would a rival drug lord get his hands on a warhead?"

Jakes nodded to himself, pursing his lips. "Here's a scenario: A certain number of displaced nuclear armaments may have been diverted during the breakup of the former Soviet Union. It's possible some of these lost assets may have fallen into the hands of terrorists. These slimeballs do a better job of eliminating each other than we do of apprehending them."

Scully stared at the curled photo again. "With a nuke? Isn't that going a bit overboard?"

Major Jakes sidestepped the question. "We also know that the revolutionary group *Liberación Quintana Roo*—the gentlemen shooting at us this evening—have been gathering up weapons for their hopeless fight against the central Mexican government. We are greatly concerned that one or more of these missing tactical nuclear weapons may have fallen into their hands. We believe the guerrilla group would hold few compunctions against using it in a major populated area."

Scully nodded, concerned to see the actual reasoning behind the drastic actions Major Jakes and his commandos had undertaken. She pressed her lips together as her thoughts whirled, wondering if the murders of the archaeology team had something to do with gun-running activities or weapons sales to drug lords. Could the illegal revolutionary group have been using Xitaclan as a secret base, undiscovered, until a nosy team of American scientists came in to poke around?

But that didn't help Mulder, who had run off in the direction of the pyramid two hours ago. She hoped he hadn't been taken prisoner by the revolutionaries, or shot.

"That still doesn't tell me why Xitaclan," Scully said. "Why here? These isolated ruins have been untouched for centuries. There are no roads, no facilities, no power—obviously it's not a high-security compound. There's nothing here. Why an all-out strike in the middle of nowhere?"

Jakes reached over into the control panel of the all-terrain vehicle. He switched on the flatscreen grid, which glowed gray and silvery blue before the images resolved into a topographical line drawing of a close-up of their location, centering down from the overall Yucatán Peninsula. Jakes punched several commands, and the map zoomed to a smaller and smaller scale. A pulsing light throbbed from a location on the map like a sonar signal or a heartbeat.

"This transmission emanates from here, Agent Scully. Prior to the strike on Xavier Salida's fortress, the signal appeared on our military receivers. It seems to be encoded. We cannot determine its origin or its purpose, but we believe the signal is linked to these activities. Therefore my team has been given orders to penetrate whatever defenses might surround this isolated jungle base—and to destroy the transmitter."

Scully watched the pulsing signal, the hypnotic pattern of flashing light on the screen. "How do you know that's a military transmission?" she said. "If it's in a code you don't understand, you have no reason to believe it could be a threat. That's quite a leap of logic."

Major Jakes remained staring at the screen, his dark eyes intent. "Our intelligence has classified it as a military threat."

"What intelligence?" Scully said, gripping the side of the vehicle. "What do they know beyond what you're telling me?"

"It's not my place to question them, Agent Scully," Major Jakes said. "I need only to know the target and the objective. My commando squad is tasked with carrying out those orders, not in debating them. From experience, we know that's best for all concerned."

The first injured soldier staggered up to the all-terrain vehicle, panting. Scully noted that the narrow gash in his side had split open again, spilling fresh blood into his uniform. "All set up, sir. Ready to rock and roll, as soon as you give the order."

"Very well—the order is given." Jakes straightened, crossing his arms over his chest. He did not turn to face Scully. "Let's take that pyramid down."

Scully looked toward the silhouetted ziggurat in the flickering flames from jungle fires, wondering if Mulder had found shelter.

"Let 'er rip!" a young voice shouted.

Scully watched in horror as the commandos began to launch explosive mortars into the ruins.

30

Xitaclan derelict ship
Wednesday, 2:41 A.M.

When Mulder finally recovered from the shock of finding Cassandra Rubicon, caught in the derelict ship like a fly in a spiderweb, he stepped back. He drew several deep breaths, calming himself, remembering to focus, to study all the details, acquire all the information, before he did anything rash. Assess the situation....

He stepped as close to the suspended figure as he could without touching the strange, gelatinous barrier, then he paused to consider what he should do. He couldn't risk damaging anything here… and he had no intention of becoming trapped, as the young woman had been.

But this was incredible!

Forcing himself to turn away, he spun around, scanning the amazing room, looking for more clues. With a start, he saw that other small, dim chambers similar to the one that imprisoned Cassandra dotted the walls around him—dim alcoves like empty coffins in a mausoleum… empty except for one, which held someone—something—else.

Resisting his unsettling curiosity about the archaeologist's daughter, Mulder moved to the single other occupied chamber in the control-room wall, dreading what he might find there.

"Let's see what's behind door number two," he said.

The figure lay crumpled, a mound of wadded rags and desiccated flesh, as if he had been struck down where he stood. The mummified, hardened remains were distorted like a lump of mahogany driftwood, stripped of all moisture, barely more than tatters of iron-hard tissue that held crumbling bones together.

At first glance Mulder couldn't tell if the mummy was actually human. He recalled similar dried corpses he had encountered while investigating other cases—in a high-schooler's grave in Oregon, in a buried boxcar in New Mexico—desiccated remains, possibly of extraterrestrial origin, possibly not.

With a sense of amazement tinged with desperate hope, he wondered whether this forlorn figure could have been one of the original occupants of the derelict craft. Perhaps even Kukulkan himself?

Scully would never accept that conclusion until she could do an autopsy herself. But when taken together with the other evidence—the buried ship and its artifacts, the Maya carvings of spacemen and feathered serpents—this long-dead inhabitant would be compelling enough even to the most hardened skeptic. Even to Scully.

He turned back to the murky, bizarre chamber that held Cassandra Rubicon, and the differences between the two… specimens… struck him. Whereas Cassandra hung perfectly preserved in a coffin of petrified light, as if time had somehow stopped for her, the other occupant looked as if time had rolled over him with a steam roller and left him like roadkill in the dust. This dried-out corpse had suffered some kind of mishap. Mulder wondered what had gone wrong.

He resisted going inside the mummy's alcove. Not yet. The walls of the main chamber blistered with the pulsing light that sent a vibrating tingle through his head. A message only recently sent out to a distant people who must have stopped listening a thousand years before.

Tearing himself away from the mummified corpse and the trapped figure of Cassandra, Mulder studied the limestone walls, where metal had fallen away in the main chamber. He saw chiseled images similar to those on the temple at the apex of the pyramid. But these images were less stylized and more realistic.

As far as he could tell, the scenes depicted a tall silhouetted form, a godlike figure, an alien surrounded by Indians who seemed to worship him… or fear him. The godlike image—Kukulkan?—stood accompanied by several monstrous feathered serpents.

Mulder felt a shiver crawl down his back. These were well-rendered images of the creature he had seen in the moonlit shadows two nights earlier. Slithering, glossy… unearthly.

He followed the succession of carvings that paraded across the walls, impressions of the Maya people building temples, erecting cities in the jungle, treating the ancient astronaut with great reverence. In each scene the visitor had his back turned, his head lifted up, his unseen face toward the sky… as if waiting for someone to come. A rescuer perhaps?

But for whatever reason, Mulder thought, "Kukulkan" had intentionally come back inside the derelict ship, placing himself into one of these chambers to stay… to die.

Unless there had been an accident.

Mulder approached the young woman's frozen alcove again, straining to see if she had moved—blinked her eyes, drawn a breath… but nothing had changed.

Through the "amber," Cassandra did not look lifeless, though. The flush of blood still colored her face, a sparkle of tiny injuries on one cheek as if she had been sprayed with splinters. Her hair seemed sweat-dampened, her skin dusty as if she had worked her way through the partially crumbled catacombs in the pyramid above. She looked exhausted, overheated… frightened.

But not dead. Mulder had seen enough corpses to know.

Assuming that this place was indeed a buried spaceship, he wondered if this could perhaps be some sort of suspended animation chamber, a stasis booth where time would stop for extraterrestrial explorers making an incomparably long journey across the void of space. He had seen the same idea in plenty of science fiction movies… maybe the aliens had thought of it for themselves.

He searched the walls beside Cassandra's glowing doorway, but found no controls, no status indicator, no colored buttons that might show him how to thaw the frozen substance.

So, instead, he reached out to touch the cold, dim gel himself, imagining that perhaps he could just take Cassandra Rubicon's hand and raise her up out of her glass coffin, like the prince awakening Sleeping Beauty in the forest.

He hesitated before he let his fingertips brush the tangible substance, afraid that it might somehow suck him in as well, like alien quicksand—two specimens for the price of one. But he had to know. He had to risk everything. Mulder pushed his hand through before his doubts could grow stronger.

When he touched the cold gelatinous wall, it… burst, popping like a soap bubble. Puddles of slick, volatile liquid splashed across the floorplates.

Coughing and gasping for breath, Cassandra Rubicon lurched at him, already running, as if she had paused in the middle of a panicked flight. Dripping wet and horrified, she crashed into Mulder and screamed. He reached out to defend himself as she drove him to the floor, pounding him weakly with her fists.

"No!" she croaked. "Leave us alone!" She grabbed the heavy flashlight that hung from her waist and swung it at Mulder as if it were a large metal club.

He reached up to defend himself. Using his best hand-to-hand combat training, he grabbed her wrist, used his other arm to snatch the flashlight away, and pinned her hands in the air. "Easy! I'm with the FBI, Federal Agent. I'm here to save you."

She trembled and held herself motionless, but coiled, vibrating like a tightly wound spring. "There was someone shooting… and a bright light." She looked around, her muddy green eyes unfocused. She smeared thin slime away from her face, shuddering and dazed. She seemed to drift in and out of coherence, as if her brain had not yet entirely unfrozen.

Mulder sat up guardedly, still keeping his eye on her. He knew he must look a frightful mess—battered, muddied from the climb down the slippery walls of the cenote, sweaty from days of trekking through the jungle. But coated with the volatile ooze, the young woman looked far worse.

He brushed at his shirt. "I take it you're Cassandra Rubicon?" he said. When she nodded, he continued. "You and your team have been missing for over two weeks."

"Impossible," she said, then coughed again, wiping her hands on her pants in disgust. "We just got here a few days ago." She sniffed her wet shirt. "What is this stuff?"

Mulder shook his head. "Your father contacted us a week ago Tuesday. My partner and I came with him to search for you here at Xitaclan." He hesitated, but she needed to know. Better to give her all the shock at once—though he couldn't bring himself to tell her about her father just yet. "I'm afraid we found the other four members of your team dead—shot, and then sunk in the cenote."

Cassandra blinked and looked around, clearing her throat. Her voice was rich and resonant, filled with more anger than fear. "Those men, men with guns," she said. "Bastards. What did they want? Who were they?"

"I think they're part of a violent revolutionary group. They've been keeping us company outside tonight."

Cassandra looked down at her fingers, blinking but seemingly not seeing. These events had happened for her only moments before. "So how... how did I get away?" She clamped her teeth together and hissed, "Bastards."

"We found the other four, but you were still missing," Mulder continued. "I've just discovered you here by accident. You were trapped in... and I set you free from... whatever it was you had gotten yourself into."

Cassandra wiped at her eyes and stared at the metal walls around her. But her vision did not seem to focus. "This stuff burns my eyes... can't see very well."

Mulder used his sleeve to dry her face. She continued talking. "I ran into the pyramid to get away... got lost... stumbled in here. Then I don't know what happened. Light gushed all around me, drowning me, burning and cold." She sat down on the floor next to him, deeply puzzled. "Did I hurt you?"

Mulder shook his head. "Good thing you don't know karate," he said, rubbing his bruised arm.

Then he suddenly realized that the throbbing SOS signal had ceased as soon as he had released her from the alcove. The diaphanous light throughout the main chamber began to fade. The signal had stopped, and now the derelict ship seemed to be... waiting, settling back to sleep.

Tears streamed out of Cassandra's reddened, irritated eyes.

Mulder wiped her face again and decided it would be too much to tell Cassandra he believed they were inside a derelict ship, an extraterrestrial space-craft buried beneath the pyramid of Xitaclan. Or that he thought she had stumbled upon a lifeboat. She must have activated its automatic system which placed her in suspended animation.

Mulder stood up and helped her to her feet. Cassandra stretched, flexing her arms experimentally. The cold, wet gel began to dry into a thin coating on her clothes and skin. She swayed dizzily for a moment, then drew a deep breath.

Mulder looked around, but the pulsing signal had not resumed. He wondered again if her actions had triggered a distress call, a homing beacon. Perhaps the original inhabitant had tried the same thing, but hadn't succeeded because his lifeboat had been damaged somehow.

Mulder decided it was time to get moving. "Thanks to your explorations, we know there's a passage through to the pyramid level. Good thing, too," he said. "I don't look forward to climbing the cenote wall again."

"I still can't see very well." Cassandra followed close beside him as they picked their way away from the main chamber, then she asked in a hesitant voice, "My father… did he come with you?"

Mulder swallowed, his heart leaden. The passages around them grew darker. "Yes, he came with us. We tried to have him wait for us back in the States, but he wouldn't hear of it. He wanted to help you himself," he said. "But Dr. Rubicon… he was another casualty of the people who tried to kill you. I'm sorry."

Cassandra stopped in midstep and swayed, leaning into the rough wall where metal plates had loosened and fallen to the floor. She looked as if Mulder had just punched her in the stomach.

She said nothing but slid down to sit, shuddering, where the wall met the floor. She drew her knees against her chest. She stared at her dirty hands.

Mulder looked down at her, understanding. He quickly ran a hand through his hair, then touched her lightly on the shoulder. She needed to be alone.

"I'll go on ahead and find the way out," he said. "You take the time you need."

Cassandra nodded, intensely weary. With a last glance back at her, Mulder set out, trudging up the slope. His heart pounded, heavy with grief for her, filled with amazement for the things he had already seen, yet with an equivalent amount of dread for what he might encounter up above—the battleground, the snipers, the explosions. He hoped Scully had managed to keep herself alive and safe.

The passageway became dimmer, the walls made of vitrified stone. The deck plates transformed into a limestone path under his shoes. He realized he had emerged into the pyramid levels again. Up ahead, he recognized the same area he had seen when he went looking for Vladimir Rubicon, though now he stood on the opposite side of the fallen barrier. Elation surged through him—home free!

Then he turned the corner and came face to face with Carlos Barreio. The police chief's flashlight beam shone through the dimness, pinning Mulder like a moth in a specimen box. Barreio held out a nickel-plated revolver, pointing it at Mulder.

"Agent Mulder," he said. His lips formed a humorless smile. "I thought I might find you inside the pyramid. Unfortunately, I cannot allow you to leave here alive."

31

Xitaclan ruins, Pyramid of Kukulkan
Wednesday, 3:27 A.M.

Reflexively, Mulder took a step backward, but found no escape.

Barreio's police revolver pointed directly at him, unwavering. Mulder could not see the man's finger on the trigger. He would never know when it began to squeeze, when the gunshot would ring out.

Once again, Mulder wished fervently that Major Jakes had left him with his own weapon.

"Let me make a wild leap of logic," Mulder said, taking another gradual step back, "and guess that you were the one responsible for killing the archaeology team members." He carefully began backing down the corridor.

Barreio, with the gleam of the hunt in his shadowed eyes, stalked after him, gun forward. He answered only with an enigmatic smile, his large mustache folded in the cleft of his cheeks.

Mulder pressed, "So you let the archaeologists uncover new treasures for you— priceless pre-Colombian relics that brought fabulous prices on the black market."

Barreio shrugged his broad shoulders. "*Liberación Quintana Roo* needed the money."

Mulder took another step backward, the flashlight beam dazzling his eyes. Barreio seemed amused at his attempt to escape.

"And I suppose Fernando Victorio Aguilar would find customers for you?" Mulder said. "He's in this too, isn't he?"

"He only made himself rich." Barreio growled. "It is distressing to see a man with no drive or purpose other than his own greed."

"Yeah, I can see how you're much more admirable," Mulder said.

The slope was steep. He continued backing down, kept talking. Barreio followed, confident, watching his victim proceed deeper and deeper into the trap. "But why kill the archaeologists?" Mulder continued. "You just called attention to yourself.

They were Americans on a visit sanctioned by the central Mexican government."

Barreio shrugged again. "The government knows nothing of the problems of Quintana Roo. We have our own land, our own history. We should be our own country like Honduras, like El Salvador, like Belize."

"Don't you have a brochure or something I could read?" Mulder said. "Instead of giving me the whole speech?"

"We had intended to take the Americans as hostages. That is all. Political hostages."

Mulder raised an eyebrow. "I suppose they were shot trying to escape? And then you had no choice but to throw them into the cenote?"

"Some of our revolutionaries still believe in sacrifices to the old gods," Barreio said, shoving the revolver closer. He shone the flashlight directly into Mulder's eyes. Mulder blinked and held up his hands to ward off the bright beam, stepping back toward a corner. "We all have to make sacrifices," Barreio observed.

Mulder backed around the corner, unable to believe that Barreio kept stringing him along, kept playing him.

The police chief followed him, closing the distance for the last time. Barreio grinned, flashing white teeth in the dimness. Mulder knew his time had run out.

As the burly man rounded the comer, Cassandra Rubicon stepped out of the shadows, holding one of the metallic plates that had fallen off of the walls. She hefted it over her head and brought it crashing down against the side of Barreio's skull. His policeman's cap toppled to one side; his body toppled to the other.

Still barely able to see, Cassandra dropped the plate with a loud clang, amazed at what she had done. Carlos Barreio grunted in pain and shock, reeling, stumbling into the wall. He was not dead—not even unconscious, just stunned for a moment.

Mulder did not want to risk grabbing for Barreio's revolver. He snatched Cassandra's arm as she blinked her eyes. He yanked her after him. "Come on, we've got to run!" he said. "That was one of the men who shot at you." She jogged after him, hustling back down toward the control bridge.

"That man killed Cait and John, Christopher and Kelly?" she said, her voice icy.

"Yes, I'm afraid he did," Mulder said.

"Then I should have hit him harder," Cassandra answered.

Mulder helped her as they both ran down the slippery slope. Moments later, with a bellow of rage, Carlos Barreio came charging after them. He fired his revolver twice, and the bullets plowed gouges along the walls, ricocheting into the darkness.

Gasping for breath, Cassandra said, "Men shooting guns. This was what led me down here in the first place. I still can't see… my eyes—they burn!"

They ran back into the tunnel, whose walls still sizzled with a faint light that grew dimmer by the minute. The corroded, half-collapsed metal-and-crystal outcroppings gave a drastically anachronistic counterpoint to the Maya glyphs carved on the exposed limestone in the walls: symbols that ancient priests had added in hopes of restoring the damaged or pilfered artifacts removed from the derelict.

Mulder led her along, guiding her as she tried to clear her vision and find her way. He guided her behind one of the glistening metallic mounds. "Stay down here," he whispered.

"Do you actually have a plan?" Cassandra said. "Or are we just running?".

"Running seemed like a good idea at the time." Mulder swallowed and came to a stop in the confusing but awesome control chamber.

Then Carlos Barreio staggered onto the bridge, weaving unsteadily on his feet. His eyes seemed unfocused, and he blinked repeatedly, as if to stop his ears from ringing. Blood poured from a gash in his scalp, wetting his dark hair, dribbling around his ear and down his cheek. He had left his policeman's cap back in the outer tunnel where it had fallen.

Leaving Cassandra huddled behind the shelter, fighting to regain her vision, Mulder backed away in another direction. Carlos Barreio caught the movement. He swung his revolver and fired spasmodically, but his aim was off. Several bullets ricocheted off the metal wallplates. One struck inside the dark lifeboat chamber holding the mummified remains of what Mulder believed to be Kukulkan.

"Where are you?" Barreio croaked, wiping blood out of his eyes, smearing it on his cheeks. He roared with pain as he inadvertently touched the wound on his head. "What is this place?" The burly man seemed barely able to focus on his amazingly unexpected surroundings. Mulder wondered if Cassandra had given him a concussion.

Barreio staggered forward and swiveled the revolver around, shooting blindly. The bullets struck the central mound of metal shapes and crystals, sending up sparks and blue-green fire that rippled out in icy cold flames.

Hoping to distract the police chief somehow, Mulder grabbed a small, broken lump of crystal from the rough floor and hurled it, hoping to strike Barreio in the head—but he missed. Barreio caught the swift motion past his face and whirled, hearing the chunk strike the wall inside the narrow alcove—the chamber that had held Cassandra suspended. The police chief charged toward the sound like a five-hundred-yard-dash runner, waving his pistol.

Barreio fired once and strode into the lifeboat chamber.

Suddenly a flood of light poured over the police chief like a waterfall of lightning. Instinctively, Mulder shielded his eyes. Barreio thrust his hands out, trembling, his jaws clenched, his eyes opened wide. Dazzling, ethereal gel suddenly congealed around him, as if solidifying from the air itself. His nostrils flared—then he froze exactly in place, pinned by the lifeboat's automatic stasis systems. The amber hardened.

Barreio hung motionless, like an exhibit in a museum, one breath half indrawn, his eyes still hot, though dazed, the blood petrified along his cheek.

Mulder heard the dull throbbing begin again inside his head as the derelict's signal thrummed once more from within the wrecked ship—the SOS, the reactivated homing beacon.

But whom it meant to summon, Mulder could not guess.

Cassandra picked herself up from the floor, panting. She brushed herself off, looking satisfied. She shook her head to clear her thoughts. Creeping forward, she stood just in front of the glowing light wall, squinting slightly, trying to focus her eyes.

Mulder took his place beside her, staring in, feeling his heart pound.

The young woman shook her head and directed a cool smile at Barreio. "At least I'm on the right side of the wall this time," she murmured. "I like it better this way."

32

Xitaclan ruins, Pyramid of Kukulkan
Wednesday, 3:51 A.M.

When the thunder started from above, Mulder turned up to see the control chamber's ceiling vibrating, trembling. As a second pounding thump reverberated through the walls, he feared another volcanic quake might be striking Xitaclan—and this time he was trapped inside a crumbling underground derelict that did not look as if it could withstand such severe stresses.

With another loud, discrete boom, he hunched down. Dust pattered from above.

"Those sound like explosions," Cassandra said, crouched beside him.

"Yes," Mulder agreed. "It's bombs exploding. I think Major Jakes's military tactics have heated up just a little bit—and I don't know if this old ruin is going to take much more pounding. I'm not too keen on the idea of being buried alive, are you?"

Cassandra's face turned pale and she shook her head. "My goal in life is not to become a specimen for some future archaeologist."

"Let's try this again," Mulder said, leading her toward the upper exit. "We'll make our way to the pyramid levels. If Barreio could make his way down here, the passage must be open."

"At least for now," Cassandra said.

Together, they scrambled up the steep ramp, leaving the murderous police chief trapped in his coffin of light. If everything turned out all right, Mulder could always come back and arrest Barreio later.

Cassandra led the way upward, her hair flying all about her face. Mulder shone his flashlight ahead as the passages became dimmer, where the skeletal remains of the derelict gave way to limestone and hand-carved blocks.

Eager to escape, Cassandra pulled ahead of him as they reached the partially blocked passage where the stones had tumbled across the corridor. The barrel-chested Barreio had opened a wide enough passage for both of them to crawl through.

Cassandra scrambled up and into the dusty opening, wriggling her way ahead. Mulder gave her feet a push, and the muscular young archaeologist disappeared into the shadows. She twisted around and returned, reaching across for his hand to help him up. With surprising strength, she dragged him across the broken stone and into the cramped opening. He pushed his way past a shard of rock and tumbled beside Cassandra, into the upper corridors of the Xitaclan pyramid.

Mulder looked around and brushed himself off.

More thunderous booms sounded from above and outside, closer now. Mulder shone his flashlight beam to see a snowfall of dust pattering down through the ceiling stones. One of the support beams began to groan from the strain.

"We'd better hurry before it gets even cozier around here," Cassandra said. Running along the winding tunnel, they followed the line of vitrified blocks of the inner temple that covered the entombed derelict like a shrine.

"Just a minute!" Cassandra reached into her back pocket and pulled out a crumpled piece of graph paper on which she had sketched her explorations through the pyramid's lower levels. "Let's check our route. You'll have to read it—I still can't focus well enough."

"I got to this point myself two days ago," Mulder said, remembering how Scully had called him upon finding Vladimir Rubicon's body in the cenote. "I didn't get any farther though," he said. "I was… interrupted."

Cassandra did not pick up on the grimness in his voice. She licked her lips and said, "Well, in my mind it's only been an hour or so. I believe it's this way." She turned down a different passageway leading upward.

Another explosion struck much closer. The pyramid floor and the thick stone walls rocked. The hand-hewn limestone blocks rattled together like chattering teeth.

"That sounded awfully loud," Cassandra said. "The good news is, we must be close to the opening."

"Let's hope so," Mulder said, then he heard another thump and whoosh of air, moments before another equally loud detonation. "Hey, those are mortars. Somebody's launching mortars." Then he swallowed hard as he remembered Major Jakes and his covert search-and-destroy mission. "I think they're aiming to take down the pyramid."

"Nothing like respect for antiquities," Cassandra said.

They turned the corner and just up ahead saw the opening that led out into the wide plaza. Outside, the night was lit by fires in the jungle and dwindling white flares from burning phosphorus.

"I'm not sure it's a good idea to run out into the middle of that," Mulder said. "Keep your head down."

Just then he saw the flash, heard the whistle, and instinctively grabbed Cassandra. He dove with her against the wall. One of the mortars hurtled into the stairstepped facade just above the doorway, detonating with a monstrous roar of fire and smoke and blasted debris. The shockwave made his ears pop.

An avalanche of rubble, rocks, and chiseled limestone blocks collapsed to block the entrance. The low ceiling of the claustrophobic corridor split open and fell in as Mulder dragged Cassandra deeper into the tunnels, both of them blinded by the flash and the sudden darkness.

He breathed a searing mixture of hot gases and pulverized limestone dust, choking and coughing. They staggered back the way they had come. "This is getting ridiculous," Cassandra wheezed. "We'll never make it out of this pyramid."

"Back to the drawing board," Mulder said. "Let's try the passage I used to enter this place. Third time's the charm."

Down, down, deep underground, Mulder followed the image in his excellent memory, though he cheated a little by spotting his own footprints scuffed in the dust of the long-abandoned corridors.

"This passage leads out to the cenote," Mulder said. "Once there, we'll have to climb up, hand over hand."

"The cenote?" Cassandra said. "We must be below the level of the water. Are we supposed to swim, or what? At least I can wash the rest of this slime off."

Mulder looked at her, surprised. "Oh, I forgot to tell you—the sacrificial well is just a big empty hole in the ground now, thanks to the last tremors."

"Tremors? What tremors?" Cassandra asked.

"You've been sleeping for a long time."

They arrived at the ancient door hatch, the metal bulkhead that Mulder had reached by climbing down the cenote walls. Standing in the mysterious entrance to the derelict, Cassandra stared out at the dripping corkscrew walls of knobbed limestone. The empty well remained wet, still stinking of sulfurous volcanic gases.

"I've heard complaints about how pristine archaeological sites are destroyed as soon as outsiders arrive at the scene," Cassandra said. "But this goes beyond my worst nightmares."

Up above, flashes from continued mortar fire and smoldering forest blazes lit the sky.

"Steady." Mulder reached out to take her hand as they both stepped out onto the algae-encrusted limestone ledge. "We're on our own for the first half of the climb," he said, "but from that point we can use the ropes we hung down."

"Ropes? What did you need ropes for?" Cassandra asked.

Mulder swallowed. "Well, my partner, Agent Scully, used your own diving suit to go underwater to explore. That's where she found the bodies of your team members… and I used the ropes to retrieve your father. We found him floating here in the sacrificial well."

Cassandra's lips whitened as she pressed them together. Then she nodded. "I'm glad you got him out before all the water drained into the ground… though I couldn't imagine a more appropriate burial for a hardened relic digger like himself."

Mulder reached up for the first handhold and climbed cautiously, finding the ascent somewhat less terrifying than the downward climb. This way he could look up and see his goal, rather than slipping and working his way down to the unknown depths of a bottomless pit.

Wiry like a wildcat, Cassandra found tiny outcroppings that even Mulder didn't dare try. They picked their way around the circumference, ascending at an angle, completely encircling the sacrificial well until they reached the right height to grasp the ragged ends of the dangling ropes.

From deep below, volcanic vapors continued to gurgle and belch and gasp. Mulder knew that the eruption had not yet peaked, but had merely paused to gain its second wind.

His shoe slipped, and he dropped, grabbing for a hold. Cassandra reached out, her hand as fast as a rattlesnake strike, as she grasped Mulder's wrist. His other hand maintained its grip on the rope. "Thanks," he said.

"Any time," she answered. "Just make sure you do the same for me."

Once he regained his footing, they climbed the last few meters up to the edge of the cenote, the flat limestone rim where drugged sacrificial victims had once been hurled down into the deep well that would swallow them up for thousands of years.

Silently deciding to keep themselves low, Mulder and Cassandra raised their heads up, peeping over the edge to where they could see the Pyramid of Kukulkan silhouetted in the firelight.

Half of its side had sloughed down. Mortar explosions had gouged great craters into the carefully crafted hieroglyphic stairs. Mulder saw other people running in the plaza, dim forms scurrying for cover.

Both of the carved feathered serpent stelae had toppled over, and only one of the tents remained upright. Mulder could see cautious figures scrambling about in camouflaged uniforms; one wore a different outfit. Scully.

Before he could haul himself over the ledge, though, a renewed outcry came from the jungle, shouts in the guttural Maya language. A loud crackle of gunfire came in a staccato burst as the regrouped guerrillas charged out of the cover of the trees. The revolutionaries fired at the surviving members of the military team, who responded in kind.

Gunshots grew into a deafening hail of sound in the sky. Two more phosphorous flares soared into the night, overwhelming the light of the moon.

Mulder held on, and watched, thinking of the relative peace inside the derelict spacecraft.

33

Xitaclan ruins
Wednesday, 3:26 A.M.

Scully covered her ears as the mortar launcher fired another projectile toward the half-demolished ziggurat. She cringed, and the other soldiers ducked away, also covering their ears.

The mortar struck the base of the great pyramid, dead on target. With the explosion, fire and smoke and shrapnel blossomed outward, hurling chunks of broken rock in all directions. After the impact, cracks appeared along the steep ceremonial stairsteps—steps she had climbed only days before to get a panoramic view of the surrounding jungle.

The pounding had continued for nearly an hour, but the ancient structure withstood the most vigorous barrage from Major Jakes.

So far.

Scully had repeatedly argued with Jakes, insisting that he cease the destruction, that he and his troops stop pummeling the archaeological treasure. But foremost in her mind was an engulfing dread about where Mulder might be. She didn't know where he had run—but no matter what, she knew Mulder would be in the thick of things.

"How long are you going to keep this up?" she screamed, her voice muffled in her ringing ears. "There may be people inside that pyramid!"

"Regrettable casualties," the major answered.

"Don't you care?" she said, grabbing his sleeve like a persistent child… and feeling as helpless. "Can't you see what you're doing?"

Jakes turned his emotionless gaze down, staring at her. The weird light splashed colors across his dark skin. "No, Agent Scully—I don't care. I am not allowed to care. That's too dangerous."

"Is that what you tell yourself, just to keep ignoring your ill-advised actions? Can't you think about the consequences?"

He didn't move. "My mind is my tool, capable of accomplishing seemingly impossible missions—but only because I never allow myself to deviate from orders. Too much thinking creates confusion, double-talk, doubts.

"I have been through hell numerous times, Agent Scully. The maps called it Bosnia, or Iraq, or Somalia—but it was hell." Now his eyes flared with embers of emotion. "And if I ever let my conscience get too heavy, then I would either be insane or dead by now."

Scully swallowed, and the major turned back to face his remaining men.

After repeated direct hits from the mortars, the ancient pyramid looked ready to collapse. Heavy blocks jarred loose from where they had rested for centuries, tumbled down, smashing the intricate carvings and glyphs. The pillars of the apex temple platform had all fallen over, the feathered serpent statues blasted to dust. An avalanche began along the eastern face of the ziggurat, roaring down the steep stairs and adding to the nighttime din.

"We've almost got it," Major Jakes said. "A few more direct hits, then our mission will be accomplished. Gather the casualties. We can fall back."

"No! We can't leave Mulder!" Scully shouted. "We have to find him. He's an American citizen, Major Jakes. Your actions have put him into the middle of an illegal military action—and I hold you personally responsible for his safety."

Jakes looked at her again with his placid dark eyes. "Agent Scully, I am not even here. My team is not here. Our mission does not exist. We are not officially responsible for you or anyone else."

Then a bullet took him high in the left shoulder, spinning him around and hurling him into Scully, knocking them both to the ground. He grunted, but did not cry out in pain.

"The snipers are coming back," one of the commandos yelled.

The other soldiers scrambled away from the mortar launcher as a renewed shower of gunfire came from the jungle. The guerrillas howled their challenges.

The commandos took shelter, ducking beside the all-terrain vehicles and the mortar launcher. They leveled their automatic weapons and shot at will, targeting on the bright spitfire that came from the shadows, the surging forces of the *Liberación Quintana Roo* guerrillas who charged out of the trees.

Major Jakes heaved himself off of Scully with a barely restrained hiss of pain. He stood up and squeezed his shoulder. Blood welled up in his uniform. He looked down at her, and she saw the splatters of blood staining her own jacket.

"I apologize for bleeding on you," he said, then offered her a hand up.

The commando closest to the mortar launcher fell backward without an outcry, his head suddenly splashed with bright red.

"Another down," Major Jakes said. He looked at his own bleeding shoulder. "My team is dwindling with every moment."

"Then we've got to get out of here," Scully said, clamping her teeth tightly together. "Find Mulder and go."

"The mission is not yet accomplished," Major Jakes said.

The guerrillas, bolder now, came out of the trees, firing. Major Jakes's commandos shot back, though their defense seemed to be crumbling. One of the soldiers launched a grenade into a knot of *Liberación Quintana Roo* fighters. It exploded right in their midst. Broken bodies flew, arms and legs akimbo, hurled into trees that also burst into flames from the backwash of the exploding grenade.

The viciousness of the response caused the guerrillas' surge to falter. Major Jakes grabbed Scully's arm. "Come on, I want to get you back to your tent. You'll take shelter there, so I can concentrate on our defenses."

"I'm not going back to my tent," Scully said. "I need to be out here, looking for my partner."

"No, you don't," Jakes retorted. "You'll follow my orders. Period."

"That tent isn't going to offer me any protection whatsoever."

"It'll offer enough," Jakes said. "The attackers won't be able to see you. You won't be a specific target. That's the best I can do."

"I didn't ask you to—"

"Yes, you did," Major Jakes said. "You said I was personally responsible for your safety. Therefore I want you away, where I don't have to worry about you—and where I don't have to listen to your constant insubordination."

With his good arm he wrestled her into the flap opening of the tent. She struggled and turned around, shouting at the top of her lungs, "Mulder!"

"He can't help you, wherever he is," Major Jakes said. "I'm trying to protect you, ma'am."

She glared at him. "I need for him to know where I am."

"Just get inside the tent, ma'am."

She bristled. "Don't call me ma'am."

"Don't force me to be rude."

Defeated and helpless in the middle of a war zone, Scully crawled into the dim confines of the tent, huddling among the blankets. Major Jakes dropped the tent flaps back down.

Scully felt as if she were inside a cloth tomb. The sounds outside were muffled. Moonlight filtered through the heavy canvas, intermixed with staccato bursts of light from flares, gunfire, another mortar launch, and distant explosions.

She listened to the deafening, chaotic sounds of the assault and knelt on her blanket. She rapidly lifted up her pillow, checking that no scorpions had snuggled under the rolled-up cloth.

More gunfire rang out. Scully heard a gasp from Major Jakes and a thump. Outside she saw silhouettes, shadowy figures—then a bullet tore through the tent, missing her head by inches. Another small circular hole ripped through the fabric, singed around the edges.

She ducked down, flattening herself to the ground, and listened as the fighting continued outside.

34

Xitaclan battleground
Wednesday, 4:06 A.M.

Mulder helped Cassandra over the limestone lip of the sacrificial well, then stretched out, relieved just to be on solid ground again. Exhausted, he tried to decide which direction to run that would have the least likelihood of getting both of them killed.

Mulder felt sick in the pit of his stomach as he watched the destruction of the pyramid continue. The artifacts buried in the derelict ship would answer the questions archaeologists had wondered about for nearly a century. But every blast pummeled and crushed the evidence of extraterrestrial influence on the Maya culture. Now the answers were reduced to rubble and debris.

He and Cassandra sprinted for cover every chance they could, stealing around the perimeter of the ziggurat. He intended to reach the base camp in the plaza. Despite its dangerous openness, the plaza was the most likely place for him to find Scully. That was his first order of business… that and preventing them from getting killed.

Another mortar sailed high and dropped like a wrecking ball onto the top platform where ancient priests had performed their bloody sacrifices. The pillars that supported the delicate Temple of the Feathered Serpent had already crumbled and collapsed, slumping down into a mound of debris.

Rubbing her eyes, Cassandra watched in dismay, her face seething with anger. "First my team, then my father—and now this… this desecration." She snarled and then stood tall, balling her fist and shouting into the night. "You can't do this!"

As if to defy her, another explosive detonated. The shockwave blasted debris from one of the stairstep terraces directly above them, causing a rain of broken blocks.

"Look out!" Mulder said and dove toward Cassandra, but the shattered rubble dropped down on her like the proverbial ton of bricks. A jagged chunk of stone emblazoned with a partial Maya glyph clipped her across the top of the head. With a thin gasp of pain, she collapsed, bleeding from her scalp, a scarlet stain oozing into her mussed cinnamon hair.

Mulder bent over her, cradling the young woman's head in his lap as a few remaining chunks of shrapnel pattered around him. Miraculously, he himself suffered only a large bruise on one shoulder blade and a nasty cut in his right leg.

The side of the great pyramid seemed to sag as rubble and stone blocks sloughed toward the base.

"Cassandra," Mulder said, pushing his face close to hers. "Cassandra, can you hear me?" Her skin had a grayish color, and sweat broke out on her forehead.

The young woman groaned and sat up, blinking and stunned. She shook her head and then winced. "Bullseye," she croaked, pressing a hand against her temple. "Ouch."

Mulder gingerly felt around on her scalp, probing the seriousness of the gash. Though she bled profusely, it seemed to be a shallow wound. His main concern was that she had suffered a concussion or fractured skull.

"We can't stay here, Cassandra," he said. "We've got to find some kind of shelter, or we'll have a lot more to worry about in a few minutes."

He looked around, trying to focus in the uncertain strobelight of flares against the enveloping darkness. "If we can find my partner Scully, she'll be able to give you emergency medical attention."

He scanned the plaza, watched the scurrying figures, the smattering of gunfire like deadly fireflies blossoming into the night. Ahead, in the open plaza, he saw a tall figure hustling a woman's petite form—obviously Scully—toward the tent. The two seemed to be arguing, and then the man pushed her inside, dropped the flap, and stood up to stand guard beside the tent.

Was the man protecting her… or holding her prisoner? Mulder couldn't tell if he was one of the American commandos or one of Carlos Barreio's guerrilla freedom fighters.

"Come with me, Cassandra," Mulder said, draping her arm over his shoulder and helping her to her feet. She groaned, and her eyes blinked, unfocused, her pupils dilated in their muddy-green irises. The blood continued to flow down her face.

"Hey, I can walk," she said, but her voice came out with a quaver, like a child trying to impress her father with her bravado. Mulder loosened his hold, but Cassandra began to slide toward the ground like overcooked pasta.

"Maybe I'll just help you out after all," he said, placing his arm around her for support. The two of them stagger-walked toward the plaza. Mulder kept his eyes toward the indistinct figure standing next to Scully's tent.

Continued gunfire prevented even an imagined moment of peace. A chain of popping sounds cut through the scattered background noise. The commandos scattered again, but the guardian figure beside Scully's tent did not move fast enough. Mulder watched as the rain of automatic-weapon fire nearly ripped him in half. Several bullets tugged at the peak of the tent like thick darning needles, and Mulder prayed Scully had kept herself low.

"We have to get over there," he said, with greater urgency. Cassandra stumbled as he walked with her, hunched over to present a smaller target. He expected to be shot at any moment.

He and Cassandra reached the more distant of the two feathered serpent stelae at the edge of the plaza. Both carved pillars had toppled over, smashing the already disturbed flagstones. Some of the rubble had fallen across the tarpaulin-covered corpses he and Scully had fished out of the cenote—but the victims didn't seem to mind.

Mercifully, Cassandra seemed too dazed to recognize her team members, or even to know what the shrouded forms might be. He helped her to crouch beside the fallen limestone monolith, taking shelter.

Then, to Mulder's surprise, the din stopped. The combat field grew still and oppressive... as if a blanket of silence had descended upon Xitaclan. Mulder stopped moving, letting Cassandra lean back against the fallen pillar. He craned his neck to look around. As he waited, the silence seemed to grow louder. Something strange began to happen.

He felt his skin crawl, and the hairs on the back of his neck tingled with static electricity. Mulder huddled next to Cassandra behind the stela. Some force in the air compelled his gaze upward.

He watched the light come down from the sky.

The glow came from inside and out of a huge vessel poised in the night. He saw it for only an instant—but his imagination supplied the remaining details. It was an immense construction, a dazzling chiaroscuro of angles and curves forming a geometrical shape that no architect had ever conceived. A blaze of light glowed around it like a halo, keeping all details indistinct.

A ship.

He knew it had to be a ship. When Cassandra Rubicon had accidentally fallen into the lifeboat chamber, she must have triggered a pulsing message, a distress signal transmitted across the starlanes… a beacon shining along an infinite distance.

Until finally the rescue craft had arrived.

Mulder recalled the blurred images of Kukulkan on the walls of the buried control chamber: the towering extraterrestrial visitor staring hopefully up at the stars. But the rescue craft had come more than a thousand years too late for him.

"Cassandra, look at that!" he said, glancing down and shaking her shoulders. "Look at it!"

She groaned and blinked her eyes. "It's too bright," she said.

Mulder looked up again. The moment the luminous craft reached the partially demolished pyramid, long spikes of searing light burned from the ship's belly… glowing, pulling an invisible thread. Mulder gasped and shielded his eyes from the dazzling glare.

Beneath him, the ground trembled, strained, ripping like a thin sheet of iron tugged by a powerful magnet. Temple blocks flew off the top of the ziggurat. The rubble blasted away on all sides. Debris pounded down around them like meteors.

He tried to look again, but the blazing light blinded him, and he had to cover his eyes. Mulder heard the strange craft continue its excavations, oblivious to the covert U.S. squad, to the Central American guerrillas, to the FBI agents. The powerful beam knocked the entire broad-based pyramid down, razing it one stairstep layer at a time, like a child toppling a house made of building blocks.

Mulder understood everything now, knew his speculations must have been correct. Kukulkan had never been rescued because his lifeboat chamber had failed, entombing him—but Cassandra's accident had once again summoned help from the stars.

And now the rescue ship had come to excavate the derelict.

The ground bucked and heaved as the dazzling craft devastated the remainder of the pyramid, leaving only ruins. Shouts and panic rang out from the jungle and from the surviving U.S. commando fighters.

Cassandra groaned again. "Please don't break it," she said.

"Not much I can do to stop it," Mulder answered, trying to make out details through the cracks between his fingers. The light grew brighter, hotter, in the belly of the hovering ship. More glaring beams lanced out. Mulder watched, drinking in the details, still awestruck.

Finally, the inner pyramid lay bare—the original structure that enshrined the derelict ship. Sudden darkness fell again, disorienting Mulder as the rescue craft floated silently over. He supposed it was probing, scanning... and then the brilliant beams ripped out again, titanic forces stripping away layers of the ground to excavate the skeletal remains of Kukulkan's ancient ship.

The earth cracked and shook—until finally, with a great rending tear, the piercing light from the hovering ship ripped free the remains of the crashed craft. Mulder was hurled to the ground as metallic girders and curved hull plates protruded through the base of what had been the great Xitaclan pyramid. Risking blindness from staring at a light as bright as the sun, Mulder tried to watch as the rescue ship heaved Kukulkan's derelict entirely out of the ground, like a Maya blood priest ripping out the heart of a sacrificial victim.

Dirt and stone showered all around them. Mulder ducked, confused by the garish shadows that had become razor sharp in the backwash.

Defying gravity, the crushed remains of the derelict rose into the air. The glowing rescue ship gained altitude with astonishing speed, tugging the skeletal girders along with it. Debris pattered around them, a blizzard of rubble that sprayed the entire site.

Mulder gazed into the sky, his mouth dry, watching all hope for finding artifacts and incontrovertible evidence rising into the sky... forever out of his reach. The rescue craft had come like a soldier crossing enemy lines to bring back the dead. Mulder had no idea where the craft might go, what descendants of Kukulkan might mourn his mummified remains.

Eyes stinging with tears, he stared as the brightness compressed itself and shrank into a blinding star that streaked off into the night, leaving him only with colorful afterimages on his eyes.

With a shock, Mulder realized that the Mexican police chief Carlos Barreio remained trapped in one of the lifeboat chambers. Perhaps Barreio would survive the passage. Or perhaps he had already been killed during the unearthing of the derelict. Either way, the extraterrestrial craft took the revolutionary leader along with it.

Mulder knew this was one abduction he would not mourn, one alien kidnapping he would never bother to investigate. He looked at the gaping, smoking crater where the pyramid had been. "Good riddance," he said.

35

The ruins of Xitaclan
Wednesday, 4:19 A.M .

Feeling helpless and trapped, Scully huddled in the imaginary shelter of the tent while she listened to the tumult outside, destructive sounds like the end of the world... or at least a Maya version of the last days of Pompeii.

She heard explosions and crashing stones, but they did not seem to be coming from continued mortar fire. The commandos had dashed for cover, and the launcher had fallen silent. Several more bullet impacts had ripped holes like tiny skylights in the top of her tent. Scully heard nothing more from Major Jakes or his surviving men.

She tried to decide how long to wait before she made a break for it. She hated being sequestered in here, like some princess locked away in a castle tower. Jakes had thrown her inside this smothering enclosure just because she was a woman, or a civilian—but she had no better chance of survival cowering in a tent than if she actually dashed out across the plaza, to the ruins, to the jungle, in search of Mulder.

"Enough waiting," she said. "I'm getting out of here."

Scully yanked open the tent flap and crawled out, keeping low, expecting one of the soldiers to shove her back inside at any moment. A harried Major Jakes might even bash her in the head with the butt of his rifle, she thought, just to keep her under submission "for her own protection."

But no one noticed her. She crouched beside the tent, ready to dive for cover. But no shots rang out to strike the flagstones at her feet.

She stood up on shaking legs to look around, blinking in the uncertain light of the burning jungle. Xitaclan seemed to be quivering in shock.

Scully found Major Jakes where he had fallen. Heavy-caliber bullets had ripped his chest apart. He lay sprawled in his own blood, staining the flagstones like another sacrifice to the ancient Maya gods. Even in death, his face remained expressionless, as if it were all part of his beloved mission.

A frantic soldier ran toward her, dodging fallen stone blocks and uprooted trees, his uniform torn and stained. His rifle dangled from his shoulder, out of ammunition. The clips on his utility belt hung empty, as if he had already used every one of the grenades and throwing knives he had carried.

"We're under attack from the sky," the soldier said. "I've never seen an assault like this—but we can't resist! They've already destroyed the pyramid." His face dripped with perspiration, his eyes opened wide and white.

Then he looked down to see the bloody corpse of Major Jakes. "Oh, damn," the soldier moaned, glancing quickly at Scully in embarrassment. "Excuse the language, ma'am."

"Don't call me ma'am," she muttered, recalling what she had said to Major Jakes, but she didn't expect the young soldier to understand.

"Okay, it's fallback time!" the soldier shouted to his unseen companions. He looked at her, his eyes haunted. "Ma'am, you'd best make your own way out of the jungle as soon as possible before that ship comes back. You can request asylum from any authorities you may encounter. Our team, on the other hand, does not have that option. If we're captured, we're dead. Only three of us left now."

Without another word, the soldier dashed back across the plaza, holding his empty rifle in front of him, sprinting for the cover of the trees. Scully turned around to stare at where the tall Xitaclan pyramid had once stood—but now she saw only a gaping crater.

"My God," she said, awed, feeling an uncontrollable urge to cross herself. The rubble lay piled up, massive blocks thrown hundreds of meters as if tossed by some titanic force. She glanced down at the major's motionless form. "It looks like you accomplished your mission, Major Jakes."

Deep in her heart, though, she suspected that no amount of mortar fire or grenade blasts could have leveled the centuries-old structure so utterly. She thought of what the soldier had said—an attack from the sky. Some other military force, an air force? A bombing raid?

Another tactical nuclear weapon, an atomic artillery shell?

"Scully!" The shout sounded like music in her ears, and she whirled around upon hearing Mulder's voice. "Scully, over here!"

She saw her partner, bedraggled and exhausted, supporting another woman who staggered next to him. The two of them worked their way across the plaza.

"Mulder, you're safe!" She ran toward him.

"Let's not come to any premature conclusions," he said. His face was flushed, his eyes glazed with shock—or amazement. "Scully, did you see it? Did you see it?" He gestured frantically over to the crater where the pyramid had once stood.

Scully shook her head. "I was stuck inside the tent, so I didn't see much of anything," she said. "Major Jakes is dead. So are most of his men. We've been told to move out as soon as we can. We're all by ourselves, Mulder."

Finally, as if getting a second wind, more sporadic gunfire popped through the trees, and Scully felt very vulnerable. Major Jakes's three surviving commandos had already fled, piling onto one of the all-terrain vehicles. They roared off into the jungle without waiting for stragglers.

"She's hurt, Scully," Mulder said, indicating the reddish-haired woman he supported. "She was hit on the head by a piece of shrapnel from one of those mortar explosions… but at least she's alive."

Scully looked at the woman's head wound, saw that the blood was already clotting, matting her hair in place over it. "Mulder, is this Cassandra? Where did you find her?"

"It's a long story, Scully—and I'll tell you right now you're not going to believe it. But she's here, living proof."

Before Mulder could explain further, the ground began to writhe yet again. The flagstones shimmied from side to side, as if some legendary titan buried beneath the earth's crust were trying to break his way out using a jackhammer.

"I don't think it's kidding this time," Scully shouted.

A section of the flagstones blasted skyward as a geyser fountained up. The entire plaza shifted sideways as underground plates moved. The stress became so great that a fissure ripped the courtyard in two, tumbling the wall of the long-abandoned ball court off to the side of the pyramid ruins.

"The ground here is unstable enough." Mulder shook his head as if to knock the dazedness from his brain. "With all the explosions, I think Xitaclan is about to become a thing of the past."

Gouts of sulfurous ash spewed from the pyramid crater, an upside-down waterfall of lava and smoke. The limestone rocks cracked, igniting like candle wax. The ground split open, collapsing the sides of the drained and hissing cenote.

"Remember that new Paricutin volcano from 1948?" Mulder said. "My guess is that this place is going to erupt and keep erupting until we've got another national landmark on our hands." He helped the dazed Cassandra to her feet again. "If it's all the same to you, Scully, I'd rather not have my name on a little memorial plaque near the Visitor's Center. Let's get out of here."

The gunfire had ceased, the guerrillas having scrambled back into the destroyed jungle, their victory complete now that virtually everything standing at Xitaclan had been destroyed.

Scully pointed to the remaining all-terrain vehicle. "We can take that ATV, get better speed through the jungle… though I have no idea where we're going."

"How about away from here?" Mulder said. "Do you know how to drive this thing?"

Scully looked at him. "We're intelligent people, Mulder. We should be able to figure it out." But as she said it, she wasn't terribly convinced herself.

"Don't be so sure," he said. "It's military technology."

As she and Mulder helped the injured Cassandra Rubicon, they staggered toward the remaining vehicle under the lava firelight and the conflagration of the jungle.

36

Yucatán jungle
Wednesday, 5:01 A.M.

Orange gouts of lava shot up into the sky behind them as Mulder fought to control the all-terrain vehicle.

"You have to hurry, Mulder," Scully said, her face flushed, her expression urgent.

Scully had settled Cassandra Rubicon into one of the vehicle's seats and looked at the injured young archaeologist while glancing over her shoulder at the flames, the cracking ground, and the shooting fire and steam.

"I'm used to driving Ford rental cars," Mulder said. "This is a bit more challenging."

The ATV's engine had started up with a cough and a roar. Mulder worked the pedals, the gear shift—and they lurched off with all the ease and comfort of a plane crash. They followed the trampled path hacked through the jungle by the commando team earlier that night. The vehicle's thick tires swiveled and rolled over the dense underbrush, smashing down ferns and fallen branches.

Scully did her best to prop up Cassandra Rubicon's groggy form. She used a torn strip of cloth to probe her head injury, studying the seriousness of the gash. "What is this substance coating her?" she asked.

The young woman winced and tried to squirm away from Scully's ministrations. "I'm all right," Cassandra croaked, and with a sigh slumped back to half-consciousness.

Mulder plowed deeper into the jungle, but their pace remained maddeningly slow as he dodged tree trunks and boulders and crashed through thin streams and shallow trenches.

Flames from the fresh crack in the earth backlit the jungle. Spewing magma boiled up from the open wound where the immense alien rescue craft had excavated Kukulkan's long-buried derelict. Greasy gray smoke roiled where the grenade launchers had blasted parts of the forest.

With the loud rumbling behind them and the continued hissing of the eruption in progress, Mulder could hear few subtle background noises, but he thought he spotted running figures scrambling through the underbrush. Some of the shadows might have been guerrilla soldiers fleeing, others might have been the surviving members of Major Jakes's commandos trying to make their way back to a safe rendezvous point.

"This woman needs medical attention," Scully said, "but she'll be all right for the time being. Nothing serious, just a little banged up… but everything I see here are fresh wounds—not weeks old." She looked over at Mulder, her blue eyes filled with curiosity, her eyebrows raised. "So where has she been all this time?"

"She was trapped down in the pyramid, Scully."

Scully frowned skeptically. "She doesn't look like a woman who's been in hiding for days and days. I see no signs of malnourishment or physical stress."

He looked at her with a deep intensity, feeling the passion of his convictions bring a flush to his cheeks. "I'll tell you everything once we get out of this alive."

Scully cradled Cassandra's lolling head so that it did not bang against the side of the ATV. Far behind them another huge explosion ripped through the night, spraying more ash and lava into the sky, spitting fire in all directions. Mulder flinched, then tried to coax greater speed out of the groaning all-terrain vehicle.

The front left side of the ATV smashed into the bent bole of a tree, and Mulder overcompensated by swerving to the right, then zigzagging back to return them to their course. In the darkness and the chaos he had already lost the beaten track. Maybe, he thought, he could stop at a gas station for directions.

He squinted ahead and swerved again, struggling to find a reasonable course through the overgrown jungle. "I hope we're not lost out here in the wilderness for the rest of our lives. I've got season tickets to the Redskins games."

He looked down at the high-tech apparatus and control panels that equipped the vehicle. "Check in the glove compartment, Scully. See if you can find a Triple-A map."

Scully reached over and scanned some of the screens. "Major Jakes showed me a dossier file—satellite images of an enormous crater left behind when a local drug lord was supposedly attacked by a tactical nuclear device. You'd probably consider it the result of some sort of alien technology gone awry… but let's not get into that. The major had precise maps, topographical contours, detailed studies of the jungle." She shuffled around before letting out a defeated sigh. "But all of that was in the other ATV, of course."

On an impulse she switched on a flat grid in the dashboard unit, which displayed a digital compass and a glowing LCD map of the Yucatán. "Well, here we go," she said. "I couldn't find the cigarette lighter or the radio, but this should do the trick."

Mulder heaved a sigh of relief.

Suddenly a slim and wiry figure charged out of the underbrush, striding in front of the ATV's path. He looked sweaty and exhausted, his khaki vest torn, his ocelot-skin hat lost somewhere in the jungle. But his dark eyes narrowed with a fanatical gleam as he held a wicked-looking automatic assault rifle, no doubt taken from one of Major Jakes's fleeing men.

"I will shoot you now, or I will shoot you later," Fernando Victorio Aguilar said, thrusting the rifle toward them. "But either way you will stop. Now."

37

Yucatán jungle, near Xitaclan
Wednesday, 5:26 A.M.

Wrenching the controls, Mulder pulled the all-terrain vehicle to a halt. Aguilar's leveled rifle provided quite an incentive.

With the denseness of the foliage, the tight-packed trees, and tangling ferns and creepers, he didn't have enough momentum or enough confidence in his driving ability with the clunky military vehicle to roar forward and trample the long-haired guide. If he missed the man on his first attempt, Aguilar could easily dodge them and shoot at point-blank range. He wouldn't risk Scully or Cassandra that way.

From her seat, Cassandra groaned and brought herself close enough to consciousness that she blinked at Aguilar. "Him," she said. "Bastard! Abandoned us…" Then she slumped back, as if that effort had cost her all the energy reserves she had managed to rebuild.

Aguilar looked at her in shock, then jabbed his rifle at them. "Where did you find the archaeologist's daughter, eh? Barreio's men searched for days, but they kept getting lost in the pyramid."

"She found a very good hiding place," Mulder said.

"In fact, Señor Barreio found the same spot—but I don't expect we'll ever see him again."

"Too bad. He was a political fool, anyway." Aguilar held up the rifle, pointing it directly between Mulder's eyes. He could feel the black hole of the barrel boring through his forehead, as if the long-haired guide were performing some sort of virtual trepanning operation.

"What do you want, Aguilar?" Scully said.

The man swung the rifle to point it at her. Mulder saw that his ponytail had come undone and his dark hair hung in greasy, ropy strands to his shoulders. Aguilar smiled at Scully. "For the moment I'd like hostages—and this vehicle, Señorita." He rubbed his cheeks with one hand as if the faint stubble bothered him. All of his supposed plans had crumbled around him, but Aguilar still seemed amused by the entire situation.

"It's too late to say that nobody will get hurt if you do exactly as I say… but, believe me, *Liberación Quintana Roo* meant to do this in a bloodless fashion. All I wanted was the artifacts, all they wanted were the political hostages. We could have gotten away without any casualties whatsoever, but alas, circumstances did not permit that. Thanks to your American soldiers, and your own stubbornness, eh?"

Mulder heard a crackle of branches overhead and glanced up at the trees. Aguilar saw the sudden movement and jerked his rifle back at Mulder. "Don't move a muscle," he said.

Mulder didn't move, though he could still hear a rustling, creeping sound through the twigs high above. Other ferns began to stir behind Aguilar, but the guide kept his attention on the vehicle.

"We were obtaining artifacts from lost Maya sites," Aguilar said. "*Our* Maya sites. It was like stealing, but no one got hurt, no one lost anything. *Bueno!* The jungle had buried these treasures for centuries, and now we were making money from them, eh?

"Barreio squandered his profits on political fantasies of independence and all the headaches that carried with it, while I put the profits to good use, making myself comfortable—for once in my life. I grew up on the streets of Mérida, Agent

Mulder," he said with a snarl. "My mother was a prostitute. From the time I was eight years old I lived alone, rummaging in garbage bins, stealing from tourists, huddling under a box when it rained.

"But thanks to Xitaclan I have made myself a reasonably wealthy man—and no one was hurt by it—until too many people poked their noses where they didn't belong!" He tossed his head. "The locals knew enough to leave these ruins alone. The American archaeology team should have known as much… and so should you."

"You've already promised to kill us," Scully said. "Now are you trying to gain our sympathy?"

Aguilar shrugged. The deadly end of his rifle bobbed up and down. "We all desire to be understood," he said, with a smile. "It's human nature, eh?"

Then the branches overhead snapped and broke. To Mulder's utter amazement, a giant, sinuous shape dropped down like a gleaming tentacle, a coiled mass of muscle.

Aguilar looked up and screamed, swinging the rifle—far too slowly, far too late.

There was a gleam of translucent fangs as long as stilettos, as sharp as needles. A wide, hungry mouth flared. Feathery scales spread out in a crown around bony headplates, looking like beaten scales of precious metal. The monster moved, quick as lightning.

Aguilar fell to the ground under the weight of the creature. The vicious reptile wrapped around him, squeezing its serpentine body like a braid of steel cables.

"My God," Scully whispered.

Aguilar screamed in pain as well as terror. His rifle fell away into the underbrush. He clawed and pounded at the armored, flexible body of the feathered serpent. Blood sprayed from his mouth, a fountain of red as the feathered serpent squeezed.

The man shrieked as his bones cracked like dry wood. Then the huge serpent monster moved off into the underbrush, dragging its crushed victim along until the foliage-entangled deadfalls shielded the carnage from view.

Aguilar screamed twice more, then the noise was cut off with a high gurgling pop. They could hear nothing more than rustling sounds… breaking bones and tearing meat.

Scully sat next to Mulder, transfixed, her face pasty white, her eyes wide, her lips pale and bloodless. "Mulder… I…"

Cassandra coughed groggily and croaked, "Kukulkan."

Something fast and fluid rushed through the tangled underbrush on the other side of the all-terrain vehicle, moving too swiftly for Mulder to track. It slid through the creepers and ferns, then burst up with a spray of fallen leaves and moss-covered twigs. Looking at them.

Another feathered serpent—even larger than the first—reared up in front of them like a cobra before a snake charmer, baring its long fangs with a bubbling hiss, only feet away.

"Mulder, what is that thing?" Scully asked, her breath slow and thin.

"I'd suggest we don't move for the moment," he said through clenched teeth.

The sinuous creature weaved back and forth in front of them, huge and intimidating, larger than any crocodile ever born. Its feathery scales thrust out like spines. Its breath came in a sharp, unending hiss, like steam forcing itself out of a boiler.

"What does it want?"

The iridescent, oily serpent moved with a blur like an optical illusion, as if its entire body were made out of quicksilver, as if it had been bred for a different gravity, a different set of environmental conditions.

Mulder couldn't move. He simply stared at the beast, hoping none of his actions would intimidate it.

As the monster fixed its attention on them, it stared with eyes of burning pearls, grunting with an unfathomable intelligence driven by a brain of incomprehensible alienness.

Mulder remembered the carvings, the stelae, the images of Kukulkan deep within the ship. These serpentine creatures had been the ancient extraterrestrial's pets or companions or helpers… or something else entirely.

Though Kukulkan himself had died many centuries ago, his mummified corpse nothing more than petrified tatters of flesh clinging to naked bone, descendants of the original feathered serpents had remained behind. Stranded. Over the centuries they must have made their home in the Central American jungles, surviving hidden in the densest rain forests.

The creature in front of them stared, bowing closer. The moment froze in time.

"Mulder, what should we do?" Scully asked.

Mulder met the creature's burning, opalescent gaze. They stared at each other for a moment, a flash of understanding passing across a gulf vastly wider than any simple species barrier.

Mulder realized he was holding his breath.

Scully sat wide-eyed next to him, her knuckles white, her fingers clenched against the seat. Cassandra Rubicon groaned, staring at the creature with glassy eyes.

Finally, the tension inexplicably evaporated, and the feathered serpent backed away, slithering into the underbrush. It vanished as quickly as it had come, leaving only broken and rustling branches behind.

The forest fell silent again.

"I don't think we'll have any more trouble with them," Mulder whispered.

"I hope you're right, Mulder," Scully said, then swallowed hard. "But let's get out of here before one of those things changes its mind."

38

Jackson Memorial Hospital, Miami
Saturday, 11:17 A.M.

With a clean shave and clean clothes, and after a good night's sleep, Mulder felt like a visiting relative as he entered Jackson Memorial Hospital in Miami, where Cassandra Rubicon had been taken to recover from her injuries.

Now that he had returned to civilization, the dense jungle wilderness seemed another world away, with its bugs and scorpions and snakes and miserable rainy conditions… though it had been only two days ago. The ordeal had still not faded from his mind.

With the aid of the ATV's computerized map, he and Scully had managed to work their way east toward one of the paved roads in the state of Quintana Roo. Then, like a survivalist senior citizen driving a "Don't bother me or else!" RV, Mulder barreled along the roads, terrifying shepherds and pedestrians, dark-haired Indians wearing colorfully embroidered Maya clothes.

Using a small first-aid kit she found in the all-terrain vehicle, Scully had taken care of the worst of Cassandra's injuries, giving her painkillers and applying disinfectants. She could do nothing more until they found an actual hospital.

Finally, a Mexican police cruiser had stopped them, the officer demanding to know what they were doing there in a U.S. military vehicle. Scully had politely requested to be taken to the nearest American embassy.

During the grueling drive through the unmarked forest, they had found MRE rations in the storage compartment—"Meals Ready-to-Eat"—as well as bottled water. Cassandra had been unable to talk or eat, and she seemed so dazed by her ordeal that Mulder had doubted she would remember anything to back up his theory about the alien space craft rescue, any more than he expected to find witnesses from the commando operation. Scully and Mulder ate some rations, however, and by the time of their arrest they felt relatively comfortable again and ready to go back home.

Cassandra had been treated in a Mexican emergency medical care center while Mulder made the appropriate phone calls and Scully filled out the extensive paperwork. Upon arriving in Miami, Cassandra had been taken to Jackson Memorial for observation and recovery. The young woman was so weary after her ordeal that she viewed the forced hospital stay as a relief instead of a burden.

Walking down the linoleum-tiled hall, Mulder wondered if the archaeologist's daughter would recognize him, now that he had cleaned up and changed clothes. She had never seen him in his suit-and-tie FBI uniform.

He punched an elevator button and rode up to see her. The heavy doors closed on him, sealing him alone in the small elevator—and he experienced an unexpected dread as he thought of Carlos Barreio trapped in the lifeboat chamber onboard the derelict ship, dragged into the air with the salvaged wreck… and from there to the stars.

Fortunately, the hospital elevator didn't prove nearly so threatening.

Cassandra Rubicon lay propped on the bed surrounded by bleached white sheets, her head bandaged like a Civil War veteran's. She stared at the television mounted high on the wall, wearing a look of combined boredom and amusement as she absorbed a women's afternoon talk show. The topic of the heated discussion was "Women who claim to be married to aliens from outer space."

"I should have remembered to set my VCR," Mulder said. "I wanted to catch this one."

Cassandra saw him standing at the door to her room, and her face brightened. "There are some things I don't miss out in the jungle," she said. She picked up the TV remote control and stabbed the POWER button; the picture on the tube winked out with a faint cry of dismay.

"Feeling better?" he asked, corning to stand beside her bed.

"Much," she said. "And your own appearance is much improved."

He glanced down at the uninteresting and uneaten meal on a tray at her bedside. "You should eat your Jell-O—after all, you've had a pretty rough time."

She forced a smile for him. The heavy bandages covered much of her mussed cinnamon-brown hair. "Well, archaeology isn't for wimps, Mr. Mulder."

"Please, just call me Mulder," he said. "I can't help but think that Mister Mulder was my father's name."

At Mulder's mention of his own father, the young woman's face tightened again.

"I have to ask you this, Cassandra," he said, growing more serious, "because everything we saw has been destroyed without a trace. Did your team happen to smuggle out any notes, any photographs, any hard evidence from the Xitaclan site?"

She shook her head, then winced as a flicker of pain crossed her face. "No, there's nothing. My entire team died down there: John and Cait, Christopher and Kelly—all dead, struck down at the beginning of their careers. My own father was murdered because of me, because of Xitaclan." She swallowed, then looked back at the television herself, as if wishing she could be distracted by the talk show again, anything but the discussion she was now having with Mulder. "No, Mulder. It's all gone now, including our records. The only thing I have left is my memories—and even those aren't too clear."

Mulder stood next to her, momentarily turning his attention to the blank television set, trying to find the right words.

Cassandra seemed withdrawn, as if searching for an inner reservoir of strength. When she spoke, it surprised him. "There are still a thousand unexcavated sites in the Yucatán, Mulder. Maybe when I get back on my feet I'll put together a new expedition. Who knows what else we might find?"

Mulder allowed himself a small smile. "Who knows?"

39

Scully's home, Annapolis, MD
Sunday, 1:07 P.M.

With her little dog curled up asleep on the sofa, Scully flicked on the computer and sat down at her desk, taking a deep breath. So different from wandering lost in the wet and bug-laden jungles of Central America, she thought. And quite an improvement.

Now that she had returned home, she had to get into the right frame of mind to work on her official report about Xitaclan, juggling the loose ends in her mind until she finally succeeded in tying them together. There were other cases, other investigations… other X-Files. She had to close this one and move on.

In a few hours of peace and solitude in her own apartment, Scully could finish up the backlog of paperwork that had piled up during their trip to Mexico. It felt good to be back in civilization.

She crossed her legs in her chair and rested a lined legal notepad on her knee to jot down notes, sketching out her thoughts before committing her report to the computer. She scribbled several headings, writing her ideas under broadly defined categories.

Their specific assignment—to search for the missing archaeology team members—had been completed. Scully felt grateful to be able to mark an official case CLOSED, technically at least. Assistant Director Skinner would appreciate that.

On the legal pad, she listed the names of the four murdered team members, adding details of how she had discovered their bodies submerged in the cenote, how she and Mulder had recovered them from the water. She described the apparent cause of death—murder by gunshot wounds, broken vertebrae, and/or drowning. She concluded that Cait Barron, Christopher Porte, Kelly Rowan, and John Forbin had all been killed by members of the guerrilla organization *Liberación Quintana Roo.*

She didn't know what to write under "Cassandra Rubicon." She had been found alive and unharmed—though how, Scully did not understand. She still had no satisfactory explanation for the young woman's disappearance, the lost two weeks in her life. Had she been out wandering in the jungle or hiding down in the ruins of Xitaclan while the rest of her team members lay dead in the sacrificial well? Scully could not include Mulder's talk about buried spacecraft and suspended animation chambers.

As a side note, she scribbled a sentence about how, in the wake of the Xitaclan disaster and the debacle of the U.S. military covert operation, the Mexican government had finally come in with a sufficient force to crack down on the guerrilla activities. Soldiers had confiscated the remaining illegal arms and arrested the surviving revolutionaries who could be found hiding in jungle villages.

The violent *Liberación Quintana Roo* movement had been crushed. Their nominal leader, the turncoat police chief Carlos Barreio, remained at large. Mulder maintained his own explanation for what had happened to the man. Despite Scully's coaxing, her partner had not been forthcoming with sufficient details and she felt comfortable about including Mulder's speculations in her report. They didn't have a specific bearing on the case.

As for the tactical nuclear weapon that had supposedly obliterated Xavier

Salida's fortress—their investigations had uncovered no evidence of additional black-market armaments, other diverted nuclear devices that had fallen into the hands of Central American criminals. A continued search, though, would have to be conducted by other federal agencies, such as the CIA or the State Department.

Under "Vladimir Rubicon," Scully summarized the scenario of how the old man had been killed: struck on the head by Fernando Victorio Aguilar because the old archaeologist had threatened to broadcast his report and call in additional government-sanctioned help—all of which would have interfered with Aguilar's artifact thievery.

Hesitating, she made a notation that their guide Aguilar, Rubicon's murderer, had been killed by "a wild animal" in the jungle.

Then she swallowed and procrastinated, doodling with her pencil before getting up to make herself a cup of instant coffee, heating the water in her microwave.

The monstrous feathered serpents were the hardest part for Scully to explain. Their presence posed the greatest difficulties for her rational report. She did not know how to account for the creatures, but she had seen them with her own eyes. She could not ignore their existence.

Earlier, Mulder had described his glimpses of the unearthly serpent creatures in the moonlight, and she had thought he had just been imagining things. But she herself had watched the towering, coiling beast with its long iridescent scales and curved fangs.

Finally, steeling herself, Scully sat at her desk again and picked up the pencil. Without further thought, she wrote down her own explanation, the best she could come up with.

The feathered serpents must be members of a large, previously uncataloged species of reptile, perhaps nearly extinct, but with enough representatives surviving into historical times to account for the numerous legendary images on Maya structures and artifacts. In retrospect, she realized Mulder had been right— the feathered serpent image appeared on so many glyphs and stelae that it seemed likely the ancient Maya had seen some of the creatures in life. Mulder had even suggested that the carnivorous feathered serpents could be responsible for the numerous accounts of missing people in the area around Xitaclan.

She commented on the density of the Central American rain forests, how many thousands of new species were identified every year. She conjectured that it was not completely beyond the realm of possibility that a large reptilian carnivore-—

especially one with such apparent intelligence—could have remained heretofore undetected by scientific expeditions and zoological study teams.

Agent Mulder had reminded her of how many images of similar creatures existed in the world's mythologies: dragons, cockatrices, wyverns, Chinese water dragons—and the more she thought about it, the more sense it made that such rare beasts might have indeed existed.

With the destruction of the Xitaclan site and the significant amounts of new volcanic activity there, Mulder had been unable to offer any corroborating evidence. His alien artifacts remained unconfirmed, his derelict spacecraft destroyed. She felt that, while she would include his verbal eyewitness account, she could do nothing more than let it stand on its own.

She sipped her bitter coffee and scanned over her notes as she turned to her computer. She crossed out a few lines scribbled on the legal pad, tried to arrange her thoughts on paper, then rested her fingers on the keyboard.

She would have to smooth everything out in her final report. Scully could say only that the many anomalies at Xitaclan remained unexplained.

40

FBI Headquarters, Washington, D.C.
Sunday, 2:12 P.M.

Though FBI Headquarters never shut down entirely, the Sunday afternoon quiet surrounded Mulder with a warm peacefulness unlike the usual bustle of a normal business day.

Only one bank of fluorescents shone from the ceiling, the others were gray and dark. The atmosphere inside the FBI offices surrounded him like a tangible presence: the thousands of investigations, the case files, telephones that would normally be ringing, photocopy machines whirring and clanking into the night.

The phone beside his desk remained silent—down the hall, the other computers, the neighboring offices, the adjacent cubicles equally quiet.

It was not a rare occurrence for him to come in on the weekend; Scully had often joked about his lack of a social life.

Now he sat pensive, with the miniblinds drawn and a desk lamp switched on. Rubbing the bridge of his nose, he pushed aside his stack of books on Maya myths and archaeology.

He studied a sheaf of satellite photos he had obtained through sensible use of two Washington Redskins tickets. He had invested in season passes, though his caseload rarely allowed him the time to go to the actual games. However, the tickets often proved to be a useful form of currency for getting unofficial favors done in the Bureau.

He sat down and looked at the finely detailed photos, a few of them showing the devastated crater remaining where a Mexican drug lord's private villa had once been. Curious, he turned to another photo, studying the close-in target of the hellish, blasted landscape around the ruins of Xitaclan.

The volcanic hotbed had already generated enormous excitement among geologists. That part of the Yucatán should have been geologically stable instead of giving birth to an erupting volcano, much like the mysterious appearance of Parícutin in 1948. The cone of the new volcano had already begun to take shape, and early geological reports suggested that the new eruption would continue for years.

Mulder wondered if there could be any connection between Parícutin and Xitaclan, but dismissed the thought.

He would have no chance to go back to the Yucatán. He had no reason to return, because the erupting lava and volcanic tremors would have annihilated all evidence, even down to the mundane archaeological ruins. Not a scrap of Xitaclan's ancient glory remained.

Mulder picked up the precious jade artifact, the slick-smooth stone of whitish green carved into the design of a feathered serpent.

This time, the image struck him with an eerie chill, because he had seen the real thing. He ran his fingernail along the notches in the carving, tracing the feathers, the fangs in the open mouth. So many centuries of mystery lay locked in that place, and in this artifact.

But since Xitaclan had been destroyed, no one would believe his explanations. As usual.

Mulder set the jade carving on his desk with a sigh. At least he could use it for a decent paperweight.